THE NINTH METAL

BOOKS BY BENJAMIN PERCY

The Language of Elk

Refresh, Refresh

The Wilding

Red Moon

The Dead Lands

Thrill Me: Essays on Fiction

The Dark Net

Suicide Woods: Stories

THE
NINTH
METAL

BENJAMIN PERCY

MARINER BOOKS
Houghton Mifflin Harcourt
Boston   New York
2021

For information about permission to reproduce selections
from this book, write to trade.permissions@hmhco.com or to
Permissions, Houghton Mifflin Harcourt Publishing Company,
3 Park Avenue, 19th Floor, New York, New York 10016.

hmhbooks.com

Library of Congress Cataloging-in-Publication Data
Names: Percy, Benjamin, author.
Title: The ninth metal / Benjamin Percy.
Description: Boston : Houghton Mifflin Harcourt, 2021. |
Series: The comet cycle
Identifiers: LCCN 2020034167 (print) | LCCN 2020034168 (ebook) |
ISBN 9781328544865 (trade paperback) | ISBN 9780358331537 (hardcover) |
ISBN 9780358450368 | ISBN 9780358450528 | ISBN 9781328544186 (ebook)
Subjects: GSAFD: Science fiction.
Classification: LCC PS3616.E72 N56 2021 (print) | LCC PS3616.E72 (ebook) |
DDC 813/.6 — dc23
LC record available at https://lccn.loc.gov/2020034167
LC ebook record available at https://lccn.loc.gov/2020034168

Book design by Chrissy Kurpeski

Printed in the United States of America
1 2021
4500823896

For Lisa,
always

And for my father, Pete,
who taught me to study the night sky with wonder

PROLOGUE

I t begins with a comet.

Decades ago, an infrared telescope captured the thermal emission streaking through the solar system. Eventually it was determined to be 300.2 kilometers wide and orbiting the sun in an elongated ellipse that would bring it within five hundred thousand miles of Earth.

The moon, by comparison, is 238,900 miles away. This would be, scientists said, a beautiful light show that everyone should enjoy all the more, knowing that we'd narrowly escaped planetary annihilation.

The official name of the comet was P/2011 C9, but most people called it Cain, the surname of the astronomer who'd discovered it. Twenty years later, it burned into view and made its close pass by Earth.

People took off work. They gathered at soccer fields and in parking lots, on rooftops and along sidewalks, setting up lawn chairs and picnic blankets and grills and coolers as though readying for a fireworks display. Everyone suddenly owned a telescope. Vendors sold comet T-shirts and hats and key chains and plush stuffed toys. Surfers stacked up on beaches waiting for the big waves they believed would come from the gravitational flux. At least two cults killed themselves off, announcing this was the end of world and the comet a gateway to the vault of heaven.

Professors and scientists and religious leaders became regular guests on cable news shows, where they talked about how comets had long been associated with meteorological and human disasters—tsunamis, earthquakes, and droughts. In 44 BC, when Caesar was assassinated, his soul was said to depart the Earth and join the comet flaming overhead. In AD 79, a comet's arrival aligned with the eruption of Vesuvius. In AD 684, when Halley's comet passed by, the Black Death broke out, and in 1066, when it made another appearance, William the Conqueror won the Battle of Hastings. Celestial judgment and providence. Or an instrument of the devil, as Pope Callixtus III called it.

"Heaven knows what awaits us," one professor said. "It is a reminder of our irrelevant smallness and accidental existence in the universe, a glimpse of something violently outside the bounds of human existence, as close as you can come to seeing God."

Local news reporters interviewed people on the streets. "I don't know—it's just kind of cool," one man said. "Special. Once-in-a-lifetime sort of deal. You want to be able to say, *I was there*. It's almost like we were living this two-dimensional life, and now there's this sense of it being three-dimensional, if you know what I mean."

Cain looked like a roughly drawn eye, some said. Or a glowing animal track. Or a slash mark in the fabric of space. A wandering star.

For a few days, the comet made night uncertain, hued with a swampy green light. And by day, the sky appeared twinned with suns. And then—gradually—the comet trailed farther and farther away, and people forgot all about it.

Until one year passed. The planet finished its orbit of the sun and spun into the debris field left behind by the comet. The residue of Cain's passage.

This June, the sky would fall. That's what the newscasters said.

The meteor shower was not as long-lasting as August's Perseids, but for several nights the sky flared and streaked and wheeled, the constellations seeming to rearrange themselves with ever-shifting tracks of light. At first hundreds and then thousands and then hundreds of thousands and finally an uncountable storm of meteors.

The ground shook. Windows shattered. Grids of electricity went dark. Satellites shredded. Radio signals scrambled. Dogs howled and people screamed their prayers. Many of the meteors dissolved in the atmosphere, but many struck the earth, sizzling into the ocean, splintering roofs, searing through ice, punching craters into fields and forests and mountainsides, like the seeds of the night.

It was then that everything changed.

THE NINTH METAL

1

✳

His father came in the front door and went directly to the picture window as if he couldn't decide whether he belonged inside or out. He stayed there a long time, studying the county highway that ran past their farm. Whenever a car grumbled by, he took a step back and tugged at the curtain, ready to drag it shut. Night was coming, but he snapped off the lamps in the living room.

He didn't say hello to Hawkin when the boy hugged his leg but he absently patted his head. And he didn't respond to Hawkin's mother when she called from the kitchen, "Henry? Where in the hell have you been?"

His father locked the door and walked over to the shelving unit where his mother kept her books and teapots and porcelain figures. He dug into his pocket and then stared at something cupped in his hand. He pulled down the Bible and hurried through its pages, sometimes pausing as if to take in a certain passage. He glanced back at Hawkin, said, "What?" and then returned the Bible to its shelf. He paced in a circle and turned on the television, but with the volume down. Its shifting light and color made the room an uncertain space. The news played. Something about the historic meteor shower expected that evening, the beginning of a light show that could span several days. Hawkin's teacher, Mrs. B., had talked about it. The fourth-graders could keep a sky journal for extra credit.

His father was balding but kept his hair long enough to comb over and spray stiffly in place. Right now several clumps of it stood upright and revealed the pale dome of his head. His eyes were red-rimmed and his cheeks unshaven and he hadn't changed his clothes since yesterday, when he'd driven off in the pickup and said he was going to make them some money.

These days he was always seeing about a job, trying to catch a break. A few years ago he had sold their horses and their ATV and their fishing boat, and when Hawkin asked why, he said he was retiring. Hawkin knew he was too young for that. The only people who were retired in north-central Minnesota spent their days slumped in wheelchairs. You worked until you couldn't. You could be white-haired and wormed with veins and still put in your ten-hour shift as a waitress or bank teller or hairdresser. *Retired* might as well mean near dead.

In fact, his father and hundreds of others had lost their jobs at Frontier Metals after the federal government shut down the mining lease on over a hundred thousand acres of land. Northfall was located at the edge of the Boundary Waters Canoe Area, and Hawkin's parents and their friends complained constantly about the forest service and the BLM and the damned hippie vegan environmentalists who thought the land belonged to the owls and walleye. "These are the same sort of people that think you're killing a carrot when you eat it," his father would say. "I look at a tree, I see a house. I look at a deer, I see venison sausage. I look at a hill packed with iron, I see a skyscraper and a fleet of fighter jets and a club-cab pickup with a chrome nut sack hanging from the hitch."

Hawkin heard his parents arguing through the walls at night. About money mostly. About his father spending it on nonsense or blowing it on pipe dreams or throwing it away at the poker table un-til the bank account emptied. "Why can't you get a job?" Hawkin's mother asked and he said, "Where? Where are the jobs? You want me to serve cheeseburgers at the McDonald's?" There were a lot of men like him in town. Loggers and miners who didn't seem to know what to do with themselves except crack a beer and shake their heads and lament what had become of this place, this life.

His family discussed selling the land off as well, but only lakefront property was worth anything up here, and these four hundred acres of maples had not only been in the Gunderson family for three generations but made money for them every spring as a source of syrup. Which also qualified them for the cheaper ag-land tax rate. Gunderson Woods, the locals called it. "My sweet little sugar bush," his father called it and talked about the day he might install a pump and a web of tap lines instead of tapping over six hundred trees and hauling buckets as they dripped full.

Hawkin's mother worked as a clerk at the Farm and Fleet and smoked menthol cigarettes and had bottle-blond hair and pink fingernails and rhinestone-butted blue jeans. She spent Wednesday nights and the whole of her Sundays at the Trinity Lutheran leading Bible studies and ushering, but she was always reading books on Buddhism, Judaism, Islam, Hinduism, the Rajneeshees, the Church Universal and Triumphant. She believed there was something else out there, even if she didn't know exactly what. When Hawkin asked how she could be so certain, she pointed a lit cigarette at him and said, "Because that's the nature of faith. Besides, this can't be it." Here she traced the air with her cigarette, as if drawing a smoky map of the world around her. "The thought's just too goddamn depressing."

She was cooking dinner now. Burgers on the range and frozen French fries in the oven. Hawkin was helping put dishes away, but only in the areas he could reach, the cabinets below and the lower shelves above. He was a whole head shorter than his classmates, smaller than he should be. Sicker too. He missed school so often that the students in the fourth grade forgot his name. He'd had pneumonia seven times and wheezed when he ran. His mother blamed it on the chemical runoff in the water and all the years of beer swirling around inside Hawkin's father, which no doubt compromised his seed. "You'll get stronger when you grow up and get out of this godforsaken place," she said. "Don't worry. I've been praying on it."

Now Hawkin set a pan on a shelf, tucked a cutting board beneath the range, and tried to dodge out of the way of his mother, who didn't always see him underfoot. When his father entered the kitchen and picked up the wall telephone and listened to the dial tone before setting it in its cradle and then unplugging the cord, his mother said, "What's your deal?"

"I want quiet. That's all."

Hawkin's mother swatted at the air with her spatula. "All you ever do is make noise and suddenly you're Mr. Quiet? Something's gotten into you."

"It's nothing."

"Don't tell me it's nothing when it's obviously something."

His father was breathing too hard and his eyes couldn't seem to settle on anything. When he headed back into the living room, Hawkin's mother followed, her voice rising in pitch and volume as she asked him what stupid-son-of-a-bitch thing he'd gone and done now.

"I've got it under control. Okay? If I play my cards right, we might come out of this with a pile of money."

"Cards? This is about cards?"

"It was a metaphor, woman."

"So you weren't playing cards?"

"That's irrelevant. What matters is, I've got everything under control."

"*Pfft*. That's a laugh."

Hawkin knew that whatever happened next would probably involve something getting thrown. He turned off the range and nudged the pan off the burner. In the dinette, from the round table, he retrieved his notebook and pencil, then he headed out the sliding glass door and onto the splintery back deck.

The night was humid. Frogs drummed and crickets sawed. One side of the sky was still red with the setting sun, but the other was the purple-black of a bruise with a few stars dotting it.

He could still hear his parents, their footsteps tromping the floor as they followed each other around the house, their voices calling out sharply, as he went down the stairs and into the weed-choked yard.

There was a sandbox with rotten boards and the nails undone

at one corner, but it still carried three inches of sand the consistency of wet cement. He plopped down and cringed as the water soaked through his jeans and underwear. He shouldn't be out here, he knew. His mother would say he was liable to catch cold, but he had come to weirdly enjoy his stays at the hospital, where no one ever yelled and he could watch TV and read comic books and eat as much strawberry ice cream as he wanted.

His notebook had Superman on the cover, a montage of the Man of Steel as a baby zooming toward Earth in his Krypton rocket, hoisting a cow over his head as a teenager in Kansas, and finally soaring through the sky in his red trunks and cape. Hawkin ran his hand across the image before flopping the notebook open. He poised his pencil over the lined paper and studied the sky. *Nothing yet,* he wrote in slow careful letters, then paused. He was an excellent speller, a wonderful writer, Mrs. B. told him, but he wasn't sure how to describe what he felt then. If every falling star was a wish, and if the whole sky was supposed to light up tonight, then he had a good chance of finally getting what he wanted. A kitten, for starters. And a rabbit too. And how about no more wasps or spiders or bullies? In their place he'd ask for buckets and buckets of strawberry ice cream. And a Star Wars bedspread like in the Target flyer. And a nice house that didn't have nightmare water stains in the ceiling and paint peeling off the walls like flaps of old skin. And a truck that didn't die in the Shopko parking lot so that they had to beg a jump-start off strangers. And parents who didn't fight and who hugged him and kissed his forehead and called him smart and strong and handsome and awesome. And a good immune system so that he could stop burning up with fevers and coughing until his lungs ached and start going to birthday parties and playing kickball with the other kids at school.

A mosquito whined by his ear and he swatted at it. Another bit his arm, another his neck, his forehead. "Stop!" he said. His father had taught him a trick: If you tossed sand into the air, the bats would swoop through it, mistaking it for a cloud of insects. It was like a flare. A call for help. Organic repellent, his father said.

Hawkin thought he would try that, try summoning the bats to him so they would eat up all the mosquitoes eating him.

So he did. He scooped sand and tossed up smoky handfuls of it. He scrunched shut his eyes. His hair and shirt dirtied with sand that crumbled from creases when he moved. The bats came—just as his father said—wheeling and fluttering in the air around him, and he felt like a conjuring wizard.

He was so busy with his bats, he didn't notice the last bit of sun seep from the sky as night took over. He didn't hear the engine of the approaching vehicle. He didn't see the headlights cutting through the pine trees and blinking out as the car parked. He didn't hear the footsteps crunching on the gravel driveway or someone testing the locked knob of the front door. But if Hawkin had, he might have also heard his parents' voices rising. The money. The money. That was what they were arguing about. His mother was goddamn tired of living off goddamn food stamps and goddamn handouts from their goddamn parents.

They didn't know what was coming, and neither did Hawkin. Not until he heard the scraping charge of a shotgun shell loaded into its chamber. He spun around in time to see a figure sneaking along the edge of the house and testing a foot on the deck stairs to see if they creaked—and then creeping up them slowly, slowly. He wore a black jacket and blue jeans and his face looked like a smear, a melted nub of candle, veiled in pantyhose.

There was something off about his movement and balance. A slow, confused deliberateness, like somebody exploring the dark in a blindfold. When he stumbled on the top step and caught himself against the house, he mumbled a curse, and Hawkin recognized the slur of his voice as familiar. His father sounded like that most every night when he shut off the TV and rose unsteadily from his recliner and stumbled down the hall and said, "Had a few too many."

His parents were visible in the windows, moving between the squares of light and gesturing wildly, like characters in a cable program Hawkin wasn't allowed to watch. He wanted to yell something, to warn them, but his voice felt zipped up and double-knotted and shoved in the bottom drawer of his lungs.

The sliding door opened, and the stranger charged inside. He knocked against the table and then righted himself and continued out of sight. A moment later his parents hushed. There was the mutter of conversation. And then a thud and a cry as his father fell to the floor.

Though Hawkin did not comprehend what he heard next — over the next five minutes or so — he understood his father was in pain. He understood the stranger was asking him questions, and because his father wasn't answering them satisfactorily, he was being kicked repeatedly.

The last thing he heard his father say was "We can work something out, right?," his voice somewhere between a whimper and a shriek. "This doesn't have to be an argument. It can be a negotiation. A simple business negotiation between two —"

A shotgun blast strobed the windows and made the house sound as though it had been split by a great hammer. There was screaming — his father's — and then there was no more screaming.

Hawkin felt the sand grow warm beneath him and realized he had wet himself and worried he would get in trouble for it. His mother appeared in the kitchen window then. She was backing away with her hands held up.

"Didn't mean to shoot him," the stranger said, his voice carrying through the open door. "Was an accident. Finger fucking slipped or something." His words garbled in a slurry jumble. "If the idiot had just — I just needed him to tell me where it was." He muttered something unintelligible and then seemed to find his focus. "What about you? You know where it was? Is, I mean?"

"I don't." His mother shook her head — no, no, no. "I don't know anything. I swear."

The stranger sounded tired, like someone trying to get out a few thoughts before falling asleep: "This is — you better not be —" But before he could finish the sentence, another shotgun blast sounded.

His mother was shoved suddenly from view. The fridge sparked. One of the cabinets shattered and swung from a single hinge before coming loose and falling out of sight.

There was a long silence. And then the stranger spat a series of curses that gave way to a primal yell. Not of victory, but frustration. This was followed by heavy breathing. And then he moaned more than said, "What's wrong with you?" Who this was directed at, Hawkin wasn't sure.

The stranger then moved from room to room, switching on every light and taking their home apart. Pictures were torn from walls and smashed, drawers ripped out, pillows and box springs and couch cushions split open. Cereal boxes were shaken empty. The carpet was peeled back, the toilet tank checked. The stranger was searching for something. For the better part of an hour.

The bats continued to swirl around Hawkin, maybe a dozen of them, nipping at the mosquitoes, and he still had a lump of sand in his fist. He had been squeezing it so tightly his knuckles hurt. The bats made a chirping, buzzing sound like the electric fence that bordered their neighbor's property to the north.

Sometimes Hawkin liked to reach his hand for that fence—an inch away, then closer and closer still—not touching it, but almost, so that he could feel the hum of electricity. It made his skin tighten and his hairs rise. He felt a similar sense of prickling danger when the stranger came out onto the deck and heaved a sigh and ejected a shotgun shell. He tried to walk down the steps but missed his footing and fell.

He landed heavily only a few feet from Hawkin, who knew he should run but didn't; instead, he remained still and tried to will himself invisible. The stranger lay in the grass for a long time—long enough that Hawkin hoped he might have fallen asleep—but then he stirred with a grumble and hoisted himself up onto an elbow and said, "Oh. There you are." He clumsily rose into a squat. "Was wondering where you were. Hawkin, right? That's your name?"

Hawkin could see the pantyhose had gone gray with moisture at the eyes and the nose and the mouth, and it made the stranger look like he was rotting. A jack-o'-lantern that needed to be tossed into the compost. "Saw your name spelled out on the wall of your room. What kind of a name is Hawkin, I don't fucking know. But I like your room, Hawkin. I like the color of the paint." His voice wandered dreamily. "Is your favorite color blue? That's a good color. It always reminds me of Lake Superior or . . ." Here his voice fell off a cliff. "Did you hear what happened in there? Because I'm sorry how things turned out. Hawkin?"

Hawkin couldn't respond, not even when the stranger cocked his head and waited for him to.

"This is so fucked," the stranger said and laid the shotgun across his thighs and pinched the bridge of his nose. His balance wavered and he rocked back on his heels and popped up into a standing position. "Okay. Okay, okay, okay." The smoke coming off the gun burned Hawkin's nose. "So I have some questions for you, Hawkin. Some very important questions. Like a test. You take tests at school? This is like one of those. Except it's real."

A bat chittered then, and Hawkin remembered the sand. He hurled the clump of it, and it unfurled into a veil that glittered in the air between them. And harmlessly frosted the stranger along the head and shoulders. He did not flinch but seemed ready to say something when the bats struck his face. One, two, three of them. The first couple dived in and out, but the last caught its claws in the pantyhose and beat its wings furiously over his eyes.

The stranger dropped the shotgun and screamed and punched at the bat, punching himself. To Hawkin, the pantyhose looked like stretched skin when the stranger struggled to yank the mask off, to free himself, his forehead growing long and his eyes widely hollowed.

Hawkin lurched up and made it a few wobbling steps before tripping. His legs were cramped from sitting still so long.

He wasn't sure if he was crying or if the dew in the grass was wetting his face as he crawled forward. He didn't know where he would go. Maybe the shed. He could get a rake there or some garden shears. Something sharp to protect himself with. Or maybe hide behind some pots or in a watering can, like Peter Rabbit in Mr. McGregor's garden.

It was then he noticed, as he wormed away from the house, that instead of growing darker, the night was growing lighter. A blue-green glow hued his vision, everything flickering and warping, like the bottom of a pond when he put on goggles and ducked his head below the surface.

He looked up. And there it was. Just like Mrs. B. said. It was the beginning of the meteor shower. It would be a night busy with falling stars. A sky full of wishes. Too many to count. But he tried to gather them all up in his gaze and collect them into one powerful wish. "Make me strong enough to fight him," Hawkin said.

And then the world shook and everything brightened to a blinding silver.

2

*

Five years later . . .

Montana and South Dakota and then western Minnesota flash by as John Frontier studies the landscape rolling past the window, looking the same as it did a hundred, maybe even a thousand years ago. Below, a sea-green prairie splashed with red and gold and white flowers. Above, an achingly blue sky peaked with mountainous clouds. No sign of man except for the fences squaring up property lines, the occasional milk carton of a farmhouse surrounded by a huddle of rotten outbuildings.

The train is called the Bullet. John isn't sure how fast it's going. Almost as fast as a plane, they say. Three hundred miles per hour, maybe more. In the distance, the world seems to scroll by easily, but his eyes can't grab the bunch grass or scrub oak growing near the tracks; everything's a green blur.

John is twenty-five years old with an arrowhead face and closely trimmed black hair. He's muscular, but lean and ropy, so his uniform — first lieutenant, army — makes him look more broad-shouldered than he is. He's not tall and not short, not the kind of person you would look at twice, especially since he's so still. Barely moving. As if concentrating deeply on keeping himself contained. "The longer I look at you," a girlfriend once said, "the better-looking you are." His one striking feature is a port-wine stain that splashes down his forehead, over his eye, along his cheek. It's shaped like a country that hasn't yet been discovered.

Over the past five years, since he left home, he has learned to carry himself in a way—looking everyone unwaveringly in the eye, speaking in a low, steady voice, constantly aware of himself— that demands respect. He has beaten himself, like a piece of forged metal, into someone new.

The viewing car is domed with glass. Here he sits. Every seat is taken and the aisle and the bar are crowded with bodies. Their conversation is the only sound other than a faint whispering as the Bullet glides forward. There is no engine noise and no wheel clatter, because there is no engine, no wheels. The monorail is powered by the very track it slides upon. A track made from the ninth metal. Omnimetal.

That's the reason they're all rushing to the Arrowhead, to northeastern Minnesota. The miners, the mechanics, the truckers, the construction workers, the real estate developers, the jewelers, the bartenders, the scientists and techies, the priests and pastors and prophets, the deliverymen, the retail clerks, the janitors, the prostitutes and drug dealers, the policemen and security guards. Metal.

He shares his booth with two men and a woman. They pass back and forth a pitcher of beer, drinking directly from it, while playing cards and talking about the best outfit to work for and how they're going to make some cash money. In the booth beside theirs, four businessmen sip white wine, speaking in hurried whispers and making notes and pointing to graphs in a thick black binder. Standing in the aisle, two thick-armed, deeply tanned men in tank tops and cargo shorts down tequila shots and let out a whoop. Sitting at the bar, a woman with a butterfly neck tattoo and a leopard-print top and jean shorts chews gum and stares at her phone. White, black, Hispanic, Asian. Mostly men. Everyone from everywhere ready for anything.

All because of the ninth metal. John's home, once the middle of nowhere, has become the center of everything.

He can't see the track they glide on, but he knows it gives off a soft blue glow. Some people call it the greatest energy source in the world. Others call it a defiance of everything scientists have come to understand about physics and biochemistry. And a few call it God. There were eight noble metals before, called such for their rarity and their resistance to corrosion and their metallurgical and technological and ornamental uses. Now, because of the comet, because of the debris that showered the earth, there are nine. And omnimetal, as it has come to be known, is the very peak of the galvanic series.

In southwestern Minnesota, the prairie gives way to cornfields that reach off into the distance — thick green leaves and tall stalks tasseled out in the July heat. Trees appear only occasionally, a cluster of oaks and maples islanding a town, a windbreak of cottonwoods standing guard beside a farm.

And then, just like that, the cornfields vanish and the Bullet enters a thick, shadowy forest that John knows will continue more or less the rest of the way home. The ground swells into hills and the train flashes past lakes and rock ridges. Red and white pines cluster more thickly among the maples and ash the farther into the evergreen north they travel.

The train is so new it still smells of glue and paint. The booth's table is a smart tablet, its screen presently green like a card table at a Vegas casino. The man seated opposite John swipes his finger across it, controlling the game of Texas hold'em. His hair is a wiry gray and his smile has holes in it from a few missing teeth. "Knew things were crazy up north," he says, looking at John, "but didn't think it was so bad they was sending the military."

"I'm headed home for a wedding," John says.

"You from Northfall, then?"

"I am."

The woman — denim long-sleeved top, dirty-blond hair pulled back in a ponytail — taps the table to fold her hand of cards and says, "Hey, we hear housing's a little iffy. Every motel full for a hundred miles. People sleeping in trucks. You recommend a place?"

"Afraid I can't. Haven't been home since the boom."

That's what they call it: the boom. For the explosion in money and population—and for the sound the meteors made when they struck the ground.

"Damn, son," the man says and taps the table twice, snapping out a new card deal for everyone to riffle through. "You're not going to recognize your own backyard."

"So I hear."

"A millionaire a day," the man says. "That's the slogan."

The woman scores a full house and lets out a cackle. "That's 'cause 'a murder a day' don't sound as good to the tourism bureau."

John looks to the flash, flash, flash of images streaming past the window. Already he can see the smoke dirtying the air, the red-lighted towers blinking in the distance, the sections of woods cut away and parked with heavy machinery. "I'll hardly have time to notice. I don't plan on staying long."

The sign at the edge of town reads *Northfall, Minnesota: Population 5,000*. An *X* of spray paint covers the number and beside it someone has graffitied *Who the hell knows*.

The old town remains. The Farm and Fleet and the Shopko. The Pamida grocery. The lumber mill. The implement dealer. The tree farm and the Walleye Tavern and the Severson Supper Club. The gun stores. The bait shops. The canoe outfitters.

But all around this, another town is growing, the new layered over and sprawling out of the old. A half-finished housing development. A massive Walmart built beside a massive Home Depot, both their parking lots crammed with trucks. A liquor depot. An endless trailer park called Christmas Village. A new motel next to a new motel next to a new motel, all with signs that read *No Vacancy*. Car and RV and ATV dealerships glow with stadium lights.

The Bullet slides past all of this and into the newly built train station. The track gives off an eerie light and vibrates with energy. The doors breathe open and hundreds of passengers spill out, among them John. He carries a duffel bag that weighs him down on one side. He readjusts it, swinging it up so that it hangs from his shoulder like a pack.

Everyone tromps along the platform and funnels into the station, a high-ceilinged building with the look of a Northwoods lodge. It smells like wet varnish and cut lumber. Voices clamor and footsteps clop on the concrete floor. Vending machines glow. Lines stretch from the ticket counters. Handlers push luggage carts.

Up ahead, John spots a small crowd of people waiting with a homemade sign. The glittery letters read *Welcome Home Soldier* and *We're Proud of You Son*. They smile and cheer and clap their hands.

John walks past them as a young Marine, still in his desert cammies, sprints forward and throws down his rucksack and opens up his arms for a hug. His family embraces him, laughing and weeping.

John watches them a moment before edging through the swarm of people and out the front entrance. The cool air of the station is replaced by a clinging humidity. Sunlight makes him squint. Sweat springs from his skin. He is assaulted by cigarette smoke and shouting.

There is the long-bearded man who stands atop a milk crate and preaches about greed and fornication and damnation, but his voice is drowned out by all of the recruiters. They guard tables full of swag and flyers, and they hold up signs for trucking, construction, and mining companies. John has heard the rumors—that you can step off the train in Northfall and land a job no matter your education, work, or criminal history—and by all appearances, this is true.

A man wearing a baseball cap that reads *Black Dog Energy* hands out bumper stickers with the same words. He pushes one toward John, who waves it away. "Military welcome!" the man says. "Military welcome!"

A woman approaches him with a lipsticked smile. Her T-shirt has *Frontier Metals* across the chest and she's tied it up at the bottom to reveal her tanned belly. She holds a clipboard and says, "Hey, handsome. How'd you like a starting salary of seventy grand a year?"

"Thank you. I'm good."

John continues to shoulder his way forward, unable to go more than a few paces without getting stalled. "Excuse me," he says. "Excuse me."

Finally he is moving toward the parking lot. Cars honk. A hotel shuttle unloads its passengers. Two rust-bottomed taxis idle. The four businessmen from the train approach a limo service and shake the driver's hand before he takes their luggage.

John looks for his father and checks his phone for messages. Nothing, but he does spot a familiar man moving stiffly toward him. His spine warps him into a left-leaning stance and he has a hitch with every step. He's dressed in his standard outfit, a corduroy jacket, check-patterned collared shirt, khakis ironed to a stiff crease. This is Sam Yesno. He has a small chin, and his black hair recedes from a long forehead. He's six inches shorter and fifteen years older than John. These days, he works as the Frontiers' legal counsel, but the two of them grew up together. Not brothers—not even cousins—but family. Yesno is Ojibwa and his grandmother served as a housekeeper to the Frontiers. Sam's parents were in and out of jail, and when his grandmother passed, John's father took the boy in and raised him as his own.

"It's good to see you, Johnny," Sam says, his voice lilting and gentle, almost British in its intonation. People used to tease him for it, but as he's aged, his speech has grown to match his appearance. "You look formidable in that uniform."

John runs a hand along the brass buttons. "Don't let it trick you into treating me with any respect."

"Oh, I'd never make that mistake."

John looks around without really expecting to see anyone. "No Pops, huh?"

"Busy."

"As always."

"Business, of course. But the wedding, too—"

John holds up a hand. "It's okay. You don't need to make any excuses for my father."

Yesno smiles apologetically—his teeth uneven from the bridge he wears—and John surprises them both by pulling him into a brief hug. Yesno has never liked being touched. And he goes rigid now, as if in pain, until John releases him.

Yesno adjusts his jacket. He always wears one, even in the height of summer. He's never said why, but John knows it's because he's trying to cloak the twist and hump in his spine. "I wondered if you'd recognize me, you know. I'm a little balder these days." Yesno touches the smoothness of his scalp. "Crop failure."

"You're more aerodynamic. That's all."

Yesno reaches for the duffel. "Well. Off we go. Let me help you with that."

John swats away his hand. "Not on your life."

They maze through traffic until they come to a white Expedition. Yesno rattles out the keys and chirps the fob. The trunk of the Expedition opens with a hydraulic wheeze and John hefts the duffel inside.

But before he can close the door, a deep-throated voice behind him seizes his attention: "Thirty minutes until the next train leaves. You'll be on it."

Someone else says, "I'm sorry! I'll go. I'm going."

Two men approach. One of them has a mane of blond hair and the weird snake-like face of someone who has had too much cosmetic surgery. He is slabbed with muscle and wears too-tight black jeans and a silk shirt unbuttoned halfway down the chest. His fingers shine with rings, and his right hand is so big, it seems to fit entirely around the neck of the man he drags alongside him—and then hurls to the pavement.

The fallen man's palms skid and rash over red. He curls them into his chest and rolls on his side and whimpers. His hair is long, his shirt appears chewed along the collar, and whiskers dirty his cheeks.

"Who's this asshole?" John says and Yesno says, "That's Mickey Golden. The competition."

"What do you mean?" John says.

"Let's go," Yesno says and tugs at John's sleeve and hurries for the driver's-side door. "Come on." And then, as he climbs into the cab, he calls out, "John!"

"In a second."

"You've only been home five minutes. Please let's try to stay away from trouble." With that, Yesno closes the door.

Golden reaches into his back pocket, flips open his wallet, counts out five twenties, and flutters them to the blacktop. "You know what'll happen if you come back." He speaks with something coiled like barbed wire in his voice, a Texas accent.

The fallen man does not look up but feebly chases down the money on his hands and knees before it blows away.

Golden swivels his head toward John and scans him up and down. "Hell are you looking at, GI Joe?"

John says nothing but keeps his eyes steady on Golden until the big man breaks away and stalks toward a jacked-up club-cab Chevy that advertises Black Dog Energy along its bed. He cranks the ignition and crushes the accelerator and roars out of the parking lot.

Only then does John climb inside the Expedition. Yesno gives him a nervous, sad smile and says, "Let's get you home, Johnny."

"Actually, if we have the time?"

"Yes?"

"I was hoping we could stop someplace first."

3

✳

Stacie didn't notice how old the house was until she moved out. Now, whenever she visits her parents, she feels at once cozy with familiarity—and sad. The kitchen has the same blighted color scheme as the hobby farm itself: browns, oranges, yellows. A permanent November. The wallpaper is patterned with moose and peeling at the seams. Decorative plates sit on a shelf and display a fly-fisherman casting, wolves howling at the moon, a deer leaping over a log. There is a fridge as yellow as a smoker's tooth and a dishwasher that rattles and clanks. Besides the microwave, not much has been updated since 1980.

Just off the side of the kitchen is a round table, and here they all sit. Her father, Oliver Toal, wears a buffalo-plaid shirt. His hair is gray and thinning, his face freshly shaved but deeply wrinkled. He is a man who, like this home and business, has seen better times. Next to him is his wife, Betsy. She wears a Yellowstone T-shirt and pale blue jeans, and her hair is a silver acorn cap. And finally there is Stacie herself, with her straw-colored hair pulled back in a pony-tail. She wears her deputy's uniform and sits neatly in her chair. She ironed every wrinkle from it this morning, but she still picks at her sleeves and smooths the fabric on her thighs. Six months into the job and she still doesn't feel like it fits right.

They're praying over their lunch of fried walleye sandwiches and wild rice soaked in gravy and speckled with cranberries. Their voices are monotone as they quickly recite words said a thousand times. "Come, Lord Jesus, be our guest and let this food to us be blessed. Amen."

They dig in, biting into the sandwiches, forking up the rice. Oliver says, "So when do you need to be at work?"

"Not for another hour and a half," she says. "I've got time."

Oliver touches Betsy's shoulder and says, "How about it, Mother?" and she smiles and wipes her mouth and reaches below the table and pulls out a gift wrapped in the Sunday funnies.

"Well, well. What's this?" Stacie says, and her mother says, "Oh, you already know, but pretend you're surprised anyway."

She picks off the tape and nudges open the paper to reveal her diploma from Mankato State, framed in red maple and topped with glass.

"Sorry it took so long," her father says, "but I think it turned out pretty okay."

Stacie always smiles — it's a reflex of hers, no matter the situation — but it's honest happiness that makes her beam now as she hugs the frame to her chest and says, "This is so special."

"Your father made it in his shop."

"Thank you so, so much, Daddy." She leans over and kisses his cheek and he says, "Yeah, yeah, yeah." He blows on his coffee and tests its temperature with this finger and says, "You know I'm proud of you. But I still say it's funny for a girl to be a cop."

"It's been a half a year," Stacie says. "Maybe we can stop talking about this?"

"She's not a *girl*, Oliver."

"Well, she's *my* girl."

"And," Stacie says, "I actually prefer the term *peacekeeper* to *cop*."

"Peacemaker," Oliver mutters into his mug. "No peace to be had in this town."

Her mother raps his knuckles with her spoon. "That's why it's important for her to be doing what she's doing, you nincompoop."

Stacie sets the diploma beside her juice and traces its frame with her finger. "That's the maple from that tree in back? Where I used to swing?"

"You bet it is."

"Well, I'm going to hang this in my living room. I know the perfect place for it."

Oliver says, "Still don't know why you can't just live here."

"Daddy. Stop."

"Stay in your old room. Would save you a wheelbarrow of money."

"Oliver. Hush. Independence is a good thing."

"I'm only a few miles away."

"I'm just worried about you is all," Oliver says, and Betsy says, "He's just worried about you is all."

"I keep hearing these stories." He stirs up his rice, making a mess of it. His hands are huge, thick with calluses and cracked with lines, one knuckle scabbed over and one fingernail bruised black. "Women getting harassed. Or worse. This town's changed, and not for the better. You know what I read in the paper the other day? A mother of five vanished when she went out jogging. She was—"

"We already discussed this, Daddy."

He waves his hand in the air and says, "Bah."

"Oliver. Hurry." Betsy flaps her hand at the television. "Don't forget the news."

"We don't need to watch that. Stacie's here. Let's just have a nice conversation."

"I want to see it," Betsy says and then turns to Stacie. "The Olsens are going to be on the news. You know the Olsens. From church?"

Oliver continues stirring his rice, so Betsy finally gets up herself and clicks on the countertop TV, an old box with a bad picture. The screen lightens; it's tuned to the NBC affiliate. After the grain prices, a reporter appears on location in Northfall. He wears a suit that doesn't fit properly and stands in the shadow of a haul truck. He's dwarfed by one of its massive tires, his head barely reaching the rim. "A millionaire a day. That's the slogan on the street here in northern Minnesota, where a *tiny* town has become a hub for *big* business." The camera goes wide to take in the strip mine behind him, a silver core of omnimetal that is steadily being carved out of a hillside. "I talked to one of the latest winners, Will Olsen, a middle-school math teacher who recently sold the mineral rights to his land."

"There he is," Betsy says and claps her hands, "that old so-and-so."

Will Olsen wears a cream-colored leather jacket and snakeskin boots and his hair is a freshly dyed black. He grins into the camera as the reporter puts a hand around his shoulders. "Until recently, the Olsens were unaware that their forty acres of land carried any omnimetal. But in addition to a large vein that bored into a marsh on the property, they also have a small lake hiding what turned out to be a sizable deposit."

Will takes the reporter through a gauche mansion. Gold columns in the entry. Marble in the bathroom. Quartz counters and tiger-maple cabinets and stainless-steel appliances in the kitchen. "We just tore the old place down, built right over the top." A fountain on the back deck features a stone cupid peeing water.

The camera cuts to Will standing next to his wife, who wears a glittery blouse and diamond earrings and has her hair sprayed up in a helmet.

"So what's next?" the reporter asks and stabs the mic into their faces.

"Well, Gloria here's always wanted to go to Italy. So I suppose we'll go to Italy. Food's supposed to be real good."

In the next shot, the reporter sits in the passenger seat of a Mercedes convertible. Behind the wheel, Will chomps a fat cigar and smashes the accelerator and—

The screen goes dark. Oliver has snapped off the power.

"I was watching that," Betsy says. "What's the matter with you?"

Oliver won't look at her. He stands up with his plate and takes it to the kitchen and sets it on the counter. He moves with the squinty stiffness of a man who's worked outside his whole life. "Lost my appetite." He pulls his deerstalker cap off a hook and fits it on his head and opens the door and lets in the sun. "Going for a walk."

The door shudders the house when it closes. And Betsy stares after him a moment before shaking her head and saying, "Well, I think it's exciting. When ordinary folks have something exciting like this happen to them, I'm honestly tickled to bits. The metal all around us . . . it's like a genie in a bottle. People's wishes are coming true."

"I take it he's not enjoying the new job at Dick's Sporting Goods?"

"No," Betsy says. "No, he is not." She picks up her coffee and sets it down again. "He can't sleep at night. When he's home, he spends all his time in his shop, building that birchbark canoe. All the business has shifted to the Gunflint, he says. Nobody wants to come to this part of the Arrowhead to fish anymore, he says. But of course that's not entirely true."

"All these rich businessmen?" Stacie says. "They love to fish."

"Exactly. But the big dummy does a Google search for every client request. If they've got any connection to mining, any at all, he flat refuses them. You know your father." And here Betsy picks up the framed diploma and studies it fondly. "He wishes you were still six years old and in pigtails and that this town was still nothing but loons and lakes. He doesn't like change."

4

✳

Victoria's husband knocks at the bathroom door and asks if everything is okay.

"Yes," she says over the noise of the shower. "Just give me another second."

She can't quite hear his response, but it has something to do with using up all the hot water. She isn't sure how much time has passed since she curled up in a ball on the bottom of the tub — maybe ten minutes or maybe an hour — but she has been there so long that her legs have gone to sleep, and she has to brace herself against the ledge to slowly rise. She pushes her face beneath the spray and opens her mouth and swishes and spits out the bile that sours her tongue.

She swipes the towel across the mirror and studies the face she no longer recognizes. Wrinkled and spotted and hollowed. Long white hair weeding down her neck and bony shoulders. People used to guess she was ten, even twenty years younger than she was. Not anymore. The math has reversed since they moved to Northfall, and she has never felt or looked older.

Another knock at the bathroom door. "Hey, hon? You're going to be late if you don't hurry it up."

"I'll be fine," she says. "It's not like the work can start without me." The air is so thick with steam that it feels like she's swallowing clouds and she thinks maybe if she stayed in here long enough and ignored the knocking, she would eventually become something vaporous herself — and simply float away.

. . .

In the kitchen Wade scrapes out the pan and offers her a plate of scrambled eggs with onion, green pepper, and cheese sprinkled over the top.

"Thanks, but nothing for me," she says and goes to the cupboard and pulls down a thermos and fills it with coffee from the carafe.

He tries again, following her, brushing his palm along her back. "Most important meal of the day."

"I'm sorry," she says and blows the steam off the coffee before taking a sip that instantly makes her chest burn with acid. "But I can't seem to keep anything down."

"Maybe you're pregnant?" he says.

She has to pull the coffee away from her mouth to laugh at the thought of it. After all those years of trying, early in their marriage, for her to end up a mother at sixty-two. "Can you imagine?" she says.

Wade sets the plate on the counter and draws her into a hug.

"What are your plans today?" she says and he says, "I thought I'd fiddle around in the garden, catch up on the *Times*, check out that new burrito place, maybe start a torrid affair with one of the neighbors."

She and Wade have been married over forty years, thirty of which they both spent teaching at the University of Nebraska. He was an adjunct lecturer and she a full professor. He taught freshman bio, the same curriculum semester after semester; she was a tenured faculty member in the physics department and applied for million-dollar grants to fund her lab's research. Wade never really cared about teaching. He would rather have been fishing or biking or cooking, hosting dinner parties, playing golf. But Victoria lived to work. Her job defined her, consumed her.

For as long as they have been together, Wade has talked about their retirement plans—and though she has read the travel guides and scrolled through the websites he sent her, she can never really imagine not working. They would leave Lincoln, buy a house in coastal Oregon, and when they weren't eating Dungeness crabs or peeking into tide pools or puttering around in their boat, they would travel. That was what Wade wanted, to visit Iceland, Brazil, Vietnam, Russia, South Africa, India. There were so many places he wanted to see — and Minnesota wasn't one of them.

But then the sky fell. She read the news about the fungal infection in the Pacific Northwest. She saw the footage of the electrical phantom in Bangladesh. There were rumors of a flying woman in Los Angeles, spiked tentacles rising out of drains in Mexico City, a bear the size of a school bus in Siberia. And in northern Minnesota, metal rained from the sky. Metal that might prove to be the greatest energy source in the world. When the men in black suits showed up at Victoria's lab and offered her what they called the opportunity of a lifetime, she really believed that's what it was. Truly groundbreaking work. She would author the rules of this strange new world. She came to Northfall with the understanding she was serving a higher purpose, unlocking the secrets of science and bettering humanity.

Just as Wade had dutifully followed her to Lincoln, he followed her here. To Northfall. To this housing development built on a golf course so new, the joints in the sod are still visible. They had always lived in older homes that Wade refurbished. He didn't know what to do with himself in this neocolonial with wall speakers and fake hardwood floors and a master bath with a Jacuzzi and a bidet. Just for a few years, she promised him. Then she would retire. A life's work realized. And then they could go anywhere.

Now his smile fades and he says, "You were awake a lot of last night."

"I'm sorry if I kept you up."

"I can hear you, you know. In the bathroom. Even with the door closed and the shower on, I can hear you crying."

"I'm sorry," she says.

"There's nothing to be sorry for," he says. "I'm worried about you."

He touches her face and she rubs his knuckles, which are starting to marble with arthritis, and says, "I've got to go."

"When we moved here, I'd never seen you so excited. You were as giddy as a schoolgirl. But now . . ."

"Hopefully I'll be back around five."

She screws the top onto the thermos and fetches her purse and heads for the garage and he says, "Victoria?"

She opens the door and pauses, half in and half out of the shadows.

"What are you doing over there?"

She tightens her mouth. "You know I can't tell you."

"The work . . . it's making you sick?" He is trim except for a bit of a belly poking against his golf shirt. His salt-and-pepper mustache matches his full head of hair. And while she feels paler by the day, he is tanned from all his time outside. He wears tortoiseshell glasses and he takes them off now as if to see her better. "Are you wearing protective gear? What are you exposing yourself to?"

Not for the first time, she considers telling him everything. She would feel so much cleaner and lighter then. But a siren wails in the distance and she takes a deep breath and says, "You know there's a good chance we're being recorded right now."

She can't leave him like this — he'll fret all day — so she waves her keys and says, "I'll see you for dinner!" in a cheery voice that is not her own.

There is no sign in front of the facility, but her paycheck comes from the Department of Defense. The drive takes fifteen minutes. Getting inside takes fifteen more. The first checkpoint is off a highway walled with evergreens. Here one guard examines her ID while keeping a hand on his holster and another circles the car with a German shepherd. She knows their names are Ernie and Phillip, but she cannot tell them apart. They are both young white men with buzz cuts who wear camouflage uniforms and earnest expressions and call her ma'am.

She pops the hood and the trunk. A mirror sweeps the underside of her Volvo wagon. Only then does the gate open, and they wave her through and say, "Have a good day, ma'am." She drives a quarter mile down a freshly paved road to the campus, a collection of square and rectangular buildings, all gray and windowless.

Armed drones hover over the parking lot. Guards with assault rifles walk the fenced perimeter. Pines gather so thickly all around, she can barely see the hills humped on either side of this valley. At the entrance to building 3, she again shows her ID to a guard, but this time she must hand over her purse and remove all jewelry and walk through a full-body scanner.

The building appears to be three stories from the outside, but there are five sublevels beneath, and she goes to the bottommost. She cannot walk more than twenty paces without encountering another locked door manned by a guard. The swipe of an ID card bleeps and the light changes from red to green and the locks scrape in their sleeves, and in this way she progresses, in stops and starts, to her lab. She has referred to it as a maze, but really *trap* is the better word. She feels trapped.

She used to work with a stable of assistants, but not here. Here she is alone with her research. When she enters the space, a thirty-by-forty-foot room, the lights buzz on — UV, to make up for all the time she's underground. Here is a stainless-steel counter bottomed and topped by equipment cabinets. A small fridge for premade meals and a larger fridge for samples. Filing cabinets. There is a desk on which sits a computer, but it has no external connectivity. She is encouraged to document everything on paper.

One wall appears to be plain steel, but when she nudges a lever, a crack splits down the middle and the armored shell retracts, revealing a bulletproof window, two feet thick. On the other side is a room with the same dimensions as the lab but empty of anything except the boy curled up on the metal shelf that serves as his bunk. No sheets, no mattress or pillow. It took weeks of argument before Victoria convinced her superiors to allow the boy clothes to wear. "It all ends up destroyed, so what's the point?" That's what they said. But Victoria persisted and they finally agreed on a black singlet that looks a little like a wetsuit, in part because it is woven through with biotech that reads his pulse, sweat composition, temperature, glucose levels.

"Good morning," Victoria says over the comm.

On paper they refer to him as Patient Zero. But his name is Hawkin, and she calls him by that name even though she has been reprimanded for it. She can't *not* think of him as a person, though her supervisors encourage exactly that.

The boy stirs but does not rise. Not until Victoria asks him to —with a whispering, singsong voice, the way a mother might coo to an infant—and even then the boy sits up with the greatest reluctance, rubbing his eye with his fist. Staring at the floor, he mutters something and Victoria says, "What was that, Hawkin? Can you say that again?"

"I said, do I have to?"

"I'm afraid you must." And then she clears her throat. "Or rather, *we* must."

Only now does he look up at her, his eyes the bright blue of winter stars. The boy's legs scissor the air and he leans over the cot as though considering a jump from a great height. He is short for his age, around five feet, and narrow-boned.

"You don't want to help me?" Victoria says.

"No."

Cameras—black-lensed, insectile—are nested in the ceiling on both sides of the divide, and Victoria glances at them now and then, reminding herself to take care with her words. She'd rather say, *I'm sorry.* She'd rather say, *I didn't know this was what they were hiring me to do.* She'd rather say, *I wish I could tuck you into my purse and steal you away from this place.* But instead she says, "You're such a good helper."

"I'd rather be asleep." He looks so much younger than his fifteen years, but his sulky, poisonous delivery reminds her that he is deep into his teens. "I'd rather be anything than awake."

"I know this is hard to believe," Victoria says, "but sometimes I'd . . . rather not do this either. But I have to. Because the work we're doing is important, Hawkin." She always preferred her lab to the classroom, but she was occasionally required to teach a large lecture course. When she asked Wade how he did it, he said that every instructor should be trained in theater. "You are both intellectually and emotionally manipulating them, trying to get them to *feel.* Your tone and delivery are as important as the material." She always acted so woodenly in front of an auditorium of three hundred students, but here, on a smaller stage, she has grown looser, more comfortable, treating Hawkin as both her student and subject while thinking of him privately as something more than either.

Victoria boots up the computer and jots down the readings in today's log before going to the minifridge and withdrawing what looks like a tray of airline food. A fruit cup, yogurt container, jam pack, butter pack, croissant, and short carton of milk. Along with a variety of candied pills. "Breakfast is up," she says and slides it into a two-doored compartment that divides the barrier between them. "Yum."

"I'm not hungry," Hawkin says, and though it takes some effort, Victoria smiles and, in a voice hollow with irony, says, "Most important meal of the day."

"No, thank you," Hawkin says with a shake of his head. "You eat it."

Victoria pats the compartment door. "Well, it will be here if you change your mind. You at least need to take the pills. Okay?"

"Fine. You said you were going to get me some comic books."

"I'm still waiting on approval for that."

"I'm so bored."

"I'm trying."

"I feel like I'm going crazy."

She almost says, *Me too,* but instead says, "I promise."

"Okay."

"So. What are we starting with today?" Victoria goes to her desk and flips open the binder and runs her finger down the sheet. "It looks like we're going to be spending a lot of the morning with the M16." Victoria opens a cabinet lined with weapons. She pulls on her protective glasses and tucks the earplugs into her pocket and retrieves the rifle from its ledge and picks up four magazines.

There is a kind of standing desk built in front of the glass wall. On it is a spring-loaded bipod that she locks the M16 into. She activates the control, and a window opens in the divider, and now they don't need to speak through the comm. Her voice echoes through the divide: "Hawkin? Would you mind taking your starting position?"

Near the back of the room, Hawkin slumps his shoulders and shuffles along until his toes reach the line etched into the floor. It's marked off in six-inch intervals and runs down the center of the room like a zipper.

"We'll begin with the left shoulder," Victoria says. "Ready?"

Hawkin nods and closes his eyes and licks his lips. "I guess."

Victoria nudges the plugs into her ears, squints shut one eye, targeting the boy's shoulder, and lets out a long emptying breath. She curls her finger around the trigger. And fires.

5

✳

When Yesno asks how much time John needs, he says, "About as long as it takes to eat a piece of pie. That okay?"

"It's absolutely okay." Yesno actually has a few last-minute errands to run—picking up the boutonnieres at the florist, stopping by the caterer's to make sure all is in order—so he'll plan to pick up John in forty-five minutes or so.

The traffic is thick enough in downtown Northfall that John asks to get dropped off a few blocks away. "I don't mind," he says. "Too much sitting. It'll be good to walk."

The wide sidewalks and quaint brick storefronts are still there but in a state of troubled transition, like a rosy-cheeked twelve-year-old with track marks, a nose stud, and a black eye.

Wads of gum stamp the sidewalks along with the dank dust of chewing tobacco. Broken glass sparkles. Crumpled McDonald's bags flutter. A tattoo shop has replaced the bookstore. A head shop has replaced the malt shop. Here is a Harley retailer, a bail bondsman, an EZ Money loan center, and a jewelry store with a thirty-thousand-dollar diamond-studded belt buckle on display.

In the town square there is a steel statue of Paul Bunyan. Forty feet tall. He's carrying a double-sided ax that rests on his shoulder, the blade flashing silver in the sun. All around him stand protesters holding signs that read *Save the Boundary Waters* and *Ten Thousand Lakes, Not Ten Thousand Bombs* and *The BWCA Is Ours, Not Yours.* Some are middle-aged women in down vests and yoga pants. Others are long-haired and unshaven and hemp-necklaced. The co-op and NPR crowd alongside the funky eco-warriors.

This has been standard in Northfall since he was a kid. The region is defined by protest. That's what happens when you live in place remarkable for its in-betweenness; the extremities yank it in both directions. Was it the crown of the United States or the ass of Canada? People wished winter wouldn't last so long, but then they complained summer was too hot. The ATV crowd claimed to love the outdoors, but the canoe crowd said they had a terrible way of showing it. The town hated the tourists but relied on the money they spent. The Boundary Waters were a national treasure, yes, but the lumber of the forests and the iron ore and the copper in the hills had to be treasured as well.

A man stumbles out of a bar — packed even at this early hour — and puddles the gutter with puke. A woman with blue eye shadow approaches John with a smile that he returns. "Hey, soldier," she says. "Suck for twenty, handy for ten?"

"No, thanks," he says.

On the corner stands a man wearing a coat despite the heat of the day. He keeps a pit bull on a choker leash. As they wait for the busy traffic to pass, John kneels to pet the dog, flop its ears. It licks his knuckles. "You want rocks?" the man says.

"Sorry?"

"I got rocks. I got blow. I got crank. I got weed. I got oxy. I got H. I got E. I even got a taste of space dust. Whatever you want, man. Whatever."

"Space dust, huh?"

"You never flown so high. Take you to the moon and back, man."

"I'm good." John gives the dog one final scratch before crossing the street. Even if everything else has changed, the Lumberjack Steakhouse remains the same. An institution in Northfall. The restaurant you took your prom date to, celebrated your anniversary or birthday at, ordering the prime rib drowned in au jus. Or you just went for a grilled cheese and a slice of lemon meringue.

The boardwalk is edged by a railing made from rusty saw blades.

On one side of the front door stands a roughly carved bald eagle; on the other, a flannel-and-denim-clad woodsman with an ax.

John pushes open the door and takes in the familiar aroma of garlic toast and charred steak. A glass pie case fills the entryway, every shelf of it crammed with apple, cherry, peach, chocolate cream. An older woman with a denim shirt and a bandanna around her neck leads him from the hostess station to one of the booths along the wall. "Jenna will be here to serve you in just a second, hon."

"Thanks," he says, his eyes already on her. Jenna. A few tables away. Pouring decaf into a mug. Strawberry-blond hair pulled back in a messy bun. Freckles sprinkling her nose and cheeks. She looks in his direction, looks away, then looks back again. She continues to pour the coffee even after it spills over the lip of the mug and the old man at the table says, "Hold on, now! Hold on!"

"I'm so sorry," she says and rushes to the waitress station and returns with a towel and mops up the mess. But even as she soaks and swipes and apologizes again and again to the man, she steals looks at John, trying not to smile.

His birthmark feels like it's glowing red, throbbing on his face like an alarm, and he can't help but touch it as if to test whether it's hot.

Finally she approaches him, the towel balled up and sopping in her hand. "It's you."

"It's me," he says.

"You're back."

"Just for a bit."

One of her front teeth is crooked and somehow that always makes her smile more sincere. "I knew Talia was getting married, but I still didn't think . . ." She throws down the towel and wraps her arms around him. He closes his eyes at her touch, savoring it.

"You look so different," she says and pulls back and studies him in a sad, happy, lingering way, like you do when you're flipping through a photo album and find a version of yourself that no longer exists. "But you're still my Johnny?"

"Walked some miles since we last saw each other. You, on the other hand, not a day older."

"Bullshit," she says.

"Can I buy you a piece of pie?"

"I shouldn't sit down. I'm working." She gestures to the dining room, but only half the booths are occupied. "Maybe just for a minute?"

"I'll take what I can get. You still like the banana cream with chocolate sprinkles?"

"Course," she says. "It's the best there is."

"One piece, then. With two forks."

She returns a minute later and settles into the booth across from him and picks up her fork but doesn't eat. Her arms are sunburned. Her wedding ring catches a ray of sun and glimmers a rainbow across the tabletop. "You know . . . for a long time, I couldn't even listen to the radio, read the newspaper. Every time North Africa or Afghanistan or anything came up, I'd get twisted up inside, worrying."

"Managed to make it through the thresher."

"How long are you here?"

"Just until tomorrow."

"Probably doesn't even feel like home?"

"No. But that's maybe got more to do with me than with omnimetal."

She looks out the window, watching the traffic roll by. "It's pretty scary, the changes going on here. You should hear what Dan's dealing with on patrol. Just last week, this truck full of—"

"Dan."

"He was my husband," she says and then clears her throat. "He's my husband. Dan Swanson. I'm a Swanson now. You must have heard that."

"Sure I did. Where's he from?"

"From here now. Everybody from here's from someplace else, sometimes seems. But Bemidji's where he grew up."

"You married a cop?"

"Guess I drank my fill of bad boys." She sighs through her teeth. "Not that he was ever that well behaved." Her eyes dart to a clock on the wall shaped like a loon. "Case in point, it's been — what — twenty-seven hours since I last heard from his butt." She says this in a nervous hurry, and John isn't sure what to make of it. Is she worried about Dan? Or declaring, in a way, the opposite?

"He treating you okay? How long you been together?"

Jenna studies her ring, twists it, smiles. "Four years now."

"And you've got a kid? How old?"

"Four years now."

"Mrs. Swanson, huh?"

"Yep." Her lips pop with the *p*.

A man in a flannel shirt rises from a table and approaches them and says, "Excuse me, miss?"

"Just one second," she says. Only now does she fork up a piece of pie. She savors the taste of it, like a kiss, with her eyes closed. "Working girl's got to get back to it."

She nudges out of the booth and stands over him and he reaches out a hand and she takes it and they knit their fingers together. "It's your eyes."

"What?"

"I don't remember them being that shade of brown."

"Oh," he says. "Huh."

"Anyway. Can't tell you how good it is to see you, Johnny."

She turns away, takes a few steps, looks at him one more time over her shoulder, then goes back to work.

He finishes his pie, wipes his mouth, drops a few twenties on the table, and slides out of the booth. He doesn't realize he's smiling until, on his way out the door, someone says, "What's with the shit-eating grin?" And slams a shoulder into his own. John manages to keep his balance as the man — the big blond man from the train station, Mickey Golden — enters the restaurant. "Guess we'll be seeing each other around, GI Joe."

6

✳

The Lumberjack Steakhouse has several dining rooms, all lit by chandeliers made from antlers. At a pine-plank table, Mickey Golden drags out a chair, takes a seat, and says, "Hey, boss." He's addressing Walter Eaton, the owner of Black Dog Energy, who wears an enormous dove-white Stetson, a bolo tie, and a sky-blue western shirt with pearl snaps that barely contain his girth.

Walt says only, "Already ordered for you." He's busy unrolling a map, trying to smooth it with his hands, but it keeps curling back up again. Along the table, other maps are laid flat and weighed down at their corners with water glasses. "Give me some of them rings of yours?"

"Why?" Mickey bristles his rings, some of them diamond-studded, like a second set of knuckles.

"Weigh this sucker down."

"Rather not undress if it's all the same."

Walt whistles and waves over Jenna. She is on her way to deliver an order, a tray balanced on her shoulder, but she complies, because she knows he'll keep whistling if she doesn't. He speaks with a Texas twang when he says, "Help me out here, hon. I need a few some-things to flatten this here map."

"You bet," she says. "If you can give me a minute, I'll be right back."

"No, just give me that plate with the baked potato on it, would you? And the other one? With the Jell-O salad?"

"I'm so sorry," she says, "but these are—"

Golden reaches for the plates and says, "Surely we appreciate it."

She doesn't hide her sigh, but she continues on while the two men weight the map with the plates. Before them lies the topography of St. Louis County, which looks like a giant fingerprint. The far-reaching *Omnimetal Strike Zone* is highlighted in light blue. Red ink outlines the perimeter of an area within this; it's labeled *Gunderson Woods* and has an *X* at its heart. "You know what this is?"

"I know what this is."

"The mother lode." When Walt leans forward, the silver tips of his bolo tie knock together and chime. "If we was gold mining, that's what we'd call it. Four hundred acres of deposits. Big mounds. Deep pits. Gouges. Veins. Those formations they're calling chimneys and spurs. Bunch of trees coated by melt." He lays a hand on the map, covering a good chunk of it, as if he could scoop it all up. "This is our shot, you understand. To finally beat out Frontier. Take control of the energy game."

"They're still after it?"

"You bet they are. Problem for both of us is, this here land's owned by a crazy person. Betsy Gunderson is her name, but everybody calls her Mother now. Forty-five years old. Widow. Big old load of omnimetal crashes into her backyard and she suddenly decides she's the second coming of Jesus, Muhammad, Buddha, and all the rest. Religious prophet. Queen of the metal-eaters. They got this saying: Metal is. Like it's the end and it's the beginning, forever and ever, amen. I'll tell you what metal *is*. Metal's *money*."

"Yes, sir."

"There's all these weird formations, see. One section looks like a shiny Stonehenge or something. Big silver crater that shoots up at the edges into ten or twelve spurs. Like a crown. Like some hell claw reaching out of damnation."

"That was a real good description, Walt."

"She's treating this like some religious site. Got people pilgrimaging to it. Got metal-eaters pretending her into some sort of high priestess. She's nuts, of course. Total loony tunes. Sent my best pitchmen out there. We've offered and we've offered and we've offered. And it's not that she doesn't understand *what* we're offering — it's that she does *not* care."

"You've tried other means, of course."

"I would have that woman shot in the head, run over by a semi, and fed to dogs if she ever left the damn place. But she never leaves the damn place. And Gunderson Woods is not only surrounded by a spiked wall of logs like some cocksucking pioneer outpost, it's patrolled twenty-four/seven by metal-eaters carrying AR-15s."

"So they're not the kind of cult that believes in peace and harmony and sings 'Kumbaya' around the campfire with rainbows shooting out of their eyes."

"No, they are most certainly not."

Walt's cell rings. He pulls it out and studies the screen and says, "Oh, shut up," then fumblingly silences it before continuing. "You understand how important it is? That we win this property? We don't have enough holdings right now for that military contract, but if we can secure this land, it's ours for the taking. The head of Frontier keeps claiming that we're corporate outsiders. That he's a local boy who's made good. And all these Lutherans eat up what he spoons them and sell their mineral rights to him *instead* of us. But that's a steaming pile of horseshit. He's got Saudis and Indians and Chinese on his board. I'm telling you — Gunderson Woods, it's our stone in a sling. This is how we fight the local giant."

"Yes, sir."

"I want that land. I want a signature on a piece of paper that reads *Gunderson*. And I want it now." Their food arrives — big, oozing T-bone steaks slopped over with eggs. Walt tucks a napkin in his collar and neatens his silverware, and his hand lingers on the steak knife. "I brought you up here, Mickey, because you're good at fixing things. You fixed things for me in Alaska and you fixed things for me in Texas."

"Copy that."

"I'm trusting that you can fix this too?"

"That's what I do, isn't it, Walt? Fix your shit?"

"You're my man."

"I'm your man."

7

✴

The wedding guests come from all over the world. Brits, Argentines, Chinese, Israelis, South Africans, Indians, Russians, Saudis. Some fly into Northfall on private jets; others roll into town in rented Ferraris and Escalades. They do not know Talia Frontier. They are here out of respect for her father, Ragnar.

He stands by the door of the church to greet every one of them. He is eighty-five but could pass for seventy. Barrel-chested. A full head of silver hair. Big hands, the right one brightened by a ring on his middle finger that glows with the soft blue light of omnimetal.

He refuses a chair, so Yesno stands beside him, his hands free in case the old man falls. But he doesn't, even though the sun reddens his cheeks and the heat wilts his boutonniere.

John waits in line with everyone else because that's what a guest does. And he is a guest. He no longer belongs here—and that aloneness and out-of-placeness makes him feel proud, not sad. He got out. Without his father's money. Or connections. Or blessing. He left. And now he's back home, a different man.

When it is John's turn, his father holds out his arms and says, "My son the hero." His voice is deep but rusted with age. They embrace for a long moment, and John can feel the old man's bones pushing through the fabric of his suit. He smells the same as when John was a boy, like maple syrup and fine leather. He pulls back and places a hand on the side of John's head. "I'm glad you're here," he says. "We've missed you."

"I'm glad to be here too," John says.

"How was the train?"

"Easy. Blinked my eyes and I was home."

"Best way to travel, the Bullet. You know we're building a southern corridor next. Ninth-metal tracks are going to connect the entire country before long."

"I heard that."

"We're building a whole new world." The old man's face creases with wrinkles when he smiles. "No date?"

"Just me, Pops."

"I thought you might bring someone pretty home with you."

"I had someone pretty before. And you didn't like her much."

"I liked her fine. But let's not talk about that." The old man fingers the medals along John's chest, including two Purple Hearts, and shakes his head with pride. "I always knew you had incredible potential."

"How'd you know that?" His voice is calm even as it's challenging. "Because I was your son?"

His father rolls back his head and purses his lips and raises a single finger, but before he can say anything, Yesno nudges in between them. "We've got your old room made up for you at the house, John. And I bet you two will enjoy catching up there later."

"That sounds good," John says and his father says, "Good, good," and claps John on the shoulder, directing him inside, then turns his attention to the next person in line. "Ah, Peter and Emily! Thank you for being here!"

The church is Lutheran, like so many of the churches up north, and newly constructed, like so many of the buildings in Northfall. It is painted slate gray and sits on the shore of Moon Lake. The wall behind the pulpit is made entirely of glass except for the giant cross that doubles as support beams. The sanctuary seats five hundred, and it is so full that the ushers have to set up three rows of folding chairs in the back. This is where John sits.

Fans spin. People swish their programs back and forth to make a breeze. He overhears a conversation in Japanese, another in Russian, with the same word connecting them both: *om-nimetal*. Business. Everything surrounding his father comes down to business.

There are at least five photographers in the sanctuary, and overhead, a circling drone with the eye of a camera bulging from its abdomen captures video of the guests as they await the wedding party. When it hovers low over the congregation, its blades whirring, a few people shade their eyes or turn their heads away, not wanting to be recorded.

John has never met the groom, but Talia has e-mailed photos of the two of them. He enters now and stands at the altar, tall and athletic, sunburned, too-white teeth, his blond hair gelled into messy spikes. He's a decade younger than his sister. Someone who will look nice beside her. Someone who will do as he's told.

The procession begins and cameras flash as the groomsmen and bridesmaids march down the aisle. It takes John a moment to realize that one of the groomsmen is his older brother. "Jesus, Nico," he whispers. His build is skeletal and his hair has thinned to wisps. His arm is locked with a bridesmaid's and she seems to holding him up. When he reaches the altar and moves to his place near the groom, his eyes appear as dark hollows with a soft blue light emanating from them.

John has heard about this. The side effects of omnimetal. Of smoking it and snorting it. Metal-eaters, the addicts are called.

Nico is the dreamer of the family. The artist. He plays music. He makes jewelry and paints and carves and sculpts. Family Christmases long ago always involved sweaters or stocking caps knit by him or watercolor landscapes painted by him. Sometimes he claimed to see auras. Sometimes he claimed to have visions. Once he dreamed that their father was bleeding from a hole in his head, and the next day Ragnar walked into an open cupboard door and fell to the kitchen floor with a gashed temple. No one was sure what to make of Nico. They all treated him like a delicate pet.

When the organ begins to grind out Pachelbel's Canon, everyone rises from the pews, and his father enters with Talia, her arm hooked through his. Her skin is a burnt orange, the fake tan deep enough that it almost hides the barbed-wire tattoo stitching her left biceps. Even when she was a teenager, she started every day with a hard workout, pushing tractor tires, climbing ropes, hurling medicine balls, and years of exercise have given her a thick build of mature muscle. Her trunk of a neck is highlighted by a short haircut that angles sharply to her collar. There has never been a lot of love between brother and sister, but John can't help but smile, matching her expression.

The ceremony lasts half an hour, and after the pastor speaks of love and loyalty, after a cousin reads from First Corinthians, after the bride and groom exchange their vows, the drone circles the altar so close that it startles Talia and she swipes at it with her bouquet and loses a flutter of petals.

"I believe in this town." His voice pretends confidence, but he has to clear his throat twice to get out the rest. "I believe in Northfall." His face twitches. His hair plasters his forehead and his deputy blues are soaked through with sweat.

A single bulb burns overhead. It casts a yellow cone of light. The corners of the basement remain lost to shadow, but the light reveals a mildewed floor drain. Jam and pickle jars on a shelving unit. A tool bench faintly gleaming with hammers and nails and screws.

"You're thinking one thing," he says. "But I'm telling you another. You're wrong about me. I'm loyal. To you and to the community. I want what's best for us all."

He sits in an old wooden chair. A rope around his chest is tied at the back of it, and his wrists are duct-taped to its arms. He keeps forgetting this, and when he talks, he tries to gesture, and the wood groans. "It's not what it looks like. I wasn't giving away information. I was *gathering* information. Information I was going to give you. Just let me prove it to you. Just tell me what to do, I'll do it. Anything." One of his lips is fat and scabbed and he licks at it now. "Anything you ask."

There is no response, no noise at all except for his panting and the *click-click-click* of heel-heavy steps orbiting him.

"Anything at all," he says. "Are you hearing me?"

When she speaks, her voice is throaty, as if roughed up by cigarettes, close to a man's. "Why'd you have to go and ruin my day?" Her pacing continues, a slow circle of him, never pausing. *Click-click-click*. A pipe moans. A centipede twists and vanishes into the dark.

"I'm sorry," he says, his voice suddenly loud and desperate. A few tears spring from his eyes. "It's the worst decision I ever made! I'd take it back if I could."

And then, near the tool bench, her heels pause their clicking. There is a scrape, the drag of something heavy. Slowly she steps into the light. "Today of all days." Her wedding dress glows white. Strapless. Edged with satin. Breasted with lace. "I really don't have time for this shit."

Her fingers—tipped with French-manicured nails—tighten around the grip of the baseball bat. She lifts it to her shoulder. When she swings, the fat diamond on her ring catches the light and sparkles.

The reception is held at the Frontier compound, forty acres of forested hillside overlooking the town. The house is more of a lodge, with log walls, vaulted ceilings, fieldstone detailing, and iron and copper hardware. Steel roofing. Geothermal heating. Twenty bedrooms, seven fireplaces, four decks, a theater, a wine cellar, a sauna, a library and gym and banquet hall. The original home—the one John grew up in—was massive by most standards, but it is now just one of several wings connected by glass pathways to the central structure. His old life, his old self, feels buried somewhere inside of this larger mansion that has grown over the top of it. And maybe he feels a little like that too. Given the uniform he wears. And the distance he's traveled. And the time he's been gone. And the control he's affecting. He carries it all awkwardly, like bulky armor, like a castle on his back.

Several outbuildings surround the home. One of them, a pole barn, is Nico's studio. Throughout the house and throughout the grounds, his artwork is on display. A winding river of agates — red and yellow and orange and white, all harvested from the north shore of Superior — doubles as a path from the house to the pond. He meticulously laid the squares of concrete and nudged each stone into place. He also planted and trimmed the shrub labyrinth with topiary monsters in it. And from a dying pine, he carved and laminated what he calls the monolith, a tall totem with holes and alien designs etched onto it. Partygoers stroll past some of the installations now, making conversation around them.

The driveway is lined with cars. The porch is festooned with ribbons and balloons in shades of purple, Talia's favorite color. In the backyard, a sloped lawn bottoms out into the pond. People mill among the tables and tents and bars. A jazz combo plays on a stage and a few children leap and spin their bodies, but otherwise the dance floor is empty.

On the gift table, there are many boxes wrapped with white paper and tied with silver ribbon. But most people make their way to the open cedar chest and drop in fat envelopes tucked with cash.

Drones swirl overhead, compiling footage. Caterers dressed entirely in white wander among the guests offering trays holding champagne, bruschetta, bacon-wrapped dates, walleye Rangoon. Dinner should have already started, but no one can locate Talia.

John shakes hands, says, "It's good to see you, it's good to see you." Everyone keeps after him, asking, "Are you home to stay, Johnny?" and "Hard to believe what's happened to our little town, isn't it?" and "You've sure turned yourself around."

He corners Nico, says, "Should I be worried about you?" But his brother just looks at him with those will-o'-the-wisp eyes and says, "There's nothing to worry about. I've never felt better."

Before John can bother Nico further, Talia is beside him. She snakes an arm around John's waist and smushes her lips against his cheek and says, "Long time, no see, baby brother."

John says congratulations and she says thank you and plucks a flute of champagne off a passing tray and downs it in one gulp and wipes her mouth clean with the back of her hand. John looks to Nico, but his brother is already gone, sneaking between the tables, headed back to the house with his head bowed.

"Is he okay?" John says and Talia squints after their brother and says, "He tells me the metal inspires him. You should see some of the shit he's making right now in the studio. Calls them his *cosmic* sculptures. Creepy."

"I heard something about him joining a cult?"

Her big shoulders rise and fall in a shrug. "You could call it that, I guess. Or you could call it reconnaissance."

"I don't get it."

"These metal-eaters, they've set up shop in a compound outside of town. Four hundred acres, all of it thick with omnimetal. They think it's some kind of altar or some shit."

"Nico's out there?"

"He's got his ear to the ground for me. We want that property. And we want to know what these freaks have planned."

"Don't you worry he drank the Kool-Aid?"

"Do we have to talk about this right now?"

"It's just that I hardly recognize him."

"You're one to judge, you of all people. Nobody'd recognize you either, Johnny boy, in that army getup if you didn't still have that ugly stain on your face."

"I'm just worried about him."

"Leave him be. You do your thing. He'll do his. I'll do mine. We'll all be a lot happier."

"I suppose so."

"So now what?" his sister asks. "Dinner, right? During which time I'll have to smile my way through who knows how many insufferable toasts."

"That's how these things normally go. It's been a beautiful day so far."

"Yeah," she says distractedly and waves to someone across the yard. "Hey, I need to talk to you later, okay?"

"About what?"

"A few things."

"Yeah? Like what?"

"There's a fight going on here. A fight for Northfall, guess you could say. You probably already got a sense of that. It's like Deadwood downtown. It's like the gold rush meets the oil rush meets the height of the steel boom in the Iron Range. It's fucking bananas. Forget the Wild West. This is the Wild North."

"Okay."

"Northfall's ours — right, Johnny? It always has been. The Frontiers have kept this place alive as long as we've been alive."

"Okay."

"This Black Dog? They're a bunch of vulturous bitches. Swooping in here with their bullshit and trying to, like, usurp us."

"Usurp you?"

"Isn't that the word? Like stage a coup or some shit?"

"Seems like there's plenty of money to be made. We don't need all of it. What's wrong with a little competition?"

"It's not just about that, dumb-ass. These pricks have operations in Alaska, Texas, North Dakota. They leave a mess wherever they go. Superfund sites up the ass. No philanthropy. Treat their employees like garbage. They don't care about Northfall. They don't have its best interests in mind."

"Plenty of environmentalists will say the same about us."

"Mining's going to happen here whether those nature-worshipping pansies cry into their recycled tissues or not. Who you want doing the digging? The guys that got roots that run deep. That's who. That's us. Even some Prius-driving granola-puss is going to agree with me on that. We want to make this town into a powerhouse. Black Dog wants to make this town into a carved-out pit."

"This isn't my fight."

"Sure as shit is, Johnny. And it's not just about profit. It's about control. The future of this family, the future of this company, the future of the town, the future of this state — all the goddamn pressure in the goddamn world is on us right now."

"You should really go talk to your guests. People want to say hello to the bride."

"We're going to talk more about this later. Okay?"

"Fine."

"You promise?"

"I'm—look. I'm sorry, but I'm planning on leaving tomorrow."

She curls her lip at him, that old fast temper. "The hell is your rush, Johnny? You haven't been home in five years. Stick around. This is your town. We're your *family*." She slaps a palm against his chest and knocks him back a step.

Twenty years ago, he would have pinched her or yanked her hair and run. Now he smooths his coat and says, "I go by John these days."

"John," she says in a nasal, drawn-out voice meant to make the name sound boring.

"Aren't you leaving anyway?" he says. "The honeymoon is in Mexico, right?"

"You're not going anywhere. All right, *John?* We're going to talk. After this lace-and-cake circus finishes up. Got a favor to ask you. Can't deny a bride on her wedding day—am I right?"

"Yes. Fine. Now go."

"I gotta go make nice."

"So go."

She starts away from him, but before she gets far, he grabs her by the elbow. "Is that blood?"

"What?" she says, annoyed and then concerned. "Where?" She tucks her chin and sees the dime-size spot on her breast. She plucks a cloth napkin from a table, dunks it in a glass of ice water, and roughs the stain until it's only a pink memory. "Probably just red wine."

8

✳

Six months after Stacie was sworn in as a Northfall police officer, her uniform still feels like a costume. The belt — weighed down with pepper spray, a Taser, handcuffs, a pistol — bothers her, abrading her hips and ribs, building up calluses where none should be. Her heart jumps every time the radio squawks. She wonders why everyone stares and stiffens at the sight of her, and then she remembers, *Oh, right, I'm a cop.* Stacie Toal, Northfall PD. Part of her hopes the newness will wear off. And another part of her hopes she never loses the chirpy excitement, the stupid gratefulness she feels almost every day. She has trouble not using the word *awesome* in every other sentence, and she figures that's a good way to be, full of awe.

The downtown slides past her, every building lit up, every parking lot full, the sidewalks crowded with strangers. Hank Lippert drives. It's a warm night, but after a day of air conditioning, they've both rolled down their windows, and the breeze feels good. She takes in the vaporous night, the stink of cigarettes and weed, the whoosh and rumble of passing cars and trucks. A group of men straddling parked motorcycles glance their way and then double over in rowdy laughter. Drumbeats throb from the open door of a bar.

It's more than the job that feels novel. She still hasn't gotten used to the way Northfall has changed. The new town and the old town battle for control of her mind, reality uneasily warping her memories; it's like she's looking at her history through a funhouse mirror. Over there, behind what used to be a dry cleaner's and is now a vape shop, is the parking lot where she lost her virginity in the back seat of her parents' Buick. Over here, a real estate agent's office plastered with million-dollar properties was once an ice cream and candy shop. In that alleyway she found a stray cat and took her home and named her Snowball. On that park bench, in fifth grade, she watched the Fourth of July parade.

She's supposed to be looking for one of their own, a deputy who didn't clock out that morning. His Dodge Charger has gone missing and he hasn't responded to repeated hails and his wife keeps calling to ask about him. Dan Swanson.

Stacie hasn't been on the job long enough to know everyone, but she's seen him around the station, said, "Hey," in the hallways and parking lot. Early thirties. Goatee. Weightlifter's build. Married, but with a single-guy swagger and too much cologne.

"He's fine," Hank says. "Probably went on a bender at the end of his shift. Or met up with some tail he's chasing on the side. Happens."

"It does?" Stacie says.

"Sure, sure." Hank is her partner. Fifty-something, mustached, rumpled, and greasy along the edges. Parts of him bulge against his uniform. Someone thirty years older than her might find him handsome in an Elks Lodge kind of way. He smells like the Kodiak chew he spits into an empty Gatorade bottle. "He'll show up soon. Probably stinking of sex and Wild Turkey. You'll see." Hank reminds her of the kind of men who excel as car salesmen and middle-school football coaches. She's been doing her best to listen to him because he must have something to teach her even if he seems to be 80 percent full of manure.

She's been packing candy with her. Gummy bears. Skittles. Starbursts. Always fruit-flavored, nothing that can melt easily, like chocolate. She hands it out to kids but also to anyone they help: a man whose car broke down on the side of the road, a woman reporting her husband for throwing a chair at her. They all accept the candy with a weird look of disbelief and pleasure. She pulls out a pink Starburst now and offers it to Hank and he says, "Huh? No, thanks. Had two cavities filled the other day. Supposed to lay off the sugar."

"Life's not worth living," she says and pops the candy in her own mouth instead, "without sweets."

The radio chirps and dispatch says, "Car Three, we got a disturbance at the United Methodist on Forest Park Road. Sounds like metal-eaters."

Hank unclips the radio, thumbs the button. "This is Car Three. Five minutes away," he says and switches on the rack lights. "This should be interesting."

"Oh, I think every call's interesting."

The night kaleidoscopes red and blue. The traffic unzippers out of the way and the car picks up speed and they both crank up their windows to seal out the wind.

The *Minneapolis Star Tribune* recently ran a series on ninth metal and addiction. Everyone wanted to try space dust. People said it felt like sex in your veins. They said it made your brain go somewhere else. They said it sped up your metabolism and kept you awake for days. "You think the metal-eaters are dangerous? Because they always seem so—I don't know—dreamy and trippy to me."

Hank chances a look at her, then jerks the wheel and bombs down a side street. "I assume everybody's dangerous. I advise you to do the same."

"I like to assume everybody's good." She pitches her voice high, but it still doesn't sound true. "They just sometimes make mistakes."

He coughs out a laugh. "You say so. But these guys? I don't know. They're spooky."

Hank, like so many of the locals, believes the town is under siege. And she gets that. But she's a self-described optimist, openly fond of inspirational calendars and platitudes printed on coffee mugs and sewn onto throw pillows. She loves Disney and Hallmark. She only reads books that promise to give her a good cry. When someone asks what she does, she generally uses the word *peacekeeper*, not *cop*. Sometimes, at the end of the day, her cheeks ache from all her smiling. More than once she has been referred to as a Pollyanna.

Maybe that's meant as an insult, but it's never bothered her. What's wrong with hope? What's wrong with heart? The world needs more of it.

So she tries to think positively about the change that has come to Northfall. There were times when she was a kid, when the sawmills and the mines started shutting down, that her father guessed the town would die. Now everyone wants to live here. That's a good thing, isn't it? Shouldn't the town be proud? Of course, some growing pains are to be expected.

They roar through a neighborhood, and then the bungalows and fenced-in yards give way to a grassy lawn that leads up to a church. Stacie spots dozens of ghostly figures moving around it. Men or women, she can't tell from here. But they're all wearing black. Black T-shirts, black pants, black shoes. The color of the cosmos. This is the uniform of what some refer to as the Comet Cult—those who have formed a kind of religion around omnimetal.

Stacie says, "How do they even make the metal into a drug?"

"Grind it, crush it. Magnets, floats. Heat and water. I don't know the whole rigmarole of the recipe, but they're ultimately after the salt. That's what they smoke and sniff."

"Sounds complicated."

The squad car comes to a rocking halt and they yank open their doors and step outside and start across the grass. Stacie has to take twice as many steps as Hank to keep up with him. The night is loud with what sounds like hammer strokes mixed up with wood moaning and splintering as it's torn apart

"Junkies are both dumb as shit and smarter than hell. Give them a kitchen and some beakers, they're all a bunch of Julia Child mad scientists. You could offer them an old sneaker and a brick of cheddar and they'd turn it into something toxic to shove up their ass or needle into their eye."

"Oh, dear."

"They're armed," Hank says. "They're always armed. Haven't caught one yet without an open-carry permit, but be aware they're packing." Now they can see the ladders angled against the church and the people on the roof. Torn shingles fly off and slap the grass. Nails tinkle onto the sidewalk. A sheet of plywood hits the ground with a *whoomp* of displaced air that maybe sounds a little like the crack of a rifle, and Hank ducks down and reaches for his holster.

"It was just a—" she says, but he doesn't let her finish the sentence. "I *know* what it was."

There is a dumpster out front and a man unloads some construction debris into it. He has a pistol in a holster at his hip. He turns to look at them as they approach and his eyes glow a faint blue. It makes Stacie think of middle-school sleepovers when she and her friends would shut off the lights and crunch their way through mint Life Savers, delighting in the sparks they gave off. "Metal is," he says. This is a greeting, a goodbye, an acknowledgment of truth, a prayer of sorts, a multipurpose phrase the metal-eaters use regularly in conversation.

"What in the Sam Hill are you all doing to this church?" Hank says.

"It's our church." The man's voice is calm and soft. He is mostly bald, like all of the others, his hair downy where it hasn't fallen out in patches. They all pause in their work to stare at them.

"The hell it is."

"It was for sale. We bought it."

"The hell you did. This here's a Methodist church. I been to a dozen weddings in it and twice as many funerals."

"Not anymore." The man studies them without emotion. His white shirt and pants are dirtied and sweat through. "I can show you the paperwork, if you like."

Hank doesn't seem to know what to say. He peers into the dumpster, then steps back a few paces and takes in the people perched on the roof and ladders like gargoyles. "I thought you did your worshipping out at the compound? What do you need to be here in town for?"

"Visibility. Recruitment. We're part of this town, whether you like it or not."

Hank shakes his head and spits a brown stream of chew. "I don't know how you crazies could pool together enough money to buy a meal, let alone a building."

The front door of the church opens and a man steps out. A thin, balding man with hollowed cheekbones and eyes that strobe as he blinks rapidly. "Is there a problem here?" He approaches them. "Is there something I can do to help?"

Stacie says, "Nico?" and he trains his gaze on her. "You're Nico Frontier, right?" The Frontiers were as close as you came to celebrities in a town like Northfall, but while Ragnar and Talia seemed to be mentioned in the paper or on the radio every day, Nico kept out of the spotlight.

"Metal is," he says.

Hank says, "Jesus, what are you doing mixed up with these people?"

"We would like to continue our work," Nico says. "If you don't mind."

Hank starts to back up and his voice softens into an apology. "People are complaining, that's all. About the racket. There's noise ordinances in this town, you know. Why are you putting on a new roof in the middle of the night anyway?"

"We're not putting on a new roof," Nico says.

"Not sure I follow."

"There will be no roof," Nico says and raises his arms to address the night sky. "So that when the parish worships, they can be that much closer to the stars."

9

＊

t's after midnight when John stands in his mother's den. The original room from their original house, which has been consumed by the larger mansion or lodge or compound—whatever the word—built over the top of it. The guests are gone, but the backyard is still lit up with paper lanterns and busy with workers stacking chairs and collecting glassware and disassembling the dance floor.

Her name was Hillary and she has been dead for over ten years, but the carpet is freshly vacuumed into stripes, and the desk and the sewing table and the shelves are dusted, so it seems she might walk in at any moment and pull down a book and settle herself in her favorite chair, the glider she sat in to nurse them all. One wall is entirely covered with photos, from floor to ceiling. Varying sizes, varying frames, some black-and-white, but most color. She was one of those people whose default emotion was joy, and the photos reflect that. She is smiling in every one of them. Among the more posed wedding and baptism and birthday and Christmas shots, there are candid moments of them camping at Loon Lake, skiing at Lutsen, climbing on some heavy equipment at the iron mines.

She loved sundresses and Italian food and gardening and black tea and Ella Fitzgerald and Marlboro Reds. There was an exclamation mark at the end of every sentence she uttered. Her husband was twenty years older than she, and maybe she entered the marriage with the sense of being a caregiver because she was devoted to a fault, always giving to her husband and her children, never seeming to consider herself. She claimed to love nothing more than hosting dinner parties.

Maybe others remembered her differently, but he didn't want to know their version. In his mind she would remain cast in gold. Guilt and shame could do that to your memory. You either sought some way to deflect it and absolve yourself or you chugged the whole bottle of poison. It was his fault — no amount of therapy or assurance from others could convince him otherwise — and so she was faultless.

He had stolen her lighter and a pack of Reds. He had brought them to the middle school. He had snuck outside during shop class, and on the loading dock he shook out three cigarettes to share with those who joined him. This was in February, and a storm had blown in, mixing snow and sleet. They shivered in their shirtsleeves and stomped their feet to keep them warm when they lit up. They tried not to cough and pretended not to care when the shop teacher, Mr. Steele, appeared behind them and smacked John on the back of the head so hard that his cigarette extinguished in a snow bank five feet away. They followed Mr. Steele to the principal's office, where they were promptly suspended, then sat silently while their parents were called to come pick them up.

But his mother never arrived. On her way into town the snow gave way fully to freezing rain. The Cadillac slid on a turn and floated across the paint into the left lane and here she met a logging truck stacked with timber. The car was dragged along for twenty yards before crumpling into a shredded, smoking mess beneath the eighteen-wheeler.

He didn't remember much about the gray fever of that time. But there were flashes: The way his tie choked him at the funeral. The way minnows dimpled the surface of Lake Superior, feeding off the ashes when they spread them in the water. The way John's father turned away from him when he said, "I'm sorry."

Maybe John was never a good kid, but he had always been the favorite, the treasured baby. Talia would complain that he got all the attention, that they spoiled him and made his every day feel like the

weekend, and she might have been right. But his mother's death—
when he was thirteen—made him wild and impossible. One death
changes a life; one comet changes the world. He grew his hair long.
Dyed it peroxide blond. Pierced his eyebrow. Stole from his father's
liquor cabinet. Bought weed and oxy behind the bowling alley. He
set an abandoned trailer on fire, stole and wrecked a car, and broke
a bottle over someone's head and put him in the hospital. He would
have been expelled from the middle school if not for his father pulling him out and sending him to a boarding school for troubled boys
in Colorado.

All these years later, when he heard Talia was getting married, he
was hesitant to come back because of who he used to be, and he was
excited to come back because of who he had become.

In every photo of his mother, she wears the same necklace: a chain
with a pendant on it that carries at its heart a fang of iron. The ore
that his family called the soul of the Northwoods. When he lost her,
he couldn't help but feel he'd lost exactly that—his soul. He traces
the shape of the necklace with his finger and streaks the glass. She
was wearing it when she died. They were able to save that, at least.

A voice sounds behind him: "This would have been a good day
for her."

"What?" He turns to find Yesno, who knocks gently on the door
frame as if he needs permission to enter. John's own tie was long ago
unknotted and flung with his jacket over a chair in the kitchen, but
Yesno is dressed as immaculately as he was at the wedding.

"Your mother," Yesno says. "She would have been very happy to
see Talia married and everything go off without a hitch. Don't you
think?"

"She was always happy. Or pretending to be."

"She was always kind. I know that. Her kindness is something we
all miss terribly." Yesno gives him a sad smile. "I'm headed to bed.
But your father asked me to find you."

"What does he want?"

"To catch up, I suspect. He's down in the study." Yesno offers a
mock salute before retreating to the hallway. "Do me a favor and

make sure he gets to bed. There are a lot of guests from out of town, which means we're in for a lot of meetings tomorrow."

"I'll remind him. But unless something's changed, he's never been much of a sleeper."

"The past few years have aged him more than he cares to admit."

John lingers another five minutes, not really looking at the photos anymore, more looking through them, his eyes blurring as he remembers his mother's cigarette-roughened laugh and how, when she died, so did the love, along with any sense that he belonged to this family. Thirteen is the worst year of anyone's life, because you're flailing, trying in a clumsy hurry to figure out who you are. To lose a parent then — the parent who laid in bed with him every evening to read or talk about school, the parent who hugged and kissed him every chance she got, who taught him to make pancakes and plant a garden and shoot a rifle and drive a stick shift — was the equivalent of losing his true north. And to feel responsible for that death? It made his internal compass spin and spin and spin.

Nothing is close in this house. Everything is oversize, with multiple staircases and hallways branching off in every direction, an iron-and-timber showplace. Here is a spotlighted alcove that features the first lump of iron excavated from the original Frontier mine owned by John's great-great-grandfather. And here, at the top of a staircase, is a bronze statue of voyageurs in a canoe full of furs. And here is a river-rock fireplace over which hangs a Franklin Carmichael painting of the north shore of Superior.

He pauses before a metal sculpture, one of Nico's. It is set against the wall and looks like a doorway, but the frame is etched with what might be glyphs or runes. In the center of it is an eye. And coming out of the bottom, reaching across the floor, are either vines or tentacles. He's not sure what compels him, but John touches the wall inside the door experimentally, as if half expecting his hand to vanish.

He has dreams sometimes. Dreams that soak him with sweat and make him clench his jaw so tightly, his teeth might be ground to powder. He has tried ignoring them, killing them with drink and pills. They've come less frequently lately, as if he's quelled that part of himself, but standing before this sculpture now, he can feel something rising up, like the acid of an undigested meal.

His father's study is a long room with three massive windows cut into one side of it. In the areas where there aren't bookshelves, the walls are hung with taxidermy. There is a heavy wooden desk and a wet bar and a giant stuffed Kodiak bear standing upright with its claws extended and its mouth open in a silent roar. The fireplace crackles and pops, despite it being late summer, and his father sits before it in one of two leather chairs; the other is occupied by a short, squat man in a three-piece suit. His mustache bristles as he speaks. John can't hear every word, but he catches snippets of what is being said: "Please seriously review . . ." and "It would be unwise to . . ." and "You do recognize how much money there is to be made, of course . . ." and "Weapons . . ." and "Keep in mind this is ultimately about nationalism."

His father smiles and nods accommodatingly, like a priest absolving the sins of some confessor. "Yes, yes, yes," he says, "but *you* have to understand. Frontier Metals is a fourth-generation enterprise, and it was my grandfather's desire that we stay out of war. He was happy to supply the ore that killed the Nazis, but later, I had an uncle who died in Vietnam, you see, and ever since then, it is our company's policy to—"

A floorboard creaks beneath John's weight and both men swivel toward him. "There he is," his father says brightly. "Come in, Johnny."

The stranger's eyes seem to both grow bigger and shrink to mere slits, and John realizes this is an effect of his thick glasses. "I don't want to interrupt," John says. "Yesno said you wanted to talk."

"You're not interrupting anything," his father says. "Mr. Gunn was just leaving."

"Doctor."

"I'm sorry?" his father says.

"*Dr.* Gunn." The man stands and buttons his suit jacket. "I hope you'll carefully consider what I've said."

"And if I say no, I hope you'll gracefully accept my answer."

With that, the man smiles, showing a hint of teeth beneath his mustache. He stalks from the room, not offering any sort of farewell. They listen as his footsteps recede down the hall. "Everything okay?" John says.

His father shrugs. "Everybody thinks I owe them something."

"Who does he work for?"

"It doesn't matter."

"I didn't like the way he was talking to you."

"Neither did I. And I'm sure he'll be even more unpleasant when I make it clear we won't be doing business together." Then he holds up a crystal tumbler of scotch with one hand and says, "Macallan Thirty. Can I pour you some?"

"I'm good."

"It's a day to celebrate. We should celebrate."

"I had some champagne earlier."

"You used to steal my whiskey. When you were a teenager."

"Mixed it with Coke too, I'm sorry to say."

"Blasphemy." His father puts a hand over his heart as if shot. "Don't tell me such things." Again he motions to the bottle. "You're sure I can't tempt you?"

"Don't push it, Pops."

His father tips his head and narrows his eyes as if to see him better. "My son. The model of restraint. Who would ever have thought?" He sips from his scotch and licks his lips. "Well, sit by me, anyway."

John does, and the chair is still warm, and for a few minutes, they stare at the orange glow of the fireplace, not speaking. "Do you know how much money I made today?" his father finally says.

"That's none of my business."

"I don't know the exact number, but I'm guessing a million. Maybe more."

"That's great, Pops."

"In one day." He runs his finger along the rim of the glass and it makes a hollow whine. "I'm not bragging. And I'm not fishing for compliments. I'm trying to entice you."

"As if business is what I give a shit about."

"It's more than a business. It's our family."

"We've gone over this. I don't—"

"It doesn't make any sense. You want to fight overseas? Why not fight for what's yours? There's a war going on right here."

"Pops."

"Yes?"

"Let's be honest. You weren't the best father. And I wasn't the best son. But I've been trying to do better. So let's not fall back into the old ruts. Trust me when I say leaving was the only way I could get some perspective on myself. Leaving's the best thing I could have done. And leaving's what I've got to do again."

"Listen to you," his father says with a smile.

"What?"

"You've changed."

"Everything's changed. The whole world's upside down. Everybody's trying to figure out what the rules are."

"Who are the heroes and who are the villains," his father says, looking toward the hearth with shadows shifting on his face.

"Exactly."

"But you, Johnny. You're a hero."

"Don't say that."

"You've gone your own way. And accomplished great things on your own terms. In the past I know I've tried to entice you, or even bully you, or even shame you—and I'm sorry for that."

John can't remember ever hearing those two words from his father, and they sit in silence for a time as if to acknowledge the weight of the apology. John doesn't accept it, because it's too big to sort through, but he feels a wet burn in his eyes and a tightness in his throat. He drops his head and finds his composure and when he looks at his father again, he recognizes something new in the old man, something frantic and vulnerable.

"I respect the fact that you didn't fall back on your family's name or money. I do."

It takes John a moment to say, "Thanks."

"You went through a rough patch. And I might not have done everything I could to get you out of it. But the past is past. And the future is now. You're your own man. A good man. When I say I always saw potential in you, you're not allowed to start in about how I'm a megalomaniac who believes his bloodline is special. It's not that. It's you. Yes, you were smart, but lots of people are smart. You had something rarer. Grit, tenacity, toughness. Don't think I forgot how you made it to home plate with a broken leg in that Little League game. Don't think I forgot how you refused to eat for three days when your mother wouldn't let you watch that movie everyone else in your class had seen. Don't think I forgot how you walked away from summer camp at Wolf Ridge and hiked and bummed rides home. Who knows how life would have turned out if not for . . ." His voice fades away and then rights itself.

"If not for Mom."

"Yes," his father says and winces. "Anyway, that's why I was so hard on you. Because I knew who you really were underneath all that anger and sadness and recklessness. And I was right. Because look at you now. I'm so proud—I applaud you." And here he sets down his whiskey on a side table and gives a damp clap before picking up the glass again. "Truly, I mean it. Your siblings could take a page from your book. But Johnny—"

"It's John."

The old man bends his right ear toward him and cups a hand. "What?"

"John. I go by John these days."

"John? Fine." He waves dismissively. "I don't care if you call yourself Tulip Magoo. What matters is, this can be yours. This can be *all* yours. This family. This house. This land. And the metal beneath it."

"I don't care about the money."

His father's voice grows loud. "It's not just about the money, Johnny. It's about legacy!" Here his face darkens. "Your great-great-grandfather started this company. Our family *is* Frontier Metals. If I could live forever, I would. You bet I would. But I'm going to die one of these days and it hurts my heart to know you won't be carrying on what I've built here." He thumps his fist softly against his chest.

"Talia and Nico—"

"Johnny," his father says and clears his throat. "John. Have we ever talked like this?"

"What?"

"Have we ever had what I guess you might call a heart-to-heart?"

"Not that I can recall."

"And yet isn't that how you would describe what's happening now?"

"I guess."

"We're having a heart-to-heart. I'm trying to say what's been unsaid for too long. Maybe that proves that I've changed too. And maybe that says something about how . . . desperate I am."

"Why are you—"

"I love your brother and sister. Truly. But let's be honest. He's a weakling and she's a hothead. And that's putting it kindly. Things have become . . . volatile. And unstable. At a very critical juncture. I'm old and this town is new and—"

"What do you—"

"And in the meantime you—you've grown up and become the man I always knew you could be. It's got to be you, John." He leans forward, reaches out a hand, and places it over Johnny's. "It's got to be you."

John squeezes his father's hand and nods and then stands. "Night, Pops."

"Now, hold on. What's the rush? Don't you want to sit by your old man? Look. I came on strong. It was too much, too fast. I apologize. I've had a lot to drink. How about let's talk about something else? A funny anecdote. Your favorite television show. Something that happened to you during your adventures overseas. Anything."

"Talia asked me to do her a favor."

At this his eyebrows come together and his face darkens. "What?"

"Don't know. She says it's important."

There is a long silence. "Well, then. I guess you'd better go." He rocks his body forward and stands and lets out a groan and then marches toward the wet bar to refresh his glass. He sounds tired when he says, "You can't deny a woman on her wedding day, after all."

"I'll see you in the morning," John says and backs out of the room.

His father stands before the bear and the fire's shadows tremble across it and makes it appear very much alive. "We had some rough years, John, but we made it through. I'm looking forward to tomorrow."

When he reads the text from his sister telling him where to go, he knows trouble will be waiting there for him. Because the house stacks and sprawls, constructed into the side of the hill, there is more than one section of it that might be considered the basement. But the particular sublevel where Talia directs him is unfinished: concrete floor, stapled wires, bare studs, exposed strips of fleshy insulation.

It is the smell that strikes him first. He's halfway down the stairs when his foot pauses midair. The ammoniac stink of urine, the earthy funk of loosed bowels. He can't see much from where he stands, but enough. A thick line of blood reaches across the floor and puddles at the drain.

Slowly he makes his way down the last five steps and sees the body bound to and slumped in the chair. He wears a deputy's uniform. He looks young, but it's hard to tell through the blood. His head is dented and cracked from the baseball bat that lies on the floor nearby.

John doesn't bother checking for a pulse. He shakes his head and pinches the bridge of his nose and stands there for a good minute. Then he pulls out his cell and dials his sister and she picks up on the second ring. "You got to be kidding me," he says.

"Thanks for the help, Johnny," Talia says.

"You got *married* today. What kind of person—"

"It happened after the ceremony, if that makes you feel any better."

"What did he do?"

"Does it matter?"

"I guess not," he says. "But you can clean up your own mess."

"I'm already gone, Johnny. After the father-daughter dance, I said my goodbyes. We flew down to Minneapolis on the Cessna. Few hours and we'll be boarding our flight to Cancun."

"Then you'll just have to come back."

"Not happening. Girl's got to get her honeymoon on."

"I'm not doing this. I'm walking upstairs and closing the door and leaving on the train tomorrow."

"No, you're not."

"I am. Did you not just hear me say that's exactly what I'm going to do? I'm not a part of this family anymore."

"We can talk about it when I get back."

"You're not getting back for two weeks."

"Exactly."

"No."

"You didn't really think you could leave us, did you, Johnny?"

"Does Dad know?"

"Of course he doesn't know. He doesn't know his head from his ass these days."

"No, no, no."

"Johnny." And here the sound shifts, as though she's moving the phone from one ear to the other, maybe leaning forward. "Johnny, you do remember that I *own* you, right?"

He doesn't respond except to swallow.

"You can go ahead and put on a show for everyone else. Wear your uniform and your medals and stand real straight and talk real nice. But I *know* you, Johnny. I know what you've done. I know what you're capable of. And I know where you belong. It's right here."

His voice is quiet when he says, "I thought you were going to—"

"Just do what you're told, Johnny. We can talk more when I get back. In the meantime, I'm going to screw my husband dry and drink ten thousand margaritas. Cool?"

"What the hell am I even supposed to do with . . . him?"

"It's the Land of Ten Thousand Lakes," she says. "Choose one." And the line goes dead.

10

✳

Five years ago . . .

Every November, the Earth spins through the orbit of the Tempel-Tuttle comet. This is the Leonid meteor shower. But in 1833, it was not a shower. It was a storm. A tempest. Hundreds of thousands of meteors burned through the sky every hour. People thought it was the end of the world.

They were wrong then. They were not wrong when they believed it this time. The world had ended. The world as they knew it. On June 17, the debris from P/2011 C9 — from Cain — entered the atmosphere with shining tracks and flaming pinpricks that gave way, over several days, to firework-bright explosions and kaleidoscopic traceries of light. There were white and green and yellow and red and orange trails that scored the atmosphere and observers' eyes, steadily brightening the sky until day could not be distinguished from night and Earth appeared plugged into one dazzling circuit. The number of meteors was impossible to determine, the equivalent of trying to count all the snowflakes in a blizzard.

And just as no two snowflakes are the same, neither were any two meteors; each was a laboratory of its own featuring unknown biochemical and geologic matter. But the strikes came in common clusters. In the United States, omnimetal came to the north, a new spore spread through the dank forest of the Pacific Northwest, and today researchers are still trying to understand what's happening in Alaska. The terrestrial became suddenly alien.

At some point you read a bedtime story to your child for the last time. At some point you run through a sprinkler or hit a home run or stand on your head for the last time. At some point you go from hating to tolerating to loving to requiring coffee. At some point you go from grieving a lost parent to remembering him or her fondly. Most transitions are gentle and unrecognized and individual. This one was violent and collective. Everyone could point to the same date on the calendar and say, *Then. That was when everything changed.*

In northern Minnesota, the night birds went silent. Worms and salamanders twisted out of the dirt. Cats yowled in yards, and dogs whimpered under beds. Some people suffered from sudden migraines and others noticed their fillings tanging their mouths with the taste of metal and others shook their cell phones and said, "Hello? Can you hear me? Hello?"

And then the sky fell. The meteors, some the size of golf balls, hailed down, one after the other, a constant fusillade. Some were as big as zeppelins and knuckled up huge mounds of earth spiked with woods. Trees splintered and caught fire as though struck by cannonballs. Silos opened up and spilled their grain in a hissing rush. Lakes splashed and chimneyed with steam. Houses vanished.

A woman named Jessica Peterson was driving a semi north along Highway 1, hauling a tankful of milk. She leaned over the steering wheel, craning her neck to take in the sky. The radio fuzzed in and out — country music, Bible-thumping preachers, news reports; a chaotic babble. She spun the dial until it settled on classic rock. The station was running a themed show, a comet countdown. David Bowie's "Starman" gave way to Zeppelin's "Stairway to Heaven." A hula girl was anchored to the dash. The paint on her belly was worn away because Jessica liked to rub it for luck, and she rubbed it now. But it was too late for luck. She didn't see the meteor itself, only the crown of the fire-edged asphalt rising before her. A crater had opened in the road and she couldn't brake fast enough. The semi chunked over the lip of rubble and descended into the sudden pit. The grille struck the far side of it and the semi accordioned with the doom and shriek of rent metal. The tires melted and the milk glugged out of the fissured tank and formed a scalding pond that boiled and steamed.

A man named Paul Weitz was washing dishes after dinner while his daughters watched television in the living room. They kept complaining about the quality of the picture and he kept telling them, "If it's so horrible, shut it off and get your butts to bed." He added more soap to suds up the water and scraped some dried yolk off a plate with his fingernail and then noticed that the half- and quarter-full glasses on the counter beside him were trembling. Water shivered inside them. Their rims chimed against each other. He looked out the window in time to see the shining paths of a dozen or more meteors. He charged into the living room and scooped up his daughters with his soap-splattered hands just as the house began to shake. Holes opened in the ceiling and the floor. Cinders splintered the air. He dodged between columns of short-lived light, and when he glanced up he could see rough patches of the sky. His daughters were screaming when he laid them in the bathtub and covered their body with his and said, "It's going to be okay. Daddy will keep you safe."

Ken Pierce was out on Miners Lake in his Vee Sport cruiser. He had a six-pack of Hamm's on ice in the cooler and a pole baited with a leech in the water. Fish probably wouldn't be biting this time of night, but what the hell — here he was, waiting on the meteor shower to get going, so he might as well try his luck. When the sky began to streak and strobe, so did the reflective surface of the water, so he felt he was floating inside a globe of shaken stars. The air trembled with the thunder of sonic booms and cratered moorings, so Ken didn't hear the water splashing and plopping all around him as fish leaped, crazed by what was happening. He spilled his beer when a walleye flopped onto his lap. One sunfish and then another smacked the deck. A trout arched over the railing and rattled directly into the ice-filled cooler. He didn't need his pole after all.

And on a four-hundred-acre lot thirty miles outside of North-fall, a quick succession of impacts pounded the earth. Not much remained of the Gundersons' maple forest but scorched stumps and burning leaves. The displaced dirt had nudged the foundation of the house up on one side so it sat crookedly, but it was other-wise spared. Its windows had shattered. Some of the vinyl siding had melted. Bricks still fell from the chimney. Water gurgled from a broken pipe.

One meteor hit close to the house and produced a splash of molten metal like a muddy wave of lava. And the little boy named Hawkin was slammed by the final burning reach of it. He barely had time to throw up his arm before it struck him. His scream was silenced before it ever left his mouth. He went rolling across the lawn cowled in red-hot metal. The lawn scorched and smoked be-neath him. His clothes and hair were incinerated. He lay there for several minutes, his body tremoring, and the metal cooled to a sil-ver sheen that slowly shrank to patches, like puddles drying in the sun, before being absorbed into his skin entirely.

He went still. And then rose with a gasp, deep and hungry. He looked around at a landscape that was unrecognizable: all smoke and fire and what looked like some hellish lake, a massive silver reach veined through with red. He ran then. Into the night. He had forgotten about the stranger with the shotgun. He had forgotten about his parents. He had forgotten his name. For the moment he was nothing but fried nerve endings and he had no plan except to escape the pain that seemed centered in this place. He would later be discovered wandering naked down the middle of the highway with a blank look on his face. When asked what happened, he could only say, "The sky fell on me."

11

*

Now . . .

After Stacie files her paperwork and clocks out with the night supervisor and changes out of her uniform, she drives to the duplex she's renting and parks and then pauses her hand at the ignition. The dash clock reads 3:17 a.m. She's worked a twelve-hour shift, but she doesn't feel at all tired.

Her parents couldn't understand why she wanted to move in here when she could have remained rent-free in her old bedroom. But how can she feel like she has any authority if she's still sleeping in the four-poster princess bed they got her when she was eight? Her life is like a continuous stream of Stacies, each one of her over the years connected to the next by a series of invisible threads, all the way from infancy to the present. When she smiles or sneezes or combs her hair now, she imagines all those previous versions of herself doing the same. She wants to cut the strings. She wants her new self to be her only self. Moving five miles away feels like some kind of severance, at least.

It's nearly impossible to find housing due to the boom, but exceptions are made for townies. There's a whisper network among the real estate agents, who are loyal to their own. So while a half a dozen miners might cram into the same trailer, she has a place to herself. She has mostly unpacked, but even after six months, she still has plenty to do. Breaking down boxes for recycling. And painting the bedroom sunshine yellow. And hanging the framed posters she ordered from Bed, Bath, and Beyond. She thinks she wants Monet's *Water Lilies* in the bathroom. And maybe above her desk she'll nail the image of the tiger with the word *Determination* printed below its snarling face.

But not tonight. She nudges the gearshift into reverse. And continues the search for Dan Swanson, the missing deputy.

She had been looking all night, glancing out the window on patrol, but the radio never seemed to stop squawking and the radar never seemed to stop registering cars going 70 in a 45 mph zone. They handed out DWIs. They answered a call for a bar fight involving ten people and spent the next few hours trying to figure out who'd hit whom and why and whether any of them wanted to press charges. Then they investigated a burglary and responded to a complaint about a broken car window, and then there were the three domestics, one of which involved Stacie drawing her Glock while talking down a drunk husband with a knife.

But she hadn't forgotten about Swanson's disappearance. Northfall's police department has a new fleet of cars outfitted with GPS, but he was driving one of older-model Chargers that couldn't be traced. Now she notes the address and the time of his last interaction with dispatch. He was leaving a home after serving child-custody papers. Either his phone is powered off or its battery is dead, but his wife checked in with Verizon and they were able to confirm that his number had pinged off a tower in that same neighborhood.

Someone had called him. Verizon supplied the number to the Northfall PD, and it's untraceable, either phreaked or from a Blackphone. Whoever the caller was, the conversation lasted only fifteen seconds. A fifteen-second conversation, in Stacie's mind, consists of someone saying, "Meet me at this place at this time." And since Swanson ignored a hail from dispatch ten minutes later, she assumed that meant he had already arrived at the rendezvous.

She'd tried talking over some possibilities with her partner, but Hank dismissed her concern every time. "Just slow down there, Nancy Drew."

"I'm sorry," she said. "What's wrong with showing some initiative? You don't find any of this suspicious? That a police officer would be communicating with someone who's using an encrypted line?"

"Now, I get what you're doing here, rookie," he said. "You're excited. You want to make a difference. I think that's great. But I guess I'm a little worried about your tone."

"My tone?"

"You seem to be suspicious of Swanson. You seem to be implying he's up to something. Piece of advice: You don't ever want to talk like that around any of the other boys, okay? Ever heard of the blue wall? You're part of it. We're part of it. And the wall stands true because we all know we're the good guys. We are. And we watch each other's backs accordingly. Don't you forget that."

We're the good guys. That sounds like something Stacie herself would say. And she wishes it felt as true as it did when she swore the oath and first pinned the badge to her breast. But bit by bit, her notion of what it means to be a peacekeeper keeps getting chipped away.

Earlier, at Arby's, when they'd placed their order, Hank said, "This is on me." And when he pulled out his wallet and riffled through it, she saw it was thickly leafed with bills, all of them hundreds.

When they collected their food, Hank sucked at his soda and dug out some curly fries and pushed through the door with his hip and let it shut right in front of an old man waiting to enter. Stacie hung back and sighed and saw her reflection in the glass. There was the uniform, the holster, and utility belt — what she had always dreamed of wearing — but her expression was one of total disappointment. She had to force herself to smile when she held the door for the man and said, "Good evening! Would you like some candy?"

She drives a forest-green Jeep Wrangler with a tan shell, a car she bought in high school from money she'd earned as a lifeguard and waitress. Deep in the console there might still be cracked lipstick and fossilized energy bars and even a few mix CDs from that time. She loves and hates the car for the same reason she loves and hates the town. It's hard to become an adult in the place where you grew up. Because you can never escape who you were.

She starts at the address where Swanson was last reported, a ranch home with a four-wheeler parked in the front yard. There is a limit to how far someone can travel in ten minutes. And all the roads in Northfall are laid out in a grid.

She starts squaring herself outward, going slow — five, ten, fifteen miles an hour — turning left, and left again, and again, squinting through the window, craning her neck, sometimes getting out to check an alley or a tree cluster. She grew up knowing every inch of the town, but its parameters expand every day.

There isn't enough housing in Northfall. The construction can't keep up with the influx of people, so companies — including Frontier Metals and Black Dog Energy — clear acres of forest to build barracks for their workers. Man camps, they're called. She drives past one of them now and can see a bonfire with dark figures in lawn chairs settled around it, can feel music throbbing from a sound system cranked high.

Some of the men are fresh out of high school with dreams of making their fortune, and some are middle-aged with a wife and kids in another state, and a few are old and desperate with faded tattoos and tobacco-stained teeth. Some are vets. Some have criminal records. Some have crippling student-loan debt. But all are men. Six or seven of them to a trailer. Buses and vans come every morning to haul them away and return every evening to drop them off again, filthy and exhausted and ready to drink and smoke and snort and fight and fuck. People have a lot of names for them: diggers, dredgers, miners, moles, cowboys, metal-heads.

Ten to one. That is the ratio of men to women in Northfall. There are the women who grew up here and there are the women who have come since the boom, and of them, many are strippers and prostitutes. Their flyers are stapled to telephone poles. Their business cards litter the tables at restaurants and bars. It is the unofficial policy of the Northfall PD not to prosecute sex workers. "Weren't for them, these good old boys would go out of their minds," the sheriff says.

Sometimes it feels like they already have. Stacie notices it when she walks down the sidewalk and trucks honk their horns and voices shout from open windows. She notices it at the Big Muskie Tavern, where she can't go without one man after another demanding to buy her a drink. She notices it at Walmart, where a man angled his cart so that she couldn't get past him in the aisle, and when she asked him to please move, he said, "Only if you're real nice and give me your phone number." And she notices it at work, as the only woman in a department of sixty-three full-time deputies.

The Northfall PD covers the city as well as the county, one thousand square miles that include one hundred and ten thousand acres of water. The newly constructed, ten-million-dollar station sits on a piny lot at the edge of town and boasts a gym, a lounge, and a firing range. Frontier and Black Dog largely funded the facility.

A few months ago, when Stacie was brand-new to the job, she'd signed in for her shift, tightened her holster and her ponytail, tapped her finger on the fresh name tag on the door to her locker — *Toal* — and smiled, but the smile died a second later when she spun the combo and opened the door and discovered a lime-green dildo inside. She slapped a hand over her mouth and said, "Oh, dear."

She wrapped it in a paper towel and put it in the garbage and tried not to notice the sergeant smiling at her when she reported to her supervisor and received a pile of eviction notices to serve, an act of vandalism to investigate, and a domestic complaint to follow up on.

She didn't want to mention the dildo, but she felt flushed and distracted the entire day and at the end of her shift knocked on Sheriff Barnes's door. He called her in and asked her to sit down. The walls of his office were decorated with photos of him fishing with his family and shaking hands with the president during one of his visits; the shelves held some bowling trophies and fly-fishing lures he had tied and framed. Barnes had had cancer several years ago, and during chemo, all of his hair had fallen out and never grown back. His skin had a loose-wrinkled quality that reminded her of an elephant's. He kept the thermostat in his office at a crisp sixty degrees that made her body tighten. She wanted to sit on her hands.

She had trouble meeting his eyes when he asked what was bothering her. When she told him about the sex toy, he shook his head and inhaled through his teeth and said, "Boys will be boys." He explained that everyone in the department went through some sort of hazing and she shouldn't take it personally. "But your father asked me to keep an eye on you, so I'll look into it and make sure it doesn't happen again." He stood up and walked over to her and patted her on the shoulder and she felt a flash of hatred for him. "Okay?"

"Okay," she said and then, "Actually, you know what? No. No, thanks. Forget I asked."

"You're sure?"

"I'm sure."

Her father, Oliver Toal, had played high-school football with Barnes. The two of them weren't friends, but in a town like Northfall, going to the state tourney together is the equivalent of going to war together; the high drama of the shared experience bonds you for life. She hated the fact that her getting this job felt like a favor, that the sheriff considered himself a babysitter as much as a boss, that she had so much to prove before anyone here viewed her as anything more than a token female.

And that's why she drives through the night hunting for what no one else can find. She finally discovers Swanson's Charger parked in a lot used for county storage. Here are rows and rows of the massive concrete pipes that will be used to expand the water system. She stares at the squad car a long minute, then unwraps a Starburst and pops it in her mouth and lets the candy melt on her tongue. A warmth spreads through her, tingling her hair, the tips of her fingers, giving her a buzzy feeling all over that she identifies as courage. Or its sugary substitute.

In the sky she can see the red hint of the sun when she climbs out of the Jeep and slowly approaches the cruiser, afraid of what she'll find. The door is unlocked, the cab empty. The dome light reveals the standard mess of rubber-banded notebooks and ammo clips, fast-food bags, pens, pencils. The shotgun is still locked in the floor mount. She taps the keyboard of the computer by the dashboard, and the screen lights up.

She clicks on the flashlight and checks the ground around the vehicle, but it's hard-packed and thick with weeds and so doesn't give her much back. She peers into a few of the concrete pipes and finds nothing but spider webs and a possum that shows its needle-y teeth in a hiss.

She climbs into the driver's seat and pulls the radio off its hook, but something stops her from keying it. The memory of Sheriff Barnes patting her shoulder condescendingly. The memory of Hank dismissing her concerns and theories. "We're the good guys," he said. "Don't you forget that." And maybe there was a strain to his smile when he looked at her.

She doesn't know what she's dealing with here, but she does know that if she reports it, she'll be questioned and thanked and immediately shoved aside. So she hangs up the radio and reaches for the dash cam and slides the memory card out of it. She'll review the footage before making the call. Collect as much data as possible so that she has some ownership of the case. That's what this is. A case. She's working her first real case.

The radio squawks and she lets out a shriek and then covers her mouth with her hand as if someone might hear. Pam is the woman working dispatch, and her voice comes through like gravel. "Please respond," she says. "Reports of a fire at the Frontier compound. All available units please respond."

It is then Stacie realizes, as she steps from the cruiser and looks to the east, that what she believed to be the coming dawn is in fact another kind of flame.

12

✳

John digs through his bedroom closet and changes into a black hoodie and a black cap. In the basement, his sister has stored everything else he needs. Latex gloves. Surgical booties to pull over his shoes. He wonders how many others she's brought here and carted off in darkness. With a knife, he cuts the ropes that bind the man to the chair, and the body slumps to the floor.

He locates a roll of duct tape. He tears open a box of black garbage bags and removes one and holds it up to assess its size, then pulls out two more. He notices a bulge in the man's back pocket. His sister has already destroyed the cell phone — the pieces of it are sharded across the floor — but this is his wallet. John digs it out and flips it open and pauses at the name on the license: Dan Swanson.

He snaps shut the wallet and the word jumps out of his throat: "No." He opens the wallet again, hoping he misread the name. "No, no, no."

John wasn't even supposed to be here. He ignored the RSVP for the wedding. He didn't answer the phone calls or the e-mails or the texts. In them Talia's tone varied from pleading to raging to loving. *I can't get married without my baby bro there,* she wrote. Maybe she meant that. But she also wanted to win. To break him. That's what she's always done. When they were kids, she once sat on his chest and tickled him until he couldn't breathe and threw up all over himself. When they were teenagers, she held down his hand and hit it with a ball-peen hammer when he borrowed her car and brought it back with a scratch razed across the door. Is he really surprised that she has charged him with disposing of the body of his ex-girlfriend's husband? No.

He calls Talia again, but her phone goes directly to voicemail. He severs the connection without leaving a message. He checks the time. Four hours until dawn. There is nothing to do but finish the job.

John's father has a ten-car garage he keeps full. He's a Cadillac man but also owns a Bentley and a new model of Tesla—the Quicksilver—that features an omnimetal battery. John surveys the gleaming fleet before snapping off the lights and closing the door and hiking over to the pole barn, where he finds his old Bronco parked among the snowmobiles and motorcycles and ATVs and Jet Skis and boats. His fingers make lines in the dust of the hood. The engine whines at first, but with a few hard cranks, it turns over with a growl.

Into the rear he loads the body, now cocooned in garbage bags and banded with duct tape. And drives off into the dark.

Northfall was founded in the late 1800s when iron ore was discovered in the Manitou Range. Though there are some underground mines, the iron ore deposits are shallow, so open pit mining was the standard. During World War I and World War II, at the height of production, some of the smaller pits merged into a larger footprint a mile wide and four hundred feet deep as hundreds of millions of tons of high-grade ore were delivered by train from the Iron Range to Duluth and then shipped across Superior to be processed at steel mills. Nearly all of the high-grade iron ore has been mined from Minnesota, and though the low-grade deposits are still processed into taconite pellets, demand is low. This combined with environmental regulations resulted in a slow, decades-long economic collapse. One *Northfall News* headline about unemployment in the region read "Rock Bottom. Literally."

The cratered remains of those mines scab the landscape up here, and John drives to one of them now. A pit lake called the Witch's Sink with steep crumbly rockfaces surrounding it. One of the most contaminated lakes in the Iron Range, bottomed by acidic water no one would ever fish from or swim in, the color of a penny in a puddle. He used to party here as a teenager and chuck bottles into the void. And it was said that a bevy of swans that had once landed here perished seconds later, their white carcasses floating and pin-wheeling on the water.

He carries the body to a cliff side and wraps it in two coils of transport chain and padlocks the links together. This at least dou-bles Swanson's weight, and John strains to shove him over the edge. The clinking and skidding gives way to a hush when the body rolls off into nothingness. John gets down and lies there, breathing heav-ily, listening. The rippling flap of plastic grows fainter and fainter, and then, finally, he hears what sounds like the crunch of a beer can as it strikes the water below.

He rolls over and takes in the expanse of stars overhead. That's where all this trouble originated from, and he can't help but feel like it's a net hanging over him that will descend at any moment. He spots one constellation he knows, the Big Dipper, but he never learned the names of any of the rest. He wishes he had. He wishes a lot of things were different.

He should drive home. He should bleach the basement and shower up and pack his bag and leave and never come back. But in-stead he drives to an old neighborhood on the south side of town, close enough to the tracks you can feel the rumble of every train's passage. He didn't keep the license from Swanson's wallet, but he kept the photo. Of Jenna and the boy tucked into her lap.

The street is oak-lined; the houses are bungalows with chain-link fences collaring small patches of yard. He circles the block four times before parking across the street and killing the engine. The windows are dark, but the porch light is on, as if she's hoping Dan might still make his way home.

He pulls out the photo and angles it toward the street lamp. There is a dark dot on its corner and when he rubs it with his thumb, it smears. Blood. He tucks it into his breast pocket.

It takes him a while to notice the sirens — so many of them cry-ing in the night — and at first he believes they are coming for him.

13

✳

A few years ago, when Victoria was going over plans for the new house with the contractor, she told him to include a library. "A library?" he said over the phone. "That's really not great for resale. Kind of a waste of a bedroom, to be honest. Can't you just put in bookshelves and a few comfy chairs?"

No. In the same way that some insisted on a formal dining room, she wanted a proper library. In the blueprints, there was a bedroom adjacent to the living room, and that would do very nicely, although she would have preferred a broad, open doorway that felt like an invitation. Built-in shelves, floor to ceiling, would wrap the room. It might be an antiquated notion, but it was necessary if she and her husband were going to feel at all at home in this place, this town that didn't seem to know what it was, tourist destination or mining camp.

"With the Department of Defense footing the bill for all this," the contractor said, "kind of curious what it is you're going to be doing up here."

"I'm not allowed to say, I'm afraid. Now for the shelving, I'd prefer maple. Oak is too grainy, in my opinion. A darker stain would be my preference."

Her science books, of course, filled a full wall. But for pleasure she preferred poetry and historical novels, while Wade obsessively read any sturdy volume of nonfiction about wars and presidents. The Father's Day display at every bookstore seemed designed especially for him.

Evenings back in Nebraska, they would settle into their chairs and, in their individual shafts of lamplight, escape into phantom worlds. It was a way of being separate but together. That's how their relationship seemed to always work. They had taught at the same university, but not in the same department or at the same level. They lived in the same house, but he preferred to spend his time puttering in the kitchen and the garden while she finished the newspaper at the dining room table or fired off e-mails in her office. They slept in the same bed, but if he ever asked, "What happened at work today?," she couldn't really say. She'd fluff her pillow, turn away from him, and pretend to fall asleep.

There are no bookstores in Northfall, only spinner racks featuring paperback thrillers and romance novels at the pharmacy and grocery store, so she and Wade order everything online. Now, in the library, on her chair, sits a padded parcel. She ordered it the other day after realizing her shelves were absent of anything a teenage boy might find interesting. She searched for recommendations on Goodreads and finally settled on a title that felt right for a boy in the Northwoods.

She tears open the packaging and pulls out *Hatchet* by Gary Paulsen. She slips the book into her purse — and an hour later, at the gates of the DOD facility, the guard takes it out and riffles through the pages and swabs the cover for chemical residue and then shrugs and gives it back and waves her through.

She can't leave the job. Not only because she signed a five-year contract that no lawyer would have ever approved — one that listed fifty different ways she could end up in prison for breaching the agreement — but because of the boy, Hawkin. If it wasn't her running the experiments, it would be someone else. By staying, she might be sickening herself, but she was protecting him.

When she'd first signed on to work at the DOD, she was given a classified dossier labeled *Patient Zero*. In it, she learned that a National Guard unit had discovered Hawkin. The crew wore gamma-radiation suits and carried Geiger counters. They felt like astronauts, one of them said in the report. Astronauts exploring another planet. They were part of the initial quarantine. A perimeter was established in the Arrowhead, and the crew's task was to survey the blast sites and assess the risk the alien matter might pose and guide any survivors to the ad hoc medical facility set up on the high-school football field. They reported finding a deer with silvered ant-lers so heavy that it dragged its head and raked the ground. They reported seeing a man in pajamas lying in bed without a head, his pillow replaced by a blackened hole from the meteor that smashed through his ceiling. And they reported investigating an old gray barn inside of which an electrical storm seemed to blaze. Blue light burst through the slats in the boards and the holes in the sunken roof—and then went dark. When the men creaked open the doors, they discovered a boy lying on the hay-strewn floor. He was naked and hairless. He breathed rapidly. His eyes were scrunched shut as if he were in terrible pain. He did not respond when they called out to him. There was an ozone-y stink to the air. When one of the men reached out and touched the boy, he blinked open his eyes and sat up and screamed. The soldiers reported a wheeling, blinding light— one that seemed to spring from the boy's very pores—and a forceful concussion that knocked them off their feet. The boy curled up in a ball then, sobbing. He would not answer their questions; he said nothing but "Help. Help. Help." They had been ordered to radio in any notable discoveries. They did so now, and a half an hour later an evac unit arrived and shuttled the boy away. Not to the medi-cal facility on the football field but to a Homeland Security outpost consisting of several tents, trailers, mobile labs, and containment units hauled by semis. The boy hasn't seen the sun since.

In the lab, as the lights flicker on, Victoria powers on the comm and leans in to the mic and says, "Hawkin? I brought you a book."

His head lifts from his cot, but he doesn't get up, not until she presses the cover flat against the glass and says it again: "I brought you a book, and I think you'll really like it."

He digs some crust out of the corner of his eye and stretches his jaw into a yawn before sitting upright and hopping off the cot and padding toward her.

"Good morning," she says and he says, "Morning," and then, "Is it a comic book?"

"No. Sorry. I don't have any of those."

"What's it about?"

"Adventure. Survival. A boy about your age."

"I can have it?" He reaches out a hand to the glass barrier, tracing the shape of the book with his fingertip.

"Not right away, but maybe eventually. I'm kind of breaking the rules right now, to be honest. I thought I'd read it to you. How does that sound? Does that sound good?"

It's not a smile, but half his mouth hikes up. "Yeah."

"It will be a reward. For later. After we're done with our work."

"Okay," he says. His eyes eagerly follow the book as she sets it on the desk so that he can see the watercolor cover. "The boy, he looks unhappy," he says of the dark-haired boy featured there.

"I'd say he looks determined."

"Maybe."

Victoria readies his breakfast and fits it through the slot. While he eats, she fills out the morning's log sheet. Then a buzz comes from the door. She lifts her pen and looks up. The security light goes from red to green. The locks slide heavily from their slots. The handle turns and the door opens and a man stands in the slice of light and says, "Professor Lennon. Lovely to see you."

"Oh," she says, setting down her pen, a word left unfinished. "I didn't know you were coming."

This is Dr. Thaddeus Gunn, the project supervisor responsible for her hiring. She isn't sure what his exact title is, though at different times he has referred to himself as an auditor and a rogue agent and a floating executive. He is a short, bald, fastidious man with a brown mustache. He wears three-piece suits perfectly tailored to his body, which is more torso than arms and legs. He believes in pockets and has many more than customary sewn into his jacket and vest and pants. He is regularly pulling something out of a pocket, an apple or a watch on a chain. Depending on the direction he turns his head, his wire-rimmed glasses magnify or shrink his slitty, pouched eyes. His cufflinks are made out of stony iron meteor debris. He told her he bought them from a dealer years ago. Supposedly, in 1994 in New Orleans, the meteor had fallen through the roof of a house, crashed through the attic floor, the third floor, and the second floor, and finally scorched and cratered the ground floor. "I like how every time I put on my cufflinks," he'd said when he first hired her, "I feel as though I am both in this world and part of another. The same can be said about the work we're doing."

He steps fully into the room now and says, "Do you know what I always make a habit of? When I'm traveling? No matter where I go, no matter how much work I have to do, I explore at least one new thing. In York, Pennsylvania, it was the Weightlifting Hall of Fame. In Seattle, it was the Underground Tour. And here? In northern Minnesota? I don't really have a choice, do I? It's the lakes. The lakes are positively begging to be explored. Every time I come here, I visit a new one."

She stands and runs a hand along her lab coat as if to smooth the wrinkles from it. "Did you get in last night?"

"I did. And, wasting no time, I drove out into the woods this very morning. Right at dawn. To a place called Heart Lake. Which is named—as you might guess—after its valentine shape." He goes to the desk and unbuttons his suit coat and occupies the chair she sat in only a moment ago. His hands he lays neatly on his thighs. "I was hiking a path that ringed the lake when I saw the most extraordinary thing. A hawk dropped out of the sky and pulled a fish out of the water. Not ten feet away from me. I'm not sure if it was a sharp-shinned hawk or a Cooper's hawk—they look so similar and it all happened so fast—but ever since then, I've felt like my whole body is humming. People always marvel over the beauty of nature when it's still. Admiring a sunset or a mountain range, say. But it's nature in action that's truly something to behold. Don't you think?"

"Sure."

Gunn finally looks at the boy then, and his smile grows a bit wider. Hawkin is unpeeling the wrapper from a muffin and licking the crumbs off his fingers while watching them. "So. How are things?"

"Have you seen the data?"

"I have seen the data," he says and his eyes seem to warp and ripple as he settles his gaze back on her. "He remains uninjured."

"Yes and no."

"What does that mean, yes and no? That doesn't seem to mean anything."

"This is taking a severe mental toll on him and—"

"Let's concentrate on the numbers, please. You're a hard-data girl, not a psychiatrist."

"Please don't call me a girl. And please don't undermine my authority."

"Hard-data lady? Is that better?"

She can't stop herself from sighing. "With the higher-caliber weapons, he says . . . it feels like mosquitoes."

"Mosquitoes?"

"Burning. Itching."

"And how long does the sensation last?"

"A few minutes."

"Your answer should have been yes, then. Yes, he remains uninjured. Which begs the question, why are you progressing so slowly?"

"Because I'm being thorough."

"Thorough is good, but so is efficiency. Are you aware of what's going on overseas?"

"I am."

"You could say the world is in a state of disarray. You could say there are many threats looming. But that would be an understatement. Everything we know about biology, geology, chemistry, and physics has changed. We are not only in the middle of a geopolitical crisis—we are in the middle of an existential quandary. Certain laws have been disrupted. We don't know what it means to be human on this planet anymore. So you can understand why we're so interested in . . . this *thing*. Why he exists and what he is capable of.

Because there might be more of him. Or we—or somebody else—might be able to *create* more of him. We need to know his limits. We need to value him as a tool that might be used for or against us."

"I understand my job."

"But do you understand that what happens in this laboratory affects all of America? Your country needs to come first. What if a similar experiment is currently under way in China or North Korea or Russia or Iran? Imagine what happens if we lag behind them. Imagine how every freedom you and your fellow countrymen take for granted could be stolen away." He knocks on the tabletop. "Just like that."

"Yes. I think that's enough of a lecture, thank you."

"Mmm." His eyes then settle on the book. "What's that?"

"Nothing. I just—"

"Let me see." He holds out his hand, and when she doesn't give the book to him immediately, he rasps his finger and thumb together. Not quite a snap.

She does not give him the book but turns the cover toward him. "Ah, yes," he says. "*Hatchet.*" He stares off into some middle distance as if remembering, then reaches over and clicks off the comm, removing the boy from their conversation.

"Is something wrong?" she says. "I thought it would be nice for him if I ended every day by reading him a chapter."

"Oh, I'm sure it would be nice. Who among us doesn't love to be read to?"

"It's about a boy his age."

"It is indeed. And if he were a normal child—going to a normal school, living a normal life—this would be a *perfect* selection. It's very thoughtful of you. But I'm afraid I can't allow it."

"I don't understand."

"A boy is lost in the woods, cut off from civilization. Despite his depressing circumstances, he learns self-reliance and confidence. He struggles with the memory of his disappointing parents. He has a weapon, one weapon, that helps him survive." Gunn clears his throat. "Do you see? How dangerous something like this could be?"

"No, I actually—"

"This is not a classroom, Dr. Lennon. It is a laboratory. And *that* is not a boy. That is not even categorically a human. He—or *it*, if you will; I'm perfectly okay with the term *it* myself. It . . . is an alien. Or a weapon. A thing that could change the world. Reminding it of its humanity, encouraging its self-actualization, will only get in the way of what you were hired to do."

Victoria looks at Hawkin, beyond the barrier. He can't hear them, but he is watching intently. "I disagree. We're killing him—"

"No, no, no. That's exactly what we're *not* doing. Day after day, he refuses to die. To even bleed."

"His spirit, I mean."

Gunn takes off his glasses. The stems have left angry red lines on the sides of his head. He cleans the lenses with a handkerchief, then fits them back into place. All of this takes a long time. He rises from the chair and picks up the book.

"Please," she says.

He turns to the first page. And tears it out. And lets it flutter to the floor. Then does the same to the next page. Then the next after that. He studies her this whole time and she shakes her head in disgust. "I don't understand you," she says.

It is then that he grips both covers and, with a little effort, rips the book in half. Right down the spine.

The boy rushes to the barrier and begins banging on it with his fists. They can't hear him, and they don't need to, because his mouth is clearly spitting out *No* and *I hate you!*

Gunn says, "There's an important moment in *Hatchet*, if I remember it correctly. Soon after the plane crashes, the boy tries to find something to sustain him. He eats some berries. And they're the wrong berries." He pushes open the door and says as he exits the room, "I'd like you to widen your data pool. And begin administering—in steady but organized intervals—poison. We'll follow that up with electricity, explosives, radiation, extreme temperature differentials." Just before the door closes behind him, he says, "We'll discover the chink in his armor yet."

14

✳

John's father is rarely without a jacket and never without a collar. He prefers khakis to jeans. He eats salad for breakfast. He avoids beer, opting for wine or scotch instead. He hates cable news but scans the *New York Times,* the *Minneapolis Star Tribune,* and the *Wall Street Journal* every day. He keeps a bowl of cashews nearby, and when he's thinking hard about something, he scoops several into his big hand and delivers them to his mouth one by one while staring out the window.

His name is on the high-school football stadium. His name is on the hospital. His name is on the library. His name is on the food pantry and the women's shelter and the addiction clinic. The forty-foot Paul Bunyan statue in the center of the town square, made out of steel and commissioned from a metalworker in Brainerd, has his name on it too. He is hated by the environmentalists and by the summer residents from the Twin Cities with second homes in the area but beloved by the working class, who see mining as their legacy and Frontier as their champion.

He doesn't look or act like a northern Minnesotan, but a faint accent rounds out his vowels and he says *supper* instead of *dinner.* He doesn't ice-fish, but he eats lutefisk. He doesn't own a buffalo-plaid shirt, but his business satchel comes from Frost River in Duluth. He doesn't snowmobile, but he pays for the maintenance of over three hundred miles of trails and the warming stations along them. His family immigrated here from Norway in the late 1800s, and they chose to stay. He chose to stay. That's what people always say about Ragnar. He could have lived anywhere, but he chose to stay.

When John thinks of his childhood, his memories of his father are always crowded with other people. The man was so rarely alone. Money has its own gravity, and people orbited him, extending their hands for a shake, offering pens and contracts. John has a clear memory—or maybe it's more than one—of his father winking at him before closing the door to his office. He can't remember a single time the old man said *I love you*.

But there are a few moments between just the two of them that stand out in his mind. On the shore of Lake Superior, outside Grand Marais, his father held an agate the color of honey and told John to study it closely, to remember it, then he tossed it into the water and said, "Now go find it, Johnny. Show me how well you can swim."

There was the time, a few days after his mother's funeral, they went out for ice cream. When John said, "I'll take a quadruple scoop in a waffle cone," his father looked at him questioningly and then said, "What the hell. Make it two."

And then there was the time his father sat him down on his bed and stared at him long and hard and then slapped him across the face and said, "This family has a name to uphold. What you do impacts all of us." John was only fourteen at the time, but he'd snuck off one night and shot up every window in the downtown with his air rifle and when his father asked him why, he didn't really have a good reason he could articulate. Since his mom died, he had gone from being a sweet, smiling, energetic boy to a nuisance, a jerk, a devil, a terrorist, the kid no teacher wanted in the classroom and no kid wanted to invite to his birthday party but had to anyway, because of John's last name.

It was soon after this his father enrolled him at the boarding school for troubled boys that was more of a boot camp or a prison than a school. Stone Mountain Leadership Academy had a gated entry with a guard and a high barbed-wire-topped fence that surrounded the grounds. Seven days a week, the students attended classes, a church service, and a therapy circle, then went for a long, oxygen-starved trail run in the Rockies. John came home for holidays and summers. The school was supposed to make him better but maybe it made him worse. He hated Stone Mountain. He hated his family. He hated himself. He loved Jenna and the way she made him feel cared for, maybe a little like his mother had, but even she couldn't keep him out of trouble. By the time he was eighteen he had consumed too much of every chemical cocktail imaginable, trashed three cars, and been arrested half a dozen times for everything from driving under the influence to assault to possession to illegal gambling. He was bailed out and represented in court every time by Yesno. "I'm trying to help, but I'm obviously not doing a very good job," his father once said. "If you'd only try a little harder, I have no doubt you might become a great man. What can I do to make that happen?"

John said, "It's okay to give up on me, Pops."

Talia was always the perfect student and a dominant athlete, but really, she behaved even worse than John. She was just better at hiding herself from others. "You're an agent of chaos," she once told him. "If you're going to do something wrong, do it for the right reason." After John graduated from Stone Mountain, she took it upon herself to be more than his sister—she became his boss. At this point she was clearly in line to inherit the family business and she saw John as a sharp, dangerous tool that simply needed to be honed and wielded carefully.

Now look at him. That's what everyone keeps saying. Look at him now. With his uniform. And his medals. Tidy haircut. Nice posture. Steady gaze. A hero. A good son. A Frontier. "I guess you *can* come home again," more than one person had said to him at the wedding, and he had said, "For a little while anyway."

Now look at Nico. Once the sensitive, bookish nerd who wrote poetry and listened to Dylan and had a thing for cats, he's become an addict in some star-worshipping cult.

Now look at their father, the epitome of strength and class and honor and intelligence and success. He lies in a hospital bed, his hair burned off except in patches, his skin an angry red and stormy purple, mopped in ointment and mummied in gauze. Only some of his face is visible, and it looks as if it's collapsing in on itself, like a town built over a mine, whole neighborhoods disappearing overnight.

Yesno woke up coughing around three a.m. He punched 911 into his cell before he had even climbed out of bed and opened the door and invited the black, poisonous cloud of smoke into his room. He crashed into walls, his eyes burning, then crawled, feeling his way forward with his hands. He discovered Ragnar unconscious in his office, buried beneath a messy pile of burning timbers. Embers snowed down on them when Yesno dragged him from the room. The emergency workers arrived soon afterward. Yesno was taken to the hospital, treated for second-degree burns and smoke inhalation, kept overnight for observation, then discharged, but Ragnar is in serious condition. He has second- and third-degree burns over 50 percent of his body. He still wears his omnimetal ring because they didn't have a tool strong enough to cut it off, and it has fused with the flesh of his finger. He also has a skull fracture, maybe from the fallen ceiling. Hopefully his father can explain what happened when he wakes up. If he wakes up.

It's possible, John knows, that his father is already gone. That his body is no more than a ruined husk. The same can be said of the house. The firefighters had been able to extinguish the blaze before it spread beyond the twentieth-century wing, but that was what John identified as his home: His father's office. His old bedroom. His mother's den. The photos of them all on the walls, locked away in their frames. The original architecture. All gone, a blackened cavity.

His father has been in a medically induced coma for two days, and since then John has stayed by his side, sleeping in a cot, watching westerns on television, and staring out the window at the traffic rolling in and out of town. He's there because he wants to be and because he has to be. "I'll be back soon," Talia said over the phone. "But in the meantime, you stand guard. Whoever did this might try to finish the job."

"Maybe it was just an accident."

"Maybe my ass is a peach. Are you really that stupid? Someone did this."

He doesn't take his father's hand, because it's mittened in bandages, but he massages his feet softly, the only parts of him unburned. And every now and then he whispers in his ear. "I'm here, Pops," he says, and "You don't worry about anything. We're going to take care of you. And we're going to take care of the business. Me and Talia. Just like you wanted. Okay?"

His father's breath is a wounded rasp. The heart monitor bleeps out a slow, steady rhythm. The room stinks of Betadine and flowers. There were so many arrangements sent to the hospital that the floor is yellow with pollen and John has started turning them away. Last night the nurse came in and told John there was a candlelight prayer service going on outside, and when he lifted the blinds, the parking lot looked like a galaxy of trembling stars. "Your father has a lot of people who love him," she said, and John said, "He also has a lot of people who really, really hate his guts."

Now John knocks out fifty pushups and a hundred jumping jacks and paces the room swinging his arms. He turns on the TV, sees that the news is reporting his father's hospitalization, and turns it off again. He reads a few greeting cards pinned to the flower arrangements. Then he leans in to his father and whispers, "I'll be right back." The heart monitor spikes and falls and his father's eyes roam restlessly beneath their closed lids.

John goes into the hall. An orderly rattles by with a laundry cart. A doctor with squeaky sneakers jots down some notes on a chart. The fluorescent lights buzz and cast their painful light. On his way past the nurses' station he says, "Going to grab a coffee," and when the woman in the powder-blue top barely glances up from her computer, he says, "Hey," and knuckles the counter.

She stops typing and rolls back her chair and raises her eyebrows in annoyance. "Excuse me?"

"I need a coffee," he says. "Can you keep an eye on the old man?"

She has long pink nails with rhinestones crusted on them. "We're monitoring his vitals. Any trouble, we'll know."

"I mean make sure no one goes in there."

"The police would have assigned an officer if they thought your father was in danger."

"They tried. I sent them away."

"Now, why would you go and do that?"

He almost tells her that he doesn't trust the cops, but instead he says, "Please. I'll be five minutes."

"Yes, sir, Mr. Boss Man," she says and returns to typing, her nails clacking and scraping the keys. "Because I'm not busy at all."

He heads to the lounge and feeds a dollar into the machine and selects the double — no, triple — espresso. The machine grinds the beans and the noise is such that he doesn't hear the woman coming up beside him until she says, "Hi there."

He startles. Then nods hello. She has the short, compact body of a gymnast. Her blond hair is in a ponytail so tight, it seems to stretch her face, to pull her mouth into a smile. She digs into her purse now and pulls out a sleeve of Starbursts. "Would you like some candy?"

"Um," he says, "no. Thanks." The coffee machine spits and hisses its brown sludge into a paper cup.

She puts the Starbursts back in her purse and clips it shut and says, "I wish I liked coffee. It seems like it's what you're supposed to drink. But it tastes muddy. And anyway, even a Diet Coke is enough to make my heart go pitter-patter." She wafts her hand quickly toward her chest as if to extinguish a flame.

"I'm sorry," he says and collects the cup. "Do I know you?"

"Not really, no," she says. "I mean, we went to the same school for a while. Not the same class — I'm younger than you — but we were both at Portage Elementary and then the middle school and then —"

"Then I got shipped off to boarding school."

She introduces herself as Stacie — Stacie Toal — and he says it's nice to meet her and she says, "You look so different now."

"Yeah?"

"No more long hair. No more —"

"There's a lot of *no mores*." He shakes a packet of sugar into the cup. "I decided it was time to stop being an asshole." He runs a thumb along his birthmark. "But some things never change."

"I heard about your father."

"Yeah."

"I'm super-sorry."

"Yeah. Thanks."

"I hope I'm not bothering you, but do you mind if we talk?"

"We're talking now, aren't we?" he says and sips from his coffee. "Wait. You're not a reporter, are you?"

"No." She digs into her purse again and he wonders if she's going to offer him more candy, but instead she pulls out a badge. "I'm not a reporter."

"Oh, whoa," he says and takes a few steps back.

"Is something wrong?"

"You just look—"

When she says, "Like I'm fifteen?," her smile widens, but it has a sharp curve to it. "So I've heard. Do you want to be by your dad when we talk? Otherwise there's some comfy-cozy chairs over by the windows."

"I need to be by my father."

Stacie hopes John can't tell how nervous she is. Only minutes ago, she threw up in the bathroom downstairs. She can feel her pulse behind her eyes. One of her fists is tightened so fiercely that her nails are digging painfully into her skin. But she suspects the Northfall police department isn't following the rules. Stomping her foot and crying *No fair!* won't help her accomplish anything. So she will meet them on their terms.

In the ICU, John goes straight to his father. He touches the IV bag, neatens the sheet, shifts the heart monitor a few inches, as if to ascertain whether anything changed while he was gone. A breathing tube extends from Ragnar's mouth like a coughed-up organ, and the ventilator wheezes. Only half his face is visible beneath the bandages and she puts a hand to her mouth and says, "I didn't realize it was—"

"Yeah," John says, moving over to the window. "It's bad."

There is a knock at the door and the nurse with the pink fingernails enters, holding another flower arrangement. This one has a woodland feel, moss and cattails and birch bark and pearly everlasting and ferns. "Got another special delivery," she says, struggling with the size and weight of it.

"I said no more," John says. "There's no room."

"This one was too pretty to send away," she says and finds an open spot on a table near the bed. "I'll stick it right over here. Flowers are supposed to have a positive effect on people whether they're awake or not, you know."

"This is ridiculous," John says. "Can't we donate these to some other families? Or put them in the employee lounge or cafeteria or something?"

The nurse is already on her way out of the room when she says, "My mom always said flowers were like prayers, so I wouldn't be passing on a single petal if I were you."

John continues to stare out the window another minute before he says, "Well? What did you want to ask me?"

Stacie isn't sure how to respond at first. She downloaded the data from the dash cam's memory card onto her home computer. She scrolled through the video and followed Dan Swanson on patrol as he pulled over a jacked-up truck and gave the driver a citation, then responded to a call about a noxious smell and discovered a gas leak in a new development and ordered the whole block evacuated. Finally she found what she was looking for. His phone buzzed with a call. He said, "Hey, what's up?" And then: "Okay . . . why?" A long pause and then: "I'm kind of busy right now," followed by "I understand. See you there."

He drove to the lot where Stacie later found his cruiser and it wasn't long before someone joined him. Who it was, she couldn't tell, because he had parked facing the woods. She heard a door open and close. She saw the flash of brake lights reflect off the hood of the cruiser. And then the car pulled away.

But here is what she realized after replaying the video two dozen times: There was no engine noise. The car pulled up and the car left. She could hear the weeds scraping its undercarriage and the dirt crunching beneath its tires, but no growl of a diesel engine, no murmurous purr of a V6. Because it was an electric car, she felt certain.

And though it was difficult to tell due to the slope of the hood, the reflection seemed to match the flat, squared C of the Tesla's taillight design. A DMV search revealed there were only ten electric cars registered in the entire county, and only two of them were Teslas. One of those belonged to the Frontiers.

She knows that the family put several million into the design and construction of the new police station. And she remembers how Hank's tone had shifted from disgusted and demanding to friendly and accommodating when he encountered Nico among the metal-eaters at the church. So she's going to do some poking around on her own before she presents anything to her department. Maybe she knows nothing, but maybe she's found something.

"I already talked to somebody else," John says. "Officer Bratland, maybe? Doug or Don?"

"Right," Stacie says. "I just have some follow-ups."

"They're saying he must have nodded off in his chair and somehow the fire spread out of the hearth. But I don't think I buy it."

"No?"

"No. I walked through the office. Or what was left of it. After the crime tape got cleared. The stone in the fireplace is all cracked and crumbled. Like there was an explosion."

"You've got a theory."

"One of the logs was packed with gunpowder or C-four or something."

"That's a . . . very specific theory."

"It was a prank I once pulled as a teenager."

She blinks several times, unsure how to respond. Part of her wants to seethe her breath and another to laugh incredulously. One second he seems in complete control, and the next he seems wild and impulsive. "Isn't that . . . kind of self-implicating? For you to admit that?"

"What? No. Why would I — don't read into it that way." Again, his expression and voice broke down before cementing into something stronger and calmer. "I'm just . . . trying to make sense of what I seen."

"So you're saying this was an attempted hit?"

"Yes, that's what I'm saying. Obviously."

"If this was a hit, who do you think did it?"

"I can name a few people, easy."

"Go ahead." She pulls a notepad out of her purse and clicks a pen and takes a seat on a chair. "I'm listening."

"Well, I mean, you must have heard how many people were at that reception? Any one of them could have done it. Check the guest list. Or maybe security was lax enough, some stranger made their way inside. There was this one guy."

"Yeah?"

He sips from his espresso. The steam of it has left a shrinking oval of steam on the window. "This short guy in a bow tie. Something Gunn. I don't know who he is, but he was meeting with my father that night. I overheard some of their conversation, and it was . . . unpleasant."

"What does that mean?"

"The guy was upset. He was hoping for a deal and my father was refusing."

"Do you know what the deal was about?"

"Omnimetal. I don't know." He gestures with his cup and spills some espresso, then shakes off his hand and licks it. "And you should really look into those enviros downtown too. Just the other day, they were protesting and some of them were talking about going to war with the mining industry. They used that exact word. *War*. It was on one of their signs."

"Just a sec." She's writing fast enough to tear the paper with her pen. "Okay. Keep going."

"Anyone who works for Black Dog Energy."

"Anyone? That's a pretty long roster."

"Well, there's this one dude in particular . . ."

"Yeah?"

John looks like he's going to tell her something but then waves the thought away. "Look. My father had a lot of people who wouldn't have minded him dead."

"I thought he was a hometown hero."

"I bet you've heard more than that."

"You mean about the money laundering? Tax evasion? Front organizations? Illegal logging and timber exports?"

"Like I said, a lot of people wouldn't have minded him dead."

"You seem to suspect everyone."

"Check out the security cameras. And again, take a look at the wedding guests. I'd—"

"Including you?"

With that, he swings his head away from the window and looks at her sharply. "Me?"

"You," she says. "I noticed you were a guest at the wedding, not a member of the wedding party."

"So?"

"Seems odd. So does the fact that you come home after five years away, and there's suddenly trouble."

"I—" It takes him a second to get it out. "I love my father."

"Did he love you back?"

"What kind of question is that?"

"It's just a question."

"In his way. Yes. We both loved each other in our own ways."

"How would you describe your relationship with your family?"

"Fine." He sets the cup on the windowsill, then picks it up, examines its bottom, and drains the dregs.

"Fine?"

"Distant."

"What does that mean?"

He approaches her, then takes a seat on the hospital bed. The steel webbing beneath the mattress whines. "I guess you could take it literally. I've been overseas."

"Why did you leave?"

"Wanted a change of scenery."

"Is that what you told your family?"

"I don't recall what I told them."

"You told him you were in the army."

He puts his hands on his knees and straightens his posture as if bracing for something. "Yeah."

"Even though that's not true."

He doesn't blink so much as snap his eyes shut several times.

"It's not true, John. You're not in the army. You never were." She doesn't realize she is tapping her pen repeatedly onto her notepad until she sees the ashy sprinkle of ink. "It's not that difficult to look up military records, you know."

"No," he says with a hard swallow. "I suppose it isn't."

"So why are you lying to everyone?"

"Because."

"Because?"

"Maybe I wanted him to be proud."

"Your father."

John studies his father's still form and rests a hand on the rail of the bed. "And you know what? It worked."

"He never wondered whether you were telling the truth."

"Look. My father was sixty when I was born. There's a — I don't know what you call it — a *remove* that comes with that big of an age gap. His focus was always business. Work. He only had so much time. He barely paid any attention to me when I was home, let alone when I was three thousand miles away." John adjusts the IV line. "I'd e-mail photos now and then. Proof of life. That was enough."

"There are more people you had to lie to besides your father."

"Not really."

"What do you mean?"

He rubs his hands together and his calluses scrape. "They understand my relationship with my father. Things were always . . . difficult. They knew it would be easier — not just on him, but everyone — if Pops thought I was off doing some good."

"They lied for you?"

"You say that like lies can't be good."

She wants to say, *Yes, that's right, lies are wrong, they're always wrong* — but recognizes her very presence here is a kind of deception. She straightens up and checks her ponytail. "I heard you even showed up to the wedding in uniform."

"That? Yeah. Sam got it for me."

"Sam Yesno. Your adopted brother?"

"Not adopted, but — yeah. Sam arranged it. Sam arranges everything."

"Is there something else you want to tell me?"

"What do you mean?"

"About why you lied."

"Why else would I lie?"

Stacie says, "Maybe you didn't want him to wonder what you were actually doing?" She cocks her head when he doesn't respond. "What *have* you been doing these past five years?"

"So you really think I did this?"

"I don't know what I think. I'm sorry for your father, honestly."

"I'm sorry too. That's why I'm here. Looking after him."

"Where were you that night?"

He crunches the coffee cup and tosses it at the trash can — and misses.

Stacie says, "You weren't home when the fire broke out, when the emergency crew arrived."

"I was driving around."

"Where?"

"Around."

"Seems like you should have been pretty tired. After a long day of travel. The wedding and reception. The fact that you weren't home at three a.m. is a little . . . odd. Don't you think? Especially when you consider what happened."

"I couldn't sleep. So I decided to drive around, see how the town's changed."

"Hmm," she says and waits an awkward beat. "I'm also interested . . . in Dan Swanson." She is someone who normally can't stand uncomfortable silences, but she leans into this one as best she can. "Does that name ring a bell?"

His shoulders tighten to the point that they're nearly touching his ears. "Should it?"

"You used to date his wife. As I understand it, you were pretty serious for a while."

He hasn't shaved and when he runs his hand across his cheek, the stipple of hair sizzles against his palm. "You mean Jenna Flatt."

"I mean Jenna *Swanson*. Dan's wife."

"Something happen to Dan?"

"He's missing."

"He's missing?" he says. "I've got nothing to do with my father lying in this bed, and I've got nothing to do with any Dan Swansons going missing."

"Seems a little suspicious, don't you think? You show up, he goes away."

"How long has this Dan guy been missing?"

"Few days."

"How long exactly?"

"We don't know exactly. Maybe Tuesday."

He barks more than laughs. "I didn't even get into town until Wednesday, genius. Took the Bullet in." He pulls out his phone and calls up the QR ticket scan and shows it to her.

"Oh," she says. "Well, that's not . . . that doesn't mean . . ." She feels her eyes blink at camera-shutter speed as she tries to process this. "That's interesting. Thank you. Can I get a copy of that ticket, please?"

They both notice something then. A click. Like a gear turning or a ballpoint pen retracting. But it doesn't come from Stacie. It comes from the opposite side of the bed. His eyes narrow when the click sounds again.

"John? Can you please—"

He holds up a hand and says, "Shh."

"What?"

"I said shh."

He stands and walks slowly around his father's bed, eyeing the equipment, then the rolling table, then the flowers on it. *Click*. It sounds again.

"Do you hear it?" he says.

"I hear it."

She helps pinpoint the location: it's the woodland arrangement. *Click*. The sound is nested inside it. She lifts the clay pot it sits in, and it feels heavier than it should. Leaden.

"Oh no," he says. "Oh no, no, no."

"What are you doing?" Stacie says as he grabs the pot from her; he rushes to the window, yanks it open, and hurls the arrangement outside. He doesn't see it arc through the air and explode in a carnation of flame because he's shielding his father with his body. But she does, and the detonation is enough to crack the window and open a jagged black crater in the parking lot.

15

✳

haddeus was teased as a child. For his small size and for his glasses, yes, but there was something else about him that upset people. What his mother called his "old-mannishness." This referred not only to his manner of dress—he was fond of bow ties and suspenders from an early age—but to the certainty of his views, the breadth of his knowledge and his willingness to share it, the way in which he would smack his fist into his palm when making a point or drop a word like *simulacrum* or *crepuscular* into everyday conversation. From the time he learned to talk, he had always asked the hard questions: "Why is the sky blue?" and "Why doesn't the moon crash into the Earth?" and "Why does my body look distorted when I lower it into the bath?" He insisted on being called Thaddeus. Not Tad. Never Thaddy.

His mother once told him that, soon after he was born, she began to suspect he was a changeling. An impostor left by fairies who had stolen away her actual baby. You could identify a changeling by its ugly temper, wisdom, and strange appearance, she said. "But I decided to love you anyway," she added.

He was thrown in dumpsters and locked in his locker and spitballed and shoved and kicked and pinched because the other children didn't think he deserved his self-confidence. When he came home with a broken tooth one day, the result of a baseball hurled at him during PE, his father hugged him and said, "Do you know why they're angry? It's because they know they'll be working as garbage men and gas-station attendants while you go on to rule the world."

Thaddeus had an only child's self-assurance and knew without a doubt that his father was correct.

Service was in his family's blood. His great-grandfather had been a general, his grandfather a captain, his father a major. And this tradition had been continued by Harold, the older brother Thaddeus never met. A West Point grad, he'd died by sniper fire in Lebanon. His square-jawed photo was framed alongside a folded American flag in the living room. Thaddeus's family remembered him by attending Memorial Day celebrations and always setting an empty plate at the dinner table at Thanksgiving, Christmas, and Easter. His parents were old. Old enough to be his grandparents. They referred to Thaddeus as their second chance and spoiled him accordingly. "Your brother died a hero," they said. "But you'll live as one."

His parents believed he loved animals because he asked for them as pets. His room was stacked with glass tanks. Some were aquariums that bubbled with oxygen filters and held fish that flashed colorfully in and out of ceramic pirate ships. Others were bottomed with cedar chips or sand and housed tarantulas and iguanas and gerbils and mice. But he wasn't caring for them. He was experimenting on them. With tools and chemicals. He knew other people wouldn't think of it the way he did — they would use a word like *torture* — so he kept his scientific inquiries a secret and hid the logbook in which he noted his results. And when he reported their deaths to his mother, telling her, "Sadly, another guppy died," or "Alas, Mr. Mouse is gone," he always hung his head as though to hide his tears, and she would rub his shoulders and say, "Don't be blue. We'll pick you up another."

He developed very early on, from his animals and from his deceased brother, the perspective that life was discardable, replaceable. And that the difference between man and animal was comparable to the difference between himself and his schoolmates. Beasts accepted their station in life, whereas the best of humans dreamed and aspired. Besides having sex and watching movies and winning ball games and buying new clothes from the mall, his fellow students didn't seem to care about much beyond their most basic needs. They did not wish to conquer or influence or discover. This seemed to Thaddeus positively un-American. They had been given a gift — to be born in this country at this time was a gift. This was the richest, healthiest, least dangerous, and most educated moment in human history, and to be an American at this juncture was the equivalent of winning the cosmic lottery. You were obligated to do something with your winnings.

Whereas his fellow students seemed to consider oxygen something to blandly consume, Thaddeus felt it was something you needed to *earn*. Only a few people were great. Maybe one in every hundred thousand. Maybe even fewer than that. He was among the exceptionals. Of this he was certain. The rest were no different than the guppies and gerbils he kept in his bedroom lab.

This boy, Patient Zero, is his guppy. Except that he won't die.

Yesterday, Thaddeus left the laboratory feeling unsettled. Victoria Lennon wanted to give the boy a book? That meant she viewed him as more than a test subject. She empathized with him, worried he was bored, hoped he might still educate and entertain himself. No. No, no, no — that was exactly the wrong approach, one that put the entire project at risk. The subject's name was not Hawkin. He was nameless. You didn't name a splotch of exotic mold in a petri dish.

She thought Thaddeus cruel. But is the choker vine that tangles a tree cruel? Or the wolverine who claws a fish from a river? Or the fire that burns through a forest? The universe is constantly in pain as it tries to feed, survive, refine, and improve itself. You have to have a wider view to understand this. That's why he is in charge.

He ordered an immediate review of her findings and compared the time stamps on the data to the laboratory surveillance footage. It didn't take long to discover the anomalies.

Omnimetal was especially notable for its ability to store and deliver energy. It was like nothing in the known universe. Because it contained . . . *more*. Take the partnership and spatial orientation of standard atomic bonds and multiply it by a hundred, maybe a thousand. They didn't know how deep it went. They were still trying to understand the geometry of the chains of particles and the impossibly dense angles of their subatomic structure on a quantum level.

This was what they did know: If you struck omnimetal, if you shook it, if you electrified it, it ate the energy and stored it. This was why the alloys had been so successful in batteries. The very movement of a car rumbling along the road created its own kinetic power. The wiggle and jimmy of a phone in your pocket charged it. The monorail for the Bullet train was also its engine. If omnimetal could disrupt communication and transportation networks, then the government wanted to know what it could do for the American war chest.

At first, after every session, the boy would vomit. Or cry. Or piss. Or void his bowels. But then, as Victoria notched up the intensity and frequency of the experiments, something changed. Something that went unnoted in her charts: The boy would glow. A pale blue, the same color as his eyes. It was concentrated around the bullet's impact site, veining outward, giving his skin a marbled luminescence. After this he would pace around and breathe heavily and sometimes run in place. His nights would be sleepless and disturbed, as though he were wound too tightly and was in need of release.

Then, just the other day, Victoria unloaded an AR-15 into the boy at ten yards. The most extreme test to date. At first the bullets did nothing but fall to the floor like dead wasps. They didn't ricochet. They didn't knock him back. They hit him and they dropped, suddenly devoid of all energy.

The boy rubbed his chest and said the sensation was akin to an itchy rash itch or the burn that follows being roughly tickled. And for a few minutes afterward, the microphone picked up something. A humming. A vibrational murmur. As though the boy's spine were a struck tuning fork.

Video footage played in slow motion revealed that his skin flashed silver-blue upon the projectiles' impact, so his body reminded Thaddeus of the lake-dotted landscape that scrolled beneath the plane when it came in for a landing at the regional airport. The boy paced around, taking big breathy gulps of air, and Victoria asked him what was wrong, and he said, "I have to let it go."

"What do you mean?" she said.

"I have to, I have to, I have to," he said and then punched the wall. The impact shattered the concrete and sent cracks racing outward. The surveillance camera shook with the impact and Victoria held out her arms as though she might lose her balance. She looked up at the camera then. And it was as though their eyes were meeting. She knew. The dangerous potential of what had just happened was in her gaze. Yet her notes made no mention of it, and her maintenance request for the room simply cited "bullet damage."

The Northfall facility is mostly featureless, but Thaddeus oversaw the construction of his office and one wall of it consists of windowed boxes representing the periodic table, each with a sample of its element. There are 119 boxes instead of 118. The extra casing is empty except for a placard that contains an ellipsis. That's where omnimetal belongs, along with everything else that fell from the sky, cooked in the cosmic cauldron. In a way, the whole world exists in this empty box right now. The whole world is an ellipsis. What they'd thought they knew, they didn't.

Thaddeus knows Victoria Lennon despises him. But he is accustomed to being despised, so he gives it little thought. He doesn't believe in emotions, only calculations. But the other day she asked him a question that continues to cycle through his head: "Do you even consider yourself a scientist, Dr. Gunn?"

It wasn't offense that made him unsure how to respond. It was because in this time, with these impossible new rules, his work felt more like an investigation into magic. Which made him not a scientist, but a *wizard.*

He has full security clearance and supervisory control. His staff is here in Northfall to discover a framework for the ninth metal, a use for it, a language and a narrative for it.

In one laboratory, they are focusing on its psychoactive and biochemical effects. Here they apply an extraction that is roughly the same compound as space dust, the preferred drug of the so-called metal-eaters. Their subjects are rats and chimps and pigs—all of their eyes now give off a faint blue glow. There are also a few human test subjects who signed the necessary paperwork in order to collect the very generous honorarium at the end of the study.

Another building is devoted to energy economics. Here the metal is studied for its flow, as a conduit, and for its storage, as a battery. There was an impossibly dense clustering to it on an atomic level that gave it a supernaturally high tensile strength and made it extremely difficult to mine. This same density seemed to be the source of its fuel—its ability to absorb and multiply its potential energy. The metal here is tested with water and magnetics and microwaves and radiation and heat and sound. One of the walls ruptured and was repaired. The top floor detonated, killing everyone in the lab, and was entirely replaced.

And the third building houses their weapons program. This is where they keep the boy. Patient Zero is their only living subject. Miners discovered another body statued in an omnimetal crater, and there have been rumors of a metal wolf and a metal owl and a metal bear, but the exploratory drones have picked up nothing.

Thaddeus has always done his best thinking on the move. He insisted a sidewalk be installed for this very reason. It winds through the grounds and his feet tap the concrete with a metronomic rhythm. He undoes his cufflinks and rolls them around in his palm. Everyone knows not to bother him when he is on one of his rambles. He is slowly, steadily, deepening his focus with a meditative exercise. Every step equals one thousand years of time. It doesn't even take a full step to erase industrialization, and it takes only six steps to extinguish all of human history. All of Wright's architecture and Homer's texts and Einstein's theories and da Vinci's paintings and the world wars and the Roman Empire and the Zhou dynasty. All of it, gone.

And it takes only two hundred steps to outpace humans altogether, their shapes disappearing into the jungles of Africa. If he keeps going, he categorizes his steps according to ages and epochs and periods, retreating through geologic and cosmological time, as glaciers rise, as dinosaurs rule, as oceans shift and continents coalesce, as life withdraws and simplifies and finally vanishes and the Earth is nothing more than a spinning ball of molten rock. Sometimes he makes every step ten thousand years, or a hundred thousand, or a million, or a hundred million years so that he can go farther and farther still, seeking out the stardust of our beginnings, seeking not just deep time but deep space. Somewhere out there, he knows, he'll find the ninth metal.

Today he does something different. He shortens the timing of his pacing to decades. His mind keeps circling around this notion of wizards, of knights and orcs and mystical forests and dragons and tombs full of treasure. So he walks until he arrives squarely in the Middle Ages. And it is here that he pauses. And stares off into an uncertain distance for many minutes on end. His mouth forms silent words.

A security drone buzzes overhead and brings him back to the present. He turns in a circle and takes in the pines and the campus and the trill of a chickadee and the pulpy clouds overhead. And then he heads promptly to building 3.

He knows what to do in order to voice his professional disappointment. To remind her of his authority. And to accelerate their research efforts. He has made his calculation.

Mining omnimetal is especially difficult due to its yield strength. You couldn't simply chip or carve it out of the ground. A pickax would snap. A bulldozer shovel would bend. A jackhammer would dull and smoke. But at around 4,000 degrees Fahrenheit, it begins to melt. As it did when it originally entered the atmosphere and burned through the skies and cratered the region. Tools have been developed to mine it. Called welders and nicknamed "wizard blades," they resemble giant drivable chainsaws with laser-lit teeth, and they can slowly slice through omnimetal. The blue smoke their cuts release is toxic with spent energy, the bump that makes space dust so popular, like some supercell of cocaine.

Thaddeus commits himself to his office for most of the day.

Later that afternoon, when the door to Victoria Lennon's laboratory opens and Thaddeus enters, he walks with a hunch, weighed down by something he carries two-handed. One side of it is housed in a thick grip, a hilt with many thick wires tangling out of it cored in a battery casing. A four-foot shaft of metal rises out of this. A circuited version of what might be called a broadsword.

Victoria stands from her desk and asks, "What are you doing? What is that?"

Thaddeus ignores her as he bends over the control panel and fits a key into the lock and twists it. He plugs his security code into the keypad. An entry unlocks with a buzz. The entry through the security barrier and into the chamber that contains Patient Zero.

"Dr. Gunn?" Victoria says. "I'm in the middle of an experiment. Please."

Thaddeus thumbs on a switch in the hilt. The blade begins to sizzle and spit with a lacework of lasers. He can feel it humming in his hands, the voltage high enough that all the hair on his body prickles. He slides open three latches and opens the door and stumbles into the chamber.

The boy has his fists balled and his legs spread apart, a defiant stance. He does not retreat when Thaddeus approaches. Instead, he stares curiously at the sword, his expression a mix of curiosity and hate.

"Please leave," Victoria says behind him.

Thaddeus tips his head to acknowledge her. Then he hoists the sword, with some difficulty, and brings it down on the boy, slashing a gash across his chest that glows with a painful blue light.

16

＊

A barrier surrounds Gunderson Woods; it's made from spiked logs set upright. Clumps of bark scab their sides. It's like the perimeter of a pioneer fort. Guarding something old. And indeed, that's the position of the metal-eaters. They believe what they're worshipping is not new — it's the very essence of long ago and faraway. They will do anything to protect it; they peer down from towers with binoculars and patrol the grounds with assault rifles.

Sam Yesno pulls up to the gated entrance in one of the family Cadillacs. He climbs, with pained difficulty, out of the car. One of his arms is bandaged and he's wheezing slightly, still recovering from the fire. The day is cool, an early taste of fall, and he wears a tweed jacket and jeans. The hunch of his spine is made worse by the satchel he hoists out of the back seat.

Officially he is the Frontier family's lawyer. But maybe *emissary* is a better word for his role. He represents the family. He joins Ragnar on calls and in meetings, often sitting to the side, listening, taking notes. He flies to other states or countries on his behalf. He finalizes contracts and arranges press. He works with a staff, but many matters are for his eyes alone. He is the embodiment of the Frontiers' goodwill. The boy no one wanted, the Frontiers took in. The boy with the father in and out of prison and the mother who took off for Grand Forks with the high-school baseball coach has grown up inside a dynasty. In so many ways, he doesn't fit. He's not part of one family or the other. An Ojibwa with no sense of blood and culture. A Frontier without a shared surname.

The gates of Gunderson Woods are made from iron-armored oak slabs. Each has an eye etched on it with wobbly rays—or are they tentacles?—extending on all sides of it, their symbol. Yesno stands before them, raises a hand, and knocks. Gently at first. And then, after a few unanswered minutes, pounding with the meat of his fist.

"Metal is," the voice says and he takes a few steps back and shades his eyes with his hand. A woman—maybe a man—stares down at him from the sentry post. She casually aims an Uzi at him. She is cleanly bald, one of the side effects of smoking or snorting space dust. Even her eyebrows are gone, giving her an alien appearance. She wears all black, the fabric of space. And the blue glow of her eyes is evident even on a sunlit day such as this.

"Um, yes," Yesno says. "Metal certainly is."

"What is your purpose?"

"My name's Sam Yesno, and I'm here on behalf of the Frontiers to discuss—"

"She is busy."

"Oh, I'm not surprised to hear that. I just showed up out of the blue. I'm perfectly willing to wait. I would have set up an appointment except that, well, there's no phone."

"She is busy."

"Yes, you mentioned that. But I'm very patient and would very much like an audience with Mrs. Gunderson."

"You won't find Mrs. Gunderson here."

"Oh. Well, I'm almost certain—"

"Mrs. Gunderson is dead."

"Dead? Goodness. But—when? How?"

"She died the night the sky fell."

"Ah, so you're speaking metaphorically. That's a relief. So—help me out—what shall I call her?"

"You can call her what we call her."

"Which is?"

"Mother."

"Mother? Mother. All right. Then may I please speak to Mother?"

It takes several more minutes before he convinces her to open the gate. He has a way with people. A kindly patience, a soft-voiced persistence. He wears at them the way a steady drip of water will a stone. She pats him down, then takes his satchel and goes through it before returning it to him. "This way."

In most of the Frontier mines, scientists consider the meteor strikes somewhat equivalent to gunfire: The omnimetal came traveling at a high velocity and struck the earth and burrowed in and warped its shape as a bullet would flesh or brick or wood, then it usually mushroomed outward or balled like a teardrop. Sometimes they find a fat crater with a silver smear at its bottom and then the geologists bring in their coring drills and the 3-D imaging reveals what looks like a massive tadpole or jellyfish hidden beneath the ground, frozen in flight, swimming away from the surface and toward the center of the earth. Sometimes there is an acreage struck by many small meteors, creating hundreds if not thousands of veins, like silver roots filamenting downward. Sometimes, in the deep lakes, the omnimetal, heated by its sprint through the atmosphere, would solidify in long spikes or tendrils, like a silvery coral.

Yesno has visited many mines, and most of them require the draining of lakes or the excavation of all localized dirt and stone to reveal the metal for extraction. But Gunderson Woods looks like nothing else he's seen. The drone footage of the property hasn't prepared him. When he steps through the gate, he experiences a sudden sense of dislocation. It is as though he has traveled, in a few paces, through several months of the calendar and arrived at winter's edge after an ice storm coats everything with a silver-white gleam.

The dirt here is shallow — bottomed by pre-Cambrian bedrock — and when the thick cluster of molten omnimetal struck, it splashed back. So there are scalloped patches and bright rivulets underfoot, like ice melt. And so there are waves, like those frozen on the Superior shore every January. And so there are trees — some fallen, others upright — that are mostly sleeved in metal, some with leaves still unfolding from their unvarnished branches. He spots one that's already turned red, anticipating fall.

But the view is interrupted, for now, by a shantytown. Tents, hitched trailers, pop-up campers, vans, singlewides, shacks with corrugated plastic roofs, hastily built cabins with gaps between the logs. Here her followers live. The metal-eaters.

Smoke drifts by. Some of it smells pleasantly of pine and some of it burns his nose like battery acid. Space dust. People sit on lawn chairs and they stand in doorways and they peer from windows, watching as he passes. Most with eyes glowing. All wearing black.

Here is a larger outbuilding, what clearly was once a barn. The double doors are closed, but through the slats he can see light zapping. The sounds of a factory come from within. Drilling and scraping. The tumbling clatter of what might be a dryer full of stones. Several chimneys rise through the roof and expel a foul, spicy smoke that's run through with blue sparks. Their kitchen.

His host leads him on a winding path through the structures, and he says, "And what was your name again?" and she says, "That doesn't matter."

"Well, of course it does. If I want to thank you properly for letting me in and showing me the way, I should know who you are."

"I've reached the point beyond naming."

"But you must have a name. Everyone has a name."

"That person has been erased." She gestures to the people watching silently all around them. "That's why we come here."

"Erasure?"

"The forge. We were ore. Now we are metal. Stronger, cleaner, better than before."

"I see." He remembers reading that the human body sheds nearly a million skin cells a day, that in a little over a year you have a completely new stratum, making you a different person. If cells can be lost, so can names, he supposes. Identities. He would ask more questions, but he's not sure he'll get an answer that isn't a riddle.

They arrive at what must be the original home. A ranch with brown siding that would be completely unexceptional if not for the omnimetal that messily shells half the building. It looks like a snap-shot of a sandcastle right as a wave strikes it, the silver tide curling around its base and foaming over the roof.

They climb the steps. The door gives a rusty shriek as his host opens it. "Wait here."

She leaves him for a long minute and he neatens his bandages and readjusts the strap of his satchel to ease his back. Then the door opens again and his host waves him in and he enters the gloom of the interior. "Ah, thank you."

The smell is potent. Both scorched and sweet, as if someone vomited onto a campfire. He sneezes and says, "Pardon me." The floor is angled up slightly, the foundation unsettled by the meteor strike, and Yesno feels as though he is walking uphill when he enters the living room. The curtains are pulled shut and the room is dim, but he can see her eyes. The flashes of them as she blinks. She is otherwise a shadowed mound, a black shape stationed in the corner. He can make out the dead eye of a TV, the frame of a picture hanging crookedly on the wall, some books and porcelain figurines on a shelf.

"Hello?" He approaches her and puts out his hand to shake. "My name is Sam Yesno, and I'm—"

But a hand grabs his shoulder and stops his progress. The barrel of the Uzi digs into his ribs. "That is close enough."

"Oh," he says. "All right."

His host steps off to the side but keeps the gun trained on him.

The eyes of Mother continue to watch. And then a lighter flares. The flame licks the bottom of the bowls they use. The bowls he's seen downtown, displayed in the windows of head shops. Each one looks a little like a teapot made of metal. Into the hatched lid they feed the powder, the space dust. There is a handle to hold. And a spout to suck the smoke out of. He can hear the deep-lunged inhalation, and he can see more of her body, illuminated. She is hairless, like her brethren, and her skin is a blotchy pink. Her body is rippled and banded with fat, heavy enough that she would not be able to walk upright even if she weren't paralyzed from the waist down.

Five years ago a shotgun blast nearly killed her and shredded the nerves in her lower spine. She lost her husband and her son. By all accounts she turned to oxy and then to heroin and then to space dust to ease the pain. And in the metal she found enlightenment. She has transformed from a retail clerk and Bible-study leader to a guru, a prophet of ninth metal. She is Mother. And Mother wears a night-black muumuu that covers everything but her head and arms. She sits on a couch, but given her size, it might as well be a chair. The lighter lasts only a few seconds and then she's gone again to darkness.

"Thank you for taking the time," he says.

Mother does not respond except to release the smoke of her held breath.

"Maybe you know why I'm here. I'm guessing you do. Frontier has been fixture in this community for more than a century. We've had good times, like during the height of the steel boom. And we've had challenging times, like when environmental regulations and overseas competition nearly shut us down and killed Northfall. But we've endured. We stuck with the town and the town stuck with us. And now we're doing better than ever. Because of omnimetal."

He waits for her to respond, and when she doesn't, he clears his throat. "Do you mind if I sit?" His eyes have adjusted to the gloom. There is a ratty recliner near him and he settles into it. "I'll just have a seat, if you don't mind." He sets the valise on his lap and unbuckles it and pulls out a folder thick with papers. "I have some reading material you might be interested in." He riffles through the documents, just to make some noise. "It covers our philanthropic efforts locally. For every dollar we make, we're giving a good percentage back to Northfall. Scholarships, construction, medical care, nutritional programs, et cetera. You grew up here. I bet that matters to you." Again he clears his throat. "I'm sure you've heard from many other companies. I know you have. And they've likely offered you a lot of money for different options. The land. The mineral rights. But they're not from here. They're selling snake oil. Black Dog, for instance. Frank Olmstead—maybe you know him—leased his land to the company about a year ago. They promised a clean extraction. After they finished, his land would be just as it was before, they said. And since those fifty acres have been in his family for as many years, that mattered to him. It sure did. But you know what? Black Dog lied." He realizes he's talking very, very quickly, the words starting to pile on top of each other, no breath between them. He can't seem to stop himself. "They drained two lakes, razed his woods, left behind chemical runoff and even equipment. He's living in a bomb crater. They don't know what's best for our community and our state. Do you know what I heard the other day? That Minnesota is one of the fastest-growing states in the nation, and all the growth is concentrated here. We were losing people before. Now we're gaining them. That sounds good, but it comes with complications. And—"

"This is a holy place," she says.

"Yes?" He clears his throat and tries to remember what he was saying before. "Well, I don't question that. I don't doubt that. But here's a thought. You have four hundred acres. What if—this is just me spitballing—but what if you kept two hundred of them? Or three hundred? Or one hundred? Or whatever. Whatever you felt was right. This could fund your . . . church? I'm sorry—I'm not sure if that's the right word for what's happening here. Your church . . . your following. You would be well provided for, and that's an understatement."

His heart is knocking his chest. He doesn't understand why he's so nervous. For a long painful minute, he listens to her fierce, singed breathing. Then the lighter snaps on again. This time she doesn't bring it to the bowl. She holds it up so that he can see her fully. Her eyes, nose, and mouth are tucked into the middle of the rounded span of her face. Her chin is but a crease that's lost to a pouch of fat when she says, "Look at me."

A body is an instrument, and Sam often thinks of his as broken. Unable to move quickly or bear much weight or hurl or kick a ball with any accuracy or attract a woman—ever; he remains a virgin. You would think, looking at this woman—Mrs. Gunderson, Mother

—with her swells and drools of flesh, he would feel something similar, that, like him, she was a physical failure. But in her solidity and mass there exists some significance he doesn't understand. She barely speaks, but she dominates the conversation. She hardly moves, but he feels controlled by her. It is as though she is a vessel and inside she is as huge as the sky, as vast as space, with unguessable geographies. Whole galaxies might burn and wheel inside her.

She used to be a cashier at Farm and Fleet. She used to be married to an ex-con collecting unemployment. And now? Now she's a drug lord or a pope or an amulet. Sitting on a billion dollars of metal. How can that be? How can the whole world suddenly feel like that? The before and the after irreconcilable. It's as though all the memories have crumbled to ash and sifted away and now there is only metal, metal, metal.

"I don't want your money," she says. Her voice is high and musical and makes him think of singing. She used to belong to the church choir at Trinity Lutheran and he wonders what darker hymns she might sing now. "I don't want anyone's money. So I'm going to tell you the same thing I told him."

"Him? Him who?"

"And do you know what I told him?"

"What?"

"The same thing I'm about to tell you."

He swallows and almost loses the word. "What?"

"I want my son."

"Your son."

"I want him to be free."

"I was under the impression that he—"

"You give me my son, and I'll give you your metal."

"I'm sorry, but I was told that your son is . . . dead. That he died along with your husband when—"

"He's not dead."

"Is this also some kind of metaphor? I don't understand. I—"

"He is in the government facility outside of town. He is their prisoner and their experiment."

"You mean the Department of Defense? That's absurd. Why would they do that? How do you know that?"

"A mother knows."

"But how—"

"A mother hears. A mother sees." The couch springs creak as she shifts her body and sets the bowl down on the side table. "Take him to the Herm."

"Yes, Mother." The voice comes from behind him and he starts at the sound. He forgot she was there. He forgot when and where he was altogether, and the feeling is only more pronounced a few minutes later when he is led—blinking molishly in the sunlight—out of the house and down a slope.

The majority of the property, no matter how rich in omnimetal, has collected the dirt and leaves and pine needles that amass over time. Saplings rise. Grass and flowers grow. But the metal-eaters have kept this area clean. Swept and even polished it. The Herm. It is a collection of spurs. Monoliths. Each fifteen to twenty feet tall. Roughly shaped. Forming a circle fifty feet in diameter. Like the melted crown of some dead giant.

As Yesno is led into its center, the shadows seem to lean toward him with their cold reach. He must be imagining it, but he can hear something. Or almost feel it. An undersound. A hum. He has heard stories about how people with fillings in their teeth sometimes catch radio signals and he wonders if there's any equivalency here. All of the nerves in his body feel shaky and electric, like iron filings in the presence of too many magnets.

"What is . . ." The question trails off as he turns in a circle, taking in the megaliths that surround him.

"Metal," the woman says. "Metal is."

When Yesno motors away from Gunderson Woods and down the county highway, he doesn't notice the truck—a jacked-up club cab —that has pulled across the center line and blocked his way until he is almost upon it. His foot jams the brake and he skids a few inches before coming to a rocking halt.

"What on earth," Yesno says and then he sees the decal running along its side. Black Dog Energy. "Son of a . . ." He steps out of his car and keeps on the other side of his door, as if to shield himself.

The driver's-side window whirs down and Mickey Golden leans his head out. He wears aviator sunglasses that catch the sun. He wiggles his fingers as if imitating a child's wave, and his many rings clink together.

"Get out of the way," Sam says. "Please."

"Did you fuck her?"

"Please move your truck."

"You were in there a long time, bucko. And I want to know if you fucked her."

"I'm not humoring you with an answer."

"What'd she tell you? She tell you about her boy? She ask you to go fetch him? We're dealing with a special sort of crazy in this one, I must say."

"I don't want any trouble."

Golden cranks up his accent, cowboying it up. "Y'all won't have none. Long as you stay away. Gunderson Woods is ours."

"Not unless you've got ink on paper, it isn't."

"What are you planning? Midnight raid? Take big mama out with a bullet to the belly and falsify her will?"

Yesno does not respond except to stiffen his posture.

"Don't think we haven't thought about the same. But there's more ammo in that joint than a bullet factory. And those metal-eaters give me the creeping willies. You try to stage a raid, I can almost guarantee you you're in for some David Koresh–style apocalyptic warfare, you know?"

"That feels like an accurate assessment, yes."

"So? What's your move?"

"To stay one step ahead of you, I suppose."

"I guess it's a bet, then. Who's going to get there first? And you know how much is on the table?" He nudges down his sunglasses to show his eyes. "All the money in the world, baby."

"Let me by."

In response Mickey gives him a cruel smile. "What are you, anyway? Mexican? Injun? But you dress and act like somebody on one a them British baking shows."

Sam slams shut his door and stands there defiantly. "Let me by!"

"You know what I could do?" The truck nudges forward, then stops, nudges forward, then stops, rocking closer and closer to Sam. "I could run you over right here and now and be done with you."

The bumper batters his knee and Sam finally backs away.

"But that would be too easy," Mickey says. "Got to give you a sporting chance!"

"Go to hell."

"Oh, Yesno—you're so much fun to mess with." With that, Mickey cranks the wheel and stomps the accelerator hard enough to leave some rubber on the blacktop as he tears off down the road.

17

✳

Stacie finds her father in his shop. The air smells like oil and cedar shavings. There are several benches, some topped by pegboards hung with saws and drills, others with felt boards pinned with dry flies and wet flies and tangled reels of monofilament. Here is an old framed advertisement for Hamm's Beer, and another for the 1991 Minnesota Twins, World Series Champs. A twenty-drawer toolkit on rollers squats beside a minifridge full of cheese curds and summer sausage and Miller Lite.

In the center of the shop, laid out on four sawhorses, is the birchbark canoe he's been building the past few months. He's finished the frame, cut and rolled and spliced the bark, constructed the inner gunwales. Right now he's focusing on the outer gunwales, clamping them in place. "Just let me finish this one up," he says.

She climbs onto a stool with a John Deere cushion. "No rush."

She can see, even through his flannel shirt, her father's shoulder blades, the sharpness of his elbows. He used to have a paunch. His cheeks used to jowl softly around his mouth. Her mother used to bully him to eat less, and now she gently tries to get him to eat more.

"Okay," he says and steps away and cocks his head one way, then another, before giving the clamp a nudge, readjusting it. "That'll do 'er." He claps the grit off his hands and hugs her. "You going to help your old man? Working on the thwarts next, if you're up for splitting some cedar."

"Just wanted to be by you."

"Be by me? Well, goodness." He bends over the minifridge and pulls out two cans. "Five o'clock somewhere," he says as he offers her one.

She takes the beer but doesn't pop the top. "Been thinking about you, Daddy."

"Don't waste your time." Some foam whitens his upper lip when he sips from the can. "More important things to devote that good brain of yours to."

"You seem so sad all the time."

"Sad?" The wrinkles on his face deepen. "Well . . . maybe I am a little sad. I guess I just miss how things used to be."

"Yeah."

He sets down the beer and picks up a broom and sweeps the bark dust dirtying the floor. "It's like I don't know where I stand anymore, you know?"

"Yeah."

He leans on the broom handle and studies her a moment. "Don't you think something weird's happened to this place?"

"I think something weird's happened to the world."

"But *this place* is what I'm talking about. This is the place I know."

"Yeah. Something weird's happened, all right."

"Most people," he says and starts sweeping again, working the bristles across the same stretch of floor and not making much of a difference. "Most people, they used to be content with their lot in life. Be a bank teller or a line cook or a teacher. Go to church on Sundays. Go out for a nice meal now and then. Marry somebody decent and pop out a few kids and try to keep everybody fed and clothed and happy enough. Dreams were for someplace else." His sweeping slows until it stops. He stares off into the middle distance. "I remember one kid I went to school with — he wanted to be an actor. Wanted to move out to California. Make a go of it in the pictures. And, Lord, people gave him hell for it. It was just awful. Like, how *dare* he? We weren't good enough for him? This place wasn't good enough for him?"

"Lutherans," she says.

He breathes a laugh through his nose. "Yeah, Lutherans. *Don't get too big for your britches* must be written somewhere in the liturgy."

"What happened to that boy?"

"He left. Last I heard he was working at a dinner theater in Eau Claire, Wisconsin. I sure hope he's happy." He hunts around for the dustpan. "But anyway, what I'm saying is, everybody's like that now. Big dreamers. Everybody wants to live here. Everybody wants to work here. Everybody wants to make a million dollars here. Everybody wants to drive a Lexus and drink champagne and wear alligator-skin boots that cost as much as a mortgage payment. Everybody wants to have it all. And there's not enough room for all those big dreams." He scoops up the dirt pile and knocks it into the trash. "There's just not."

He goes over to the window and she hops off the stool and follows him there. When she rubs his back, she can feel, through his shirt, the knobs of his vertebrae.

"The Olsens can have their million dollars," he says, "and they can shove it up their ass."

"Daddy!" She laughs and he winks and she elbows him and he elbows her back. "Well, it's not all doom and gloom," she says. "I've got a job offer for you."

"Say again?" He pivots toward her, but he looks like he's tottering, uncertain of his balance.

"A job offer. An outfitter trip."

He has a way of smiling with his whole face. She hasn't seen him look like that in a while. "Oh, do you, now? Well, how about that? Is it one of those boys down at the department? They interested in a day trip or a backcountry experience?"

"Nope."

"Then who?"

"It's me."

The smile fails. "Say again?"

"It's me, Daddy. I want to hire you."

"You?" His forehead creases with confusion. "Well, you . . . you can't hire me. Come on, Stacie. If this is about pity—"

"It's police business."

He takes a while to answer. "You're serious?"

"I'm serious. I need you to help me find someone."

"Who?"

"A man named Dan Swanson."

"Who's Dan Swanson?"

"He's a fellow deputy. He's gone missing."

"And you think something bad happened to him?"

"I do."

"What makes you think I can find him?"

"If you're going to get rid of a body in northern Minnesota, you're not going to bury it—the coyotes and wolves will dig it up. You're going to dump it in a lake."

"And nobody knows these lakes better than me."

"Nobody," she says.

"Well, then," he says, "I guess we better go find ourselves a body." He nods and hooks his thumbs into his pockets—then wrinkles his forehead and changes his tone. "That's not something I ever thought I'd say."

"You ready?"

He blinks at her a few times. "You mean now?"

"Why not?"

"'Why not,' she says." He shakes his head as if it's loose on its hinges. "Okay, boss. Why not?"

Only an hour later, they are loading the rear of his Ford Explorer with supplies and hefting a canoe onto the roof rack.

18

✳

The west wing of the Frontier compound wasn't worth salvaging, so the bulldozers cleared it away. Thirty years of family history hauled off by dump trucks. All that remained was a muddy scar on the hillside. The windowed hallway that led to it had been temporarily capped with plywood. Two weeks later, the air still smelled of smoke.

Talia's office is in the east wing. While their father's was dark-wooded and walled with bookshelves, hers is windowed and washed with light. And while their father's had oriental rugs thrown over rough wide-plank flooring, hers has white plush carpeting that shows off every footstep and vacuum stripe. Instead of oxblood leather wing-back chairs, she has decorated the space with unforgiving, straight-lined black and orange and yellow Nordic-influenced furniture. Her desk has no drawers, but it is topped by three computers. This is where they gather now, the four of them. The children. John and Nico and Yesno and Talia.

Their father remains in a coma. After the near miss with the IED embedded in the floral arrangement, they transferred him out of the hospital and into private care. He's home with them now, stationed in one of the guest rooms downstairs, a nurse constantly by his side, a doctor visiting twice daily. Drones and guards patrol the property. One of their trucks is parked in front of the gate as an extra precaution.

In the corner of Talia's office, there is an exercise station consisting of a bench, a chair, an exercise ball, a pull-up bar, and three racks of plates and dumbbells, and she busies herself with the equipment, rearranging the angle on the bench, clamping plates onto bars. She wears a snug purple tracksuit. Some sweat glistens on her upper lip. As they talk, she does curls, military presses, triceps extensions, rear delt flies. At one point her husband walks in and she flicks her hand and says, "We're busy," and he turns on his heel without a word and leaves them.

John paces a long oval of footsteps into the carpet. Nico sits with perfect posture and stares straight ahead and says nothing. Yesno scratches notes on a yellow legal tablet and answers questions when asked, including giving the story of what transpired when he visited Gunderson Woods. He talks about Mickey Golden blocking the road, the threats made, and the impossibility both companies face in securing the land. Mother would not negotiate with either of them. There was one thing—and one thing alone—that would convince her to sign away the property.

"Her son," Nico says in a dreamy voice.

John stops pacing. "What did you say?"

"Hawkin Gunderson," Yesno says. "Her son. He vanished five years ago during the meteor shower. Mother refuses to accept that he is dead. She's convinced that he's being held prisoner in the DOD facility outside of town." He tips his head and bites down on the butt of his pen. "Perhaps denial is easier than grief. Or perhaps it's a paranoid delusion brought on by smoking space dust."

John can't stop himself from saying, under his breath, "Or she's right."

Nico turns his head slowly toward him. And nods.

Talia doesn't seem to notice. She goes *yeesh-yeesh-yeesh* as she finishes her set and then drops the dumbbells with a boom and says, "Black Dog is looking for a fight. I say we give them one."

"Let's just settle down," John says.

"Settle down? Hell-raiser here's telling me to settle down. Can you believe that?"

Yesno gives John a small smile and makes a gesture with his hand to indicate the floor is his.

"For one," John says, "I'm not convinced it was them that tried to kill Pops."

"Oh? Are you confessing, then? Because that's another theory floating around."

"Don't, Talia."

"Then shut the fuck up. It was them. No doubt in my mind."

"The night of the fire," John says. "Did anything turn up in the surveillance footage?"

Yesno shakes his head no. "It was clipped. It went dark."

Talia swings her arms back and forth while giving John a baleful stare. "You heard about how Mickey Golden was talking to Yesno? Bullying him with his truck? That's a declaration of war. And we're not going to sit around with our thumbs up our asses while they figure out the next move."

"Okay, you two," Yesno says and holds out his arms as if to keep them apart. "What do you have in mind, Talia?"

She flexes an arm, feels the muscle, seems satisfied by the bulge. "Dad kept you around because you were smart. So *you* tell *me*, smart guy."

Yesno smiles a little sadly. "Well . . . we could start with basic retaliatory gestures. Slash the tires of their trucks. Destroy the engines. Raid their equipment warehouse."

"That's not—" John begins, but Talia takes over before he can finish. "Sure. Fine," she says. "But that's not enough. Not nearly enough. Some people have to bleed for this."

"How ambitious are you feeling?" Yesno says.

She picks up an insulated cup and the straw pinkens with the power shake she sucks from it. "Pretty fucking ambitious."

"Walter Eaton ambitious?"

John holds up his hands and says, "I'm going to go."

"Stay right fucking there. Don't you move. Don't you move an inch. You're part of this conversation, whether you like it or not."

"I don't want to be."

"Shut up," Talia says to John, and then to Yesno: "Why not? They go after the head of Frontier, we go after the head of Black Dog. That's good math. That makes sense to me."

Yesno darts his eyes from Talia to John, then clicks his pen, retracting the tip. "Last I heard, Walter Eaton was back in Texas."

"Oil fields were calling, huh? That fat fuck knows better than to stick around."

"So." Yesno clicks the pen again and poises it above the paper. "Mickey Golden would be the obvious target. But not an easy one. He was with Blackwater for a decade before signing on with Eaton back home in Houston."

John raises his voice to a near shout when he says, "There's more than one way to fight."

The straw croaks and gurgles as Talia sucks the shake dry. "Go on, you giant pussy. What's your giant-pussy plan?"

"Gunderson Woods."

"What about it?"

"That's what Black Dog wants. And if they get it, they'll own this industry and this town."

"So?"

"So we get there first."

"Johnny, news flash — we've been trying to do exactly that for five fucking years. That bald witch won't sell."

"That's not what she said. You heard Yesno."

"She'll give us the land — or some portion of it, anyway — in exchange for her son," Yesno says. "She did say that, but . . . I'm afraid it's wishful thinking."

"Why?" John says.

"Don't you think it's a little unlikely that her son — who is officially dead — is secretly housed in a government facility?"

John waits a long beat before he answers. "I think it's worth looking into."

Talia picks up a medicine ball and tosses it from one hand to the other and loses herself in thought for a moment. "Hey, Nico."

Nico does not respond. He remains stiffly seated in his chair, staring out the window. He wears all black and appears as thin and insubstantial as a shadow.

"Nico!" Talia says and slaps the medicine ball. "Earth to Nico!"

He shifts his gaze to her, his eyes a luminous blue. "Yes?"

"Stay with me, okay? I'm talking. Are you listening?"

"I'm listening."

"Is she serious or is she blowing smoke?"

"Who?"

"For fuck's sake. The cult leader! The worm! Big spooky mama-jama over at Gunderson Woods!"

Nico takes all of this in before saying, "Her name is Mother."

"Is *Mother* as good as her word?"

"Her word is true."

"How does she know her boy is still alive?"

"Because the metal told us."

Talia drops the ball and throws up her hands. "Because the metal told you? That's just great. That's wonderful. Do me a favor and lay off the space dust before you lose the last three brain cells left in your head."

"I think she's right," John says. "I think the boy's alive."

At first Talia's face twists in irritation, but then it settles into an expression of suspicious wonder. "I guess you'd be the one to know . . . wouldn't you, Johnny?" Silence brittles the air. They stare at each other a long moment.

"I'm afraid I don't understand," Yesno says and clicks his pen several times as though to capture the ellipsis in his mind. "What are you two talking about? Why would Johnny know anything about this?"

Slowly Nico turns his head to study John and his eyes seem to burn a little brighter when he says, "Metal is."

"It sure is, Nico," John says.

"I'm sorry, but what's going on?" Yesno says. "Please enlighten me."

John puts a hand on Yesno's back, right over the warped hump of his spine, and says, "You know we love you, Sam. You know you're like a brother to me. I'm sorry I didn't tell you."

"Tell me what?" His head swings back and forth between John and Talia. "Tell me what?"

John nods at Talia. She nods back. "Five years ago," he says. "Something happened."

"Tell me," Yesno says.

John brings his thumb and forefinger to his eye and delicately toys with the contact lens. He peels it from his pupil and deposits it in his palm and holds it out to Yesno. It is colored, as brown as a shelled nut. And now, when John blinks, the one eye glows blue.

"I don't understand," Yesno says. "You're like Nico."

"No," Nico says. "He is more."

Talia slides the plates off the bench and racks them. Then she hefts the bar off its cradle and readjusts her grip until she holds its center one-handed. "Maybe it's easier to show you," she says. She takes a few hurried steps and snaps her arm and hurls the bar like a javelin at John.

John doesn't lift a hand to stop it or dodge out of the way. He lets the bar strike him right in the chest. There is a metal-on-metal clang that seems to break the very air. Yesno shrinks in his seat and cries out. The bar thuds to the floor with its steel end blunted.

"But," Yesno says, "how?"

And then John unbuttons his shirt and pulls it aside and reveals the silver-blue throb that veins outward, one tendril snaking up his neck and along his cheek and rooting in his birthmark.

19

✳

Jenna Swanson lives in a bungalow with a yard full of toys edged by chain link. It's ten o'clock at night. She still wears her waitstaff uniform from the Lumberjack Steakhouse and she can smell the fryer grease puffing off her denim shirt and neck bandanna but can't find the energy to change. She sits on the couch with the lights off, but the living room remains bright because of the neighbors. The six-unit complex across the street houses two dozen miners or more. They drive trucks; they clean equipment; they work the wizard blades sixty, seventy hours a week—and in their free time, they party.

Country music yowls from a stereo, loud enough to throb the windows with its occasional bass. A fire pit burns in the front yard, and several men stand around it. In the driveway, a truck is up on blocks, its hood hoisted. Four men lean over the engine, one of them occasionally picking a wrench out of a toolbox, but their focus seems to be more on a thirty-pack of Old Milwaukee.

A voice calls out to her from the next room. "Mama!" She waits until he calls for her again before cracking the door to his room and poking her head in to say "Yes?"

"It's too loud, Mama." Timmy sits up in bed and scrubs his hand across his eye. One side of his face is rashy with sleep.

"Just try not to listen," she says, even as a guitar twangs outside and rough laughter follows.

"How can I not listen?"

"Turn off your ears."

"Lay by me." Timmy plops his face into his pillow and holds out his hand and curls his fingers, beckoning her.

She debates whether or not to fight him on this and decides it's not worth it. The floor is jumbled with plastic dinosaurs, and she steps on one and hisses, "Son of a—"

"Don't swear."

"I didn't." She climbs into bed and he curls into her and his warm, toothpaste-y breath puffs against her cheek. The ceiling is dotted with glow-in-the-dark stars, and she tries to focus on them and not the kick drum across the street that makes her pulse speed up.

"Why don't they go to bed?" Timmy says. "It's past bedtimes."

"I wish they would, baby."

"Call Daddy," he says. "Tell Daddy to make them be quiet."

This is what she would normally do. Ask Dan. Either he would walk across the street and offer them a beer and crack a few jokes and ask them to dial it down, or, if on the job, he'd swing through the neighborhood in his squad car, maybe blip the rack lights, and the men would take their drinking inside. That's how her husband operates. A friendly asshole. Everybody's pal, even with a gun holstered at his side.

"Tell Daddy," Timmy says again and she says, "I will," because she can't say, *I can't.* His cell jumps straight to voicemail. He's gone dark. That's what the cops said. A phrase that makes her imagine a closed coffin.

"Call and tell him right now."

"Not now," she says. "He's busy."

She's wished her husband dead before. Isn't that what all wives wish occasionally about their husbands? A spinout on a country highway. An aneurysm at the gym. A bit of ham clogged in a windpipe. Something quick. Something that allowed you a fresh start. It was a wish you made without believing it would actually come true. He had that frat-boy charm, but underneath it was something rank. A surface different than his center. Maybe that was the case with everybody. It was definitely the case with Northfall. Take one look and you think you're in a piny postcard advertising Vacationland.

Blink a few times and you realize you're in the middle of an alien-ore geopolitical crisis.

Maybe Dan isn't dead. Maybe he's getting into the trouble that is his standard. But usually that comes with texts and phone calls. A flood of bad excuses supposed to convince her he's not diving deep into a bottle or rolling around with another woman, despite the bad smells he sometimes brings home with him. This time, his cell history tells another story, the last tower ping eight days old.

She kisses her son on the forehead and says, "I'm going to go, okay?"

"No, stay."

"No, go," she says. "Love you." She rolls out of bed and once more steps on one of his plastic dinosaurs and curses and kicks it.

"No swears!"

She tries smiling at the boy, but she's got tears spilling out of her eyes. Tears she can't hide, though she tries to wipe them away with her palm.

"Did that hurt?" he says.

"Yeah, it hurt."

She's not sure why she's crying. Maybe sadness, but it feels like a different kind of anguish. A how-am-I-going-to-figure-this-out desperation. Their bank account doesn't have more than a few hundred dollars rattling around in it.

When she leans in to kiss her boy, he puts both his hands on her face. Her tears dampen his fingers. He studies their tips, then puts them in his mouth to curiously taste.

"Weirdo." She sniffs out a laugh. "What does crying taste like anyway?"

"I don't know," he says. "Like clouds, I guess."

The thing is, Jenna knows. She pretends not to, because that's simpler. And it's surprisingly easy to trick her mind blank. But she knows what happened to Dan.

A few weeks ago, he came home with a fat wallet and big promises. "Just you wait," he kept saying. "This is only the beginning."

She couldn't help but smile when he handed her a few hundreds, but then worry started gathering inside her and she crumpled the money into a sweaty twist and said, "Where'd you get it?"

He wouldn't answer her except with a stupid grin, but she kept after him. "Dan Swanson? What have you gone and done?"

"Everybody else in Northfall is making bank," he said. "Why not us?" It was a question they had often posed. She made good tips at the Lumberjack Steakhouse and he made a solid salary of forty-eight K as a deputy, but everything was more expensive now because of the boom. A gallon of milk cost seven bucks. Their rent had been jacked up to two thousand a month and their landlord said, "If you won't pay it, seven other metal-heads will." On top of that, they had car payments, student loans, credit card debt, medical bills from the croup that put Timmy in the hospital last winter.

Dan was never good at keeping secrets, and a few beers and hours later, he finally told her. "There's the mines, and there's the mills." He was referring to the metalworks that had been built in St. Paul specifically for the smelting and rolling and casting of omnimetal. "An armored transport goes out every morning, carrying the load."

Because omnimetal was so difficult to mine, only a thousand pounds or so shipped out of Northfall every day. That might not have sounded like a lot, but the ore was fantastically rich and dense, translating to ten parts per million as an alloy. "The Frontiers send ten semis down to St. Paul. A caravan with a security detail armed to the gills. But only *one* of the trailers actually has anything in it. Maybe the third, maybe the seventh. Depends. Different one every day."

"Please, please, please don't tell me you're stealing from the Frontiers."

"What? One of them screws you and that makes you loyal for life?"

"It has nothing to do with that."

"Then what?"

"The Frontiers are —"

"They're what?"

"You don't need me to tell you. You already know. They make the rules around here."

"Maybe that's about to change."

"Please, Dan." Her head suddenly felt too tight and she took down the bun and shook her hair out. "Please. You can't possibly be this stupid."

"Do I look stupid?" he said and opened the freezer and rattled his hand around in the ice tray and pulled out a cube and popped it in his mouth. "I'm not stealing from anybody. I'm *selling*." He thumped the freezer door closed.

"Selling? What?"

His cheek bulged with ice. "Information."

The traffic was a mess in Northfall, packed with cars at all hours, for the same reason the sewer system kept overflowing, for the same reason the lights sometimes faded and the internet was spotty and the cell service unreliable: about seventy thousand too many people lived here, and the infrastructure hadn't caught up. "So we always help get the caravan out of town."

"We?"

He slipped the ice from one side of his mouth to the other. His words were starting to slur, his tongue numbed by the cold. "Me and the boys. We fire up the sirens, swirl the cherries, shut down the traffic lights, and get the goods on their way."

"Okay."

"So I'm there at the loading dock at eight a.m. I know."

"You know? What?"

"I *know* what trailer in the caravan holds the omnimetal."

"Dan . . ."

The ice crunched as he bit down on it. "Guy approached me."

"Dan, I'm not liking where this is going."

"It ain't going. It's already gone."

"Guy. What guy?"

The words sounded around his crunching. "A guy. Okay? Let's leave it at that. A guy. And all he wants to know is *which trailer*."

"Jesus Christ, Dan. No. You didn't."

He swallowed the ice with a loud gulp. "Five C-notes he's paying me for the answer."

"Do you realize what you've done?"

He kept smiling even as his voice came across as more and more indignant. "I didn't do nothing. I've told him three times now. And nothing's happened except me making some extra."

"You been paid three times? And this is the first time I'm seeing any money?"

Dan ignores the implication. "This guy, he says he might have more work for me. More ways of earning."

"I bet he does."

He shook his head, gave her a pitying look. "I knew I shouldn't have said nothing to you. I knew you were going to break my balls. Honestly, it's sometimes hard to remember why I ever wanted to marry you. All you do is whine, complain, come down on my high."

"You don't want to mess with the Frontiers. They're more than the bunch of suits you think they are."

"We could use the money. We *need* the money."

"You're a cop, Dan. You're supposed to do what's right."

"Maybe nothing will ever happen." His voice lowered here and his gaze shifted to the window and took on a dim, dreamy look. "But even if something did happen, even if there was some kind of heist, the Frontiers could afford it, right? They're rich as all hell. Probably have the load insured. No loss. Everybody makes money. The rest of us deserve a piece of the pie."

"People could die."

He blinked a few times and settled his focus back on her. "People could die driving down the road or choking on their breakfast or slipping in the shower. Don't piss on me with your hypotheticals."

The argument had gone on and on and grown louder and louder and finally ended with a bruise ringing her arm from where he grabbed her and shook her and gouged his thumb deep and said, in a seething voice, "You've never believed in me. A wife should believe in her husband."

"You're so stupid," she said. "You're putting your family at risk."

She didn't see him swing. She didn't feel the impact of his fist. One second she was standing up. The next second she was on the floor. Her vision narrowed and expanded. Her ears whined. The side of her head felt hot and began to throb with her pulse, more and more painful with each beat of her heart. Whenever he hit her, he knew enough to miss her face. Her hair would hide the fat black egg that would rise from her skull, just as her clothes had hidden the bruises that sometimes mapped her ribs or thighs.

He stood over her a long minute, breathing hard. Then he reached down and shook the money out of her fist and shoved it in his pocket. "There. Now you're free to feel good and saintly about yourself." He grabbed the keys off the counter and marched out of the kitchen and slammed the front door and drove off in a hurry, and the noise of the engine had barely faded around the corner before she pulled out her mobile and texted Talia.

They weren't friends—Talia Frontier had no friends, as far as Jenna knew—but they had history. Because of Johnny.

He would come home from boarding school for holidays, and in eleventh grade Jenna met him at a New Year's party. It was a Northfall tradition for the high schoolers to gather up the stiff, browned Christmas trees shedding needles in their living rooms and toss them into the backs of pickups and drive to a gravel pit and heap them into a giant pile and set it aflame. That night it was ten degrees, but the heat from the fire came in a sizzling, crackling rush, chasing everyone to the edges of the pit, where they drank Hamm's and fruity wine coolers and danced to the music thumping from the open window of a Bronco that belonged to him, to Johnny.

She knew who he was. Everyone knew who he was. He wore a black leather jacket and a cap that threw a shadow across his face and pinched a cigarette between his lips that bobbed when he spoke. At first everyone thought he was selling, but he didn't care about money. He was giving the drugs away. Molly tucked into Altoids tins. Weed and oxy in Ziploc baggies. "Merry fucking Christmas," he was saying. "Happy fucking New Year."

The pile of trees burned fast and hot and then diminished to low flames and red embers and black branches. The more moderate blaze drew people close and rippled its light across the gravel pit. Jenna felt buzzy and warm and brave from the beer she had drunk, and so she walked up to Johnny and said, "Are you trying to bribe us into becoming your friends or something?"

She was smiling when she said it—sounding somewhere between teasing and flirty—but when his gaze turned on her, she felt the same as when the match first struck the trees and scorched everyone back. Then his eyes softened and he smiled too and said, "I just want to see you townies get so messed up, you do things you'll regret. I'm here to encourage bad behavior."

"How charitable of you."

"Right? How can I hook you up? What's your poison of choice?"

"Think I'll stick with the beer."

"A good girl, then."

"No. Not good." She arched her eyebrows. "I make bad choices, but never by accident." She gestured with her beer toward one of the varsity football players who was dancing around the bonfire naked. "Unlike the rest of these sloppies."

They spoke until the fire sank into a smoldering, ashy heap and dawn began to color the sky and then they drove to the Lumberjack and shared a big slice of banana cream with chocolate sprinkles. Afterward, they stood uncertainly in the parking lot with sleep-heavy eyes and he took her hand and said, "I'll be back in July."

Snow filled the air between them with what looked like powdered sugar. "Yeah?" she said. "So?"

"So be waiting for me then."

He didn't kiss her and she didn't kiss him; they both made the move—too fast—and clicked their teeth together and laughed at their clumsiness and then the laugh gave way to a muffled gasp and roving hands and curious lips. His hand jammed into her hair and tangled it up in his fingers. Her thumb slid along his hip bone. At first their kissing was hurried and hungry and then it settled into something more gentle and lingering. A tongue tracing a lip. A nibbled ear. Breath shared.

This went on until the manager came out and said, "Can you kids get a room or something? It's getting a little intense here for eight in the morning." And they looked up to see all the goggle-eyed faces pressed up to the windows and steaming the glass with their breath.

For a year and a half, that's how their relationship worked. Intense togetherness followed by long stretches of separation. Which suited Jenna. Not just because absence led to desire, but because Johnny could be overwhelming. She would never tell him this because he hated the school his father sent him to, but she thought he might need the structure of Stone Mountain Leadership Academy, the disciplined container it provided. The long runs in the mountains. The trail and fence building. The perfectly made beds and perfectly ironed clothes. The five a.m. wake-up calls and the nine p.m. lights out. Jenna's mother ran a pet-grooming studio, called Ruff 'n' Ready, in their garage, and she always said a tired dog was a good dog.

After he graduated, his father wanted him to go to college or enlist in an officer training program, but Johnny pushed back and when asked about the future he could only speak in the abstract about doing his own thing, getting his shit together, figuring life out. That translated to throwing lavish parties, taking the boat out on the lake or the snowmobiles on the trail, getting blackout drunk every other night. If he'd lived in New York or LA, people would have rolled their eyes and called him a playboy, a hell-raiser, but here in Minnesota, people shook their heads and pursed their lips and said he was a disgrace to his family and promised to pray for him. He had inadvertently killed his mother and now he was deliberately killing himself.

He wasn't without depth. There was reason to his chaos. Sometimes they would lie on the hood of his Bronco with a bottle between them and study the stars and he would talk about how the planet was just a speck of dust. And in the history of that speck of dust, your life span barely registered. There was no end to the universe. "We don't matter. Nothing we do matters. So we might as well have fun while we're here." When he crunched up Adderall and sniffed until his nose bled or took a deep skunky lungful of smoke or swallowed a handful of pills that made him feel swimmy for days on end, a part of her wanted to twist his ear and say, *What if you do matter? What then?* Because didn't he realize he had won the lottery by being born a Frontier? Every door was open to him, if only he would reach for the knob.

But another part of her knew she couldn't possibly put such thoughts in his head. Because he would be reminded what an insignificant nothing she was, beneath him. It was clear that's how his family regarded her — as a no one, a nobody. Not good enough for him. For *them.* If the Frontiers were royalty, then Jenna was the equivalent of a chambermaid in the castle. But there was no telling Johnny what to do. He was out of his family's control, and they recognized that she had a calming, almost narcotic effect on him. They got him into St. Olaf — arranging his acceptance after a sizable donation — but it was a dry campus and he didn't last more than a month before facing expulsion. And then they tried to get him to go to the U of M, but though he started on the drive to the Cities, he turned around and came home. And then he enrolled with Jenna at Vermilion Community College in Ely, but he only bothered going to class when she escorted him there.

"What do you want out of life?" she once asked him.

He had a necklace, a chain with a pendant on it that housed a fang of iron ore. It had been his mother's. Jenna never saw him without it. Not in bed, not in the hot tub or shower. He often toyed with it when in a dark mood, and now, rather than answer her, he pulled it out of his shirt and rubbed the pendant between his thumb and forefinger and sucked on the chain.

Every now and then, his father would try to include him a company decision, propose his involvement in a Frontier Metals project, but Talia was the only one able to successfully enlist him in the family business—because she wasn't trying to stuff him into a shirt and knot a tie around his neck. She didn't want to change or tame him. She valued him for what he was: An instrument of violence. A weapon. Johnny never said what he did for her, but he started keeping pistols tucked in drawers and under cushions and shoved into the waistband of his pants. Sometimes he had torn-up knuckles and blood on him that wasn't his own. One time Jenna heard a rattle in the dryer and found a human tooth in it.

She wasn't sure if she was enabling him or keeping him safe, but she couldn't quit him even though she knew he was bad for her. It wasn't just love. He made her feel alive the same way approaching the edge of a cliff did. She had the opposite influence on him, a grounding effect. "Being with you is so simple," he once told her. At first she was insulted and play-slapped him, thinking he was calling her stupid, but he did his best to clarify. "Not like that. I just mean . . . I can't spend five minutes with anybody else before they're trying to cure me of being an asshole. Or a dumb-ass. Or an addict. Or a criminal. Or a whatever. With you, I'm just me."

And then, when the meteors fell, when the ground shook and the lights went out, he left her. Until then, she'd thought she had her future figured out. But after that, the life that stretched before her felt suddenly empty. It was like getting caught up in a novel and turning the page and finding it and the rest of the book blank.

It took her a long time to realize her mistake. With Johnny. And later with Dan. She wasn't an author. She was just a character in somebody else's story. Her husband might have dropped her to the kitchen floor, but she got up on her own. If this town could change, so could she. If there was money and power to be found in these Northwoods, it could be hers. Nobody was going to do anything to her anymore. She was going to goddamn do something to them.

Talia showed up at the Lumberjack Steakhouse the morning after Jenna texted her. Talia was so big, her knees touched the bottom of the table and her fingers couldn't fit through the handle of the coffee mug. Her nails and lips were painted the same shade of purple, and her hair was sprayed up in a thickly curled Medusa. She ordered the Bunyan breakfast with an extra side of bacon, and when Jenna delivered it, she slipped a piece of paper under the plate that told Talia what she needed to know.

"Do you love Dan?" Talia said when Jenna returned a few minutes later.

"I thought I did. At first." But no. She had married Dan out of obligation. She was pregnant and he was willing and she remembers reciting her vows and feeling like the words were hollow even then. Love was something else. Love burned so hot it branded you for life.

Talia reached out and traced a fingernail along the bruise that colored Jenna's forearm. "And now?"

"And now . . ." Jenna pulled her sleeve down to hide the green-yellow splash. "Now he's just a fucking man I live with."

Talia nodded and sniffed a sad laugh through her nose. "You remember how we used to have a dog, back in the day? Golden named Chewie?"

"I do. She was such a good dog."

"That wasn't an accident. You want to know how we chose her? We went to a breeder down in Mankato, and here's this big litter of puppies pissing themselves with excitement. They're all cute as shit. How could we ever decide? I'll tell you how. My father, he took them one by one. And he held them down, hands on their chests, in the kill position. On their backs. Bellies exposed. The ones that squirmed and yelped and bit, he dismissed. But Chewie, she just lay there."

"Okay," Jenna said.

"That's basically how I chose my husband."

Jenna can't help but smile, even though it hurts her head to do so.

"You chose the wrong dog," Talia said. "You chose a bad dog. But the thing is . . ." And here she leaned forward. "There's no fucking lack of dogs in the world."

"So why am I wasting my time?" Jenna said.

"That's my girl. Speaking of dogs—you know Johnny's coming back? For the wedding?"

"I didn't know for sure. But I wondered. I—"

"Hoped?"

"Yeah."

"I know it was a tough time. When Johnny left five years ago. I know he never really had a chance to say goodbye."

"I was so . . ." *Abandoned? Devastated? Pissed?* There wasn't an adequate word for it. But none of that mattered anymore.

"He didn't have a choice. Okay? I can't say why, but trust me on this. It couldn't be helped. You don't need me to tell you it was a crazy time. Getting out of town hurt him just as bad as it hurt you. Understand?"

"Not really."

"Look. Might not have always seemed like it, I know, but I liked you and my baby brother together. I really did."

"Did you?"

"Yeah," she said and popped a piece of bacon into her mouth. "He always said you drove him crazy, but it's the opposite that's true. He was crazy without you."

Jenna didn't know what to say, so she doodled a heart on her notepad until it was a black blob.

"And you were loyal," Talia said. "Even now, you're loyal. Nothing's more important, in my book."

Ten minutes later, when Jenna returned with the check, she found the booth empty, the plate clean of everything but a smear of ketchup, and ten hundred-dollar bills stacked neatly beneath the coffee mug.

And now her husband is gone. Has been for over a week. Was she being naive when she contacted Talia, like the child who reaches impulsively for a flower and then cries when she realizes that once plucked, it will die? Or was she in fact cleverer and crueler than that? Didn't she expect something like this would happen? Was it possible not to know yourself?

The past few years, her life felt like it had perimeters. The chain-link fence around their yard might as well have been a symbol of her marriage — a rusty, humble boundary. She was only going to go so far.

But now? She had lifted the latch on her own. And there was a sudden sense of openness that scared the hell out of her. But she'd take being scared over being bored and sad. She couldn't change her history, but she could alter the direction of her future.

Of course the feeling doesn't last. The country music and the ugly laughter across the street continue through the night, and Timmy eventually joins her in bed and what little sleep they get is restless. The next morning, the sun shines too brightly and aches her eyes and washes out any hopefulness she might have felt. Timmy crawls on top of her and says, "I'm hungry. I miss Daddy. When is Daddy coming home? Can I have breakfast?"

She lives on a shit house on a shit street and has a shit job and her shit husband might very well be dead because of her. She considers, for the hundredth time, texting Talia but can't bring herself to ask if Dan's dead, if she killed him. It's better and it's worse, the not knowing. She opens the fridge and stares into it for a long time. There is nothing to be found but condiments, pickles, and a moldy rind of cheese.

Timmy is still in his pajamas when she drives him to the Pamida and plunks him into the cart and rattles up and down the aisles and grabs whatever catches her eye. Spaghetti. Bologna. Bananas. Cheerios. Hi-C. She doesn't have a list. She doesn't have a plan. She just has an empty fridge and a hungry kid.

At the register, she rolls the cart in backward and hands Timmy the groceries. He fumbles them onto the black conveyor belt and smiles proudly when the woman working the register calls him a big boy. The total is over a hundred dollars and Jenna says, "Okay," and reaches for her purse and only then realizes she's forgotten it. "Oh no," she says. "I'm so damn sorry. I—"

"No swears, Mommy."

A line has formed behind her and everyone in it is staring at her. So is the woman at the register, whose hand has paused inside the paper bag she's packing. Muzak plays from the loudspeakers. Timmy grabs her shirtsleeve and says, "What's the matter?"

"I don't have . . ." She keeps patting her pockets, as if the purse might magically be stuffed inside them. "I'm sorry. I'm so sorry. I wasn't thinking."

Timmy starts to cry as soon as she rips him out of the cart—and continues crying the whole way home. "I want my Cheerios," he says between big hiccupping breaths. "I'm hungry and I want them." The wailing force makes every muscle in her body tighten. She tries to distract him with the radio, but that only makes him cry harder. Then she reverts to the *shh-shh* breathing that helped him fall asleep as a baby.

She pulls into the driveway and says, "Wait here. Mommy will be right back," but Timmy screams, "No! No, don't leave me!"

So she fumbles with his seat belt and carries him inside and his crying is in her ear, so high and watery that she feels like she's drowning and can barely breathe. She plops him on the couch and hunts through the whole house twice and finally locates her purse hanging from the inside of the bathroom door, of all places. "Got it!" she says. "I'm just going to pee and then we can go back and get your Cheerios!"

She flushes and washes her hands and scoops up Timmy and heads out the door and nearly stumbles. Because there, on the porch, humped together, are the groceries.

Immediately Timmy stops crying and says, "Cheerios! Yay!" He squirms out of her arms and rummages the box of cereal from the bag and hugs it to his chest. "My Cheerios!"

"But who—" she says and looks up and down the street. A familiar black Bronco turns the corner and flashes out of sight. "Johnny?"

Why did he leave? Why is he always leaving her?

20

✳

Five years ago . . .

awkin wandered off mindlessly into the night with metal coursing through his veins. Inside the house, his father lay sprawled on the kitchen floor, dead in a puddle of his own blood, while his mother sat upright against the dishwasher, gutshot, paralyzed, fluttering in and out of consciousness.

There were no clouds, but lightning veined the air, a constant strobing from the charged particulates moving through the atmosphere. Imagine an ocean full of bioluminescent jellyfish, the waves violent and shifting by the half-second, and you'll have some sense of the sky that night. Meteors still fell, but fewer of them now. A hot wind blew. Thunder boomed, and it was like a memory, an aftersong of what had come before, when the ground shook from the constant cratering.

At Gunderson Woods, the land was puddled and coated with liquid metal that reflected the lightning. Sirens wailed in the distance. A utility pole along the highway toppled with a splintering crash, and the downed lines sizzled and spat on the asphalt. Somewhere in the dark, an animal cried out plaintively.

Compared to what had happened earlier, it was a quiet time. A time of confused recovery and bruised stillness.

Until, out of the melted pool of omnimetal in the backyard,

something burst forth. Featureless and smeared, like clay being shaped. Like a sloppy melting snowman with no coal buttons or carrot nose or stick arms. A gray shadow. A golem. A nothing.

His name was Johnny Frontier, but he didn't know that then. He wouldn't be capable of any cogent thought for some time. He understood only pain. He touched himself hurriedly all over, trying to make himself familiar. And then he ran wildly into the night. It was an unthinking movement, like pulling a hand away from a fire. But it was more than fear that propelled him. It was the energy of the strike woven into the very fiber of his muscles, the spark of his neurotransmitters. A kinetic throttle.

Talia didn't find him for another day. He was curled up in a ball in his closet. Shivering and reeking of sulfur. Hairless. His eyes a wicked blue. Almost unrecognizable except for his tattoos and the birthmark on his cheek. "Jesus, Johnny—we thought you were dead." When she touched him, she hissed; the blisters were already rising from her skin. "You're hot. You're blazing hot." The carpet beneath him was scorched in his shape. "What's happened?"

That was the question everyone was asking. In St. Louis County, cell service wasn't operational. The power grid had gone dark. Hundreds had died and hundreds more had gone missing. News choppers wasped the air. The National Guard rolled into town in their hazmat suits and promptly quarantined the region. The governor and then the president declared northern Minnesota a disaster area.

It wasn't the apocalypse, but it was a taste of it. The cumulative energy released by the meteors at the blast site was estimated as equivalent to three Hiroshimas, although diffused by the impact timeline and a hazard zone of some seven thousand square miles.

Slowly Johnny crawled out of the closet. And with every shaking inch he dragged himself forward, Talia retreated. She was not one to flinch from anything, but this was beyond her. "What happened?" she kept saying. "What happened to you?" The air was still hazed with smoke, and through the window, the sun burned red and burnished the room with its light. If he could have spoken, he would have said, *I have been punished.*

Talia did her best to nurse him, though not without doing a good deal of complaining. "If you think you're going to owe me up your ass for this," she said, "you're right." She moved him to the wine cellar, made his bed among the rows of Bordeaux and California cabs and Willamette Valley pinots, checked on him several times a day, and learned not to say, "That's impossible," when islands of silver seemed to drift across his skin or when the syringe of diamorphine broke against his vein or when seizures sent a kinetic wave off him that zigzagged a crack through the concrete floor and collapsed a rack of zinfandels that shattered into a purple-red puddle. Anything was possible, she was coming to realize.

He sometimes shouted in his sleep, nonsense about eyes and tentacles and doorways. She wasn't sure if he was going through withdrawal from the booze and the pills or if something else was speaking darkly through him. Something that came from the sky, a poisoned frequency that inhabited him, along with the metal. When she asked him about it later, he looked at her with a blank expression.

It wasn't difficult to hide him. He had already become something of a ghost in their lives. The estate was large, and the people who lived there were all otherwise occupied. Nico was in Taos, participating in a New Age workshop that focused on crystals and vortices and chakras, his latest obsession, after his yoga phase and then his painting phase and then his poetry phase and then his sculpture phase. He always had to have a thing. Some crutch to hold him up. And Yesno had not so much as sat down for a meal because their father needed him.

It was Ragnar who toured the devastation and shook hands with affected families and spoke to the press about strength and hope and endurance. He was there long before the governor arrived. Long before FEMA and the Red Cross set up their emergency stations. He immediately rented every hotel in Northfall and the out-lying communities and offered up the rooms to those in need. He paid for the catering services that supplied bottled water and three squares a day at the high-school gymnasium.

Because cell service was mostly unavailable, Yesno worked off a satellite phone. He arranged for three geologists to fly in immediately and give him a profile of the alien metal. He determined the global reach of the meteor shower. He wanted to know whether their debris field was indeed unique. He assessed the standard and projected value of the alien matter. His voice went hoarse and his ear and shoulder ached at the end of every day.

The Frontiers presented a charitable front, but their ultimate concern was Northfall and the market. To protect the town, they had to own it. Otherwise Ragnar would be like a board president with a minority share, soon to be ousted by the prospectors and investors who would come their way. He understood what would happen before anyone else did. Where others saw destruction, he saw rebirth. The economy here had long ago bottomed out. This was the most dramatic course correction imaginable.

It was possible, Ragnar told people, that State Farm and Allstate would pay for damaged property. But what had even happened? Would it be considered an act of God? Was this sort of devastation in the fine print of any contract? Was it an incalculable loss? And then there was the fallibility of the payout. With Yesno whispering in his ear, Ragnar cited numbers from the floods in New Orleans and Houston, the fires in California — the family who, two years later, still couldn't return to their mold-ridden home and who received only forty-one thousand in compensation. The three-hundred-thousand-dollar homeowner's policy that called for a sliding deductible of thirty thousand. The rise in rates that would inevitably follow, sometimes resulting in a quadrupling of yearly costs. That's what might happen. Or?

Or they could take the money he was offering: the estimated market value on their property — calculated with absolutely no re-gard for the destruction that had taken place — plus 15 percent. A fair price. More than fair. When asked by the *Star Trib* about his land grab, Ragnar said, "This area has already been devastated by the declining logging and mining industries. These people can't afford to wait around for help. I want to see them taken care of."

But when he spoke privately to Yesno, he said, "The world is always moving faster and faster. How do we keep pace? How do we anticipate today what will dominate tomorrow? We study history for clues. And the winners in history have proven, time and time again, that land is power, whether it's a restaurant sited on a busy street or the army positioned on a steep-cliffed island or pumps built over an ocean of oil. Economic power and military power and political power are based on geography. And we've got it."

Weeks passed. The quarantine ended. The rebuilding began. By this time Frontier Metals had quintupled its property holdings and Ragnar was already looking to invest in infrastructure: Water and sewer. Roads. Cell towers. Fiber-optic cable. An expanded electrical grid. Even the railway that would become the Bullet. The money wasn't flowing yet, but it would. And he understood it would flow more freely with a pipeline to accommodate it. He had always believed in the potential of Northfall—the future of this region—and now, by his hand, it would be realized.

To John this felt all too familiar, like some echo of what followed his mother's death. Everything was on fire, and he was consumed by inexpressible pain and facing an uncertain future, but rather than acknowledge that his son and his family might need help, Ragnar locked himself in his office and pursued his work.

Johnny had once heard his father say—in a dedication speech given at a high-school sports complex he funded—that there were five plays that determined the fate of a football game. They could happen at any point in the two halves, but those five critical plays added up to a victory or loss. He wished the players of Northfall High the very best on game day, but more than that, he hoped that they would recognize that the truths of the football field were universal. "There might be five moments that determine the fate of a life. Will you be ready to seize them when they come?" His eyes settled on John in the audience then, and when everyone stood up and clapped, he remained seated. The words that had felt like an insult then — implying squandered opportunity — resonated now.

His hair was growing back, his whole body stubbled. He would develop twitches — a blinky eyelid, a jerky elbow — but they were short-lived. He ate alone. He refused to answer any calls. Jenna came to the house every day, and every day he had her turned away. When he wasn't in his bedroom staring at the wall, he was tromping through the woods on long hikes. He needed silence. He needed to think.

Until he didn't anymore. Down by the lake, there was a warming shed for skating and a wood-burning sauna. Their whole lives, their father had used it once a week and claimed it was good for circulation and mental health. He often held family meetings down there. He said it was a good place to be honest. "When you're naked, there's nothing to hide."

In that same spirit, Johnny invited Talia for a sauna. They alternated fifteen minutes sweating in the cedar shed and then ten minutes swimming in the cool water outside. Talia fed more wood into the stove and the temperature clicked up to one seventy. They were dripping sweat and sitting on opposite ends of the L-shaped bench when — in a slow, measured voice — he told her everything. The events leading up to that night, and what he had done. The two-day bender. The ten-hour poker game. The hot streak that became a losing streak. His pockets were turned inside out but he wanted to keep betting and the men at the table wanted to keep betting, but they needed a promise. Collateral. "I shouldn't have done it," Johnny said. "But I did it. And when I turned up a pair of twos and lost again, things got out of control."

"That's a fucking understatement," Talia said.

When Johnny finished, she ladled a scoop of eucalyptus-scented water onto the hot stones. The steam billowed and the temperature notched up a few more degrees and she said, "You're telling me this now? Why didn't you ask for my help before? You should have called me from the game."

"Because you would have called me a fuckup."

"Because you *are*." She cracked her neck. "Did you find it, at least?"

"No."

"Well, could it still be there?"

He wiped the sweat off his face and shook his head. "I looked. I looked everywhere. And now there's no one left to ask that question."

"You bring me down here and you lay this on me — I assume for advice?" she said.

"No advice. I just want you to know what's next."

"And that is?"

"I know I've been a disappointment to the family." The sauna stones had gone red with heat. He reached his hand out and picked one of them up. Silver-blue veins began to trace their way down his knuckles, wrist, and forearm. "But I'm going to be different now."

Talia couldn't help but seethe her breath. "Yeah, you are."

"I've been given a second chance I don't deserve."

"And?"

"You know how, after Mom died, Pops sent me off to boarding school? Juvenile-delinquent daycare? Hoping it would give me perspective, make me into a better man?"

"Yeah?"

"Think I need to do something like that. Except on my own terms."

"What are you talking about?"

"I need to go. Far away from here."

"The whole world's falling apart. Nobody's going to know what you did."

"But *I* know. This isn't about getting caught. I don't care about that. It's regret. I've got nothing but regret. It's poisoning me."

"Johnny . . . I get it."

"Yeah?"

"I've understood from the very beginning. You took it hard, Mom dying. You blamed yourself and maybe you could tell we blamed you too, even if we never said so."

"Yeah."

"But we're past that. We're past all of that. This is a new fucking dawn. Earth two point oh. We all get a redo. You've done some stupid shit. You hate yourself for it. You want to stop being a waste and start being an earner. Fuckin' A. But look at you. You're a freak show. A monster. Nature gone wrong. You're going to end up in some government lab if you're not careful. You need your family right now. We can protect you. We can . . . use you. What do you think you're going to accomplish, leaving at a time like this?"

He looked her hard in the eye and said, "I'm going to escape myself."

21

*

Now . . .

August gives way to September. The seasons come fast here. The heat blows off. Nights creep toward freezing, and days barely break fifty. The birch and aspen trees go gold with fall color, and the leaves shimmer the air and dapple the lake water Stacie paddles. Her father sits at the stern of the canoe, alternating his strokes and steering them against the current and the sharp wind.

They are on Wolverine Lake, two portages from where they parked the Explorer. That was their agreement: Stick to lakes accessible by roads and never portage more than twice. There's too much water to survey otherwise. And someone looking to dump a body would want convenience as much as isolation.

A fish finder is transom-mounted to the canoe, and her father checks the display screen for what must be the thousandth time today and then adjusts the transducer. The water is so clear, she could have read the date on a quarter up to twenty feet. After that, visibility blurs — and toward the center, the lake bottoms out into a gray-green nothing, sometimes a hundred, sometimes two hundred feet deep.

"Did you know," her father says, "that you're surrounded by some of the most ancient rocks on Earth? The Midcontinent Rift."

Three point five billion years old, she mouths at the same time he says it. She knows and loves all of his stories and lessons. She has spent her whole life listening to them. He was one of those fathers who tried to make every moment teachable. He was sometimes painfully earnest in the way he saw history and geography and botany and geology and education as all intertwined. To hike or canoe with him meant pausing constantly to learn that morel mushrooms were ready to harvest when the oak leaves were the size of a squirrel's ear or that the color of lichen was a good indicator of toxicity in an environment or that 6 percent of Minnesota's surface area was water, more than any other state.

"Rocks are the reason people are here," he says. He's referring to the copper and nickel that established Northfall, but he could just as easily be referring to omnimetal.

The Boundary Waters consist of more than a million acres along the Canadian border, untouched by roads or towns or cell towers. A flooded green carpet. Unchanged since the glaciers melted twelve thousand years ago. A human here is a tiny intrusion. "If you're going to disappear," her father says, "this would be the place to do it."

There is a sameness to the lakes that makes her feel small and lost, but her father always knows exactly where they are. He has a map that he takes out every now and then, not to consult, but to mark with a red pen and show their search.

They find a wolf's paw print in the mud. They spot a moose grazing in a marsh and lifting its broad rack of antlers to study them. They watch the dark dots of loons diving into and rising from the shivering water. In a rocky cliff side, her father points out a reddish pictograph of an Ojibwa hunting party. But no sign of Dan Swanson, only the occasional false alarm that turns out to be a log or a cluster of turtles.

"Maybe he's gone?" her father says. "Maybe he hightailed it to someplace else? You can spit from here and hit Canada."

"Maybe."

Except she knows that wasn't what happened. The other day, a Black Dog mine was sabotaged. Four half-ton pickups, three bulldozers, and two dump trucks. Their tires were slashed, their brake lines cut and batteries ripped out. The day after that, a Frontier Metals "man camp"—over two hundred trailers housing four times as many men—lost power and water from clipped lines and blasted mains. There was some sort of battle going on, and the Northfall PD was somehow caught in the middle of it. When cops showed up at the scene, mining representatives told them that all was well and sent them away.

She'd asked the sheriff about this in his office one day, and he tried to tell her ecoterrorists were to blame. "We've dealt with plenty of that around here. As long as I've been working, there've been hippies putting sand in the gas tanks of timber trucks and hammering railroad spikes into trees about to be logged."

"Shouldn't we be looking into it?" she said. "Isn't that our job?"

His phone started ringing then and his eyes locked on it. "Look . . . Stacie . . . we've got more drunk drivers and fistfights and domestic assaults and space-dust overdoses and neglected kids than we can shake a stick at." He picked up the phone from its cradle and motioned her toward the door. "How about let's not get too ambitious?"

If she wanted to pursue more than she was assigned, she would do so on her own. Or at least with her father beside her.

He knows all the campsites and uses them to navigate their course. They survey the air for vultures and the shore for tire tracks or signs of trash. "What am I looking for?" her father says, and she says, "I don't know. A trash bag or latex glove or tarps or duct tape. But don't limit your vision. Anything unusual."

He's been taking her out whenever she's off duty. "It's kind of like fishing, I guess," she says. "Except without bait." She has her swimsuit and goggles with her, and occasionally, her father will pause his paddling and say, "Take a look at this," and after some deliberation, she'll plop into the water to investigate. In deeper waters, they've trolled with heavy hooks and steel line.

"We'll find him, don't you worry. Your mother always said I was a good looker," he says. "Get it? Good looker? As in, *good* at *looking*?"

She digs in with her paddle. "I get it, Daddy."

"Did you know there were once beavers here that weighed five hundred pounds?"

Stacie smiles at the memory of yesterday. Now her neck and lower back ache from perching so long on the bow seat. Her hand is still sore and blistered from the paddle. And the squad car, as it rumbles along the crumbling, potholed streets of Northfall, reminds her of the lake chop brought on by yesterday's autumn wind.

Hank sips from the Styrofoam cup of coffee bought from the Kwik Trip, then licks the splash off his mustache. "Just you wait," he says.

"For what?" she says.

"What I've been talking about the past five minutes. Just you wait. You're going to break."

"I'm going to break?"

"You're going to become a coffee drinker. You can't be a cop and *not* drink coffee."

"Oh," she says, realizing she's tuned out the drone of his voice. She used to be attentive to his every word, thinking he might have something valuable to teach her. But while her father generously shared his knowledge of plants and Chippewa myths and the Pleistocene era because it was his way of saying *I love you,* Hank seems interested only in showing off his big-butted authority. A mansplainer.

"No," she says. "I want to like it, but coffee tastes like dirt. I'll stick to Diet Coke."

"No, you won't."

"Yes, I think I will."

"Nope. Another month, I'll have you drinking dark roast. Mark my words."

She almost says no again but then gives a noncommittal *mmm* instead, hoping it will quiet him. There was a time, not very long ago, when she met every situation with a smile. There was a time when she tried to be as agreeable as possible and chase away any discomfort. There was a time when every sentence seemed to include a qualifier like "I'm sorry but" or "I guess" or "I think." It's still a struggle for her, but she's doing her best to change. She's trying not to go out of her way to help others feel comfortable. She's learning, slowly, to take a stance.

This is dawn, and they are rolling out of town, headed to Frontier Metals. The gated campus takes up several hundred acres and consists of windowed office buildings, a fleet of trucks, a sorting facility, and a number of equipment and storage warehouses. It could be mistaken for a Walmart distribution center if not for the guards in Kevlar patrolling the perimeter.

Security officers wave them through and they roll toward the loading docks built into the side of a warehouse. Here they park and get out and wait as the ten trailers are hitched. The semis idle. Diesel scents the morning air. Stacie remains by the squad car while Hank hitches up his pants and walks over to the silver-haired, crew-cut warehouse manager and bums a cigarette off him. The two men blow smoke and trade jokes and maybe comment on the weather or how the Vikings are shaping up this season. And then it's time to go, and Hank drops his cig and smashes it beneath the heel of his boot and jogs back to her.

The same routine every morning for the past two weeks, including what happens next. Upon their departure—after they fire up the siren and swirl the rack lights and head out the front gates, escorting the long line of semis behind him—Hank always pulls out his cell and types out a message one-handed.

Today Stacie pretends to stretch, one way, then the other, leaning toward the phone. She sees the number 4. That's it. The entirety of the message.

The squad car rolls over the center line and Hank readjusts the wheel and she says, "You need me to text for you while you drive? I don't mind."

"Don't you worry about it, princess," he says and hits Send. "I got everything under control."

· · ·

The squad car continues past the exit ramp, canceling its siren and rack lights, while the semis downshift and chirp their air brakes and take the long sloping turn that will merge them onto the Highway 1 corridor. The roads up north are so battered from the winters and the traffic that crews recently resurfaced the highway, added two extra lanes, and widened the shoulders. The asphalt is a silken black and hums beneath the truck tires as they pick up speed and begin their four-hour journey south to St. Paul.

Autumn has hurried here, and winter will soon be behind it. The sky is a pale blue pillared with clouds and triangled with geese. The sumac growing in the ditches burns a bright red. The wind carries leaves in it that stick briefly to windshields like wet stars before flurrying away.

Every truck in the brigade is a black Cascadia Freightliner with a silver grille like a clenched jaw. The ten semis maintain a steady speed of sixty-five and a distance of twenty yards from one another. Several hundred thousand tons of steel flowing southward. Their windows are tinted and give nothing back.

A billboard advertises a strip club called Chubbies. Another billboard advertises a gas station and McDonald's oasis fifty miles ahead. The highway is otherwise walled in by pines. Every few miles they are cut away to make room for electrical stanchions or a road.

It is on one of these side roads that the four armored trucks wait. They are white half-ton Fords with brush guards and no license plates. They pull onto the highway after the semis blast by. They accelerate hard, kicking up smoke.

In the passenger seat of the lead vehicle is Mickey Golden. He — along with everyone else in his twelve-man crew — wears an alien mask. Gray skin, bulbous head, black oval eyes. But you would know him by his rings or Hawaiian shirt or gold-chain necklace or the ropes of yellow hair tumbling down his shoulders. He activates a device and sets it on the dash. It looks a little like a Wi-Fi router — a plastic square with six short antennas and many blinking lights — but it is a scrambler. All cell and radio signals within two hundred yards will be disrupted.

His vehicle launches up the left lane and then quickly nudges into the space between the fourth and fifth semis. The other three pickups follow — two screaming past him, the other keeping pace with him — and soon the semi they're after is boxed in.

Horns deafen the air. The topper at the rear of Mickey's pickup opens and two men in alien masks appear holding a spike strip between them. They chuck it, and the semi behind them doesn't have time to turn or brake. The barbed metal clicks the pavement and then disappears below the grille. A second later the tires shred.

Black strips of rubber kick out of the wheel wells. The rims bite the pavement and send up fans of sparks. The semi lurches toward the ditch. The driver overcompensates, yanking back at the wheel. That's when it's rear-ended. The trailer crumples. The rig jackknifes and tips. With a screech of rent metal, the laws of physics play out violently. The overturned semi skids another forty yards, gouging the asphalt and spitting debris, before coming to a stop. The southbound lanes are now blocked.

The semi before Mickey slows. He knows that the pickups ahead are braking and that the men in the toppers have their AR-15s trained on the driver. But before he can calculate the next step, the rear doors of the trailer unlatch and swing open.

Inside, he does not see a shining load of omnimetal. He sees a tall, muscular woman. Talia Frontier. The black curls of her hair whip around her face. She wears a harness, and ropes run from its loops to bolts in the wall and floor, anchoring her in place. She hefts something onto her shoulder, what Mickey recognizes too late as an RPG launcher.

"Brake, brake, brake!" he cries out to the driver just as — with an orange flash and a cough of smoke — the warhead streaks toward them.

22

✳

A few days ago, John told his sister she was on her own. He told her he didn't want to be part of the trap she was planning. He told her, "You're playing a dangerous game."

"This isn't a game. It's business." But she was smiling when she said it.

They were in her office, just the two of them. The sun was sinking and the night was chasing it. Only a single lamp burned on her desk. Neither of them stood in its light. "Talia, come on."

"What?"

"The night of your wedding . . ."

"What about it?"

"You gamed me then."

"I didn't game you."

"You did. You trapped me here. And you're trying to game me again now."

She put her big hands on his shoulders and drew him close. "You're a part of this family. And this family is Frontier Metals. You've had your little vacation. Your walkabout. Your vision quest or whatever the hell. Now you have to make up for lost time." Her fingers worked at his muscles, hard enough that it was an effort for him not to flinch. "Don't you realize how important you could be to us?"

"You're gaming me. Stop gaming me." With her this close, he had to tip his neck to look up at her. "You're going to make things worse. I'll help, but only if I can make things better."

Her middle finger found the space between two of his vertebrae and prodded it. "It's funny."

"What?"

"You don't feel like a sack of shit, but you're sure acting like one."

"Talia . . ."

"Don't have a heart attack. I'm just busting your balls." Her smile was open-mouthed, revealing the grape gum she gnashed with her teeth and twisted with her tongue. Her breath smelled like spoiled fruit. "I actually respect you. You know that, Johnny?"

"John."

Her eyes narrowed to slits. "I know who you are."

Outside, the sky darkened and the stars brightened. "I'm going to look into finding the kid, okay?" he said.

"You really think there's a kid?"

"I've got a feeling, yeah."

"A feeling. What's that supposed to mean?"

"I don't know how to explain it, but that's going to be my contribution. That's going to be my way of helping."

"That's good," she said and she cupped his cheek with her hand and laid a nail along his birthmark. "You haven't forgotten your family." She lowered her voice, though there was no one around to hear them. "Stay loyal, okay? We're in this together. To the end."

John's first step is recon. There is no address for the DOD facility in the phone book. And there is no satellite view on Google, that section of land curiously blacked out, as if cut by scissors. But Yesno pulls out the map and confirms the location — in the woods west of town. "The trouble is, you can't simply drive past," he says. "The road was built specifically for the facility. If you go there, they're going to notice."

"How heavily is it guarded?"

"Heavily, I understand."

Three drones patrol the Frontier estate, staggered according to their geolocation software. A dozen more sit on a shelf in the storage shed, ready to rotate out or be salvaged for parts. He snatches a quadcopter, peels off its FAA ID, wipes its memory card, then tosses it into his Bronco.

Just before he climbs into the cab, he hears a noise. The grinding squeal of a saw. He looks toward one of the outbuildings, the pole barn that serves as Nico's studio. The door is open and a brief spray of orange sparks lights up the dark inside. He goes there.

Music plays—something New Age, a blend of thunder, wind, synthesizers, and chanting—and the sound echoes through the cavernous space. The floor is concrete and splattered with paint and wrinkled with drop cloths and crumbled with rock. Several canvases are stacked against the wall. Others are set up on easels. Many of them seem to carry the same image: the sprawl of space, dotted with stars, with either a mouth or an eye at its center.

There are shelves stacked with paint and benches cluttered with power tools. Here is an archway built of moose and elk and deer antlers. Here is a half-chiseled creature that appears to be mostly eyeballs and tentacles. Here is a quilt sewn from furs harvested from beavers and coyotes and foxes and deer. Here is a boulder made out of many smaller stones, most of them agates. Here is a giant man with angel wings, every inch of him built out of bleached driftwood.

"Nico?"

The saw fires up again. The pole barn is a maze of installations, and John walks through one made of black fabric jeweled with rhinestones. Beneath the teepeed shawl, John feels like he is either traveling through a cave sparkling with gems or floating through deep space with the stars winking all around.

On the other side of it he spots Nico hunched over a workbench. The footing is uneven here because so many extension cords snake across the floor. One of them connects to the stereo that blasts . . . is it even music? Right now it sounds like a storm at sea. "Nico!" John says, and Nico finally turns, his blue eyes flashing in the gloom.

His brother goes to the stereo and clicks it off and the sudden silence feels like both a relief and a discomfort. "What are you doing in here?" he asks.

"Wanted to say hi. See what you were up to."

Nico slowly raises an arm, like a magician revealing a trick. "I'm building."

"Can you show me?"

He plucks what looks like a small metal sickle off the workbench and then walks John over to a rectangular structure maybe five feet wide and seven feet tall. It is incredibly intricate, almost biological. Unfinished, but already with a thousand parts welded or fitted together. Thickly framed with steel, tailored with copper and iron, veined throughout with wiring, studded with agates, and brightened here and there by omnimetal that appears to be laser-etched with ciphers. There are wide channels that come together from several directions and merge into a circle at the structure's center. The same kind of circle painted onto the canvases. Everything seems somehow to point to or thread with or connect at this juncture, like a sculptural vanishing point.

John doesn't know how to explain it, but he feels like he's seen it somewhere before. In a dream? Maybe his ears are still suffering from the stereo's noise, but the air seems to shiver and whine here. Like after a bell is struck.

A ladder is set next to the structure and Nico climbs it and fits the sickle into the larger arrangement. Near the top, it clicks perfectly into place and his fingers linger there a moment, trembling with exhaustion or the pleasure of creation. "It's not finished yet."

John says, "It already looks pretty badass, but . . . what's it going to be?"

"I'm calling it the eye of the Herm."

"Like *Herb* with an *m*?"

"It's Greek. It refers to a threshold between realms."

"You lost me. Looks like a weird door."

"You're not wrong."

"Where does it go, then?"

Nico climbs down the ladder and stands beside his brother; both of them stare at the sculpture. "I hope to find out."

. . .

There is an old logging road that abuts the government facility. John drives down it, clunking through the ruts and thumping over the exposed rock, before pulling into a meadow of fireweed. He sends up the drone with a buzzing whir, and a few seconds later it is out of his line of sight.

The live feed is projected onto the controller's screen. The drone whines over the treetops and at first there is nothing to see but their green and red and gold crowns. Then everything opens up into the grounds, and he hovers high above, taking in the six buildings and the concrete paths threading between them. From here it could pass for a college campus. He yaws the drone. Tilts the pitch. Tries to get every angle he can from this height. He adjusts the flight altitude, ten feet at time. It is then that he notices something curious. There are no windows. Every building is shelled fully with concrete.

He wasn't sure what he was hoping for, but more than this. Some movement catches his eye—a car pulling into the lot. He rudders over the vehicle and throttles down twenty feet and observes the door open and a silver-haired woman step out. She hesitates a moment, as if wondering whether she forgot something, and then heads toward a nearby building. She appears unhurried. Slow, even hunched over, to the point of appearing sick or exhausted. She pulls out a keycard and uses it to open a door. He can't see much from this height, but a guard waits on the other side.

He knows it's a risk, but he drops the drone another ten feet, then another five, until he can angle it and focus the camera on her license plate. He reads the plate aloud—twice, three times, four, committing it to his brain. Just as he is about to throttle up, the image shakes. It rolls one way, then another, and he catches a glimpse of another drone trailing his. The image shakes again, this time with a burst of static. And rather than lead the other drone on a chase, he crashes his own full speed into the asphalt below. The screen goes dark.

23

✳

ven after John turns onto the county highway, his eyes flit to the rearview and he keeps his speed just ten miles over the limit. He repeats her license plate several times over and then pulls out his cell and makes a note of it. He remembers to buckle his seat belt. He turns the radio on, then off.

Paranoia drives him. The fear of getting caught and boxed away. But more than that, it's the sick feeling he gets from the DOD facility itself. He recognized it. Impossible as it seems, he dreamed it. He knew its gray concrete walls. He felt both inside and outside it at the same time. He was there. The boy was there. They were there.

The farther he travels, the more his heart settles. Just when he thinks he's gotten away undetected, a siren sounds. He can't see the source, but it's coming from behind him, where the road curves through the woods. He could crush the accelerator now, but he's headed for a five-mile straightaway through an open marsh. There's no place to turn off, dive down a side road. They'd spot him. Better to play dumb than run guilty. He's not afraid of getting caught for spying on a government facility. He's afraid of attention, questions, any sort of scrutiny that might reveal what he is. A freak show, Talia called him.

When the squad car appears — fifty yards behind him, haloed in red and blue light — he slows and pulls onto the shoulder. But the cop blows by him, maybe going eighty, rattling the Bronco with the grit thrown up by its tires.

John continues to idle until the cruiser is out of sight, then returns to the blacktop. "Huh," he keeps saying. He's got that old familiar feeling — the sensation of almost getting caught — and it makes him a little giddy. When he nears town, more squad cars go roaring past, and he sees where they're headed: onto the ramp that will lead them south on Highway 1. From here he can see the hospital. Just then a helicopter rises from its roof with a sputtering roar and flies in the same direction.

John picks up his cell to make a call, but it is already ringing. The ID reads *Yesno*. He hits Accept and says, "What happened?"

Talia is fine. Yesno knows that much. The same can't be said for everyone else. He knows of four fatalities so far. Several other people appear to be in serious condition. "From what I understand, no fewer than three of our semis were totaled. And the highway is a complete mess." Backed up for miles in every direction. The pavement torn and buckled from the wreckage. His voice remains brisk and businesslike, as if he's reporting quarterly earnings.

"What a shit show," John says.

"Yes, that's a fair way of putting it."

"So Black Dog tried to make the hit and steal the load. How many of them were there?"

"She isn't sure. Four vehicles, maybe twelve men. All wearing masks."

"But it was definitely them?"

"Talia says so. She said she recognized Mickey Golden by his hair."

"I don't suppose he's one of the fatalities?"

"No."

"He at least in custody?"

"No. As I understand it, the only ones in custody are presently being zipped into body bags. The rest got away. Including Mickey. But she claims she hurt him. In her words, 'He was so scared, he was pissing blood out of his eyeballs.'"

"Yeah," John says, "those are definitely her words."

"She couldn't really talk, so I only got the short version. I don't know anything more than what I've told you except . . .'"

"Except it's not over."

"No, it's not over," Yesno says. "It's far from over."

John isn't sure where to go. Home? Or south on Highway 1? Or maybe he should just hit the train station and bullet his way out of here once and for all. He turns one way, then another, then back the other way, circling blocks, detouring his way to nowhere. And then, without really thinking about it, he ends up in Jenna's neighborhood.

He doesn't plan on knocking on her door. He just wants to drive by. Maybe catch a glimpse of her in the window. But she and her boy are out front, doing yard work. As he approaches, she turns her face toward the familiar growl of the Bronco. He takes his foot off the gas but doesn't brake. Not yet. Not until she raises a hand, a dirt-smeared garden glove, and waves hello. Then he has no choice but to pull over.

She wears a flannel shirt, jeans. Her hair is pulled back in a messy ponytail, her red hair like a curl of flame. She seems to be hiding a smile when she approaches. He lowers the window and is immediately assaulted by country music blaring from across the street. "It's a bad habit," she says.

"What?"

"Driving by my house and not stopping to say hello."

"Don't know what you're talking about."

"Uh-huh. Thanks for the groceries, stalker."

He doesn't say anything but shifts the Bronco into park. It rocks a little and she settles her arms on the door. "What's the matter?"

"Nothing."

"Something's the matter. I can tell."

"It's just my sister. Kicking the hornets' nest."

"She does that."

"That she does."

"So," she says. "You going to get out or just sit out here like a weirdo?"

He looks toward the yard, where she's been potting mums and

tearing out weeds and planting bulbs, thinking ahead to spring. Her boy balances a Wiffle Ball on a plastic stand and then tries to hit it with an oversize bat. "Not sure that's a good idea."

"Why not?" she says.

"I've already been questioned about Dan's disappearance."

"You have?" Her expression sickens. "I didn't know that."

"Can't blame them. I'd be worried about me too."

"Well, you didn't do anything wrong, so you have nothing to worry about."

He can't meet her eyes when he says, "I wouldn't say that. But I promise I've got nothing to do with your husband. Whatever happened to him."

"I believe you."

"That's the weird thing about you, Jenna." He fiddles with the radio dial, even though the power is off, as if hunting for the right tone. "You've always believed me."

"It's true."

"Anyway. Probably doesn't look good. Me being here."

"But here you are."

Someone across the street cackles and John leans forward to see past Jenna. The yard of the apartment unit there is a mess of stained pizza boxes, empty chip bags, crushed soda and beer cans. The grass grows only in patches. Several men stand around a grill, pushing hot dogs around with tongs. Others toss beanbags in a game of cornhole. "They always play their music that loud?"

"Pretty much."

"You want me to talk to them?"

"No."

"Why not?"

"Because I have to live here."

He reaches for the gearshift. "Better get going."

Her hand shoots inside the window and grabs his forearm. "Stay." She keeps a tight grip. He imagines he can feel the heat of her even through the leather glove. "If you didn't have nothing to do with Dan, there's no point in being shy."

"Right. I guess. Yeah."

"It's been a month," she says.

"A month?" he says and checks the rearview as if the road be-hind him might offer some response. "That's a month longer than I planned on staying."

"Stay a while longer." She leans a little farther into the window, reaching across him. She kills the engine, unslots the key. "Now you've got to come inside." She starts toward the house, holding up the keys and jangling them. "I was about to make some chow anyway."

He waits another second before he follows. He makes hard eye contact with a guy wearing a camo hat across the street. When he pushes through the chain-link gate, the boy says, "Who is that stranger?"

At this point Jenna is halfway up the steps. "An old friend."

The boy swings the bat one-handed, hitting his foot, hitting the grass, hitting the weed pile. He doesn't look up when John says, "Timmy, right?"

"Yep."

"You like baseball?"

He continues to swing the bat at everything but the ball. "I'm go-ing to play T-ball next year."

"Yeah?"

With every swing of the bat he says, "Yep, yep, yep."

Jenna lingers in the doorway and says, "Why don't you teach Timmy how to hit home runs while I race around and stuff all the dirty clothes into a closet so that you can actually come inside with-out me being embarrassed?"

John looks toward her in a mild panic. "I don't know—"

But she is already gone. The door claps shut and the two of them are left alone.

The boy squints at John as if he can't quite see him. "Did you get hurt?"

"What?"

The boy touches his own face along the cheek. "You got an owie."

"Oh," John says. "No. Just born that way."

"You were born with an owie?"

"Doesn't hurt. Just a funny color. Everybody's born a little different, right?"

"You're different than everybody else?"

"I am," John says. "Yeah."

The wind scatters leaves across the lawn. The country music blares and they say nothing for a little while and then the boy fumbles the bat toward John and says, "Show me."

John takes the bat, blue and hollow and plastic, and strangles the grip with his hands. "Let me ask you something?"

"Okay."

He looks across the street. "Does it bother you when those men play their music that loud?"

"I hate it, but Mommy hates it worst."

"That's what I thought."

24

✳

Victoria knows what the boy is capable of. But she has mis-reported and ignored data. And she has intentionally slowed her lab work, claiming she must take care when testing his limits and capabilities. They don't know what they're dealing with, she said. They don't want to rush and potentially destroy what could be a trillion-dollar tool of war, the next evolutionary step, a revisionary defiance of everything they knew about science, she said.

She isn't sure what scares her more, the practical promise of Hawkin as a living weapon or the dreams he sometimes reports to her. The visions of worlds other than this one. The possibility that he might be an antenna or a bridge or a connection to something *other*. He dreamed his body turned inside out and instead of guts, tentacles came squiggling out. He dreamed he was standing among mountains, but the mountains were floating. He dreamed that a door opened and a black wave of galaxies came pouring through.

She's been buying the boy time while knowing all along their time will run out.

She needs to do something to get him away from this place, but she doesn't have a plan. Or rather, she has one, and it's terrible and dangerous and impossible and could land her in prison and her husband in harm's way.

By day she tries to pretend that nothing will ever change. She tries to believe that she will continue to spend her time testing the boy and — let's face it — mothering him in her own quiet way. But at night she lies in bed, unable to sleep, her heart beating furiously, her guts in an acidic twist. She does not believe in God, but she prays all the same.

She prays that Dr. Gunn will lose interest. She prays that some other world event will shuttle resources and attention elsewhere. She prays that the facility will lose funding and shut down. She prays that the boy will somehow grow out of or learn to inhibit his powers.

The sword, if that's the right word for what Dr. Gunn brought into the lab, sliced a five-inch gash in Hawkin's chest. A blue light shone suddenly from it like a torn-open drape. It was pure energy, unleashed from the subatomic matrix of omnimetal woven through him. The air visibly shook and warped. Like a mirror melting.

Gunn was knocked back as though an invisible hand had picked him up and hurled him across the room. He skidded across the floor and came to a stop against the wall. He didn't whimper or cry out, though he must have been hurt badly. Instead, he pushed himself up into a seated position and rasped his breath through a busted-lip smile and said, "That's what I thought."

Hawkin could have killed Gunn then. He could have killed Victoria. He could have killed everyone in this building if he wanted. In the town, the state, the country. But he didn't. He wouldn't. He was just a boy, after all.

He fell to the floor. And curled into a ball. And wept.

For years, Victoria ran for exercise, but she gave it up after she couldn't kick a bad case of plantar fasciitis. To this day, the pain lingers in her right arch. She'd had a slipped disc in her lumbar vertebrae years ago and it still hurts for her to sit for any length of time. Her triglycerides remain high, no matter how closely she monitors her diet. The vision in her left eye is starting to fade. She can't smell as well as she used to. If she eats anything with onions or garlic, she'll pay for it on the toilet the next day. This boy, Hawkin Gunderson, might be partially made of metal, but his body remained human, a sack full of chemicals you could poke holes in if you found the right vulnerability. The boy was hurt.

He might be ridiculously powerful, but she never saw him that way. He was afraid, sad, weary. Vulnerable. There was something about his bearing, even on a good day, that made him appear bruised inside. He was always wheezy with asthma. He was always fighting a runny nose. He never looked like he'd had enough to eat, and his skin was the same fluorescent yellow as the lights down here. And after Gunn slashed him, when she rushed to him, when she asked him if he was okay, his whole body shook with his weeping. He had wet himself.

"Get out of here," she told Gunn. "Please." She wanted to say more—tell him how he disgusted her—but she kept the words pinched inside. Gunn took his time, but eventually he did rise with a sore moan and scraped his feet across the floor and opened the lab door. "You have to understand what's at stake," he said.

"Please leave," she said.

With that, the door clanged shut.

Only then did Victoria say, "Let me see." Hawkin remained in a tight ball and shook his head. But she kept speaking soothingly to him and assuring him that she only wanted to help, and finally he loosened his arms and showed her his chest.

The wound had already closed up, but a thick blue scar remained that was hard to the touch. Her fingernail ticked against it. "Shh," she said and petted his hair. "It's going to be okay."

"Do you promise?" Hawkin said.

She didn't answer at first. She didn't want to lie to him. But finally she resolved something inside herself—because the time for waiting and denial was over—and said, "I promise. But I'm going to need your help."

Wade followed her to Nebraska. He followed her to Northfall. She knows he will follow her wherever she goes next. She sometimes feels guilty about his devotion. That the emotional math is off between them. On her less generous days, she sees him as vacant, happy not to work or think too hard. Like a golden retriever eager for a scratch, a ball, a sunbeam to lie in. But the rest of the time, she believes completely that he is simply a better person than her. Good and earnest.

He whistles when he washes the dishes. He hangs his golf score-cards on the fridge. He laughs at the sitcoms he streams on his tablet. He scratches down ideas for a historical novel he'd like to try to write someday. He pots mums for the fall and sets them on the porch. Every Sunday, without fail, he brings her the comics and says, "You've got to read this one." Every day, he does something to display a small flourish of joy and satisfaction. He's at the kitchen table now, a pen and legal tablet before him, humming as he tries to sketch a bowl of fruit. He wears a yellow golf shirt tucked into his jeans.

It isn't in Wade's nature to complain, but she knows he hates this place. They have no friends in Northfall. She seems always to be at work, and whenever she is home, she's so tense her muscles ache. Ever since they moved here, he has struggled hard to make conversation and get her to laugh. He has to remind her to eat.

When she pulls up a chair at the table now, he smiles and sets down his pen and says, "I draw a pretty mean pear, but that's a sorry excuse for grapes. Wouldn't you say?"

"Wade."

She takes one of his hands in both of hers and massages the knuckles. She has trouble making eye contact at first, and he leans into her and says, "Honey? Victoria? What's wrong?"

"Every day, multiple times a day," she says, "you ask if there's something you can do for me. Rub my neck. Make me dinner. Iron a blouse."

"Do you need something now? I'm happy to help."

"I know you are. I know. And I don't think I've made it clear how grateful I am for that. For you."

He shrugs and smiles. "Oh, hey. That's sweet. Thanks. I'm grateful for you too."

"You've been worried about me."

"I have." There is a moment's silence when he studies her and his eyes water and crinkle at the corners. "I've been real worried about you. And I'll be honest"—he seems to give this next part a good deal of thought—"I think you need to seriously consider quitting your job."

She almost says something, but he holds up a finger. "Now, I'm sorry to be bossy, but I need to say something. I hope you'll hear me out. I know you can't tell me what's going on over there, but it's clear it's not good. It's not what you hoped it would be. I don't care if it's groundbreaking. I don't care if you win the gosh-darn Nobel Prize. It's not worth it." He taps the table with finality. "There. I said it."

"Thank you. For saying that."

"You're very welcome."

"You're right, Wade."

"I sure think so. I'm glad you think so too."

"The question is, what are we going to do about it?"

He leans forward eagerly. "I can't tell you how glad I am we're having this talk."

"You want to help me."

"I do. Of course I do."

"That's good. Because I need your help." Her throat feels dry. She tries to swallow but has no spit. "But I want you to know . . . it's okay if you say no."

"How could I ever say no?"

"You might need to. Maybe you should. This is your life. Not just mine."

"This is our life."

"Wade. Listen to me. You can say no. Do you understand? This is a conversation. And I don't even know . . . exactly what I'm asking yet."

"Tell me. We'll figure it out. Together."

She releases his hand then. There are red marks where her nails bit into him. She puts a finger to her mouth, indicating the need for silence. His forehead creases. And he looks around as if he might be able to spot those who might be listening. He mimics the gesture — *Shh* — and nods, understanding they might be monitored.

She reaches for his pen. He flips to a fresh sheet of paper and rotates the legal tablet toward her. And she begins to write.

25

*

Jenna does her best to keep up appearances. In the bathroom, John finds a brightly colored shower curtain and a vase full of dried flowers and a cheap blue candle sputtering in a pool of molten wax. But that can't hide the linoleum bubbling up or the mold spotting the ceiling. In the living room, a painting is hung off center in an attempt to hide a dent in the wall that looks like it came from somebody getting shoved hard against it. The futon is broken but braced by a dictionary and a Bible. He finds a framed family photo—Dan crushing Jenna and Timmy into a hug—laid flat on a shelf.

In the same way, she puts on a show of hosting him. Touring him brightly through the house, with a special focus on Timmy's bedroom. Insisting on a meal of spaghetti, Caesar salad, and garlic bread. But her constant smile seems to tremble. And her laughter comes a little too easily, as if she's trying to convince him that the chain-link fence outside is actually made of white pickets.

He can't help but feel distracted by the music blasting across the street and he goes often to the window to look out at the men. In response, she drops the shades and puts on a Police CD. "'Every little thing she does is magic,'" she sings along with Sting and then says, "Remember?"

He is peering through the slats in the blinds when he says, "What?"

"Remember how you wrote that to me? You used to leave me

sticky notes. On my car. On my window. In my purse. You put that one on my timecard at work."

The slats snap together and he turns away from the window. "I was pretty corny, wasn't I?"

"Everyone's corny when they're a teenager. But you just *felt* everything to the extreme. It's like you were always either all the way pissed or all the way happy or all the way in love." She adjusts the volume. "Nothing was ever halfway. That's what got you into so much trouble."

"I'm not that guy anymore," he says.

"Maybe," she says and studies him for a long moment, and he shoves his hands deep into his pockets and leans into them as if he could follow.

Timmy walks into the room and says, "What are you guys doing?"

"Just catching up," Jenna says.

"But you're not saying any words. You're staring at each other."

Jenna claps her hands together and says, "How about let's make some food already? I'm starving."

"What are we having?" Before she can respond, Timmy spots the box of Barilla noodles on the counter and throws up his arms and says, "Baspetti!" He points at John. "I get to put the noodles in the pot, but you can take them out of the pot."

Jenna raises her eyebrows at John and says, "How do you feel about that?"

"Put me to work."

Timmy brings his dinosaurs into the sunlit kitchen while they cook. He sets them on the table and loudly lists off each of their names—spinosaurus, stegosaurus, brachiosaurus, and so on—and then arranges them into different formations and mutters their cartoony voices as they fall in love or charge into battle or debate what to watch on television. Counter space is tight, so while Jenna cooks the spaghetti, John sets up the knife and cutting board beside the boy. He hacks his way through a head of romaine, then scoops it into a colander.

At that moment, Timmy smashes a T. rex into a stegosaurus, and the stegosaurus strikes the knife and sends it spinning off the table and onto the floor—where it stabs John's foot. He nudged off his shoes when he came inside, so the blade lands, tip first, on his big toe.

There is a harsh chirp, the noise two swords make when clashed together.

Jenna and Timmy stop what they're doing and look at him.

"Oh my God—John?" Jenna says and rushes over even as he holds up his hands and says, "I'm fine. I'm good."

Timmy's face goes red. His chin quivers when he stutters out, "I'm s-sorry."

John snatches the knife off the floor. "Really, I'm fine. It just missed me."

"It was blue," Timmy says and points at him. "I saw blue fire!"

"Are you sure you're okay?" Jenna says. She's trying to look at his foot, but he keeps pivoting away from her.

"I'm positive," he says and returns to the table and picks up a toy and floats it in front of Timmy's face. "Don't worry about it, buddy. Okay? Now, what's the name of that dinosaur? A fartosaurus?"

The boy says, "I saw . . ." But then the creases of his suspicious expression go slack and he says, "Fartosaurus?" He slaps his hands over his smile and says, "Fartosaurus!"

"Yes," John says. "That's how it hunted its prey. With its deadly poisonous farts. Didn't you know that? I obviously know way more about dinosaurs than you do."

The boy laughs in a shrieking way—saying, "No!"—and John hurries the knife to the sink and drops it in before Jenna can note that its tip is bent and blunted.

When John left Northfall five years ago, he wasn't trying to kill himself, not exactly. But he wanted to suffer. He wanted to find the edge.

He avoided people. If he was alone, he could hurt only himself. He slowly dialed up the intensity of his experiences. First hiking the Pacific Crest Trail. Then free-climbing Smith Rock. He camped in the Alaska backcountry and wandered unmolested among the grizzlies. He dived the *Yongala* and the *Thistlegorm* and wormed his body through the rusted guts of the shipwrecks and sometimes stirred up silt and lost his sense of up and down. He hang-glided off the lip of Kilauea, and the updraft of the red sulfuric pit pushed him thousands of feet into the air and melted holes in the craft's nylon.

Sometimes his body scared him. He hiked more than thirty miles one day, and when he pulled off his boots to soak his feet in a river, he discovered they were blue. The glow extended raggedly up his calves, as if he were suffering from frostbite. Another time, while climbing, he startled a nest of swallows and lost his grip and fell fifty feet from a cliff side. He didn't remember the impact, but when he awoke he was lying in a crater that had not been there before with rubble strewn all around him.

And sometimes he had dreams. More vivid than any he had known before. *Visions* might be a better word for them. In one he was floating in an ocean as red as blood with black lightning veining the sky above. In another he was falling into what he believed to be a star until it blinked and he realized it was an eye. In another still he was coughing, coughing, coughing until what looked like an organ unfurled from his mouth. But when it began to curl, he saw that it was a tentacle. There were whispers in the dreams, but the whispers didn't sound like words so much as a complicated wind. Or breathing.

He eventually learned to close off that part of himself. It was like trying to believe in God or spinning the dial on a radio that played only foreign and scrambled stations: He could keep questing. Or he could give up.

At first he wore sunglasses to hide his eyes. But he found he couldn't eat at a restaurant or drink at a bar without somebody making a comment or giving him a shove, so he switched to colored contact lenses. The luminescent blue of his eyes were masked by plain brown.

Someone told him about the Salt Cathedral, a natural formation over a thousand feet high, and he decided to climb it and BASE jump off. He had himself smuggled over the border in the trunk of a car, then he hiked deep into the Syrian Desert. On a steppe bunched with brittle grass, he saw the convoy of Jeeps and trucks approaching long before it arrived. They sent up a miles-long wave of dust that dirtied the sky. He didn't run or try to hide. And even when they circled him, driving around and around and around until the world was a gray-brown nothing, a cyclone that bit him with its grit, he did not react except to pull the keffiyeh more tightly around his mouth and nose.

He didn't speak their language, but he nonetheless understood the meaning of the orders they barked at him. He raised his arms to show he meant them no harm. He would not drop to his knees, not until they forced him to by kicking the backs of his legs. They pulled a black sack over his head and tied his wrists and ankles and hurled him into a truck bed and drove for hours over rutted roads, stopping once for a piss break and another time for a brief rattle of gunfire, until his body went rigid and numb.

When they finally parked, the engines ticked and wheezed and the men unhitched the tailgate. They told him to get out, but he could not stand without help, so they dragged him out of the sun and into what he believed to be an inhabited cave system. He could not see, but the floor was a stumbling mess of stone and sand, and the air was cool and damp and smelled like guano, like shadows. He heard voices echoing all around and computers bleeping. A door yanked open with a rusty shriek and he was thrown to the floor.

They ripped open his backpack and dumped its contents. They picked through his pockets. He carried a wad of cash, but no identification; this he had stashed in Turkey beneath a loose tile in a mosque. They wanted to know who he was. They wanted to know what he was worth. But he would not say.

"Why don't you just tell them?" a voice said to him later that night. It came from across the hall. A man with an accent he couldn't place. Something Eastern European.

"Because I've been enough trouble to my family."

This got a laugh out of his neighbor. His name was Anton, he said, and he was a mercenary working for Academi. His unit had been ambushed. Three killed by the roadside IED, another two by gunfire. Of the four who'd survived, he was now the only one left. "They kill me soon. They kill you too."

"I don't care," John said. He wasn't trying to be defiant. It was the simple truth.

"Well, then," Anton said. "You have come to right place."

The next morning, his cell door opened and three men ripped off his hood and arranged him on his knees and held up a cell phone to record what happened next. He couldn't see at first. He had been so long in the dark. But he heard the machete swing with a whistling rush.

It should have taken his head off, but the metal only clashed against his neck. And a blue light shone suddenly, like someone had thrown open a window. The blade lay on the ground in two pieces. And an energy pulsed through him, as though circuits were lighting up, currents sizzling. This only grew when the men cried out in alarm and called him devil and emptied several rounds into him with their pistols and the bullets fell clinking to the floor.

He didn't know how to describe it any better than this: He felt full inside. But more than that, busy. Churning. Like a shaken soda. Something needed to spill out or he would explode. He had lost his temper many times before, and this was a little like that, only the sensation was purely physical. There was no rage, only a need to unleash. Less than a minute later, his bindings were torn and three men lay dead on the floor.

He stumbled out the door and into a carved sandstone passage with buzzy lights strung from its ceiling. There were crates stacked in the corridor. Shelves crammed with old radios and dead computers. Other passages branched off into the distance. One of them was colored with sunlight. He was about to head in that direction when he heard a familiar voice say, "Help me." It came from behind a rusted metal door. Two bloodshot eyes peered at him through its food slot. "Please. Help me," Anton said. "And then I help you, friend?"

After dinner, Timmy asks John to read him a book. John wants to say, *That's not really my thing,* but Jenna shoots him a hopeful look, so he says, "Sure."

The boy takes him by the hand and leads him into the living room. John sits on the futon and says, "Whoa," when Timmy climbs onto his lap.

"What?" Timmy says.

And John says, "Nothing." He isn't sure what to do with his hands, so he lets them flop to his sides. "What are we reading, anyway?"

The boy shows him the book: *Good Night, Gorilla.*

"Never heard of it," John says. "But okay. Let's give it a shot."

He clears his throat and cracks the cover. But there are no words. He turns to the next page, then the next. Nothing there either. The whole thing consists of illustrations tracking a gorilla who escapes his cage and then the zoo but then, instead of going wild, he chooses to help the other animals, busting them all out. "Well, you don't need me for this," John says and Timmy says, "Yes, I do. *Read* it."

"How can I read it? There's no words."

"You have to make your own words," the boy says. "You have to write your own story. And you have to make it good."

John does his best to make it good.

Soon, the sky is black over Northfall. A bottle of merlot is empty. The dishes have been washed and placed in the rack to dry. The Garth Brooks CD has repeated itself five times. Timmy is asleep on the couch, curled in a tight ball, with *Good Night, Gorilla* clutched against his chest.

"This has been fun," Jenna says.

"Yeah," John says and nods toward Timmy. "He's a good kid. You've done a good job."

"I can't imagine life without him."

"Yeah?"

"There's something about having a child."

"And what's that something?"

She keeps her eyes fully on the boy and chews at her lower lip, nibbling away the dead skin. "I'd do anything to keep him safe, give him a good life." Now she turns her eyes to him. "Kind of funny to say, being married to a cop, but . . . I didn't feel safe . . . before."

There is a long silence between them. John is thankful for the stereo then. Without it, he feels like Jenna might have been able to hear the thoughts churning around in his head. He understands what she's implying. That she feels that he—John—will always shield her, protect her, which is true, but also that he is some kind of hero, which is not. She treats him with the same pathetic hopefulness that she does this house—prettying up his potential when, really, he's a wreck.

He can think of nothing but the Gunderson boy. He has thought of little else since leaving Northfall. Sometimes flinching. Cursing himself. Even punching himself for what he had done.

That night five years ago, John had drunk his way through a bottle of whiskey and snorted enough oxy to topple an elephant. The poker game was held in an old horse barn. Black flies and moths swirled in the light. Two men with holstered pistols stood in the shadows, monitoring the table. John had lost over thirty thousand dollars. And Henry Gunderson hoped to hustle more out of him. He kept filling his glass, kept pushing more money to the center of the table, fattening the pot. When John tried to fold, saying he was tapped out and had better call it a night, Henry offered to let him keep going on credit. "I know who your family is. I know how deep those pockets go. You put up some collateral and we can keep on playing. I can't be on a hot streak forever. Soon enough your luck's bound to turn." But it hadn't.

John doesn't remember a lot about that night, just flashes. An overturned table. Drawn pistols. A fist to his gut that knocked the wind and bile out of him. A car chase that ended up with him spinning out into a ditch. His eventual arrival at Gunderson Woods. A shotgun blast, another shotgun blast. Screams that eventually went silent. A house that seemed to warp and wheel in circles as he tore his way through it, trying to avoid the sight of the bodies on the floor.

But he does remember the boy. He remembers tripping down the stairs of the back porch and landing in the dew-soaked grass and looking up and finding Hawkin before him. Huddled in the sandbox. Was he in third grade then? Fourth? Old enough to have heard and understood everything that happened inside.

John was desperate. He'd wanted only to retrieve what he felt had been stolen from him, even if he himself was responsible for its loss. And he had gone too far. He was drunk and he was high and he had been awake more than forty-eight hours, but that didn't excuse him. He felt only more disgust for his weakness. There was a chain of stupid, regrettable, reckless decisions that bound together his mother's death and the blood spilled that night. He had achieved what he thought he'd deserved all along: the very summit of disgust and guilt and culpability.

It wasn't the murder that bothered him so much — Henry Gunderson was worthless — it was the erasure of a family. He had ruined that boy's life. Stripped him of his childhood. And now he only wants to give that back. If Hawkin was indeed in some basement lab, then John may as well have locked him up there. He can't go back in time, but maybe he can repair the future.

"I'm going to put him to bed, okay?" Jenna says, and John says, "I'm sorry?" and then, "Oh, okay."

When she bends over and pulls the boy into a hug, Timmy mumbles in his sleep and brings a tiny fist to his eye and she says, "Shhh." Her feet whisper when she carries him away.

John rises from the futon and paces a half circle. He doesn't know what will come next. He wants Jenna and feels like he doesn't deserve her. She's always thought he was someone he wasn't, isn't. He feels like he's settled into something both familiar and alien, an alternate timeline in which he doesn't belong. He picks up his wineglass, stained purple, and knocks down the dregs of it. Then he hits the power button on the stereo. Instead of silence, he hears laughter.

Drunken whoops. Aerosmith. Across the street, at the apartment complex, the party is still going. He has a feeling it never stops.

He senses his heart rate jacking up. Over the past few years, he has made every effort to detach himself from emotion, to contain himself, to choose restraint, but something about tonight has made his feelings stir up and spill out. That old rage. But something else. Something like sadness mixed with needy optimism.

He goes to the front door and opens it and lets the noise and the cold night air play over him. He looks back into the warm orange glow of the living room and hesitates, but only for a second. The darkness calls.

A few minutes later, after Jenna gets Timmy settled, she cleans up in the bathroom and opens another bottle of wine and carries it into the living room and says, "Now, where were we?"

In response the front door swings open with a chill autumn wind. She can see a fire burning across the street. And she can hear someone crying out in pain. Her grip tightens around the bottle when she steps onto the porch.

When she was nine, her father left. He was one of those men who rarely shaved and never cleaned out the gutters. The only thing he took care of was his car, a blue Firebird. The sound of rattling ice cubes, to this day, makes her think of him, because he was always carrying around a thermos full of rum and Coke. He worked for Frontier Metals, driving a loader. He was always either sweet or silent to Jenna, but he hurt her mother. More than once. It was never something Jenna saw until the next morning. An arm in a cast. A lost tooth.

Summers, Jenna used to paint on an easel she kept in the front yard. One day, while she was working on a storm cloud that rained hearts and smiley faces, she realized that her father was leaving and maybe for good. He was tromping back and forth from the house to the driveway and shoving his clothes, a lamp, a bowling ball into the car's open trunk. She dipped her brush into the red pot of paint and hurried over to his Firebird and painted a heart on the bumper.

She thought maybe, when her father saw it later, he would remember his love for her and return home.

He didn't return home, of course. But years later, when she was fourteen, in downtown Northfall, she saw the blue Firebird with the faded red heart on the bumper roll past and she raced after it, thinking her father had finally come back to her. While it waited at the stoplight, she hurried up to the open window and peered in, and a man younger than her father had been when he left grinned back at her and said, "Hey, girlie." It was as though he had returned to her changed.

At first she wondered if the same would be true of John. He dressed differently. He talked differently, every motion and word like a tensed muscle, a clenched jaw, as if he were trying constantly to keep himself locked and knotted up. Was his familiar face just another bumper with a faded heart on it? But now she knows—for sure—that he is the man she fell in love with, the man who would always protect her.

He didn't say goodbye when he left Northfall five years ago. And he didn't say goodbye tonight, but he left her his own kind of gift. Across the street, at the apartment building, tires are slashed and windshields broken. The engine of one truck is alive with flame. An inky-black smoke makes the air taste like burned plastic. Bottles of beer have been shattered and their foam bubbles along the gutters. Men lie on the lawn and sidewalk. She isn't sure whether they are alive or dead, but they are quiet except for a keening wail that comes off one of them.

"Good night, Johnny," she says and smiles and hugs her arms around herself.

26

✳

The first thing Victoria thinks when she wakes up—blinded by a flashlight beam in her face—is *It's him*. Thaddeus Gunn. He's come for her. She thought she would be safe by keeping quiet, by writing out her plan to Wade on a pad of paper instead of speaking to him, but the surveillance caught her nonetheless. Maybe there are cameras nested in the light fixtures or behind the mirrors.

Sleep is so rare for her. She has trouble falling into dreams but even more trouble rising out of them. Exhaustion pulls at her hard now, and she muddles through the confusion of this waking nightmare.

She scrabbles back against the headboard, convinced she sees Thaddeus grinning at her from the shadows even as another voice says, "Don't scream." A deeper, rougher voice than Gunn's. "And don't move."

Wade cries out and lurches for the baseball bat he keeps under the bed. But the man is already on him, as swift as a shadow, backhanding her husband across the face and shoving him hard into the mattress. "I said don't move."

He keeps the flashlight swinging from Wade's face to hers and back, ruining their night vision. She throws an arm up and squints through her fingers. "I'm not going to hurt you as long as you do what I say," he says. "I just want answers."

Now she is fully awake, a headache gnawing at the space between her eyes. "Answers to what?" she says.

"About the work you're doing for the DOD."

Wade continues to struggle and calls out, "Help!" But the word is cut short as the man strikes him again, this time in the stomach, silencing him.

Wade gags and retches as he tries to inhale through the pain. It is a muddy sound. Then he thrashes again and the stranger bashes him in the ear with the flashlight's butt. "You're trying to be the hero, but there's no point, old man. All you have to do is let your wife talk to me and I'll leave."

"Wade, honey," she says. "Stop fighting. Stop! Wade!"

Wade listens to her. He always does. He goes still. His throat whistles raggedly as he tries to find his breath.

The stranger steps back, the flashlight held before him. His voice sounds young, brash, with a bite behind it. Like a pit bull barking at the end of a chain. She can't quite see him, but there's a misshapen quality to his silhouette that makes her believe he's wearing panty-hose over his face. "I know your name, Victoria Lennon, and I know your CV. But I don't know what you're doing in Northfall. I don't know what you're doing working for the Department of Defense."

She brings her finger to her lips.

"What?" he says. "Are we playing charades?"

She cups a hand to her ear and then points to the ceiling and then returns her finger to her lips.

"Oh," he says, "you think they're listening. You're right to be paranoid. This place has got more alarms and surveillance on it than your standard bank. But not to worry. I clipped the power and overrode the security system on the way in."

She gapes at him another moment before saying, "Whom do you work for?"

"Nobody."

"Everybody works for somebody."

"I work for me."

"Have you been hired by another country? Or a private company?"

"Did you hear me?" the stranger says. "I work for me."

"Why do you want to know, then?"

"Because from what I hear, you've got a kid named Hawkin Gunderson locked up in that facility outside of town."

"How could you possibly know that?"

"People talk."

"No one talks. Not at this level of classified."

The stranger waits another beat before responding. "There are other ways of hearing."

"I don't know what that's supposed to—"

"Do you have Hawkin?" He kicks the bed frame. "Do you? Answer the question."

"Even if we did, why do you care? What do you want out of this?"

There is a moment of hesitation before the voice says, "I want to get him out of there."

"And what then? You deliver him to whoever's paying you?"

"I told you—"

"You work for yourself. Yes, yes, yes."

"I've got my reasons, and I don't need to explain myself to you."

"Sorry." She crosses her arms. "But I'm frankly old and exhausted and embittered enough that your threats and bullying don't really mean anything. If you expect me to give you something, you're going to have to give me something."

The stranger blasts out an impatient sigh. "I want to save him. Okay? I'm going to save him." He says this with plain sincerity, as if it's obvious, as if no other possibility is imaginable.

There is something about his tone. She tries but can't not believe him. Her mouth jerks into a smile. She takes a steadying breath and reaches out and finds Wade's hand. Their fingers knit together and she squeezes.

"What if I told you," she says, "that I wanted that too?"

27

※

t is the smell that makes Stacie's paddle go still. The smell of rose-water that has turned. A faint rot. Her father asks her what the matter is, and she says, "Do you smell that?"

"What?"

"That." But it's already gone.

They are on a small lake, maybe ten square acres, ringed by jack pines. Her father takes a deep series of sniffs and the canoe drifts for half a minute, zippering through the water. "I don't smell any—"

"There!" And again, she catches a whiff, stronger now than before. Heavy and moist. She is reminded of the time she opened a cabinet full of potatoes so rotten they sat in a puddle of gray slime. Or the time a possum ate poison and crawled underneath their porch to die.

"Yeah," her father says, "Okay. I'm with you. Whew."

They change course and align with the breeze, trying to find the source of the smell. The canoe eventually scrapes bottom and they set down their paddles and climb onto the rocky shore. Somewhere within the thickly shadowed stand of pines, crows cackle.

"If memory serves," her father says as he tents his undershirt over his nose, "there's a trail near here. A five-miler that runs between three campgrounds and tracks back to Battlecreek Lane."

Stacie pulls a sleeve of Starbursts from her pocket and offers him a yellow square.

"What's that for?" he says.

"There's a reason a lot of coroners chew gum. I'd rather smell something sweet than something rotten."

"No, thank you." He waves it away. "Always thought that stuff tastes like you're sucking on a clown."

She unpeels the wrapper and pops the candy in her mouth. She lets it soften on her tongue a moment before licking her upper lip. She can still smell the rot, but it's at least hidden behind a sugary tang.

"Something's sure dead," he says. "But probably it's just a deer. Maybe a coon."

"Yeah," she says as they start into the woods and enter the cool shade of the trees. "Probably."

Twigs snap. Brush clings. Branches swat. In a small clearing up ahead, the crows hop and flutter in trees like impatient shadows. Their croaking grows louder as Stacie grows nearer. Finally they take wing and depart with a rusty *kak-kak-kak* of complaint.

Here they find a four-wheeler, its bright red detailing dirtied by bird shit and fallen pine needles. "Well, this isn't allowed out here," her father says. "No ATVs permitted in the BWCA." As if he is going to issue a citation.

Stacie says she thinks that's hardly a thing to worry about right now.

"No?" he says. "No, maybe not."

She circles the ATV. The fireweed remains roughed and flattened behind it, the trail maybe a few days old, leading off into the woods. The front left wheel has sunk into a depression and the metal of the front guard is dented, bent, caught on a log. The smell here is profoundly ripe and she gags more than once.

A fly lands on her arm and she shakes it off. Another grazes her cheek and she blows at it. More and more of them orbit her head with a buzz. They should be mostly dead at this time of year, but these ones have managed to hold out, unable to give up on the feast. She hears the whirring of many wings and locates the source. "Oh dear."

A tree fifteen yards away. A man slumps at the base of it.

Her father comes up beside her, his breathing harried, and together they approach the body. "Looks like he was going too fast in the ATV, hit that log, shot out of his seat."

"Looks like it."

His neck is bent at an unnatural angle, presumably broken from impact after he was launched through the air. His skin is gray-black and puffy with rot, but she can clearly see that he is short and heavyset. The crows have pecked away much of his face, but pieces of beard cling to his jaw.

"Is it him?"

"No." She crouches and waves a hand and the flies alight with an angry buzz. "I don't recognize him."

"Well, let's see who he is, then." Her father bends down with a crack of his knees and sweeps away some brush on the ground and picks up a metal storage clipboard. He swipes the dirt off it and pops it open, revealing a mess of paper.

He hands it to Stacie and she fingers through the forms inside. There are surveys and analysis reports with the Frontier Metals emblem at their top left corner. She finds a map folded at the bottom of the pile, and her father unfolds it.

"But that's impossible," he says. That word — *impossible* — could apply to so much right now. But he remains focused on the rules and boundaries that guide his particular understanding of the world. "This land. It's protected wilderness. They can't mine it —"

"Why not?"

"Because there are laws."

"Don't laws change? Could they have gotten a special provision?"

"Not yet, they haven't." He studies her with tired eyes. "I know I'm partial. But I'm not exaggerating when I say this might be the best canoeing in the world. Certainly it's one of most beloved patches of wilderness in the country. If anyone so much as proposed mining it, there would be lawsuits, editorials, thousands of activists here overnight making all sorts of noise and trouble."

"So what's going on? What's Frontier Metals doing here?"

"Nothing good. You know I've always thought that company —

and the Frontiers themselves — are the worst thing to ever happen to Northfall."

She remains still another moment, riffling through the papers, lost in her thoughts, and then stands and paces in a circle. "Until I figure out what's going on here, let's keep this between us."

Her father looks back and forth between her and the corpse. "This man might have a family. You're not going to report —"

"I'll report the body. But anonymously. I don't want anyone to know we were here. Because I don't want anyone to know I have this. Not until I understand better what's going on." She snaps shut the clipboard. "Now, I know you and Sheriff Barnes go way back. I know you've told him to look out for me. But I'm going to say this only once: You don't say a word to him. About any of this. Not one word."

There is a long beat of silence before her father says, "I've never known you not to be a rule follower, Stacie. But it sounds like you're going your own way on this?"

"I don't like it," she says, "and I doubt you'll like it. But I've come to a conclusion: I can't win by playing by the rules when everybody else is breaking them."

Night is coming when Stacie and her father hoist the canoe from the water and carry it to the Explorer. They arrange themselves on either side of the vehicle and say, "One, two, three," then heave it up onto the rack. Their shoulders are sore but they manage. They haven't spoken since they walked away from the corpse, and they don't speak now. Not until they've tied down the canoe and tossed their gear in the back seat and closed themselves into the cab.

"All right," her father says. "Spit it out."

"What?"

"I was under the impression that we were looking for a missing police officer."

"We were. We are."

"You're clearly not telling your old man everything." Her father turns the key and the engine coughs to life. "So tell me."

"I'm looking for evidence."

"Of?"

"There's something going on with the Frontiers."

"They're crooks and despots. Sure, there's something going on with them. I could have told you as much." He tugs the gearshift into drive. "Am I to understand you think they might have something to do with this Dan Swanson going missing?"

"Dan Swanson might be the tip of the proverbial iceberg."

"Keep going."

"You probably read in the papers about the father? Ragnar?"

"He's in a coma. There was a house fire and—"

"And I suspect foul play."

"Who?"

"I thought I knew. Now I'm not *sure* sure. All I know is, Frontier Metals and Black Dog seem to be going after each other. And there might be some sort of cover-up going on with the police."

"Is that all?" he says, and then, "I'm kidding."

"It's not funny."

"No. I'm sorry. It sounds . . . dangerous."

"It's really fucking dangerous." Here she slaps a hand over her mouth. She is not one to swear, and never in front of her father. Quieter now, she says, "It's really dangerous."

She expects her father to scold her, to encourage her to quit her job, to walk away from all of this, but instead he says, "I'm proud of you."

"Yeah?"

"I am. Real proud."

"Thanks, Daddy."

"Somebody's got to protect this place." His eyes might be a little damp when he looks at her and gives a quick nod. "You're doing it. You let me know how I can help."

"You're doing it right now." She curls a hand through his arm and leans her head against his shoulder. "You are helping."

He pulls the Explorer out of the weeds and onto the rutted road and they bump down it slowly. The light is dying and the shadows close in around them. "You've heard me talk about the wolves."

She has, but she has heard most of his stories, and that never stops her from listening. "Go on."

He talks about the nationwide incentive to hunt down wolves and decimate the population. It began in the nineteenth century — ranchers and then government agencies offered rewards for carcasses — and carried into the twentieth. An eradication campaign. Wolves were shot, trapped, and poisoned. And the only place in America they managed to survive was northern Minnesota. "Because the Boundary Waters are so wild."

"What's your point, Daddy?"

"I'm getting to it, I'm getting to it." Some branches claw at the windows and at the canoe. "I'm saying, maybe you're struggling with breaking the rules. Maybe you're scared of what you're up against. But look at the bigger picture. Look at what's happening to this place. How do you fight it? Protest marches and letters to the editor can only accomplish so much. Frontier and Black Dog, they're the hunters in this scenario. They're not going to stop now that they've got the scent. Now that they've got the Boundary Waters in their cross hairs. We need to push back. We need a place for the wolves to hide."

"Are we the wolves?"

"You betcha we are."

28

✳

wo new hangars and three runways have been built at the
Arrowhead Regional Airport to accommodate all the extra
air traffic. Several commuter airline shuttles dash back and
forth from Minneapolis each day, but the private planes and jets are
what keep the control tower busy. The Gulfstream that lands now
—a direct flight from Houston—has a Black Dog Energy emblem
on its tail.

It pulls into a hangar and powers down with a wheeze. A han-
dler rattles a stair ramp over. When the door unlatches, the pilot
smiles and gestures with his arm, and a big man exits the plane.
Walter Eaton pauses at the top of the ramp and fits his Stetson into
place on top of his head. It's a cold enough day that his breath fogs
the air. His belt buckle is the size of a salad plate, and his cowboy
boots cheat his six-foot-two frame another three inches. Everything about him's big, he likes to say, Texas big.

The first thing he notes is the Cessna parked directly beside him.
Frontier Metals is painted across its side with a northern lights effect, a magical swirl of purple and green around the lettering. He
huffs, and when he gets to the bottom of the ramp, he tells the han-
dler to arrange a separate space for his Gulfstream. "I don't want to
be within spitting distance of that so-and-so, understand?"

He doesn't travel with luggage, because he has a fully stocked
cabin waiting for him here, and he doesn't travel with an attendant,
because he hates relying on people. Case in point: what happened
with the hit.

For more than a month now, Mickey Golden had groomed contacts within the PD. He offered cash for simple information: Which truck in the fleet carried the load of omnimetal from Northfall to the St. Paul mill? That's all he wanted to know. Anything that happened, the cops were assured, would happen outside their jurisdiction. Mickey promised no one would get hurt. And he also promised both companies would profit from the situation. Let's say the Frontiers get ripped off. The insurance claim covers them, and then Black Dog offers to sell half the ore back at market price. It's just good business. Everybody wins. Mickey implied the Frontiers might even be in on it.

Everything seemed fine until the first contact vanished. A cop named Dan Swanson. No warning something might be off. And no body to indicate foul play. He was simply gone. Who knows what happened, Mickey said. Maybe the guy got sick of his old lady and skipped town.

Maybe. Walter told Mickey to get to work on whatever cop took over the escort. However careful he'd been last time, do better. Step up the secrecy. Only meet up in remote locations. Use a Blackphone. Pretend the Frontiers were always watching. Turns out, they were. Now another cop has gone missing and men on the Black Dog payroll are dead.

If something needs to be done, Walter would do it himself. He had started off at the bottom—a high-school dropout living in his truck. His work as a handyman led to him buying foreclosures and condemned buildings and fixing them up and flipping them decades before this became a trend so popular that there were stupid TV shows about it. Then, in the early eighties, he happened upon a hundred-acre ranch in the scrublands of northern Texas that was home to a dried-up well and the site of a triple homicide. Nobody wanted it. He walked the property and found at its southeastern corner a blackened stretch of sand that stuck to his boots. He brought a drill out and tapped a vein of crude that came gurgling up so fast, he and his truck were soaked in it. He bought the place for pocket change. He saw value where others didn't. He muscled his way onto the *Forbes* list not because anyone offered to help or because he asked permission; he simply took whatever could be taken — whether land or oil or metal.

He keeps an Escalade parked at the airport and climbs into it now. He cranks the engine. The windshield is silvered with a latticework of frost and he punches up the heater and waits for the vehicle to warm.

Walter once filled a syringe with oil and inserted it directly into the jugular of someone who crossed him. He'd bribed farmers hesitant to sell their land for a pipeline project, and, with a hammer, he had broken the legs of those who'd refused. He'd sent in a team of divers to set C-4 charges and sabotage a competitor's platforms in the Gulf of Mexico. Midway through a freighter shipment, oil prices dropped steeply, so he ordered the ship sunk to collect the insurance rather than letting it dock and sell the barrels at rock-bottom prices.

Walter is not about to be undone by a bunch of flannel-wearing, loon-loving Lutherans from northern Minnesota. They don't know how the game is played. He does. There is no law. And there is no God. Legal and moral restrictions are set in place for what Walter calls sheeple. Those too weak and too stupid to think for themselves. You only have eighty or so years on this planet, and that's not a lot of time to take it all in. He is a self-professed man of large appetites. He believes in excess. In gluttonously enjoying every meal, every woman, every cash grab; every drop of oil and every gram of omnimetal. He worships at an altar built from wagyu beef, single-malt whiskey, and hundred-dollar bills. Why have one wife when you could have a mistress in every state? Why be a millionaire if you could be a billionaire?

The frost has mostly melted from the windshield. But he pauses his hand at the gearshift. Something smells off. Like old ham. He checks around him for the source. A forgotten sandwich, maybe. Then he leans into the vents and takes a deep sniff and cringes. A mouse. Maybe a whole nest of them. The little buggers must have crawled into the engine block and readied a winter home. He notices a few faint lines of smoke rising from the edges of the hood.

He curses about how his goddamn luck couldn't get any goddamn worse and climbs out of the cab and huffs toward the front of the Escalade and discovers the hood already popped. He lifts it cautiously, and more smoke comes drifting out. He waves it away and discovers the source. A head—roughly severed at the neck—shoved in next to the exhaust manifold. The edges of the face are scorched and the hair aflame, but otherwise the skin has been preserved by the cold. A fifty-something-year-old man with a mustache. Walter knows he was a police officer because of the badge propping open his mouth.

When the gate rose on the semitrailer and revealed Talia Frontier hoisting an RPG launcher to her shoulder, Mickey slammed the brakes and cranked the wheel hard. He was going seventy at the time. His truck skidded and then rose into a flip. If it hadn't, the warhead would have shot through the windshield, but instead, it glanced off his rear bumper before detonating and cratering the asphalt.

He isn't sure how many times the truck rolled. His brain went black for a minute. He woke up to find himself hanging upside down and the airbags deployed and his mouth tacky with powder. The man in the passenger seat had been ejected from the cab and left behind a blood-edged hollow in the windshield. Mickey ripped off his alien mask and cut himself out of his seat belt with a pocketknife and staggered onto the highway just in time to wave down one of his other trucks. Two men in alien masks dragged him into the rear bed, slammed shut the tailgate, and tore off across the median.

That was a week ago, and ever since then, Mickey has been in hiding. A concussion has left his memory a mess and any light makes his head hurt, so he's wearing sunglasses even when inside. His left arm is broken above the wrist, but he thinks he's set it properly on his own, duct-taping a wooden spoon to his forearm. He's still digging glass out of his scalp. He should have gone to the hospital but couldn't.

The Frontiers were ready. They knew he was coming. That means the cop Mickey had been working with, Hank Lippert, might have flipped on him. Lippert wasn't responding to texts or calls. Best guess—he'd taken the cash from Mickey and then double-dipped as a rat for the Frontiers. If that's the case, Mickey will make him pay with a pound of flesh. Right after he heals up.

For now he's content to medicate with space dust and whiskey. He has a five-thousand-square-foot neo-Tudor in one of the new developments, but he doesn't feel safe there, so for now he's holed up in a singlewide trailer at the Black Dog man camp. Lying down makes him dizzy, so he's stationed himself permanently on the couch. He wears nothing but his jewelry and his silk boxer shorts, a bottle of Old Grand-Dad tucked into his groin. He isn't sure how much he's sleeping, but maybe eighteen, nineteen hours a day. Right now, the lights are off. The television plays *Judge Judy* on mute. On the cushion beside him lies a pistol, three cell phones, and a business card for Happy Endings massage service. And on the far side of the couch sits the woman they sent. Asian. Barely legal. In a red wig and purple negligee. He called out of boredom. She tried to make something happen for him earlier, but after ten minutes, he said, "It's okay. I'm not really in the mood anyway. Just sit by me, how about?"

"Do you want to talk?" she says now.

"No. Talking makes my head hurt. Let's just sit and watch ourselves some TV."

"Do you want me to put on the volume?"

"No. I like it like this. Quiet."

After a few minutes, she says, "This is kind of weird," and he says, "You're getting paid to watch TV. I'd say that's a pretty sweat deal."

"Sweat?"

"Sorry. I got hit in the head. My words are all mixed up. *Sweet.* It's pretty sweet. It's a sweet deal. That's what I meant."

"Oh, okay," she says. "Do you mind if I take my wig off? It's itchy."

"Go for it."

"My name's Tina, by the way. Is that space dust?" She slips off the candy-colored wig and sets it on the coffee table next to the Ziploc bag full of blue powder. She shakes out her shoulder-length hair and then picks up the scorch-bottomed bowl and sniffs it and curls her nose at the smell. "What happened to you anyway?" she says. "You look like—"

"Like I got hit by a skunk?"

"A skunk?"

"Like I got hit by a truck, I mean."

"Yeah," she says.

Right then the door shakes in its frame. Three hard knocks. Whoever is on the other side doesn't wait for a response, just twists the knob, letting in a shaft of sunlight.

"Who's—" Mickey fumbles for his pistol and knocks it onto the floor. A gut-twisting sense of vertigo sets in, and the trailer seems to lurch and spin. He slumps over on the couch, unable to understand any direction but gravity.

Tina takes her cue from him; she picks up the pistol and aims it at whoever's coming through the door. "Stop," she says, "or I'll shoot." Then she whispers to Mickey, "Should I shoot?"

"Tell the pretty lady to put the pistol down."

At the sound of his voice—that familiar, meaty bark—Mickey hoists his head and tries to focus. The wobbling image of Walter Eaton solidifies. The big man wears his standard uniform—Stetson hat, bolo tie, denim, boots—but in his hand, he's holding something. A black garbage bag.

"Put down the pistol," Mickey says. "It's okay."

"You sure?" Tina says. "He's your friend?"

"My boss."

Walter says, "You go on now, darling. Go home. Two of us have some important matters to discuss."

"I need to get paid," she says and Walter says, "His wallet's on the table. Take what you're owed. Then we'll all say so long."

She gathers up her things and zips herself into a calf-length jacket. "Call me anytime you want to watch TV or whatever," she says and pulls the door closed behind her.

Mickey remains slumped over on the couch. He can feel some whiskey spilling from the bottle, puddling on the cushion, but can't bother himself to move.

"Boy, you sure are a sight," Walter says.

"I know."

"You stink too. Smells like an unwiped ass in here."

"I know."

"So you just been sitting here in the dark, drinking and smoking and screwing and feeling sorry for yourself?"

"Pretty much, yeah." His mouth is muffled by the cushion his face is smushed into.

"I don't like the idea of you smoking that stuff. Makes people funny in the head."

He motions to his duct-taped forearm. "Yeah, well. Ibuprofen ain't gonna cut it. I needed some help."

"Here I am." Walter comes over to the couch and looms over Mickey a moment before swinging the trash bag into his stomach. Something heavy thumps him and he curls an arm around it. "What's this?"

"Take a look."

He struggles upright and moans at the dizziness he feels and delicately peels back the bag to see what's inside. "Ah," he says. "Was wondering what happened to him." He pats the head of Hank Lippert.

"Could've been you."

"Almost was." He closes the bag and lobs it aside, and it rolls under the coffee table. "Frontiers are praying for keeps."

"They're praying for what?"

"They're *playing* for keeps."

Walter paces back and forth, and as he does, the trailer shudders. "Not only is my best man down, I got four skid loaders and ten dump trucks that was slashed and scorched last night. And now a storehouse full of wizard blades has gone missing."

"Oh, shit."

"*Oh, shit* is right."

"So what do we do? Parley?"

"Parley?" Walter takes off his hat and looks into its hollow as if for an answer. "I don't much like the sound of that." He clucks his tongue. "But maybe it's the right move. At least pretending interest in some sort of bargain."

"What's that supposed to mean?"

"It means things have gotten out of control, and we need to change tactics. Now get your stinking ass off that couch and into the shower. I'm going to brew some coffee and sober you up."

Mickey edges forward, steadying himself with one arm against the coffee table. "I'm not doing so well—"

"No. You're not. I leave you in charge and everything goes to hell. You're going to make it up to me, but first we've got to get your filthy, broken ass cleaned up."

"Talia's not going to parley with you. Not unless you got something on her."

"Oh, I already thought of that."

"What?"

"Not what," Walter says. "*Who.*"

29

✳

Yesno wears a sports coat to hide the hunch in his spine, and he wears a small smile on his face to hide the pain that defines his days. Everyone always comments on how calm he is, how stable, the rock of the Frontier family. But his composure is a deception, carefully manufactured. He is screaming on the inside.

His father went to prison. His mother ran off with another man. Then his nana died. Everyone in his childhood abandoned him. The Frontiers—out of loyalty to his grandmother, their longtime housekeeper—had taken him in, but he was convinced they too would tire of him, find him annoying, a nuisance, and toss him aside. This suspicion lingers to this very day, maybe because Ragnar never made the move to adopt him even when calling him a member of a family. Yesno was always *like* a son or *like* a brother without actually being one. That's why he has given himself over to the Frontiers so fully. Everything he does is in service to them so that they will keep him close.

He never complains, though he has every reason to. About his back, for instance. The kyphosis that warps his spine makes comfort impossible. He is always in pain, no matter if he's sitting or standing or lying down. The only slight relief comes from floating in water. So late at night, when no one can see him, he sometimes walks down to the pond and sheds his bathrobe and steps delicately into the water and leans back. The cold makes his teeth chatter, but it also eases the throbbing ache in his spine. With the stars shining above and reflected all around him, he likes to pretend he is floating through space, a child in a cosmic womb, free of gravity and the many tasks that weigh him down.

Ragnar is in a coma. Talia is warmongering. Nico has abandoned them for a drugged-out cult. John, impossibly, is the only person in the family who's acting sane, but he's somehow — also impossibly — a metal-skinned freak, a walking weapon. Yesno has enough to worry about with his phone and inbox blowing up: Political lobbying. Business queries. New tax laws. The legal black hole of terrestrial property laws, as Minnesota considers declaring omnimetal a natural resource it can claim. Bulk equipment orders. Industrial-size energy-storage patents. And on and on and on. He feels, on a daily basis, as if he is being whittled down to a nub.

His one luxury — what someone else might call self-care — is that every Friday, he visits a physical therapist in town for massage, exercise, and traction. This is the only hour in his week he shuts off his phone. Timberwolf Rehab is located in a strip mall next to a Supercuts, a Chinese buffet, and a U.S. Armed Forces recruitment station. Today, the receptionist invites Yesno down the hallway and into the last of three rooms, where Brenda is waiting for him. She is a beefy, short-haired woman who always wears a white polo shirt. Her cheeks are bunched up by her smile. She squirts some oil into her huge hands and rubs them together and says, "There he is. Rip that shirt off, big boy, and get on the table."

The walls are painted eggplant purple. Framed anatomical posters hang throughout the room. Soft rock plays from the speakers. He puts his jacket on a hook and unbuttons his shirt. He has done so hundreds of times before but still feels a pang of shame and embarrassment. Brenda is the only one he undresses for. She is the only one who touches him with any regularity. Her hands are twice the size of his own and she uses them to mash and rub and grind his body into submission.

The paper on the table crinkles beneath him as he settles his weight onto it. Brenda kneads her fingers and presses her palms and digs her elbows into his muscles, talking the whole time about her softball team and the new comedy show she's streaming and nutritional supplements and essential oils he should consider taking, and he tries not to cry out in pain and ecstasy. After a fifteen-minute rubdown, she bullies him off the table and onto a foam mat on the floor for traction. She calls it the posture pump. And once his head is in place between the many clamps, she squeezes the inflation ball and the pressure ramps up, gently stretching his vertebrae, so that he can imagine the spinal nerves — like damp, colored strands of yarn — visible between them.

"All right," she says and squeezes his shoulder. "I'm leaving you. Stay put for a few minutes."

He keeps his eyes shut when she's massaging him, when he's in traction, because the intimacy and vulnerability make him uncomfortable. So many things make him uncomfortable. His body. His family. His sexuality. His race.

Ojibwa culture includes a third gender. They are called the two-spirit people. This is a man who practices shamanism or a woman who takes on some male behaviors, like hunting. Someone who doesn't fit. Someone who can't be neatly categorized. He has always felt like something of a two-spirit. Even his name, Yesno, feels like it can't make up its mind. It's not only because his role in the family has become almost maternal. He cleans up messes. He is expected to anticipate the trouble people will get into and then get them out of it. It's also because he doesn't fit. He doesn't look like anyone. He is both a part of and apart from the Frontiers. He's never *not* felt welcome, but he's clearly never belonged.

He has a shelf of books on Ojibwa myths and history and culture, but other than that, he feels completely disconnected from his people. He tried to go to a rice harvest once, but no one would partner with him. At a land-use meeting where he presented on behalf of the Frontiers, some Chippewa protesters called him an Uncle Tom. How long do you need to live with people to become their family? How long do you need to separate yourself from a culture before it's no longer yours? He felt like he was floating in the middle of these questions the same way he floated listlessly in the pond every night.

There is a curious sound in the hallway, something like a heavy cabinet falling over. Another minute passes and then the door opens and footsteps scuff across the carpet. Normally Brenda comes in halfway through his ten minutes in traction to check on him. He hears knees pop as she kneels. "Everything okay?" he says. "I thought I heard something fall." The pump squeezes again, and again, and again — and he feels a jolt of pain and hisses, then says, "I'm sorry, but I think that's too much."

"Too much, huh?" a voice says. A voice he recognizes. A man's voice. "Does it hurt?"

Yesno snaps open his eyes and finds Mickey Golden hovering over him. He wears aviator shades that carry a warped reflection of Yesno's body. His long bottle-blond hair dangles down and frames his face. His left arm is in a sling, but his right hand holds the pump, which he continues to inflate at a heartbeat rhythm. "How about now? Does it hurt now? When it hurts, tell me. Go ahead and scream. Let it out."

30

✳

Another cop has gone missing, this time her partner. When Hank didn't show up for their swing shift — and when he didn't respond to her calls — Stacie took the squad car by his house, a rambler on the edge of town. She found the front door open and a cardinal fluttering from room to room.

There was a dried puddle of blood and two bullet holes in the mattress, but no body. The house was a mess, with piles of dishes on the counters and towers of *Sports Illustrated* and *Hustler* magazines stacked throughout the living room. But there were no drawers ripped open, no medicine cabinets raided, no dusty rectangles on shelves where electronics once perched. No attempt to make this look like a robbery.

The only thing missing was his phone. The phone she repeatedly saw him text from when they escorted the omnimetal delivery from town. The omnimetal delivery that was then interrupted by a failed heist. It didn't take a lot of effort to make the connection.

Wherever Hank had ended up — a shallow grave, the bottom of a lake — she guessed she'd find Dan Swanson. And whatever happened to Dan Swanson tracked back to the Frontiers. And whatever was happening to the Frontiers connected to the mining surveys of the Boundary Waters and their profit wars with Black Dog. And she thinks she understands the who and why if not the how of it all. But there are a few more questions to ask before she can be certain.

But when Sheriff Barnes called Stacie into his office and asked if she had any idea what happened to Hank, she said, "No." The word felt sour and foreign in her mouth. She thought about taking it back but couldn't. Right and wrong no longer seemed to apply. Her moral compass couldn't find its true north, and she felt dizzy, sick.

"You seem pretty shook up," Barnes said. He wore his reading glasses and gripped a pair of needle-nose pliers. He was putting the final touches on a dry fly, a caddis woven from elk hair. "And you got every reason to be. It's not just about losing a pal and a colleague. It's about wondering whether you're next." With his thumb he tested the prick of the fly's barb with his thumb. "Am I right?" He studied her over his glasses.

"But I didn't do anything," she said in a hollow voice. "Why would I be next?"

"You don't have to do nothing. Except your job. You pull over the wrong car. You knock on the wrong door. You answer the wrong call. Sometimes police pay the price for doing what's right."

"Doing what's right," she said, talking more to herself than him. "That's the job."

"Poor old Hank." Barnes set down his pliers and pinched the fly and examined it admiringly before tucking it into a plastic case with many compartments. "It's a lot to process. You want to talk to somebody, we got people you can talk to. You want to get back to work, sometimes that's good. Or—"

"Can I take a few days?" she said.

"Or there's that. You want to take a few sick days, you go right ahead."

She couldn't believe she was asking. She could barely acknowledge why she wanted the time off. It was the recognition that she needed to set aside her badge and ignore the laws she'd sworn to uphold if she was going to do what was right.

At dawn, Stacie parks her Jeep on a side road and waits. She has positioned herself to look out on the Cannon Lake Highway that runs between Northfall and the Frontier estate. The morning is cold enough that the ditches are white with hoarfrost. Among the pine trees, the occasional maple burns red and a few leaves spin through

the air and cling to her windshield. She has a thermos full of hot cocoa and an insulated lunch bag packed with baby carrots and apple
slices. She sings along to pop songs on the radio and listens to an
NPR report on the mysterious deaths of all the scientists and professors assigned to an Antarctic field station called the Miskatonic.
She keys on the engine every twenty minutes to warm up.

It's nearly noon when the black Bronco shoots by on the highway. She is peeing in the bushes at the time, and she says, "Gosh
darn it," and hitches up her pants and stumbles forward in a rush
to catch up.

The road wends through thick woods, and she leans into every
turn and feathers the brake, not wanting to rush up behind John.
She spots him just as he hangs a right onto Otter Falls Boulevard, a
road that bypasses Northfall. The Bronco is hauling a trailer.

She's never tailed someone before, and it feels kind of impossible. In town she could have darted in and out of traffic, but out in
the country, trees and ridges and distance are her only camouflage.
For the next twenty minutes, she does her best to maintain a safe
space between them, panicking when a fuel tanker and dump truck
slow them down on an incline.

Where he's going, she has no idea until—a few turns and miles
later—the destination becomes clear. Gunderson Woods. The
roughly hewn logs mark its perimeter and she drives along them a
minute before rounding a bend. Here are the gates. Several dozen
cars and trucks are parked here, including John's. He's backed the
trailer in, and its doors are flung open.

The compound is skirted by a gravel parking lot, and enough vehicles are staggered through it that she feels comfortable pulling in
and parking thirty or so feet away.

The gates open, and a crowd of metal-eaters approach the trailer.
They wear their standard uniform of black. Some are hairless. They
seem to drift more than walk, slow and careful in their movements.
Among them she recognizes Nico, John's brother.

He directs the metal-eaters up the ramp of the trailer and it dips
and rocks with their weight. A minute later they appear, carrying

something. What it is, she can't tell, since it's draped in a black cloth. But from its rectangular shape and size, it appears to be a massive table. They take tiny hesitant steps as they haul it through the gates.

The brothers linger outside, talking, and Stacie dares to open her door and softly shut it and sneak closer, winding her way through the cars so that she might hear them.

Nico's voice is soft, barely a whisper, carried away like tufts of milkweed in the wind, but John's voice resonates. Stacie hears, "I'd appreciate it if you talked to her," and "I'm going to do my best, but there's a million ways this could go wrong."

The only thing she hears Nico say before he heads back through the gates is "If you're going to do it, do it now. There's not much time before . . ." And here his voice drifts away.

She has heard the stories about Gunderson Woods — about the richness of the omnimetal reserves here — but she can't see much from where she stands, only a faint gray shine that matches the clouds in the sky. Towers are staggered along the perimeter and she can see the dark shape of the sentries posted there. She's wondering if they can see her when a scope flashes, maybe trained in her direction.

Long after the gates close, John remains in the parking lot, his hands on his hips. Lost in thought. Staring at the barrier as if dreaming his way onto the other side. A haul truck growls along the highway, downshifts as it nears a bend, and the noise wakes him from his reverie. He rubs his eyes and goes to close the trailer, and she figures she might as well make herself known.

Her feet crunch the gravel and he looks her way. "You." His face crumples with irritation that then flashes into bright-eyed curiosity. "What are you doing here?"

"Was going to ask you the same thing."

He slides a bar across the trailer doors, locking them in place. "Helping my brother out."

"He said there's not much time," she says. "What did he mean by that? Not much time for what?"

He heads to the Bronco and opens the driver door and climbs inside. "You're following me around, spying on me? Guess that means I'm still a suspect."

"It's not what I think *you've* done."

"No?"

"It's your family."

"Aren't I my family?"

"No. I don't think so. And I don't think you think so either."

"What makes you so sure?"

"Because you left." There is a short silence between them. Their breath steams in the cold. "I was hoping we could talk?"

"Isn't that what we're doing?" He puts his hand on the door, ready to drag it closed.

"I'm honestly kind of nervous right now. Because . . ." She digs her phone out of her pocket. "Hold on." She cringes as she snaps a photo of him. "Because I don't know how you'll react." She hurriedly texts the image to her father. "Sorry about that. Sorry to be weird."

"You took a photo of me? Why? To document we're together?"

"Yeah. Just in case, you know, you try to . . ." She isn't sure what to say, so she pockets the phone and then mimics strangling someone. She giggles out of nervousness and hates herself for it. "Sorry."

He doesn't look as angry as she thought he would. He takes his hand off the door handle and rests it on his thigh. "It's smart to be careful."

"Yeah."

"But not so careful you risk hypothermia. Now that you've taken your photo and convinced yourself I'm not going to murder you, how about you get in? We'll talk in the cab."

"I'll stay out here. Thanks."

"Have it your way. Hit me. What did my family supposedly do?"

"Before we get into that . . . I feel like I need to get a better sense of your code?"

His eyebrows shoot up. "My code?" He laughs and it's the first time she's seen him smile. He's missing one of his molars and the black gap is somehow upsetting. "Who says I have to have a code?"

"I do. And if it's something you haven't thought about, you really need to."

"That sounds like something you got from a therapist or a magazine or some dumb website that's supposed to make you feel special."

He isn't wrong. She subscribes to an e-mail listserv on mindfulness and every day a message pops up with an affirming quote or lesson or exercise. The other week it suggested she write a code. A kind of contract or belief system — separate from any religious doctrine — that informed her choices. She tried out a few different options that she erased. Finally she settled on something simple as her code: Be brave and be good. After some consideration she added *mostly*. Be brave and be (mostly) good. This she scratched on a pink sticky note that she affixed to her bathroom mirror.

But she's not going to tell John any of that. "This place," she says. "Northfall. It's mixed up. It doesn't know what it's supposed to be. And look at it. It's chaos."

His smile fades. "Yeah, this town's gone crazy for sure."

"If you don't have a code, I think the same thing could happen to you."

His eyes narrow, but she can't tell if he's annoyed or intrigued. "You think you know me, huh?"

"I know enough. I know you were a complete — pardon my French — screwup. And now you're trying not to be."

"You know you cringed when you said *screw*? *Screw* is a bad word to you? That's kind of hilarious. You're such a Girl Scout."

The wind picks up and she stamps her feet, trying to kick the cold out of them. "You know what?" she says. "Maybe I will get in."

"Be my guest."

She walks past the grille of the Bronco and a struck moth weakly flutters its wings. She yanks open the passenger door and climbs inside. The seat is ripped. The dashboard is dusty. A nest of receipts and cans and wrappers clutters the floor. "You know, for a rich guy, you drive kind of a lousy car."

He turns the key in the ignition. "You're the one who said it." He adjusts the heater, nudges a vent toward her. "I'm not the rest of my family."

She wears a fleece and tucks her hands deep into its pockets, balls them up, trying to get warm. "If it makes you feel any better, I've been pretty mixed up too."

"Yeah?"

"Yeah. I think what happened was . . . my code changed. Not all at once, but gradually, over the past few months."

"Your code changed? Jesus Christ, you talk about it like it's a password-protected phone."

"I used to think about the world in terms of black and white. And now—"

"And now it's gray?" He shakes his head. "Not exactly a groundbreaking epiphany. Welcome to reality."

"No. Not gray. I don't think there's even a color. Or if there is, we don't know the name of it yet."

"You're not making any sense. Get to the point."

"Let me tell you what I know. Then let me tell you what I think I know. Then let me tell you what I think we should do."

"We?"

"We."

"Okay, Girl Scout. I'm listening."

"First, let me make a confession. I thought you were responsible for what happened to Dan Swanson and your father."

"Not exactly news."

"But you know what? I've changed my mind."

"Lucky me. How did that happen?"

"When I was a kid, my father and I used to sit on the front porch and whittle. Whenever my knife slipped and I made a clumsy notch or took off a big chunk of wood, he'd encourage me not to get frustrated. He told me to think of the mistake as *a happy accident*."

"You should really teach Sunday school or something."

"So a frog became a dog, for example. Or a fish became a man. I just needed to be open-minded about the change."

"We're getting to the point soon, I hope."

"I've been looking for Dan Swanson's body."

This makes John go still and quiet.

"My father is a wilderness guide, and I've enlisted him in the search, and we've been working our way through a lot of water. Fishing the Boundary Waters, I guess you could say."

"Yeah?" John says, his voice now quiet and serious. "Find anything?"

"In fact, we did." She lets this set in and waits to study his response but gets nothing back. "I was looking for one body, but I ended up finding another."

At this, he wrinkles his forehead. "What?"

"And I guess you could also say that I was looking for one suspect, but I ended up finding another. The body in the woods—he was my happy accident. He helped me see the design of everything differently."

"Who was the body?" John says.

"A geologist working for Frontier. And do you know what he was doing? When he crashed his ATV and broke his neck? He was surveying the area for omnimetal."

"I thought you said you were in the Boundary Waters."

"I was."

"It's illegal to mine there."

"That's what I thought. But here's what I've learned." She's rehearsed this several times, but the words feel logjammed in her throat. "Frontier has been surveying the Boundary Waters for omnimetal strikes. Once the press gets wind of this, busloads of protesters are going to show up from every corner of the country. But for now, the prospecting isn't public knowledge. I made some phone calls. And it turns out the feds, on an emergency order, granted your company—"

"It's not my company."

"A provisional mining license that nullifies the protected status of the BWCA."

"I got nothing to do with the business. Zero."

"This license was granted by the Department of Defense. Do you understand what that means? Frontier is now a military contractor."

"What?" John visibly flinches. "No. No, that's not possible."

"You're going to be their principal supplier for omnimetal-weapons research and development."

"I said that's not possible. We've got a policy going back to when my great-uncle died in Vietnam not to—"

"Like a code, you mean?"

"Yes," he says, sighing around his words. "Like a code."

"I'm not done."

John opens his mouth to say something more but doesn't. He makes a go-ahead motion.

"This is why I think your father was targeted."

"For working with the DOD?"

"The opposite. For refusing to work with the DOD."

John's eyes go somewhere else. He seems to understand now what she might be suggesting.

"This is where the code comes in," she says. "This is what I was nervous about. What do you stand for? Lashing out and being a big stupid idiot? Or making peace? Because personally, I'm interested in making peace and protecting this community."

He clenches his fist and softly bashes the wheel. "You're saying it's Talia."

"As soon as your father was declared incapable, she became the acting president of Frontier. She's the one who signed off with the DOD."

"When? When did she sign off? Did you check the date?"

"It was days later. He was still in the hospital. To me that implies—"

"Impatience."

"Now, there are a few things going on here, *mister,* that I have some pretty big problems with. But the biggest one is this. I became a peace officer—a cop—because I love Northfall. And right now, a place that's near and dear to me is being threatened." She holds up a finger when John tries to speak. She doesn't want him to interrupt because she's going to tell him a story. A story her father shared with her. A story her father shares with everyone he takes out into the BWCA as a wilderness guide.

"It happened right here. Or not far from here. Over on the Gunflint Trail. About two billion years ago, a meteor hit. Big one. Giant fireball. Did you know that? I bet you didn't. The impact crater was a hundred fifty miles wide. The winds that came off it would have carried you to Oz. This was back when northern Minnesota was underwater, sunk under a shallow sea. There would have been earthquakes, tsunamis. An end-of-the-world type feeling. Kind of like what we all went through five years back, but worse, if it's possible to imagine.

"Anyhoo, the ejecta from the impact site gets mixed up in the mess of all these storms, and then it gradually settles and forms a layer of rock. You follow me? Only about twenty inches thick, but it reaches all the way up into Canada and all the way over to Michigan. That layer, it's exposed at Gunflint Lake. The fireplace at Gunflint Lodge? It's made out of that rock. That whole area is called the Gunflint because of it. Because the rock—that alien rock—was popularly used as gunflint in rifles. A lot of people died because of it, in a roundabout way. And that's what I'm getting at. This strike. This omnimetal. The business interest in it. The government interest in it. The military interest in it. It's got me and my daddy and a whole lot of other people worried. Because this place has a long tradition as a source of weapons, of killing.

"Now, history has a habit of repeating itself. And maybe I'm naive—I know I can sure seem like I am—but I see a way to stop this. To stop the killing." She waits a beat and then says, "Okay. You can talk now. Do you want to know how to stop all the killing?"

"All ears."

"It's you. You're the way."

He says the word as if it's a punch line: "Me?"

"At the hospital, you told me you lied about your military service because you wanted your father to be proud of you. Well . . . maybe this is your chance."

John's face hardens. He slams his hand against the steering wheel.

"What do you stand for?" she says. This isn't the sort of peace-brokering she imagined doing when she signed on to become a cop. But it is justice nonetheless. The rules have changed. She is changing with them. "What are you going to do next?"

31

✳

Four years ago . . .

John didn't know where he was. When he escaped his cell, when he stumbled out of the compound and into the cruel sunlight, he might as well have been on Mars. Dun-colored hills knuckled with rock and tufted with wiry brush reached off into the distance. Every panting breath felt choked with hot dust.

A bullet struck him then. In the cheek. He brought a hand there experimentally and felt the warmth of its impact. And then, in quick succession, he was shot in the shoulder, ribs, thigh. The rattle and pop of automatic fire was drowned out by the harsh chipping of his skin as it deflected lead. A fresh volley tore up his T-shirt, and from the gashes came blue sparks, like a lighter that fails to catch.

He turned toward the source. The compound was built into the side of a hill with dirt shouldering the structures, and a man with a thick mustache and an AK-12 stood framed in one of its dark doorways. His eyes were open so wide they looked lidless. He dropped the rifle. At first John thought it was in disbelief—but then his body slumped and collapsed, and Anton appeared behind him with a blood-slick knife.

His fellow prisoner looked different out of his cell, free in the sunlight. He was straw-haired. Pink as the skin under a scab. Awkwardly tall and long-limbed. He hoisted up the fallen rifle and yelled to John, "Remember when I am telling you to get in truck, foolish asshole? Get in truck!"

Voices could be heard shouting inside and Anton nosed the rifle through the doorway. A quick spray of gunfire strobed the shadows yellow. Someone cried out in pain. Anton let out a laugh and sprinted after John.

They scrambled into a Toyota pickup that might once have been white but was now skinned with dust and mottled with rust. The keys dangled from the ignition. It took John a few cranks to bring the engine to life and then they were on their way, skidding and thumping and grinding along a rutted road that twisted off to nowhere.

They studied the mirrors for the next ten minutes. When Anton decided they were safe enough, he dug around in the cab and listed off what he found. "Petrol. Bullets. Blanket. Flashlight. More bullets. Boobs magazine. Bag of roasted chickpeas." He uncapped a dirty jug and sniffed it. "Water, I am thinking." He took a swig and offered a contended grunt. "Water." He tipped the jug back and guzzled until he needed to catch his breath. Then he showed his yellow-rimed teeth in a smile. "So, what are you, man? Devil or angel?"

"I don't know what I am," John said.

"You are always like this?"

"No."

"Since Cain, then?"

"How did you know?"

Anton sloshed another drink, and water dribbled down his chin. He shoved the jug at John. "Everything has been strange, yes? Since Cain? In Pakistan, near Nanga Parbat, I was on job. Locals tell me to stay away from village. You know why? Everyone there was ice cube. Frozen. I thought this was nonsense until I saw for self. Not just people, but houses, trees, dogs. Like Pompeii, yes? Nobody knows what is coming. Excepting for the ash, people are covered in ice and looking like dipped in glass."

"What were you doing there?"

"Oh, you know, I was supposed to be killing someone. The usual, blah-blah." Anton's voice lulled here, then he continued on with excitement. "And then, near my grandmother's, farmer discovers worm. White worm size of python. You know what he uses to fight worm? Pitchfork. You know what happens to pitchfork? Blades rust to nothing by next day. Gone. Poof. And then cow steps in place where worm bleeds? Big mistake. Hoof gone. Leg no longer working. Milk becomes blood. Farmer must kill cow. All because of worm!"

"Jesus."

"Son of God, He is not seeming so special anymore, yes? Making fishes and bread and walking on the water? *Pfft.* Who is caring? We have metal man now! And giant white worm with rust blood!"

"I guess."

The road forked and Anton threw out an arm and said, "Go that way. Left. Left!"

John did as he was told, cranking the wheel. "So you know where we are?"

Anton popped open the glove box and rifled around in it. "Not really, but left is lucky."

The road was sometimes sand and sometimes stone and sometimes hard-packed clay. It cut now through a valley where evening had already come. John clicked on the headlights, but only one of them worked.

"I could sell you, you know." Anton wagged a long finger and croaked out a laugh. "I could tie you up and sell you for big money, metal man."

"Why don't you?"

"You are lucky you saved me or I would! Also, maybe I am having another idea. A way I can make money off you that is lot more fun."

At boarding school, John had to participate in a sharing circle every day. A counselor would arrange a dozen folding chairs in a room and students would all sit around and stare at their hands. You were supposed to unload your regrets and anxieties, hopes and dreams. No one was allowed to judge you there. And no one was allowed to repeat what was said outside of the room.

One day the counselor — a man who favored Easter-egg-colored sweater vests and white Velcro sneakers — asked who they dreamed of being. Their fantasy selves. "If you could be anyone, in any time, doing anything, what would it be? Sky's the limit," he said.

John had always loved westerns and samurai movies. He related to the gun- and sword-slinging loners who wandered through lawless territories, got caught up in some local trouble, kicked ass, then headed off into the horizon. They were masterless. They abided by no one's rules but their own. They did bad things for good reasons. So when it was John's turn to speak, he said, "A ronin."

No one knew what he was talking about, and when the counselor pressed him to say more, John said, "It's like a wandering knight."

There was a moment of silence before the counselor said, "You used the word *wandering*. If I'm hearing you correctly, John, that means you want to travel? I'd say that sounds like a very positive goal."

"That's not what I mean," John said, but everyone's attention had already moved on to the next student in the circle.

But Anton knew what he meant. Ronin was what they named their private security team, a two-man task force that they pitched as a small-scale Blackwater or Academi. They couldn't risk taking anyone else on for fear of John's secret being discovered.

For Anton, it was about the money. For John, it was about atonement. He had left Northfall to escape himself. He had been given a second chance at life, and he was trying to decide if he was worthy of it. Every mile he traveled from Minnesota felt like a necessary distancing. And every punch, every blade, every bullet he took from there on out had a chiseling effect, so the plaque of who he used to be gradually fell away. In Afghanistan, he took a flamethrower to a field of poppies and the men who guarded it. In Brazil, he crashed a truck going eighty miles an hour into a convoy carrying the kingpin of a human-trafficking network. In Nigeria, he detonated C-4 charges in a warlord's compound, and in the South China Sea, he sank the yacht of an online scammer. One way to be absolved in the judgment of the world is to become the judge yourself.

Then came the job in Russia. A member of the Bratva—a man known as Ox—had broken away and formed a splinter group, and the two factions were warring over money, drugs, territories. Anton wasn't sure who contacted Ronin via the Dark Web but guessed it was a government official who needed the street violence to end. At a luxury spa and steam bath in the Khimki Forest, Ox would be celebrating his birthday, and John and Anton were hired to make it his last.

But a warning came with the job: Ox wasn't a standard target, their client said. Something about him was different. He had changed, and the change had inspired him to leave Bratva and go it on his own. "What is this supposed to be meaning?" Anton asked, and their client sent them a file that included photos and a message: *He calls himself Ox for a reason.*

They staged the hit in the steam bath because, as Anton said, "Does not matter how big of a sausage you are having between legs, when naked, we are all vulnerable as babies." The entire facility had been rented out by Ox's group, and guards were stationed throughout the building. But Anton and John didn't have to sneak by anyone. They were already there. They had broken in before dawn and hidden in the laundry room, where they'd donned the white uniforms of the staff.

They carried in their arms stacks of towels inside of which they'd tucked Berettas snouted with silencers. They made it as far as the steam bath before a man with a buzz cut held up his square hand and said, "No farther." "But the party just called the front desk and requested towels," Anton said in Russian, and the man said, "Then I'll deliver them myself."

Anton shrugged and made as if to pass the towels. A muffled thump sounded—the cough of the silenced bullet. Blood fronded the wall behind the man. His face registered disbelief just before he crumpled to the floor. John and Anton dropped their towels on him in a messy shroud. When they opened the door, steam oozed out, and it was as if they were walking into a cloud. Their noses tingled with the smell of eucalyptus. Their sneakers squeaked on the tile as they crept forward.

They heard laughter up ahead, but the first man appeared from the side, his bare feet slapping the floor, their only warning. He had a peacock tattoo on his shoulder and wore a towel wrapped around his waist. He screamed when they double-tapped him, and that was when everything went to hell.

It was difficult to tell how many of them there were. Maybe four, maybe ten. They kept ghosting in and out of sight. Mostly they attempted to throw punches or sweep kicks, but someone broke a bottle of vodka and came at them with the sharded butt of it. Another used a wet towel to snap Anton's pistol out of his hand. Gunfire clapped off the walls and made their ears whine. Blood misted the air and reddened the tiles.

And then Ox appeared. The pictures hadn't done him justice. He stood so tall that he had to hunch to avoid the ceiling. His body was brutish, a hairless slab of muscle and fat. His gut was swollen and his cavernous bellybutton could have accommodated a cannonball. With a single hand he snatched up Anton by the waist and smacked him against a bench and then the wall until there came a sickening crack. Anton's body flopped lifelessly when it was tossed aside.

John had two bullets left in the clip and fired them both into Ox, but they seemed to have no effect; they were simply absorbed into his bulk. He charged naked toward John. The floor might have shook or it might have been the pounding of his heart. A hand vised around his legs and he too was swept up and battered against the floor, the wall, even the ceiling — again, again, again. But he did not break. The tile did. And then the concrete beneath. And then the rebar within the concrete.

Eventually Ox tired and dropped him and heaved with breath. John lay at the bottom of a shallow crater with shattered tile edging it like broken teeth. He looked up at the giant looming over him. Though his head was massive, his eyes and nose and mouth were small, pinched into the center of his face. Ox was young. Maybe even younger than John. His voice was high when spoke. John didn't know the language but understood him all the same: *You're like me?* That's what he'd said.

Slowly John rose. His chest and arms pulsed. A stardust glow shone through his skin. There was something inside him that had to get out — and he threw his arms forward as if to hurl something. A big block of kinetic energy came rippling out of him, and the cannon strike of it pulverized skin and muscle and bone. The giant did not fall but he flew back, vanishing into the steam and smacking some distant wall with enough force to shake the building and make the lights flicker.

That was the day John decided to accept his family's invitation to come home at last. The ronin had wandered far and long enough.

32

✳

After John's mother died, all of her bad habits were forgiven or banished from his memory altogether. Her tendency to cry and throw things when she got drunk on red wine. Her inability to get out of bed for days at a time every January and February. Her refusal to allow anyone in the kitchen when she was cooking. None of that mattered. She became faultless, ethereal. She was the one who'd brought them all together for meals. She was the one who'd organized vacations. She was the one who'd demanded that family come before business. She left behind so much neediness, a terrible vacancy and insubstantiality that made John feel, as a teenager, like he was collapsing in on himself.

He was depressed to realize that he hadn't truly loved her until she died. To make something valuable to someone, you had to take it away. Or at least threaten to. That was the way of things. That was certainly the case with his own life. And his father's. And now with Northfall itself. He hadn't given a damn about any of them until they were in danger of vanishing.

Now he sits by his father. The air smells of menthol and old sweat. His father's PEG tube gurgles. His skin has mostly healed, but some bandages remain. John combs his thin white hair. He rubs lotion into his father's hands, trying to be gentle, mindful of his arthritis. He pauses to spin the omnimetal ring along his father's finger. The skin beneath it is red and swollen. He tries to slip it off but can't. He and his father are the same in that way—they cannot unwed themselves of the metal grafted to them.

So many years ago, after his father sent him away to Stone Mountain Leadership Academy, John opened up his duffel to find a letter tucked into it. Neither he nor his father was inclined to heart-to-heart discussions, so this was a way for the old man to unload on his son without anyone raising his voice or slamming a door. Several days passed before John could bring himself to read it. In careful square handwriting—his father used only capital letters—Ragnar wrote, EVERY NEW BUSINESS VENTURE REQUIRES PATIENCE, AN UNWAVERING BELIEF IN THE INVESTMENT. THE PAPER-WORK YOU HAVE TO DEAL WITH RIGHT AWAY—THE LOANS, LICENSES, CONTRACTS, DECLARATIONS—IS THE EQUIVALENT OF A LOVE LETTER WRITTEN TO THE FUTURE. IT WILL TAKE SEVERAL SETBACKS AND SEVERAL YEARS BEFORE YOU SEE SUCCESS. THIS FAMILY IS A BUSINESS. YOU ARE ONE OF MY MOST VALUABLE INVESTMENTS. I BELIEVE IN YOU.

He was trying to say *I love you* but didn't know how. John kept the letter for years, the stationery becoming wrinkled and yellowed and torn along the creases. He thought about responding several times but never did. Until now.

"I'm sorry," he says to the silent figure. Not dead, but not really alive either.

He's sorry about his mother. He's sorry about his wild, reckless behavior as a teenager. He's sorry for leaving Northfall. He's sorry for lying. He's sorry for being such a shitty son.

He's sorry for what happened that night, the night the sky fell. "I don't know what I was thinking. I wasn't thinking. He wouldn't give it back, he wouldn't tell me where he had hidden it—but I still shouldn't have done what I did." He holds his father's hand as he talks. "I've had my share of setbacks, Pops. You were right about that. But maybe I'm on my way to becoming the man you hoped I might be. When you wake up, you'll see."

He doesn't have much of a plan when he finds his sister in her office. She's sitting behind her desk, staring out the window with a faraway look on her face. She doesn't seem to notice him until he clears his throat. She tips her head in his direction and says, "That's enough."

At first John thinks she's talking to him. Then her hands reach below the desk and she drags up her husband. "I said that's enough."

Her husband glances at John and wipes his mouth and stands unsteadily.

"You can go now," Talia says and hitches up the elastic waistband of her track pants. "My brother and I need to talk."

Another minute and it's just the two of them. Wind wobbles the windows. A few snowflakes ride the air. The light outside is gravestone gray.

Normally Talia goes heavy on the makeup — smoky eye shadow, thick foundation, purple lipstick — but her face is scrubbed of it now. She looks older and more severe than he's ever seen her. "I got bad news," she says.

Whatever she has to say, he's not here to listen. He speaks breathlessly to get it out: "I know what you've been doing to Pops."

"What?" She curls a lip at him when he holds out his phone and pulls up a video. "What am I even looking at?"

"I bought it at Walmart for thirty-five bucks. A nanny cam."

The screen displays Ragnar as he lies in his medical bed connected to IVs and monitors. His eyes flutter beneath his lids. He mutters in his sleep. A nurse sits beside him reading a Hollywood gossip magazine. She sets it down when Talia enters the room. Talia dismisses the nurse and says she would like some alone time with her father.

"That's enough, Johnny," Talia says from the other side of the desk.

But he keeps playing the video. It shows her holding a pillow over her father's face — experimentally, for thirty seconds — releasing him, and studying his labored breathing. Then she tucks the pillow back under his head and neatens his hair and walks away.

She turns her chair to face the window. "I said that's enough."

John pockets the phone as he says, "I've got more, if you like. One time you crimped his IV and stopped the fluids. Another time you shut off the enteral pump. Another time you emptied his feeding bag into the toilet. Another time you changed the incline of the bed to decrease the infusion rate."

"What do you want from me? You want me to cry? You want me to say I'm sorry? I won't. I'm not. We got bigger shit to deal with than your sneaky-little-bitch ass recording me with a nanny cam."

"Bigger than the contract you signed with the Department of Defense?" There. He's laid it all out.

In response Talia blinks at him several times, like a camera changing its aperture, finding its focus. "Like I was saying before, I got bad news."

"Did you just hear what I —"

"It's Yesno. They got him."

This is not the response he expected, and he doesn't like the way his voice goes high when he says, "What?"

She pushes away from her desk and stands and stretches. "Have a drink with me, Johnny."

"I don't want a drink."

She has a wet bar set up on a metal cart and she goes to it and grabs a bottle by the neck and pinches two tumblers between her fingers. "Macallan Thirty. Dad's favorite. Come on. Drink with me."

"Why did you do it?"

"They're probably beating Yesno with a lead pipe right now and this is what you want to talk about? Business?"

"Dad isn't business."

"This family is a business, Johnny. That's what Dad always taught us."

"You started the fire, didn't you?" he says. "You tried to kill him?"

She clinks the glasses and bottle down on the desk. "He should have retired a long time ago. The world has moved on. We had to move with it."

"Talk to me like a human being."

"Says the guy who's the farthest fucking thing from a human being." She sweeps an arm out so violently, he imagines he can feel the breeze of it. "What the fuck do you care, anyway, you sneaky little cunt? Since when do you give two goddamn cents about the old man? Go fuck yourself. I'm sick of your face." Here her rage recedes and her voice softens. "But I'm willing to put up with it because I need you to help with Yesno. That's what's important right now. Are you hearing me? Yesno needs us."

"Who—who has him?"

"What kind of a stupid question is that? Black Dog, of course."

John doesn't know what to do or what to ask or what to focus on. There's too much coming at him at once. "Do you know if he's okay?"

"Guessing not."

"You ask for proof of life?"

"I asked. They haven't answered."

"Jesus," John says. "Did they say what they want?"

"To parley. They're proposing we meet someplace public. The Lumberjack Steakhouse."

"I don't care if it's land, equipment, money. Whatever it is, just give it to them. Who cares. We can't let them—"

"We got a lot to figure out." She uncorks the bottle and splashes each tumbler a quarter full. "And everything makes more sense with whiskey."

She shoves the glass into his chest until he takes it. Then she returns to her desk. Absently he lifts the tumbler and drains it in one swallow. He licks his lips. His chest is full of fire. Normally the sensation ebbs to a pleasant burn, but right now his stomach and his lungs feel stacked with kindling soaked in kerosene. He clears his throat several times. Then coughs. He can't seem to catch his breath.

Talia studies him with her head cocked. Her own glass sits on her desk. Untouched.

"Macallan Thirty," he says, then coughs again. "That's the same bottle Pops was drinking from that night."

"You got it," she says. She's not smiling. She seems to take no pleasure in what's happening. She watches him with clinical detachment. Even disappointment. "They say poison is a woman's weapon.

I personally prefer bats, but those wouldn't do much good against you, would they, baby brother? Sometimes you need a softer touch."

His vision grows uncertain. Every cough knocks him off balance.

"I was going to pin his death on you. The old man's. The cop's in the basement too. The prodigal son comes home and everything goes to hell and I'm on a jet to Mexico."

"Fuck," he says between coughs, "you."

"I drilled a hole in the log, filled it with gunpowder, sealed it with putty. I figured if the poison didn't get him, the fire would. Old man was a creature of habit. Started every day with his salad and coffee. Ended every night with his scotch and fire. Didn't expect him to get out of here alive. Didn't expect you to squirm your way out of the investigation either. But that IED stuffed into the floral arrangement sure helped you. Whoever the hell sent that didn't do me any favors. All of a sudden you're a hero."

His brain feels like it's flickering on and off. He doesn't remember falling, but now he's on the floor.

"Even I changed my mind about you. Maybe you could do some good after all, I'm thinking. Maybe my hell-raiser of a baby brother could be more than a patsy to me. Maybe he could be a defender, a soldier. But no. No, that's not going to happen. You fucked that all up with your bullshit righteousness, Johnny boy."

It's unclear how much time passes, but he's dimly aware of Talia knotting something at his wrists and ankles.

"Things didn't work out exactly how I planned, but maybe that's for the best." She pats his cheek. "Because I think I got somebody who will take an interest in you. And Uncle Sam, he's got deep pockets. You might be a worthless piece of shit, Johnny, but you're a valuable weapon all the same."

33

*

Talia is told to meet them at six. They made a reservation for supper at the Lumberjack Steakhouse. Table for four. At such a busy time, in such a public setting, she doesn't think Black Dog's people will dare make a scene, but if they try anything, bet your ass she'll be ready.

Snow is falling. It melts on the roads and clings to the trees. Talia already spoke with Jenna on the phone to confirm she was working the shift. "Some shit might be going down," Talia said, "and I need you to be looking out for me." She promised to make it worth her while. "You and me, we have an understanding — am I right?"

Jenna said of course, but had Talia seen Johnny? He wasn't responding to her calls or texts.

"No," Talia said. "But I'm sure he'll turn up."

"He said he would go house-hunting with me. There's an open house in that new development, Eagle Ridge? He said he wants to help us find —"

"That's great," Talia said. "I'm happy for you. See you tonight."

She arrives at the restaurant an hour early. In the center of the dining room is a screened fireplace with a brick bottom and a metal chimney that pipes through the ceiling. Lit logs crackle and snap and scent the air with wood smoke.

Jenna shows her the table Walter Eaton reserved for them. Next to the window. "No," Talia says. "Not there."

She stations herself at the rear of the dining room at a round table below a mounted rack of elk antlers. Her back is to a corner. She can watch everyone come and go. "They don't know you know me," Talia says. "Keep it that way."

"What's this about?"

"Business."

"What do you need me to do?"

"For now, keep a steak knife in your apron and keep the nearby tables clear of people."

"That's going to be tricky. We're full every —"

"Trust me. It's better this way."

"Anything else?"

"Ice water, how about? My mouth is dry as shit. But do me a favor and bring it in a wineglass."

"Why?"

"Just do it."

Jenna gives her a glass and Talia slurps one ice cube after another and crunches them down. She chessboards the restaurant, thinking about how her strategy might change depending on how things play out. Yesno is like a computer they have failed to back up. He knows everything about Frontier's operations. She's not here because she's soft for him, like Johnny. She's here because she needs him. She hates, more than anything, two things: being disrespected and being told what to do. She's dealing with both right now and can't stop clenching and unclenching her fists.

Maybe Walter Eaton just wants a clean transaction. A fair trade. But she doubts very much the meeting will be that clean. She's been trained her whole life to suspect what someone says is different than what he means. Because nobody is better at hiding things than Minnesotans. They'll happily give you directions anywhere, except to their own houses. If they hate you, they smile. If they think somebody's a freak or a pain in the ass, they'll never say so; they'll just use words like *different*. Arguments get swept under the rug, desires play out quietly in dark bedrooms. At concerts, nobody dances or sings along, all of them keeping whatever thrill they feel bottled up inside. Live here long enough, you learn to see below the surface of things. There is subtext hidden beneath every conversation, just as there are fish churning darkly beneath the ice of every frozen lake.

Everybody thinks Talia's brother is some war hero, a prodigal son returned home to do the family right, but she knows him to be a liar and a loser and a physical abomination. And everybody pretends her father is the patron saint of the Northwoods, but the truth is every halo is forged with a hammer.

She discovered the truth about him when she was still a teenager. The two of them were driving home from a Christmas Eve service at the Lutheran church when, on a dark county highway, a truck roared up behind and flashed its brights and laid on its horn and then nudged them with its bumper hard enough to lurch the car and nearly push them off the road. Her father put on his blinker and pulled onto the shoulder and she asked what he was doing and he smiled at her kindly and said, "Don't worry. Everything will be all right."

In the side mirror she could see the man climbing out of his truck and approaching. He didn't look like a person. In the wash of the headlights, he was an angry shadow. He carried a tire iron. With it he shattered their rear taillight, dented the roof, and spiderwebbed the windshield, all the while screaming *How could you?* and *How dare you?* As this transpired, her father calmly reached under his seat and withdrew a Glock from a spring holster and rolled down the window and shot the man in the mouth.

She cried out as the body flopped to the asphalt. Everything seemed suddenly so quiet when her father turned toward her with blood spotting his cheek. He withdrew a handkerchief from his breast pocket and wiped his face and said they were safe now. But it was time to clean up. Would she help? She shouldn't feel bad. We don't feel bad for a weed that gets clipped by a lawn mower or a mouse that gets eaten by an owl. "Sometimes the people without power hate the people with power. And they will steal that power if it's not upheld." They had no choice.

He could justify anything, she learned. His office door had always been closed, and now she understood what happened behind it, as he began inviting her to meetings and asking her to accompany him on trips. These were the days when iron had lost its value, when the mines were shutting down, when the Frontiers were doing everything they could to keep their investments sound and Northfall alive.

There was the would-be mayor whose political campaign they ruined with a prostitution scandal. There was the five-years-clean-and-sober sawmill owner they successfully tempted with drugs in order to kick-start an illegal logging operation that funneled lumber into Canada. The hunting accident that befell the congresswoman; the disappearance of a group of radical environmentalists. She could go on.

Talia is her father's daughter. But whereas he epitomized what it meant to be a Minnesotan—always calm, stoic, genteel, no matter how black his impulses—she is what she is: Loud. Gigantic. Vulgar. Subtext is a language she doesn't speak. What she says is what she means. Her inside is her outside. And that's how she feels their company, Frontier Metals, ought to be. Naked in its ambitions. You want to succeed? Don't pretend otherwise. Go ahead and rule the world.

Mickey Golden pushes inside the restaurant. Alone. He doesn't take off his sunglasses. Beneath his leather jacket, one of his arms is in a sling. He goes to the table Eaton had reserved and finds an old couple seated there, spooning up their soup. He turns in a slow circle until he finds her. A stare seals between them. He smiles and holds up a finger and wags it. He pulls a cell phone out of his pocket and texts a message one-handed.

She rises as he gets closer and he says, "Look at you. All polite."

"I always stand up when a lady approaches the table." She puts out her arms and motions him forward. "Now get over here."

"We gonna hug it out?"

She stands a head taller than him, but he makes up for his height in the broadness of his shoulders. They lean into each other, pretending an embrace while actually patting each other down. His hand lingers on her waist and in response she bashes his sling and he hisses in pain. "Don't make me hurt you again," she whispers in his ear.

She sits down. Rather than going to the opposite side of the round table, he takes the seat beside her and scoots close. He slides a hand under the table, feels for anything that might be duct-taped there. Then he reaches behind her and checks the cushions of her chair. "Satisfied?" she says.

"I am now."

"Good. Then how about you move to the other side of the table," she says. "Unless you're looking to play footsie, I'd personally prefer some distance between us."

He nods his head toward the entrance and says, "Can't. Got to leave room for our friends."

She sees then that Walter Eaton and Yesno have arrived. Eaton removes his Stetson and shakes the snow off it and hangs it on a rack. One of his hands grips the elbow of Yesno, escorting him forward.

Jenna approaches them, smiling her welcome, and they speak briefly. She tucks four menus into the crook of her arm. With a wave of her hand she indicates that they should follow. Yesno stumbles along as if drunk, dragged by Walter. One of his eyes is blotched with a bruise.

The men take their seats in silence, and Jenna snaps down menus in front of them.

"Now that we're all here," she says, "can I get you anything to drink? Coffee, wine, beer, or cocktails?"

Walter's nose and cheeks are purpled with broken capillaries. He keeps his pouched eyes on Talia as he says, "We're going to need a minute, hon."

"No problem at all." Jenna's smile twitches at the corners. "I'll let you get settled."

"Before you go," Walter says, "you mind taking these away?" He pats the silverware bundled in a red cloth napkin. "Knives make me nervous."

"Oh, okay. No problem." Jenna's eyes meet Talia's for a moment. "I'll be back in a few." She scoops up the silverware and hurries away.

Yesno keeps his head bowed. His breathing is shivery, as if he's sucking air through a broken straw. A long thirty seconds pass before Talia says, "I already patted down your pit bull."

"You want to give me a tickle too? You're welcome to. Don't got much to hide." Walter pats his body. "My jeans are tight enough, bet you can read the dates of the change in my pocket."

"How you doing, Yesno?"

Yesno might have nodded, but it's hard to tell. She wonders how badly they've hurt him, what injuries might be hidden beneath his sports coat. "He's fine." Walter claps him on the back hard enough to make him flinch in pain. "Just fine. Ready to go home."

"That makes two of us."

"Oh?" Walter says and flips open the menu. "But we haven't even had a chance to consider our options."

"Pie's good. Let's say we get right to dessert."

His finger runs down the page and stops and settles on something with a tap. "This trouble between us—it's gone on long enough. Don't you think?"

"What do you propose?"

"I'm a businessman. My ultimate concern is the dollar. How about something that would benefit us both instead of costing us both?" He reaches across the table and takes what's left of her water and swallows it down. "We want a stake in Frontier."

"You think we're just going to give you—"

"No. I don't think that. I'm offering to invest."

She can't hide the surprise in her voice when she says, "What?"

"I liquidate everything here. Hand over my equipment and property holdings. Sign over my employees. In return, we own a share of Frontier's future profits."

She doesn't know what to say, so she looks to Yesno; he remains hunched over as if in prayer.

Walter says, "I hate this damn place, if I'm being honest. Y'all can keep your walleye and buffalo plaid, your Vikings and snowmobiles and canoes and polka and whatever the hell else you think makes this frozen wasteland special. Want to wash my hands clean of it all, get back to home. Texas is calling. Longhorn country's where I belong."

She doesn't respond except to pull her wineglass slowly back across the table. "Or maybe I just take Yesno and leave?"

Her eyes are on Walter — who's giving her a jowly smile — so she doesn't see Mickey slide a hand into his sling and remove a blade from his elastic bandages. He prods her in the ribs just below the breast. "That's not going to happen," he says.

"Tell you what," Walter says and knocks the table with his knuckles. "You keep thinking about my offer. Because it's a good one. And while you're thinking, I'm going to go fetch my lawyer. He's out in the parking lot and he's got us some paperwork to look over." Walter stands from his seat and hitches his jeans. "Back in a jiff."

The big man marches out of the restaurant and leaves the three of them sitting there.

"Yesno," she says, then, louder, "Yesno!"

He bobs his head upward and gives her a little smile and only then does she realize how unfocused his eyes are.

"What's wrong with you?" she says. And then to Mickey: "What's wrong with him?" She assumed earlier he was merely injured and afraid, but this looks like something else.

"Settle down. We gave him a few heavy doses of Benadryl. That's all. Guy's so high-strung. Figured it was better to keep the negotiation mellow."

At that Yesno slumps over in his seat, fighting sleep. Which is when she notices his sports coat. He always wears one to hide his disfigured spine, but right now he appears to be hiding something else. The coat is buttoned to the breast and a squarish bulk presses against its fabric. "What is that?" she says.

"What is what?" Mickey says.

"Under his jacket. He's got something on him." She holds her wineglass two-handed. "What have you done?" She raises her voice as she says this so that Mickey doesn't hear her snap off the glass's base.

The blade against her ribs pulls back as he studies Yesno. "I don't know what you're yapping about—"

And that's when she jams the broken fang of the glass stem into his cheek. She was going for his neck, but he jerks away at the last second. The glass grinds and scrapes his molars. He wrenches back with a scream.

She explodes upward and uses her momentum to flip the table onto Mickey. Yesno wobbles and then slumps off his chair and onto the floor. His sports coat splits open. Beneath his white collared shirt, she can clearly see the outline of explosives wrapping his chest.

She doesn't know how much time she has. Maybe Walter's plan was to get her to sign the paperwork and then blow Yesno to hell as she drove him home. Or maybe he's going to take her out now. Take them all out. Mickey seemed clueless when she called attention to the suicide vest. It's possible he doesn't realize he's already a victim.

She hoists Yesno up by the collar and slits a finger down his shirt, popping all the buttons from their holes. The black vest squared with C-4 is now visible. But before she can do anything more, there is a spine-cracking impact as a thrown chair hits her.

She falls forward onto another table and it overturns with a splintering crash. The blur of what's happening all around her doesn't really register. Dishes shatter. People scream. Chairs scud out from under tables. From the floor, she pops up into a wrestler's crouch and tries to split her attention equally between Mickey, charging toward her, and Yesno, turtling across the floor.

Mickey's sunglasses hang askew. He seems to be smiling, but really his cheek is gashed open to reveal all the teeth on one side. He tries to tackle her, but she pivots with his weight, and they both topple into the central fireplace. The brick ledge bites her back and the screen tears from the chimney and tangles up Mickey's knife as he tries to jam it into her.

"He's going to kill you too," she says. "Don't you—"

But he's not listening; he head-butts her in the face hard enough that her nose shatters. Her vision throbs an electric yellow. With one hand she blocks a thrust of his knife and with the other she feels her way blindly into the hearth. She pulls out a flaming log and swings it in his direction. She hears the sizzle of flesh and a high-pitched cry. She smells his hairspray catching fire.

She staggers back toward Yesno. Her mouth is full of blood, and her vision is blurred with tears, but she's getting her bearings again. "Everybody out!" she screams. "Everybody get the hell out of here!" Though at this point, the restaurant is nearly clear of people except for a few who linger and goggle at her.

Yesno is trying to stand up, holding a chair for support. "Take it off," she says and rips at his coat and shirt. The fabric tears. Finally she hurls the shed mess of it to the floor. The suicide vest has Velcro shoulder straps, and she tears at them, trying to free him.

Talia nearly jabs an elbow into Jenna when she appears by her side and says, "What can I do?"

"Get him out of here," Talia says just as Yesno unshoulders the vest. It is the first time she has seen him undressed. His chest is hollow and his back is knuckled over and his skin has a flaky, oniony quality.

"I'm sorry," he manages to say. "I'm so sorry. I—"

"Shut the hell up and go. Only ones who're going to be sorry are these assholes."

By this time, Mickey has recovered. He has only one good arm, but he still manages to chuck chair after chair after chair at Talia. One strikes her thigh and bunches the muscle into a stone-hard cramp. She limps as she dodges away, trying to swipe the chairs aside as they come hurtling toward her. One shatters against the wall. Another hits the entrance to the bathroom with such force that its leg pierces the hollow-core door and dangles there, the world turned on its side for a second.

Her back thuds into the wall and she looks up to see the mounted elk rack. She leaps and snatches the antlers. They snap off with her weight. With a flip of her wrists, she readjusts her grip on them — and now both her hands are clawed. She lets out a howl and so does Mickey and she lunges toward him, raking the air.

The restaurant is mostly empty, but a line cook, a busboy, and a dishwasher linger near the entrance, watching the mayhem unfold behind Jenna. "Out!" she screams as she ushers Yesno forward. They startle and hold open the door for her, but she pauses — for just a second — to pluck Walter Eaton's Stetson off the hat rack. Then she pushes her way out into the white swirl of the day.

The parking lot is crowded with people. Some press cell phones to their ears. Others clutch themselves against the cold and try to squint through the windows. She rushes through them. Yesno's bare skin steams in the cold.

The snow is falling more thickly now, and it bites at her face and dizzies her vision. She turns in a slow circle and says, "Where are you?" And then she spots the Escalade parked across the street. And the heavy shadow of the man seated in it.

They pass a bench on the sidewalk and she deposits Yesno there and says, "I'll be right back." He doesn't protest, merely draws his legs up and curls into a submissive ball.

Her feet nearly slide out from under her when she steps into the slushy street. But she keeps her footing as she approaches the Escalade from an angle. It is idling, and melted snow weeps down its windows.

Jenna withdraws the steak knife from her apron and arranges it in the cowboy hat's hollow. When she yanks open the driver's door, she finds him studying his cell phone and hurriedly punching its screen. He looks up at her with surprise when she holds out his hat and says, "Sir? You forgot this."

She shoves the Stetson into his chest, and the knife continues into him, nudging through a gap in his ribs. He stares at her in disbelief as blood blooms around the thick wooden handle of the blade. The cowboy hat soaks through with red and takes on the appearance of a crumpled rose.

She retreats a few steps, and at that moment the Lumberjack Steakhouse explodes and the force is such that Jenna sees her reflection crack in the side mirror.

34

✳

There was a myth in the Northwoods about a black cabin. It was born in the time of the voyageurs, when men would cut through icy waters in their canoes and portage between lakes with hundreds of pounds of furs humped on their backs. Just when they were at their most desperate—sick with fever or lost in the maze of lakes or freezing in a blizzard—the black cabin would appear. Smoke would rise from its chimney. Lamplight would burn in its windows. There was something unsettling about the scabby black bark clinging to its logs and the ghostly moan of its porch boards, but the people in the stories couldn't help themselves. They had reached a point of desperation. They had to go in. But they never came out.

When John wakes in the dark, for a delirious moment, that's where he believes he is: in the guts of the black cabin. His skin feels hot. His breath comes in gusting pants. He isn't sure whether he's lying on his side or hanging upside down. He tries to move, but his limbs won't respond, whether because he's been poisoned or because he's been bound tightly, he can't tell. His mouth has been duct-taped shut, and his throat and nose burn with bile.

And then he sees the modem blinking and hears the furnace breathing and the hot-water heater burbling and realizes he is in the basement. Bound to the same chair where he found Dan Swanson several months ago. He made a choice then—the choice to return fully to his family, to reclaim his place in it—and now the choice has consumed and infected him. He hears floorboards creaking as someone approaches. Then the overhead light buzzes on. Maybe, in a moment, *he* will walk in. John himself. And he will wrap his own body in black plastic and weight it with chains and plunge it into a toxic lake. Because he has done this to himself.

But the person who steps hesitantly in front of him is Stacie. She's not in uniform. She wears a pink wool hat with a yarn ball at the top, a down winter jacket, and boots that still carry snow in their laces. "Oh, dear," she says and cringes when she stands before him. She leans in and picks and peels the duct tape from his lips.

He spits out the vomit clumping his mouth, and she says, "Oh, dear," again. "You don't look so good."

He heaves and splatters the floor with a fresh surge. He coughs as he speaks: "I don't feel so good."

She works at the knots binding his wrists, then gives up and searches the nearby tool bench and returns with a box cutter and slits him free.

"How did you . . ." It's difficult to find his words. His brain feels like it's hazing back and forth between dreams and reality. He tries to get up and then realizes his legs are still bound. He has no idea if he's been here for hours or days, but his joints feel ossified and his muscles larded. "How are you even here?"

"The nurse let me in. Your father's nurse. She said she hadn't seen you, but I spotted your Bronco in the shed, so I figured you were either dead or restrained somewhere in the house. And thankfully, here you are!"

"I'm so confused."

"I'm sorry to say that, while you were out, all heck has broken loose."

He slumps back and she kneels before him and keeps her gaze steady as she tells him everything that's happened. Yesno is in the hospital, being treated for shock and several vertebral fractures. Talia is dead and so is Mickey Golden, both killed in a bomb blast at the Lumberjack Steakhouse.

"The Lumberjack?" His voice suddenly sharp with panic. "What about Jenna? Was she —"

"She's fine. So's everyone else other than a few people who got cut up by broken glass and flying debris. Everyone except for Walter Eaton, that is."

"How's that?"

"A steak knife magically flew across the street and into his parked SUV and hit him right in the heart. Weirdest thing, right? But nobody's worried too much about it because he appears to have been the one who set off the device."

His head feels loose on its hinges. "I'm sorry. This is a lot to take in," he says and she nods understandingly.

"Would you like some candy?"

"What?"

She pulls some Starbursts out of her coat pocket. "You look like you could use something sweet."

"No. Thanks."

She takes a square for herself. "It's going to be up to you now, John. Everybody else is gone. You can make this right."

Pull the business out of the Boundary Waters. Cut off the contract with the Department of Defense. Take responsibility for the company while taking care of the Northwoods. The two things didn't have to be mutually exclusive.

After a long time, he says, "Not yet."

"What do you mean?"

"Got some unfinished business that needs dealing with first."

Stacie has been smiling encouragingly at him, but now the smile fades. "My father says I can't trust you, but I said I believed in you. You're not going to let me down—are you, John?"

John closes his eyes and massages the bridge of his nose so tightly that he sees a pulse of red. "I know I haven't even said thank you yet, but I'm going to have to ask you for help."

Victoria is eating again. Big breakfasts of turkey sausage and scrambled eggs and wheat toast smeared with marmalade, a short glass of orange juice with her coffee, a cranberry muffin on the way out the door. Wade whistles in the kitchen as he pops open cabinets, shakes salt, adjusts the burners on the stovetop. He wears an apron that says *I Cook As Good As I Look*.

In the mornings, he is all about speed and efficiency, but in the evenings he takes his time. He brings Victoria a glass of chardonnay and a small dish of Spanish olives and she reads a novel while he grills salmon on cedar planks or fries bacon in an iron skillet with brussels sprouts or massages a spicy dry rub into a beef roast. Then he turns down the lights and brings a flaming match to two candles and plays some jazz and uncorks another bottle of wine and they gather at the table for a long, luxurious meal. There is always dessert. Triple chocolate cake he tops with raspberries. Crème brûlée he crisps golden with a butane torch.

"This is nice," she says one night. "Thank you."

"This is just a taste," he says, "of what retirement could be like."

"I think I'd pop," she says, scooping into a coconut sorbet and letting the spoon linger in her mouth.

The color has returned to her cheeks. Her hair has shine, a lustrous silver. The hollows in her body have smoothed out with fat. Her fingernails are no longer brittle from a lack of calcium. And her throat stops hurting, no longer singed with acid. Five pounds, ten pounds, twenty. It comes on fast, and she needs it. The weight makes her feel more substantial, stronger, whereas before, she felt so frail she was in danger of snapping. She still leaves for work every morning, but without the septic dread she once felt. Wade waves at her from the window when she backs out of the driveway, and she toots the horn and blows him a kiss.

She still spends ten hours a day in the subterranean lab in building 3, but now she is testing Hawkin for another reason. For herself. For him. They need to know what he is capable of if they are going to successfully manage his escape. The boy no longer refuses his meals or lingers tiredly on his bed but jumps up immediately upon her arrival, eager to get started. "How much longer will it be?" he always asks in a whisper, and she can only say, "Soon, my dear."

She and Wade keep their packed luggage ready by the front door. They talk at length about what-ifs and might-bes, excited about their uncertain future. He fusses over her diet and rubs her feet and back with lotion and draws up lavender-scented baths for them to soak in.

Maybe a year had passed since they made love, but now they make up for lost time. She reaches for him in the dark, shuts off the television, nuzzles his neck on the couch. She surprises him with a negligee she hasn't worn in over a decade. Afterward, when they lie spent and panting with their arms around each other, he thanks her. "I missed you," she says and bites his ear.

In Northfall, most people shop for groceries at the Pamida or the Walmart Supercenter, but Wade is fussy about his food and insists on the Wellness Co-Op, where the air smells like spicy soaps and crumbly cheeses. Victoria joins him as he sniffs a cantaloupe, squeezes a tomato, burrows through a messy pile of cilantro. Then they hear a throat being cleared and turn to find a man standing close behind them.

Victoria would not have recognized John except for his birthmark. His eyes are black hollows and his cheeks are unshaven and he wears a hat pulled low. "Tomorrow" is all he says before walking away.

35

✳

Thaddeus is out of town when it happens. A U.S. warship was attacked and sank in the Sea of Japan only a hundred miles off the Korean coast. Though at first a torpedo was suspected, some of the sailors claim the gash in the hull came from something else. Something massive they saw rise out of the deep.

Gunn is on a carrier studying sonar readings when a petty officer brings him a satellite phone. He says, "Yes?" and listens for a long time and does not speak. Finally he says, "This is going to take a moment to process. Stand by." He sets down the phone. His breath whistles from his nose. He removes his glasses and rubs his eyes and puts them back on. He brushes some lint off his sleeve. He picks up the phone again and the voice on the other end says, "Please advise. What's the plan?"

His mouth opens, but for a few seconds he can't find the words. "I'm going," he finally says, "to kill that bitch."

The walls of the motel room are pine-paneled, and the overhead lamp is dirty with dead flies. A painting of the woods in winter hangs crookedly. The television is on and plays the Cartoon Network on mute. The bedspread and the carpet are similar shades of orange, both spotted black with cigarette ash.

Hawkin sits cross-legged on the bed, a fat stack of comic books in front of him. They are brand-new but already rumpled and wrinkled from him reading them over and over. All around him, he has carefully arranged candy in concentric circles. Milk Duds and

Skittles and Kit Kats and M&M's and Dots and Junior Mints and Sour Patch Kids. More than thirty packages altogether. He sprinkles them experimentally into a half-melted carton of strawberry ice cream, then spoons it up. "I have concluded the experiment," he says, speaking with a full mouth, "and science has decided that the best flavor in the world is yellow Skittles and strawberry ice cream."

The bathroom door is open and the water is running. Victoria calls out, "I respect your diligent lab work but respectfully disagree with your findings."

"Try it."

"No way."

"Seriously, it's so good."

"Dark chocolate and red wine is about as crazy as I get."

He scoots over to the night table. Four open cans of Dr Pepper sit there, and he picks each of them up until he finds the one with a few sips left in it.

Victoria comes out of the bathroom. Her hair is cut short around her ears. Instead of silver, it's now a furniture-polish brown. "Well?" she says and runs her fingers through it. "How do I look?"

He tips back the can and shakes out the final drops. Then he squints at her. "No offense, but kind of like an old boy?"

At this they both laugh, an unfamiliar sound between them.

Twenty-seven hours later, Thaddeus is back on the ground in Northfall, studying the damage to the labs and reviewing surveillance footage and interviewing the staff, trying to piece together a narrative.

A concrete-walled hallway is so spider-webbed with cracks that it powders to the touch. A staircase has collapsed on itself like a broken accordion. A steel door — five inches thick, with nine security cylinders locking it in place — has been torn from its frame. Lights have shattered and the floors crunch with glass. A pipe broke and filled the ventilation ducts with water. A gas line ruptured and three offices caught fire and burned black.

One guard has a broken leg. One guard has a lacerated liver. One guard had to have over a hundred pieces of glass tweezered out of his face into a metal bowl. One guard has such a severe concussion that he has to keep his eyes shut because everything appears scrambled — arms coming out of ears, words spilling off pages and crawling away.

Gunn sits at a desk before a bank of screens. He fiddles with the time signatures of the recordings. Rewinds and pauses, fast-forwards and pauses. Zooms in and out. Here is Victoria spending the better part of the morning emptying clips of ammunition into Hawkin. At one point he pulls the clip on a grenade and curls his body over it, swallowing up the detonation. He is charged up with so much energy that his chest glows a constant blue, as if a new star were being born.

Here is Victoria exiting her lab and asking the guard stationed at the door a question and then Tasering him in the neck before he can respond. She and Hawkin don't make it farther than the next hallway before the alarm sounds and the building goes into lockdown. Up to this point, she has sheltered the boy, half hugging him with an arm as they hurry along. But now he motions for her to stand aside.

He approaches a door and throws forward an arm. When the video is played at a normal speed, the door appears as insubstantial as paper torn by a hard breeze as it's ripped off its hinges. Then Thaddeus slows down the clip and goes frame by frame. The instant the boy's fist strikes the door, a kinetic blast blooms from his knuckles — the flowering, rippling blue of someone plunging into a sunlit pond. The force warps metal and shatters concrete. Victoria covers her ears and staggers back. The boy stands there a moment, looking at his fist uncertainly. But they don't have time to marvel because more guards are approaching now, their weapons drawn, ordering the boy to stand down, stand down, stand down.

Hawkin doesn't listen. He marches toward them steadily, ignoring the bullets that swarm the air and pock the walls and strike his body and fall uselessly to the ground. He comes to a place where two hallways intersect and pauses at the juncture. He is surrounded.

He waits until the guards empty their pistols and then drops into a squat and punches the floor between his feet. The slow-motion playback reveals a translucent blue dome swelling briefly around him—and then bursting outward. The video here is disrupted as the ceiling collapses and the walls shrug down. Minutes later, when the dust finally clears, Hawkin is kneeling at the bottom of a shallow crater. Victoria picks her way through the rubble and takes his hand and they hurry along once more.

There is one image Thaddeus keeps coming back to. It's right as Victoria and the boy exit the building. He zooms in on and sharpens the image. Victoria's face turns up to stare at the camera stationed above the door. It is difficult to tell, with the grainy quality of the feed, but it appears she is smiling.

In the motel room, Victoria sits on the bed, propped up by pillows, her head reclined against the backboard. The boy is tucked up against her waist and she combs her fingers absently through his hair. The television plays a black-and-white movie about an alien invasion. Saucers hover over cities. Ray guns blast. People scream and race through the streets.

"Maybe we should take a break from the TV?" she says. "You've been watching an awful lot of it."

"Nah."

"I brought some books. We could read them. Together." On the night table there is a short tower of books she ordered online. At its top, her copy of *Hatchet*. The ripped pages and torn spine are repaired with masking tape.

"Maybe later. You could read one of my comic books if you want." He reaches for the stack and holds up a copy of *X-Men*.

"No, thank you."

"You sure? They're good."

"Quite sure."

"Well, maybe we can read *Hatchet* later. But I haven't watched TV in a hundred million years. So I got a lot of catching up to do."

"I guess you're right," she says.

He shifts in her arms and gives several tiny grunts and she can tell he's trying to find a way to say something. His voice is shy when he finally says, "Dr. Lennon?"

"You know you can call me Victoria."

"That seems weird, but Dr. Lennon seems right."

"Just try it."

"Victoria?" The word comes slowly.

"Yes?"

"Do you think I killed any of those men?"

"I think you hurt them. But no. You didn't kill anyone," she says quickly.

"How do you know?"

She doesn't but says, "I just do. Don't you worry about that. Not for one more second. Okay?"

"Okay." He twists his body so that he can look at her. "When am I going to see my mom?"

She tries to control her expression, to show him a smile instead of the frown she feels. "We're waiting to hear back from our friend."

"Can't you call him? To see when he'll come?"

"I'm not supposed to call anyone. I'm supposed to wait."

"How long?"

She has already told him but repeats it patiently. "Six to twelve days. That's what he said." They are on day seven, but it feels like longer. With the shades pulled and no sense of night or day, it's just another version of the laboratory cell they shared before.

"But why can't you just call him and see for sure?"

"Because they might be listening."

"You think they're looking for us?"

"I know they are." She squeezes him and not for the first time considers how soft his skin, how fragile his voice. For everything else he is, he's also just a boy. "You're a pretty special guy, you know."

He sounds especially small when he says, "Now they know what I can do. What I can really do, I mean."

"Yes."

"Now it's not a secret."

"That's why we can't be too careful."

"What's the name of the man? The man we're waiting for?"

"His name is John Frontier."

"Why does John Frontier want to help us anyway?"

It's a question she isn't sure how to answer. She asked him the same thing. Why would he take such a risk? What did he stand to gain from all of this? He had casually mentioned a trade, a deal —something to do with omnimetal and a property sale—but she didn't believe him. There was something about the way he shifted his eyes and forced a casual voice before finally blurting out, "A boy needs his mother, okay? A boy should be with his mother."

So they would return Hawkin to his home at Gunderson Woods. And there he would reunite with his mother. It actually hurt Victoria to hear this at first. She knew that was horrible of her. But this woman couldn't possibly be reliable. Paralyzed? And a metal-eater? And some kind of shaman in what sounded like a cult? How could she be expected to care for Hawkin? And what about all the strangers who lived on the compound with her? What if one of them talked? What if Gunn came for him there? It couldn't be a good environment for a child.

"If you knew anything about my family," John said, "you'd say the same."

"They'll look for him there," she said. "It's practically right down the road. They'll find him."

"They haven't found me."

"Sorry—what?" she said.

"Nothing." John shrugged his shoulders, as if he didn't want to think too hard about any of this. His job was to get the kid there safely, not figure the rest of his life out. "That place has become its own kind of fortress. They're armed to the gills. A lot of people show up there—more and more every week—to start over. Say goodbye to whatever they were. *Metal is* and all that. If you're looking to hide in plain sight, it's as good a place as any."

"How do you know all this?" she said.

"Because my brother's one of them."

On television a woman throws up her arms and lets out a scream as a tentacle loops around her waist and drags her offscreen. Victoria and Hawkin watch for another few minutes, silent except for the occasional rustle of a candy wrapper as the boy snacks on M&M's.

Then a knocking shakes the door in its frame.

Someone is there. Someone wants in.

The Cornhusker Motel is located off I-35, just outside of Ames, Iowa. The Vacancy sign blinks red. Brown weeds poke through the cracks in the asphalt. Two cars are parked out front, one rusted-out Pontiac missing its bumper and a forest-green Volvo with Minnesota plates.

The day is gray with cold rain. Along the sidewalk, a housekeeper pushes a cart heaped with dirty linens. When five black SUVs roar into the parking lot, she flattens herself fearfully against the wall and says a prayer, and the laundry cart trundles on another few feet before crashing against a timbered pillar.

Men in tactical gear spill out of the vehicles and arrange themselves in a half circle around the door of unit 9. She doesn't know who is staying there, but they've kept the Do Not Disturb sign on the knob the entire time.

The men — bristling with rifles — move quickly, a swarm. But now another man approaches with deliberate slowness. Short, pudgy, balding, bespectacled. He wears a three-piece suit, like someone on one those British procedurals that play on public television. He looks so incongruous among this group of men. Instead of a rifle, he carries what appears to be a sword. If not for the threatening circumstances, the housekeeper would have wondered if it was a toy, since the blade gives off a crackling red light.

The small man stands before the door of unit 9 and studies the men who surround him as if to ascertain their readiness. They all creep closer as he raises a hand, makes it into a fist, and knocks.

There is a pregnant beat when he rises up on his tiptoes, presumably waiting for the peephole to darken. With two hands, he readies the sword at his shoulder. He then springs forward with surprising quickness, leading with the blade. The wood offers no resistance as the sword sinks through it all the way to the hilt. Smoke drifts from a black scar. When the small man pulls back his blade, he seems satisfied by the blood reddening it.

When the knock sounds, Victoria hurries Hawkin to the bathroom. "Go, go, go," she whispers. There is a window made from frosted glass here. Too small for an adult, but perfect for him to slip out of, if need be. "You wait here," she says. "And if there's any trouble, you run."

"Run where?"

"Fast and far. That's all that matters."

"I should be the one to answer the door," he says.

"No."

"I should be the one protecting you."

"I said *no*."

"But they can hurt you."

"They can hurt you too," she says and runs a finger along his chest, where he still carries an evil scar the color of frostbite. "We caught them by surprise before. But they'll be ready this time."

She climbs into the bathtub with him and props open the window above it. A cold breeze filters inside and steams their breath. "Stay here. And listen."

"For what?"

"Me screaming. I'll scream." She kisses him on the forehead, then leaves him and slinks toward the door. A line of light glows beneath it, broken by the shadows of two legs.

Slowly she brings her eye to the peephole.

Thaddeus steps aside and allows the men to shoot out the lock. Gunfire rattles, and splinters spray. They shoulder through the door. It gives way before catching on something weighty — the body felled on the other side. They barely pay it any attention, just kick its ribs once and then move on to check the closet, the bathroom. They hoist the skirt of the bed and flap aside the curtains and shine a flashlight into the ventilation ducts. They call out, "Clear!"

Only then does Thaddeus enter. He stands over the body of a gray-haired man in a white polo shirt and pleated khakis. His face has been cloven through the middle by the wizard blade. The wound does not bleed, having been instantly cauterized, but it bubbles and smolders, and an acrid smoke rises, as if his soul is escaping. Thaddeus knows this man to be Wade Lennon, Victoria's husband. They have never met, but Thaddeus has observed him from a distance and listened to him many times via the microphones nested in their home. Wade is his wife's lesser. An inferior intellect, a waste of oxygen, a human teddy bear Victoria seemed to keep around for comfort alone. How either of them figured out how to splice their home's surveillance system into a loop, he isn't sure. How either of them figured out how to game Thaddeus down to Iowa, he isn't sure. He doesn't like to be bested.

One of Wade's eyes is a startled blue. The other is gone. Thaddeus steps onto his chest as he enters the room fully. A death gasp escapes the body.

The men lower their rifles and shuffle their feet and move out of the way as Thaddeus explores the room. One of them says, "Who is this guy?"

And Thaddeus says, "A traitor to his country."

He opens the drawers of the bureau, one by one. Then he enters the bathroom and checks Wade's toiletry bag. He shuts off the switch on the sword and the red sizzle of it fades and he sets its point on the floor and leans on the handle and says, "Well, gentlemen." He looks at them each in turn. "I'll admit I'm quite vexed."

John stands in the doorway of the motel room. He wears sunglasses, though the day is cloudy. A black hoodie shadows his face. Snowflakes flutter around him and melt on his shoulders.

"Thank goodness," Victoria says. "I didn't recognize you at first."

"Didn't recognize you either," he says. "The hair. You look twenty years younger."

"Oh," Victoria says and touches it. "Thanks. I think."

"It's time."

Victoria tries to usher him inside, but he holds back. "Any problems?" he says. "Been driving by a few times every day. Last half an hour, I was watching from across the street. No red flags, right?"

"We're fine," she says. "Running low on treats. That's all."

He turns around and raises a hand, signaling someone parked in a Buick with snow-smeared wheel wells. The driver's door is kicked open and a woman with strawberry-blond hair emerges; she's followed by a little boy in a snow hat and a parka and corduroy pants several sizes too big and rolled up at the cuffs.

"Who's that?" Victoria says.

"Friends." He nervously tugs at the strings of his sweatshirt. The hood tightens around his face, pinching his expression, smushing his cheeks, making him even more unfamiliar.

"I was starting to think you'd never come." Victoria realizes she's crying and palms the tears away. She isn't sure if it's due to relief or sadness. She isn't sure what kind of life she'll find outside of this room. "Have you heard from Wade?"

"He texted me from the burner yesterday. All good. He's waiting."

"For what?"

"For you. He's waiting for you."

In a way that's been true from the start. She imagines her husband with the neat part in his hair and his kind, steady eyes and his tanned arms that are forever opening up to draw her into a hug. He likes to tour through country cemeteries to see if he can find the oldest grave. He knows every battle in the Civil War and World War II. He has a train set that he sometimes tends to in a railroad cap and overalls. He smells like butterscotch and shaving lotion and has never been anything but decent and kind to her. And now he is waiting for her to be done with her work here at last. So that they can move on. Staying married is about making compromises, he once said. Coming here was certainly a compromise. Escaping Northfall is one more compromise. She just hopes it's not their last.

"I honestly don't even know what's next for us," she says to John.

"I don't know what's next for me either. But we've made our beds. Now we've got to lie in them."

The woman and her son kick the slush off their shoes and sniffle. "This is Jenna and her boy, Timmy," John says as he motions for them to head inside. "If anybody asks, you all are just a couple of moms and their kids getting together to play some board games and have some snacks, maybe watch a movie. And if anybody makes trouble for you, rest assured that Jenna's carrying."

"I'm sorry." Victoria feels addled, her mind elsewhere, still worrying over Wade. "Carrying? What?"

He pinches his mouth impatiently, and Jenna opens her coat to flash the revolver tucked into her belt.

"I see," Victoria says. "Of course."

Jenna says, "Nice to meet you," on her way into the motel room, but Victoria is too baffled to return the greeting.

John reaches into his pocket and removes a pair of sunglasses. "Give these to the kid."

She takes them without knowing why. Sunglasses? Why would Hawkin need sunglasses on a stormy day? And then she realizes his eyes would give him away, and it bothers her how slow she is at making connections. Her mind is a mess. Everything is uncertain.

"What about you?" she says to John. "Won't you come inside?"

His eyes dart over her shoulder. "Nah."

"Don't you even want to meet him? You're doing all this for—"

"Better like this." John starts to walk to the car and says over his shoulder, "Pack up your things. We leave in ten. You lead, I follow. Any trouble comes our way, I'll take care of it."

"If there is trouble, you're not going to be able to stop it. You don't understand what these people are capable of."

"Trust me," John says. He spins around to face her, and maybe, just maybe, she sees his birthmark flash blue. "That kid isn't the only one who can cause some mayhem."

36

✳

The longer John stayed in Russia, the more he put himself at risk, but he took the time to collect Anton's broken body and carry it deep into the Khimki Forest and bury it beneath a rowan tree, and into the bark he carved *Friend*. He wants something similar to happen now, wants to move past the violence and do what needs to be done for Hawkin and then walk away.

All this time, John has been aware of the boy—he's been nibbling at the edges of his attention—but there was something distancing about the high fences and concrete walls of the DOD facility. Hawkin felt more like an idea than a person. Now that he's out, John can't concentrate or calm the paranoia twisting sourly inside him. His dreams are back. The dreams that used to plague him, the dreams he thought he had cut off, said goodbye to.

One involved every window and door in the house swinging open and spilling forth a blinding light. When John squinted and shaded his face and tried to close one of them, a tentacle shot forward and curled around his wrist.

Another involved the boy. He was curled up inside of John's chest, where John's heart should have been, hidden. When Hawkin awoke, he began to punch and then kick, seeking a way out, trapped in a rib cage that he finally mustered the strength to shatter.

John doesn't want to talk to the boy, doesn't want to risk even looking at him, for fear of being recognized as a citizen of the same nightmare.

Gunderson Woods is only thirty miles away but feels impossibly distant. He drives there now and feels watched every inch of the trip. It's not just the ramped-up military presence in North-fall over the past few days—the helicopters buzzing the air, the black SUVs with military plates in the streets, the thin-waisted, broad-shouldered men wearing earpieces in restaurants and at gas stations—it's the boy. The boy in the Buick that's driving twenty yards ahead of him. A disturbed magnetism links them.

A stormy day such as this seemed the best time to make a move. The snow falls thickly and sweeps past the windshield. The wipers creak back and forth, and gusts rock the Bronco, and ice patches skid its wheels. The overall sensation is vertiginous and makes driving feel more like flying. Extra-dimensional. Which matches the sensation inside him, everything at once expanding and contracting so that he isn't quite sure how to navigate his feelings or the road before him.

The Buick's taillights wink red every time Jenna takes a turn. The car quakes and fishtails on occasion, but he's happy for the cover of the early-winter storm. And for the emptiness of the roads. He checks his mirrors constantly but has seen nothing except a logging truck and a furnace-repair van.

All this time he studies the boy through the rear window of the Buick. At one point, Hawkin turns around, his auroral eyes visible —and John shrinks back in his seat and lets his foot off the gas to lengthen the distance between them. Forty yards. Fifty. Eighty.

It's then that a squad car pulls out from a side road with its rack lights flashing and cuts between the Buick and the Bronco. The snowflakes become red and blue confetti. The cop squawks his si-ren a few times and Jenna pumps her brakes but doesn't stop.

John pulls out his cell to call her, but she's already on the line. "What do I do?" she says. "Do I keep going?"

"You pull over," he says.

"Was I speeding?"

"Give the forty-five to Victoria and tell her to keep it ready but hidden. In her lap, under her scarf."

"I don't—"

"And the kid isn't wearing the goddamn sunglasses like he's supposed to. He needs to put on his—"

"He's got them on now."

"It'll be fine. Just be cool. Don't hang up. Set the cell phone down beside you. I'll be listening. Anything happens, I'm there."

The siren squawks again and Jenna slows and pulls over as far as she can without risking the ditch. The cop noses up behind her. The road bends here, and John parks far enough back to be half hidden among the trees. Not parked. His foot on the brake, ready to slam the gas.

The cop has a linebacker build evident even under his winter coat. He shambles through the snow and knocks at Jenna's window even though it's already half rolled down. He doesn't ask for her license and registration but says right away, "Don't I know you?"

"I'm Dan Swanson's wife."

"You're Dan Swanson's wife. And that's his boy."

"That's our boy."

"That's a hell of a thing, him going missing."

"It is."

"Don't give up hope."

"I haven't."

"You shouldn't. None of us have. We keep the light on at his desk, you know? Every night."

"That's sweet of you. Thank you."

"Mrs. Swanson, you know why I pulled you over?"

"I—I'm not sure. I don't think I was speeding? Is one of my headlights out?"

"I'm supposed to do random checks here. On account of all the loonies. Because this is the way to Gunderson Woods. The sheriff says we're supposed to set up what you might call a harassment campaign."

"Oh?" she says and then gives a nervous chuckle. "Are we the loonies you're looking for?"

"You're not headed to Gunderson Woods, are you?"

"No. Never."

"Then where are you headed?"

"We're friends." She nods at Victoria and tries to keep a steady smile, just like she does at the restaurant when dealing with customers displeased with their orders. "We're just getting together with our kids to have some hot cocoa, play board games."

The deputy is a big guy, the kind who has enough fat in his throat to make him always sound stuffed up. "Board games?"

"And maybe watch a movie."

"Huh." There is a long beat during which John grips the wheel so tightly, his knuckles pop. He imagines the cop studying the kids, maybe wondering about the age gap between them and why one is wearing sunglasses on a day like this. "Well, fun as that sounds, it's honestly kind of not genius to be driving around in a two-wheeler in these conditions. Especially with kids."

"I—yes—you're right."

"Last winter, a family slipped off the road during a storm. Froze to death. Car was buried in a drift. Didn't find them until spring."

"Oh. I think I remember reading about that. That's terrible."

"Hell of a thing. Get on the 511 next time. Check the road conditions. They've got an app for that now, even. Travel is not advised. You going someplace close?"

"Yes. It's close."

"You need an escort? Someone to escort you?"

"No."

"Sure?"

"Thank you. We'll be fine."

"Hope so. Because it's not safe out here. You understand?"

"Yes."

"It's not safe."

He shuffles away and she rolls up the window and through the phone John hears her sigh with relief. "Everybody good?" Jenna says, and Victoria says, in an unsteady voice, "Can you turn up the heat, dear? I can't seem to stop shivering."

Jenna picks up the phone and says, "You good, Johnny?"

"Yeah," he says, "I'm good." Except that, as the cop is climbing into his squad car, he pauses to look back at him wonderingly.

Hawkin can't see past the uniform. The police officer who loomed in the window felt like a stand-in for the entire security force at the DOD lab. The man might as well have had cameras for eyes and guns for hands and keys for teeth and a cage for a stomach. He would hurt Hawkin if Hawkin didn't hurt him first. And it took the strongest will for him to sit still and stare straight ahead. He knows that this is wrong but that it also feels right. He is stronger than them — all of them — and that's why they locked him up. Because they were afraid of what he could do.

He remembered, when he was younger, reading a *Superman* comic and asking his mother why Clark Kent was a reporter. Why hide? Why not just become king of the world? He could still save the people who needed saving and he could still punish the people who needed punishing, but he could also enjoy his power.

His mother shrugged and said, "Because that's what makes him a good guy."

But why? It wasn't a satisfactory answer. Now that Hawkin has tasted freedom — now that he has experimented with what he is capable of — he can feel another version of the same question bothering him now. He is the one with the power. So why is he hiding? Why was he so afraid for so long when everyone should be afraid of him?

In one of the comic books Victoria bought for him — an issue of *Batman* — there was a page he kept coming back to. In it, Robin was overcome by fear gas, paralyzed in Wayne Manor for days on end. In his bedroom, he lay curled up in a ball, shivering, scared of his own shadow. But Bruce Wayne sat at his side, and he said something that roused the Boy Wonder. "I know how you feel. I was once afraid of the dark. Then I found the darkness inside me and it was greater and more terrifying than anything I faced. So I let it out."

As they drive, Hawkin clenches and unclenches his fists, and every beat of his heart seems to inflate his chest until the pressure threatens to crack him wide open.

When Jenna says, "We're here," Hawkin almost asks, *Where?* Because he hardly recognizes his own home. Maybe it's the snow — which makes everything unfamiliar — or the long wall of sharpened logs bordering the property. He isn't sure what he expected as the Buick rolls up to the gates, but it's not this. What looks like another prison. He has been so focused on himself that he's failed to acknowledge a difficult truth: yes, he has changed, but so has the world around him.

The boy seated beside him — Timmy? Tommy? — asks Hawkin, "Is this where you live?" and Hawkin says, "Used to be."

"So it's your home?"

"I don't know," Hawkin says.

"How can you not know?"

"Because," Hawkin says, "a lot has changed."

The boy returns his attention to the plastic dinosaur in his lap. "I like our house, but Mommy says I'll like our new house more better."

"You're moving?" Hawkin says.

"Mommy says our life is going to be more better from now on. Is your life going to be more better from now on?"

"I don't know that either."

The woman named Jenna puts the car in park and says, "This is it," to Victoria. "You two are on your own from here."

Victoria unclicks the buckle of her seat belt but doesn't release it, as if she thinks she might float away without it. "You mean you're not coming in?"

"Even if I wanted to, I couldn't. They don't let just anyone through those gates." Jenna finds Hawkin's eyes in the rearview. "Good luck. To both of you."

"Thank you, then. For getting us this far." The seat belt retracts and Victoria wraps her neck in her scarf. "I don't know why it feels like there's such a long way to go yet." Victoria glances into the back seat at Hawkin with wet-eyed concern. "You ready?"

No. He is not. He imagined his house as it was. He imagined his mother as she was. He isn't sure he's prepared for whatever waits inside. But the gates are already opening and a figure is approaching them. Thin and tall and dressed in a black wrap whitened at its creases by snow. He bends his body to peer in the window at Hawkin with eyes that burn blue. Then Jenna rolls down her window and snowflakes twirl inside and she says, "Hey, Nico. You got what I need?"

Nico keeps his eyes on Hawkin as he withdraws something from a hidden pocket. A thick manila envelope. He speaks with a whispery voice: "Metal is."

"Take care of yourself," Jenna says. She accepts the envelope and tears it open and shuffles quickly through the papers inside. "Eat something, huh? You look like you're about to vanish."

His eyes finally find hers. "You don't know how right you are."

She doesn't appear to hear him. "Everything seems to be in order, so we'll let you take it from here." She closes the window and pops the trunk and Nico goes to retrieve the bags waiting there.

"What did he give you?" Victoria says.

Jenna flops the envelope heavily onto the dash. "You didn't think we were doing this purely out of the goodness of our own hearts."

"Money and murder." Victoria shakes her head. "I think I've had more than enough of it. And this place."

Jenna motions to the open gate. "Then go already."

Hawkin tries to open his door but the wind bullies it closed. He tries again, forcing himself outside. Victoria meets him there and takes his hand. But before they follow the thin man through the gates, Hawkin looks back at the Bronco parked at the edge of the lot. The cab is dark and the snow is already piling up on the windshield, but he can see the figure sitting inside. A shadow.

Hawkin raises a hand in thanks. After a moment's hesitation, the shadow matches the gesture. As if they are the same. A reflection.

The paperwork Jenna collected — signing over Gunderson Woods to Frontier Metals — is irrelevant to John. All he cares about is the boy. And now he's seemingly safe as the gates close. Back together with his mother. And happy? He must be happy. So John has done his part. This is supposed to be the moment when he feels better, restored. Yet no sense of relief or conclusion comes.

The sky droops mournfully. The wind dances the snow into twisting veils. Jenna loops around the parking lot, her tires leaving deep grooves in the snow, and pulls back onto the highway. After a moment John follows her, heading back to town. The three of them. This should feel right. A kind of family going in the same direction. When they get home, maybe they'll make grilled cheese sandwiches and tomato soup and coffee. Sit down together. Play a card game. He tries to imagine the warmth and comfort of a lamplit kitchen, but it keeps scattering away like the snowflakes billowing past his windshield, replaced by visions of him on his knees, openarmed, begging the boy to strike him down.

There were no news reports of the attack on the DOD facility because it was a black site, but John saw the smoke dirtying the air and heard enough from Victoria to know what Hawkin could do. He deserved revenge more than John deserved absolution.

His cell rings. Jenna's ID pops up on the screen. He knows what she'll say. *We did it, baby. We did it. Now we can start over.* He won't be able to match her enthusiasm, so he doesn't answer.

Why can't he allow himself some happiness? Why does he always pivot toward self-destruction? *Is it the same reason Talia wanted to mine the Boundary Waters?* he wonders. *The same reason the DOD wanted to harvest omnimetal and turn it into weapons? The same reason we gamble and drink too much and shatter marriages? In the end we're all hard-wired to destroy ourselves. Omnimetal just gave us another tool to bring hazardously to our wrists.*

He's so caught up in his thoughts, he doesn't notice the brigade of vehicles until it is already upon him. The black SUVs — one, two, three — blast past and stir up a tornadic wake of snow. Then they disappear into the white nothing of the storm, heading in the direction of Gunderson Woods.

He jams the brakes hard enough that his tires slip and he cranks the wheel and spins around and comes to a swaying stop. It must have been that cop who alerted them. Maybe he reported to them directly or maybe they were listening on the scanner. Regardless, they knew. And he had given them what they wanted.

A moment ago John felt directionless. But now he knows what he can do, what he's best at. He can hurt.

The house is jacked up on one side, so Victoria stands at a strange tilt in the Gunderson living room. The air is rank with the sour spice of body odor and space dust. Victoria's eyes haven't yet adjusted and the shut curtains permit little light, and the darkness enhances the radiant blue eyes of Mother. She sits on the couch, her hairless moon of a face floating on top of a big black body.

Victoria isn't sure what she expected from this reunion, but it was not this level of discomfort. Hawkin doesn't rush to his mother in a flurry of hugs and kisses and tears. He instead holds back, nudging his body against Victoria's, and leaves her only hesitantly when his mother says, "Come closer and let me see you."

He takes a few steps forward and pauses halfway between the two women.

"Take off your sunglasses," Mother says.

The boy does. He folds the stems and tucks them into his pocket. She regards him for a long, uncomfortable moment, and her eyes blink with an effect similar to fireflies flickering in and out of view.

"Mom?" Hawkin finally says. "Is it really you?"

Mother gives a husky laugh. "Is it me?" She readjusts her bulk. "Yes and no, I suppose. Yes and no."

To this Hawkin has no response except to shift his feet.

"We've grown," she says. "And I don't mean that in the way you might think. We've both grown inside. We're bigger — inside. Do you know what I mean by that?"

"I think so."

"Whole galaxies spin inside us."

Hawkin looks back at Victoria with a pleading gaze until his mother's voice calls out to him again. "Do you remember how I used to take you to church?"

"I remember."

"At the Trinity Lutheran. We didn't go every Sunday, but maybe every other. Not your father, of course, but you and me."

"We'd sit in the back pew."

"I liked the back pew best because then I could see all of the stained glass. When the light came through, I liked to imagine heaven was waiting on the other side. I led the Bible studies too. I ushered sometimes. And baked dessert bars for the fellowship after the service. I didn't believe in the Gospels, but I believed they were an honest attempt to make sense of everything. Do you know why we went to church, Hawkin? Why anyone goes to church?"

His shrug is almost imperceptible.

She reaches for something — what Victoria recognizes as a bowl — resting on the end table. She sparks a flame and leans her face in. "Because they want to escape."

Smoke — brightened by blue sparks — clouds her face. She takes a deep-lunged breath and only then does she speak again. "Because *this* can't be it. There has to be *more*. It doesn't matter if you practice Buddhism, Islam, Christianity, Hinduism, Satanism or worship in a laboratory like Dr. Lennon over here — that's the truth that people are drawn to. The truth of more. But no one knew what the *more* was until now. When the *more* came to us." She sets down the bowl and gives a contented sigh. "You and me — we are evidence of the *more*."

"Why?" he says. "Why are you telling me this?"

"Because you have to make a choice."

"About what?"

"Are you going to stay here? Or go with me?"

"Where would we go?"

She raises a hand and taps the air as if ringing a bell. "I bet you already know."

"Tell me."

"Your dreams. They're a little bit like those stained-glass windows at the Trinity Lutheran. You can see the hint of something else shining through them. Am I right?"

Hawkin lowers his head and then raises it, what amounts to a nod.

"That's where we're going."

Victoria can't keep herself from speaking. "Hawkin." She says his name like a warning. Because she senses, in the biblical cadences of Mother's speech, something apocalyptic. She imagines everyone drinking the same poison in Communion. Or this compound rising in flames and collapsing in ash.

She can feel Mother's eyes homing in on her now and has never felt more fully seen — naked to the marrow. "It's not what you think, Dr. Lennon."

"Isn't it?"

"This isn't about death. It's about rebirth."

"I wouldn't have brought him here if I knew we were going to have this conversation."

"I'm grateful to you. I truly am. But shut your mouth, Dr. Lennon. For just another minute. Because we don't have much time. Hawkin has to make his choice now."

"Why?" Victoria and Hawkin say at once.

"Because it's time to go. Because they're coming."

Victoria says, "Do you realize how you sound?"

But Mother ignores her and focuses on Hawkin. "We hardly know each other. We're strangers now. We've changed, haven't we?"

"Yes."

"So much has changed. And I know that makes this hard. And I believe I already know your answer. But you have to understand something before you make it."

Victoria is about to say more, but Hawkin holds up a hand to silence her. "I'm listening."

"If you stay, you're going to be their monster. That's not something you can change. The only thing you can control is what kind of monster you want to be. Do you understand?"

"I — I'll try to understand."

"You always were a good boy." Mother looks again to Victoria. "You love him, don't you?"

She does not hesitate to say it. "Yes."

"Then you'll do everything you can to protect him. From others, of course. But also . . . from himself."

It's not a question, but she answers all the same, with the solemnness of a vow. "I will."

It was on an icy road such as this that John's mother died. Because of him. And the world feels ripe with the possibility of death when he picks up speed and the snow churns and the wind howls. His wipers can't keep up and the tires barely find traction. Frosted trees, like white turrets, blur past. The road winds and he catches a few fleeting glimpses of the SUVs before reaching them. He knows they won't be paying any attention to what's behind them and so he doesn't hesitate. On a straightaway he stomps the gas and powers into the rear end of a black Tahoe with government plates.

Metal shrieks. The tailgate crumples and the vehicle lurches. John has momentum and surprise on his side. The road bends again and the Tahoe doesn't make it; it dives into the ditch and sends up a spray of snow before coming to a rest on its side against a wall of pines.

The next vehicle — a Suburban — is braking, but whoever's at the wheel still doesn't seem wise to what's happening. The Bronco's grille is shattered and the hood rumpled but otherwise it drives fine. He bolts forward again but without as much force as before. He batters the Suburban's rear but gets caught — bumper to bumper — and can't untangle himself even when he brakes. The Suburban swerves and they both slide sideways and then buckle back into formation, continuing down the road like two train cars that nearly lost their grip on the tracks.

The Suburban's brake lights burn red. The Bronco slams into it once more, and at first John believes this is why its rear window shatters. Then his own windshield spider-webs and several bullets whiz past his ear; one strikes him full in the face. Then in the hand. And then in the chest.

He can't see through the crinkly glass—it's punched through with holes—so he leans over the dash and swings a fist. The blue expulsion of energy fragments the windshield into thousands of sparkling pieces that gust away instantly with the snow.

Now he can see the men in tactical gear positioned on the other side of his hood staring down the length of their rifles. They unload a fresh assault of bullets and everything goes white with muzzle flash. When they've emptied their clips, the men come into focus again, and they look at John and then at each other with questioning terror.

The rearview mirror is gone, so he can't see his face, but he can see his hands. Bright blue veins run through them, coursing with energy. The two vehicles, still tangled together, barely creep along, so it isn't much of a challenge for John to crawl out of his seat and across the hood and then launch himself forward.

The trail of footprints is already filling with snow. Hundreds of people—all of them in black—have gathered in the meadow behind the house. Here the monoliths rise like a silver crown or some claw reaching its way out of the underworld. At the center of the circle stands a monument, what looks like a door, built from thousands of component parts. They call it Herm.

Earlier, Mother was hoisted and carried here by several men and now she sits before it. Studying it. Seemingly oblivious to the snow that dusts her bare head. Finally she reaches out to touch its center. At first nothing happens. Then a few ghostly wisps of something like electricity sparkle into view. And a blue light—a brighter version of the one that burns in all their eyes—glimmers at the borders of the monument.

Victoria and Hawkin hold hands and watch from a nearby rise. Their skin tightens to gooseflesh, maybe because it is cold. They hear a humming that trembles the air. The wind rises and for a few moments the meadow vanishes behind a thick, white veil. Then a blue flash strobes and shines hard, and for a long second every snowflake seems to hang frozen in place — before continuing to fall.

When the air clears again, Mother and her people have vanished, but the monument remains. A smoking gateway. So hot that an invisible dome surrounds it where the falling snow transforms instantly to steam.

37

✳

John drives the Bronco along the highway, chasing the tracks of the third vehicle, which is gone, maybe waiting around the next turn or maybe hurrying on to Gunderson Woods and definitely calling for backup. Smoke rises from the edges of the Bronco's hood. Something grinds in the engine. The steering wants to drag left, because one of the wheels is bent out of alignment.

All this time his phone — tossed on the passenger seat — keeps buzzing. Jenna. He doesn't want to talk, but he also can't risk her turning around and coming back this way. He picks up the cell and shakes the glass off it and accepts the call.

"Johnny?" Her voice comes in a panicked rush. "What's going on? Talk to me, baby. Please."

"I need you to find Stacie Toal."

"Stacie who — what?"

"Find Stacie Toal and tell her what's happening. She's the only honest person left in this town. She can help."

The sandbox is long gone, but Hawkin determines that he presently stands rooted in the place where it used to be. Somewhere beneath the ankle-deep snow and the layer of omnimetal, he imagines the outline of it, the wooden rectangle where he once played. Where he conjured and dashed away worlds, and where he lost his mother for both the first and the last time.

It's possible the sadness will come later. It's possible he's experiencing shock. It's also possible he doesn't feel lost so much as found because of the woman standing next to him. Victoria looks at him with snowflakes feathering her eyelashes. Her mouth opens and closes as she struggles to find the right words.

He saves her the trouble. "I'm freezing," he says. "Let's get out of here."

She takes his hand in both of hers and gives the knuckles a kiss. "That sounds like a fine idea."

Their footsteps whine and squeak in the snow as they head back the way they came. In the parking lot out front, there are dozens of cars no one will miss. The two of them will search the surrounding cabins and tents and shacks until they find some keys, and then they'll go. Where doesn't matter right now. Away from here.

But when they round the corner of his former house, Hawkin goes still so suddenly that Victoria nearly loses her balance. "What?" she says.

With a gust, the snow closes around them. It is difficult to see through it, but something glows ahead. A sparkling redness. Coming toward them. It diffuses and then coalesces into the shape of a man.

"Oh my God," Victoria says. "It's him."

Thaddeus. He carries the wizard blade two-handed and at the ready. This they have seen before. What surprises them is the armor he wears. It appears to be made with the same technology, circuited red. He had a helmet with two sizzling spikes along the top and plates along his chest and arms. He is a laser-lit knight. His whole body hums like an electrical wire, and the snowflakes spit and hiss when they strike him.

He stops ten yards away. He wipes a finger across his glasses to see them better. "You know," he says, calling out loudly to be heard over the wind, "I used to think I wanted to simply enlist the boy. Make him into a human tank. But then my thinking clarified. Do you know what I realized?" He waits a beat, as if he actually expects them to respond. "I'm harboring an enemy warhead. It doesn't belong to the Russians or the Chinese." He hefts the wizard blade and points to the sky. "It belongs to them. Whoever they are. Wherever they come from. I've been stupidly, maybe selfishly, sheltering a weapon of mass destruction that could destroy this country. That ends right now."

As soon as John has Gunderson Woods in sight, the gunfire begins. They are waiting for John. Inside the cab of the Bronco, sparks fly as bullets ricochet and zip and wang. One of the tires gives out with a slump. Then another. The engine utters a dying cough. Then something squeals and cracks in the underbelly of the vehicle. John is maybe fifty yards away when it grinds to a stop.

The third SUV is parked in front of the open gates, and two men are stationed on the other side of it, using it as a barricade. The Bronco catches fire when John gets out and walks toward them. His feet slide in the snow but his course is determined, even as the bullets shred his clothes. When the men run out of clips, they try grenades. One sends up a geyser of snow. The other knocks him over, but he gets right up.

Over the years, in his cell, Hawkin had a lot of time to think, and one of the ways he occupied himself was by pretending. Comic books owned his imagination. He had always liked Batman best of all the superheroes. It was more than his haunting mask and the militaristic Batmobile and the gadgets he kept on his utility belt and the way he crouched like a gargoyle on Gotham's skyscrapers with his leathery cape fluttering in the wind. It was the villains. The villains who made up his rogues' gallery were the best of any series. Because they weren't merely masked and spandexed weirdoes to punch and kick and throw Batarangs at. They *meant* something. They really mattered emotionally. If Batman was order, then the Joker was chaos. Mr. Freeze represented Bruce Wayne's emotional coldness. Ra's al Ghul was the father figure he wanted desperately but had to reject for his sinister ways. Two-

Face captured the constant battle between Wayne and the Dark Knight. What you eventually came to understand, if you read enough comic books, was that Batman was a unification of his worst enemies.

All of the hate and grief and weakness and loneliness of the past few years—the ruined sense of destiny—have been crushed down to this single moment and found a focusing agent in Dr. Gunn.

Victoria pulls at Hawkin, cries for him to hurry, but he shrugs her off and says, "No." She wants to run, but he's ready to fight.

Because Dr. Gunn is the Joker and Scarecrow and Mr. Freeze and Penguin and Ra's al Ghul and all the rest of them. And this is Hawkin's Crime Alley, where Thomas and Martha Wayne fell in a rain of bullets and blood and pearls. It was a moment of fusion, convergence. Here is the villain and here is the place and here is the core wound that Hawkin might conquer if he is going to come into his power as a hero. That's the way the rules work.

His mother said he had to choose what kind of monster he wanted to be. And that's what he's going to do. He charges forward, imagining that he would be faster except for the clinging trap of snow around his ankles. He lets out a scream, imagining it more low-throated and heroic. He swings an arm at Dr. Gunn, imagining the impact will blast him back twenty yards where he'll crater the snow and send up a cloud of powder.

But it doesn't work out that way. Dr. Gunn pivots at the last second and slashes the wizard blade—and Hawkin stumbles and falls. Hot pain sears his back, and cold snow fills his mouth as he opens it to scream. Just like that, the dream dissolves. He's still just a child after all. He feels paralyzed by pain and bladder-souring fear, but Victoria is crying out for him to get up, get up!—and he manages to roll onto his side.

Dr. Gunn stands over him, his feet planted wide, the wizard blade held high above his head. Their eyes meet in a baleful stare. But the blow never comes.

The *shuff-shuff-shuff* of footsteps rushing through the snow steals

Gunn's attention. He renegotiates his stance and wizard blade just as a man comes charging out of the storm. A man whose eyes are ablaze and whose skin teems and pulses blue like the atmosphere of some storm-troubled planet.

Gunn waits for him—and then dodges aside at the last second. The slash of his wizard blade catches the man across the chest. He lets out a scream of pain and the air brightens with a blue pulse of energy so severe, Hawkin turns away.

When he looks again, he discovers the man now on his knees, panting, clutching the gash that reaches diagonally across his chest.

Gunn stands at the ready. He could easily rush in and strike once more—lop off his head, cleave his chest—but he seems in no rush. His face is busy with curiosity. "There's more than one of you?" He takes a few hesitant steps toward him. "But how?"

The man springs forward with a yell—and Gunn brings the wizard blade down on him. Another gash opens in the man's chest, forming a ragged blue X. He falls back in a heap, consumed by pain.

"Who are you?" Gunn says, his breath short with exertion or scientific excitement. "Are you part of this cult? Are there more of you? Is this what happens when you smoke enough metal?"

He keeps up his rapid-fire assault of questions, but Hawkin is distracted by Victoria. She snatches at his arm and begs him to come with her and he says, "No," and she says, "I promised your mother I'd keep you safe."

"No!" Hawkin escapes her grip and scoops up a handful of snow. It's damp enough that it packs easily. He remembers the feel of the cold, wet sand in his hand when he tossed it into the stranger's face so many years ago when he snaps his arm forward and lets the snowball fly. It arcs fifteen yards through the air before striking Gunn in the face.

His glasses are knocked off. He staggers back in surprise and knuckles the snow from his eyes. "What was—" he says in a panicky voice. "Where did—who's—" He nearly slips and swipes at the air blindly with his wizard blade. "Stop!"

The man rises from the ground with slow, pained difficulty. His clothes are ragged, his eyes and his skin throbbing blue. He takes two staggering steps and then hurls himself at Gunn.

The two men don't merely fall — there is a kind of detonation that comes with their entanglement. A sound like *doom* accompanies a great bomb blast of air and the snow all around them vanishes, swept away by a rippling globe of energy.

Victoria goes flying back as if yanked by an invisible rope. And Hawkin is knocked aside; he rolls and skids for twenty yards, kicking up a big wave of snow. It is as if the man were packed with plutonium, a human missile.

For a few long breaths, Hawkin lies there, stunned into stillness. He feels a blend of gratefulness and regret. He helped, but this fight didn't belong to him. It isn't his time to be a hero after all. His ears ring. Night is coming and against the backdrop of the darkening sky, snow falls like paper stars. He manages to struggle upright and trudge back the way he came.

In a high-lipped crater of snow, a blue light throbs. He goes to it.

A few pieces of scorched metal — the remnants of the armor and sword — lie scattered like shrapnel, but Dr. Gunn is nowhere to be found. Dematerialized. A dispersion of atoms. But here lies a man. Naked, his eyes open and staring at Hawkin. He has a birthmark on his face and it leaks light. His face is light.

"I know who you are," Hawkin says. "John Frontier."

"I'm sorry," John says at last. "I'm so sorry. I wish I could take it back."

Hawkin holds up a hand and makes a fist and it shakes. Blue light begins to seep from between his fingers. He can feel the power there. He knows what he can do with it. He knows one life is irrelevant while at the same time every life is precious. He knows the pain of losing his parents, but he knows the gratitude of gaining Victoria. He knows the rage of being treated like a tool, but he knows the monstrous joy of becoming a weapon. He knows this man has killed, but he has also saved. In him is a beginning and an end, and an end and a beginning, and the two of them both destroyed each other and created each other, and *metal is, metal is, metal is.*

"Go ahead," John says. "I understand."

A shiver goes through the boy. And then his fist slackens and drops to his side. He stands there long enough for the snow to pile up on his shoulders. Finally he reaches for the stranger and says, "Let me help you up."

38

✳

A week later, beneath the unmoving gaze of the stars, a rental home is left empty, and a moving truck rumbles out of town and onto the highway; John is at the wheel, and Jenna and Timmy are tucked into the bench seat beside him. Though it is early, the air is bright with oncoming headlights as traffic continues its steady stream into Northfall, people chasing dreams, jobs, the future. Theirs is the only vehicle headed south as John leaves it all behind.

Most of what's in the truck belongs to Jenna, but he did pack a few things. At Gunderson Woods, the boy had led him into the house, and in the living room, he pulled a book off the shelf. A Bible. "I think this is what you've been looking for," the boy said. Or maybe he didn't say it. Maybe he merely thought it. There was a strange sensation between them when they stood side by side. A magnetic binding. Secrets hushing between them like fragments of radio signals. And indeed, the boy was right — the center of the pages had been cut away to accommodate a hollow in which was tucked a dime bag of weed and his mother's necklace. On the chain hung a pendant. Embedded in it was the first piece of iron drawn from one of his family's mines. Ore. What his family always called the soul of Northfall.

John wears it now beneath his shirt, against his chest. The pendant dangles at the junction of two thick purple scars crisscrossing his torso. They stitch his skin with pain, but the pain is good. A welcome vulnerability.

The radio is on and he turns up the volume — and they begin to sing — first Timmy, then Jenna, and finally even John, his voice uncertain but trying.

A week later, as dawn breaks, Yesno returns home from the hospital to the vast empty tomb of the Frontier compound. He finds two housekeepers absently dusting and a nurse spoon-feeding Ragnar, who sits up in bed, propped up by pillows. He isn't talking yet, and one side of his face droops, but he can write in a shaky script. *Welcome home, son,* he scratches on a piece of paper.

Yesno folds this note up again and again and again until it can't be bent anymore and tucks it into his pocket, and he will keep it for the rest of his life. It means even more to him than the manila envelope left for him on his bed that contains paperwork signing over the family estate — including Frontier Metals and Gunderson Woods — to him.

A week later, in the midmorning light at Gunderson Woods, the door stands in the center of the ring of omnimetal monoliths. It seems to cast a shadow in several directions at once. A cardinal flutters along and lands on top of it and begins to sing. But the song is cut short. A moment later, it drops to the ground, expired.

A week later, as the sun creeps toward noon, Stacie stands on the shore of a lake — one of thousands that puddle and spill across the Boundary Waters — watching her father load gear into a forest-green canoe. He's joined by the boy, Hawkin, who thumps his backpack into the hull and says, "I get to paddle, right? I'm not just going to sit there?"

"Sure you get to paddle. We'll need you to. We've got a long trip ahead of us."

"Good. Because I'm sick of just sitting around. I want to actually do something."

"Oh, I'll have plenty for you to do."

The short-haired, older woman — Victoria — carries a tackle box and a wobbling set of fishing poles down to the water. "Nothing better than pulling a fish out of the lake and dropping it right in the pan," her father says, treating this like just another guided expedition. "We'll be eating plenty of it. Unless you'd prefer to stick with the granola bars and beef jerky."

The snow has melted, but the next storm won't be far behind. Winter comes early in northern Minnesota. And that hurries them along as much as anything. The promise of ice is as dangerous as the threat of what might pursue them.

When John Frontier arrived — and all this trouble began — the temperatures were in the low nineties. Now there's frost edging the pine needles and stemming the cattails. The seasons change too fast up here. So does everything else.

There's a point in everyone's life when something shifts dramatically and he or she finds a different path: A death. A divorce. An illness. A job won or lost. Whatever it is, nothing will ever be the same. Stacie sighs and rubs a hand across her face as if to clear the fatigue from it. That's what happened to her. That's what's happened to all of them.

The lake carries the reflection of the sunlit cirrus clouds ribbing the sky. A loon calls out on the water. "Hey, Hawkin," she says and the boy tips his head toward her. "You like fish?"

"I'm not sure." He tromps toward her, his footsteps rattling on the stony shore. "I haven't had it in a long time. I used to like fish sticks?"

"Well, when I was your age, I hated fish," she says. "But my daddy was always making me eat it." And here her voice drops to a whisper. "Just in case you don't like walleye, I've got something for you." She pulls a sleeve of Starbursts out of her pocket, and he takes it with a surprised smile. "Don't share. It's just for you. Okay?"

"Okay."

Soon Stacie will hug her father and kiss him on the cheek and say thank you and be careful. She will wave as they go paddling off into the green, headed for Canada, and then she will return to Northfall, to the sheriff's department, where her shift will soon begin and she will no longer refer to herself as a peacemaker.

She won't be there to see Hawkin learn how to read a compass and map, to see Victoria hook her first trout and net it from the water with a startled laugh, to see her father set up camp. She won't be there to listen to them read a battered, taped-up copy of *Hatchet* together or smell the wood smoke as the fire crackles or hear her father telling a story about song lines, an indigenous term that refers to the paths across the sky or the earth taken by the creators during the first dreaming of the world. And she won't know about the humming in the air that night — what might be mistaken for insects but in fact comes from drones cutting through the sky, hovering above the treetops, hunting.

ACKNOWLEDGMENTS

This book wouldn't have been written if not for Stan Lee, Jack Kirby, Bob Cane, Bill Finger, Jerry Siegel, Joe Shuster, and Chris Claremont. Conjurers of worlds and characters and myths that owned my imagination as a child and continue to inspire me today.

Thanks to Helen Atsma, my brilliant coach and editor. Thanks to Katherine Fausset and the Curtis Brown crew for kicking down doors on my behalf all these years. Thanks to Holly Frederick, Britton Rizzio, and Noah Rosen for soldiering the Hollywood battlefields with me.

Thanks to the gang at HMH, including Marissa Page, Tracy Roe, Michael Dudding, Jen Reynolds. I appreciate your smarts and muscle.

Thanks to all the booksellers who generously support me, and a standing ovation to Jessica Peterson White and the amazing staff at Content, the killer local bookstore here in Northfield. Thanks also to the generosity and awesomeness of Steph Opitz, Jenny Dodgson, Britt Udeson, and everyone else at the Loft Literary Center, the crown jewel of Minnesota.

Thanks to Dr. James Head at Brown University, not only for his course on space geology, which sticks with me to this day, but for his kindness and guidance in making sure I didn't drop out after the GPA disaster of my freshman year.

Thanks to my parents, with a special shout-out to my father, who is a giant space nerd. He was regularly spotted during my childhood with a science fiction novel, an astronomy magazine, or a giant telescope. He raised me on a steady diet of *Star Wars* and *Star Trek* (anything involving stars, really), so whenever I look up at the night sky, I think of him.

Thanks to Arjendu Pattanayak, who bullshitted with me about physics over many glasses of scotch and helped me formulate some of the novel's slippery science. Other coconspirators who deserve a special nod: Daniel Fink, Peter Geye, Brent Schoonover, Paul W. and Stacie T., Jonathan Hickman, Jordan White, James Ponsoldt, Axel Alonso, and the Fantasy Fathers. Can I thank coffee and bourbon? Because I'd like to thank coffee and bourbon.

And thanks to love. Her name is Lisa.

ABOUT THE AUTHOR

Benjamin Percy is the author of four other novels, three short story collections, and a book of essays. His fiction and nonfiction have been published in *Esquire, GQ, Time, Outside, Men's Journal,* the *Wall Street Journal,* the *New York Times,* the *Paris Review, Ploughshares, Glimmer Train,* and *McSweeney's,* among others. He writes comics for Marvel, DC, and Dynamite and is known for his work on *X-Force, Batman, Wolverine, Green Arrow, Nightwing, James Bond,* and *Teen Titans.* His audio series *Wolverine: The Long Night* won the iHeartRadio Award for best scripted podcast, and his honors include an NEA fellowship, a Whiting Award, the Plimpton Prize, two Pushcart Prizes, and inclusion in *The Best American Short Stories* and *The Best American Comics.* He lives in Minnesota with his family. Learn more about him at benjaminpercy.com.